SHATTERED MINDS

BY LAURA LAM

The Micah Gray Trilogy

PANTOMIME

SHADOWPLAY

MASQUERADE

FALSE HEARTS

SHATTERED MINDS

SHATTERED MINDS

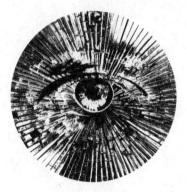

LAURA LAM

TOR

A TOM DOHERTY ASSOCIATES BOOK
NEW YORK

SHATTERED MINDS

Copyright © 2017 by Laura Lam

A Tor Book
Published by Tom Doherty Associates
175 Fifth Avenue
New York, NY 10010

www.tor-forge.com

Tor® is a registered trademark of Macmillan Publishing Group, LLC.

The Library of Congress Cataloging-in-Publication Data is available upon request.

ISBN 978-0-7653-8207-8 (hardcover)
ISBN 978-1-4668-8575-2 (ebook)

Our books may be purchased in bulk for promotional, educational, or business use. Please contact your local bookseller or the Macmillan Corporate and Premium Sales Department at 1-800-221-7945, extension 5442, or by email at MacmillanSpecialMarkets@macmillan.com.

Simultaneously published in Great Britain by Macmillan, an imprint of Pan Macmillan

First U.S. Edition: June 2017

Printed in the United States of America

0 9 8 7 6 5 4 3 2 1

*To Erica Bretall and Shawn DeMille
for reading early drafts of every book
and always being there*

ACKNOWLEDGMENTS

A gigantic thank-you to all the friends and colleagues who helped bring another book on to the shelves. This was a challenging book, but I'm proud of the end product. It would not be the book it is today without the help of my usual beta reader suspects: my mom, Sally, Erica, Shawn, Lorna, Katharine and Mike. Thank you to April, Darrel, Lewis, Jordan, Rafe, Frey, Stella, Jules, Rafael and Kai for answering questions and providing sensitivity feedback. Many thanks to my cousin, Jason, for answering my tech questions. Hugs to my aunt and uncle, Debby and Kurt, for hosting me on my research trip to Los Angeles (with a side trip to Disneyland). Thank you to my husband, Craig, for listening to me go on (and on) about various plot problems, and to my agent, Juliet Mushens, for her continued championship and possible superhero powers. As ever, merci beaucoup to everyone at Pan Macmillan on both sides of the Atlantic Ocean: editors and publicists and everyone there work magic. Last but not least, my everlasting thank-you to booksellers, librarians, bloggers and every reader that took a chance on my words.

Complacency is a state of mind that exists only in retrospective: it has to be shattered before being ascertained.

—Vladimir Nabokov

SHATTERED MINDS

PROLOGUE

THE GIRL

Sudice headquarters, San Francisco, California, Pacifica

"What do you see?" the doctor asks.

"It's a bee on a rose, just like before. And the time before that. And the time before that." The girl leans back in her Chair, crossing her arms over her chest.

"And how does it make you feel?" the doctor nudges.

"Bored."

The girl glances away from the rose and the bee. Her brain map floats above them, translucent and pink as candyfloss. *That's me*, the girl thinks. She sees the brighter spots of the neural dust of her brain implants, sparkling deep in her cortex like stars. Within those pink-gray whorls are her thoughts, her dreams, her memories.

The doctor looks at the brain map and the waves on various machines dotted about the lab. The woman is trying to solve a puzzle about her mind, but the girl has no idea what the woman is searching for or how she'll find it.

The girl has done this exact appointment five times before,

1

though she usually sees the male doctor. She likes him, and wishes he were here instead. The girl has only met this doctor once before, at the first session. She can't remember the woman's name and is too embarrassed to ask. Being able to visit Sudice has been excellent extra credit for her senior project on neuroscience. Yet each time, she wonders about the point of this experiment. Perhaps she should simply stand up, shake the woman's hand, thank her for her time and inform her she's changed her mind.

"I'm going to try something a little different today," the doctor says, her lips curling up at the corners. The girl does not like her smile.

"Where's Dr. Teague?" she asks.

"He's unavailable."

"I think I might just go," the girl says, making to stand. "I'm not feeling well. Maybe I can meet with Dr. Teague when he's back."

"I know these appointments are tedious, but the work you're doing is going to change the world," the doctor says. "Don't you want to be right at the forefront of that?"

The girl hesitates. The doctor stands, moves closer. "I'm going to dose you with our new compound, and then we'll look at the images again, see if your emotional responses differ at all."

Before the girl can respond, the doctor takes her arm and presses a syringe into her skin, just below her elbow. The girl startles and cries out at the pain.

"All done," the doctor says, her eyes bright and unblinking.

The girl's arm burns. The world goes soft and fuzzy around the edges. The doctor settles the girl back in the Chair, lays the back down flat. She fits restraints around the girl's arms and legs.

"Wh-what?" the girl asks, words slurred.

"Don't worry. It's just a partial sedative mixed with Verve."

Another sharp smile. "With a little paralytic thrown in for good measure."

"V-Verve?" the girl asks, a thrum of fear going through her. Verve is a drug the San Francisco mob, the Ratel, created; it was all over the news feeds for weeks last year. It was meant to be like Zeal, but so much worse. Not a dream you wake up from, your frustrations spent cathartically. Instead you emerge hungry for violence. Pacifica promised they'd destroyed it. What will it do to her? Her limbs are heavy. She tries to move a finger. Nothing.

Time fractures and grows strange. The girl feels a faint tickling along her skull, a strange release of pressure.

"Look at the images again," the doctor instructs.

The girl's eyes move to the wallscreen, as if she can't help it. There is the bee, its segmented eyes staring at her, its pollen dusting the blood-red petals of the rose. Its stinger is as sharp as the thorns on the stem. Something new appears—a drop of blood drips from one thorn. Above the rose, two eyes open. One is blue, one is green. Heterochromic, just like hers. There's something odd about the images. As if they're more than they appear. As if she could fall into them.

"How do the images make you feel?" The pictures segment and flash before her. A bee. A rose. A thorn. A drop of blood. Mismatched eyes. Over and over, until they blur together.

"I don't feel anything," the girl says. And it's true. All her emotions are just . . . gone. As if they've never existed.

"I see." The doctor is excited, but trying to hide it. The top of the girl's head tickles again. She looks away from the images, back to her brain scan.

It looks different. There are darker specks scattered throughout her brain, moving around like busy ants. It takes her a moment to figure out what they are.

"Nanobots," the doctor answers for her. "They'll help the code settle in quickly."

"How . . ." the girl asks. Then she realizes why her skull itches. All her pain sensors are turned off, and the doctor has opened up her skull. A piece rests on the tray next to the Chair. The girl can just see it out of the corner of her eye.

The doctor holds up the blood-slicked bone.

"It's a barbaric approach these days, to actually open up a subject like this, but there's no risk of infection. And there's something about seeing the brain right there before you as the nanites do their work. It's more . . . visceral." The doctor sets the bone aside. "Don't worry, I'll put it back where it belongs when we're done."

The girl should feel fear, but there is nothing. Nothing.

Until there is.

The nanobots converge in her brain, digging deeper, down into the very core of her. The girl's emotions switch on. She feels everything—the pain in her skull, in her brain, the full horror of what's happening to her.

She opens her mouth and screams. Alarms blare and beep in the room. She can smell blood, thick and coppery, and the taste hits the back of her throat.

"You will change the world, my girl," the doctor says, leaning over her.

The world blinks out.

ONE

CARINA

Green Star Lounge, Los Angeles,
California, Pacifica

Carina awakens with a gasp and bites down a curse.

An alarm bleeps in the Zeal lounge. The clock on the flickering wallscreen tells her she's woken two hours earlier than she should have. The room is small and close, a little grimy. All it contains is a Chair, the Zeal machine, and its body monitors. Carina paid extra for a private room with money she doesn't have to spare.

An orderly buzzes the door and steps in, his white lab coat stained about the cuffs. "700628," he says, confused. "Why are you awake?"

"Your guess is as good as mine," Carina replies. "Put me back in."

The orderly shakes his head. His hair is short and buzzed, and he's thin enough that she can see the shape of his skull beneath his skin. "If you've been booted out early, there's a reason. Something's off. It'll need to reset, and you should stay out of the Zealscape for at least twelve hours."

Carina knows something is wrong—that last dream of the

girl on the table wasn't hers, and couldn't have been. It felt . . . unfinished, somehow. Like there should be more. Between that and not getting her proper fix, she wants—needs—to go right back in.

She gives the orderly a look that makes him pause. "Reach in my left pocket," she says. Her wrists are still restrained to stop her from lashing out in the dreams and hurting herself.

The orderly reaches into her pocket, his hand grazing her hip bone. He takes out a handful of credit chips. Enough to buy himself a very nice vat-grown steak dinner at a restaurant downtown.

"Put me back in," she says, her voice low. The white-clad orderly only knows Carina as 700628. He doesn't know her name, who she used to be, what she used to do before she lost it all to Zeal. He knows enough about what she does in her dreams that his eyes skitter away from hers.

He knows Carina wouldn't mind killing him. Slowly.

The orderly shrugs. "Your call, I guess." He preps another syringe.

Carina has to be reminded of her body while she waits. She lies back on the Chair, its plastic covering crinkling. She smells and hasn't showered in almost a week, hasn't eaten in two days, and lost her third tooth yesterday (was it yesterday?), spitting it out into the sink. She can't remember if she washed it away or if it's still there.

Zeal addiction is not for the faint-hearted.

She stares at the top of the orderly's head. *Quicker, quicker.*

He restarts the machine, the air filling with the comforting whirs and clicks she knows so well. He plunges the needle into the crook of her arm, one more mark out of many. She'll have to get a vein port put in soon. As the Zeal takes hold, her eyes roll up into her head.

"Sweet dreams," the orderly says, voice flat, already turning away.

Though she yearns for her own personal heaven and hell in the Zealscape, as she does every time, a little part of her hopes she'll never wake up.

It'd be so much easier that way.

TWO

MARK

Off-grid, San Francisco,
California, Pacifica

The man coughs, blood splattering into his hand. He doesn't pause to wipe it away. His hands dance in midair, manipulating the code his ocular implants project into the room around him. The room is empty, the white walls stark. There are no windows. His body is exhausted, his lungs struggling to work. Medical advancement miracles can't cure every disease, especially engineered ones.

Sweat trickles down his temples as he works. His hands shake, and he can't afford to make a mistake. There's only one person he can trust. Or at least, trust her to want to take Sudice down as much as he does.

There. His hands fall to his sides. The code floats around him, beautiful and perfect, like a nebula of the universe made of letters, numbers and symbols. Now all he has to do is find her. Minimizing the code, he opens the government map he cracked into earlier, typing in the numbers of her new VeriChip.

There she is. Right in Los Angeles, as he suspected. And she's plugged in.

"Finally, fate gives me a break," he mutters, beginning to prep the transfer when he hears the door open.

"Fuck." His pulse spikes. He has seconds, if that. He locks onto the signal in LA. "Please, please let this work." He can't stop a sob. "Don't let this be for nothing."

The footsteps come closer. The information streams into her brain. As soon as it finishes, he manages to still his shaking hands enough to obscure the breadcrumbs of the trail. He can only hope it's enough. He turns to face his killer.

Someone shoots the lock and kicks the door open. The woman steps in and shakes her head at him. "I'm disappointed in you, Mark."

"I'm more disappointed in you, you fucking psychopath." He's still shaking, but he hasn't pissed himself. Maybe he'll die with a modicum of dignity.

She tuts. "Language, Dr. Teague. And I've never been officially diagnosed." She flashes him a mirthless smile before hefting the gun. "Now, what have you done here?"

He says nothing. She moves forward, and with a wave of her hands latches onto his ocular implants. As she rifles through his recent history, he stifles a satisfied smirk when she can't find where he's sent it.

"You've made a mistake." She points the gun at him.

"I've never been more certain of anything in my life. I only wish I could be around to see you and Sudice fall." He's proud that, in the end, he stood up to them, at least put a wrench in their plans after all they've done.

No company is entirely invincible. Sudice has been trying for decades, buying politicians and using its deep entanglement in every aspect of Pacifica's economy and government to strangle its competition. Mark knows there's always a crack, a flaw that can be used to bring the whole thing down. He's found the fissure, but he's not strong enough to give it enough pressure to break.

"Any regrets?" the woman asks with a sardonic tilt of her head. "Any last-minute confessions before you meet your maker, if you believe in that sort of thing?"

Mark regrets ever working for Sudice. Greed was why he started, and he opened his eyes to the truth far too late. "I only had a few weeks left anyway, with whatever you gave me." He shrugs. "At least I might have done some good in the end. So no regrets."

"Pity, that."

She pulls the trigger. Mark falls. He stares at nothing, the dark bullet hole on his forehead like a third eye. Roz steps over him and takes up his code, transferring it from his dying implants into her own. Face impassive, she begins her search.

THREE

CARINA

The Zealscape, Green Star Lounge, Los Angeles, California, Pacifica

Carina's drug dreams always begin the same way.

She's back in Greenview House. Her father bought it even though it was far too big for three people, outside Woodside, California, less than an hour by hovercar out of San Francisco. Nothing but trees surrounded that house that would become a crypt. She couldn't wait to leave, and now, eight years later, she still can't escape it.

Carina walks through the empty hallways, her footsteps echoing. Nothing exists outside of the house in the Zealscape, not really, and the windows only look out into a gray fog. All her dreams and nightmares take place in its various rooms. Even if the rooms can expand into streets or forests, no matter how vast, she can turn a corner and step back into those familiar corridors. She tried to change the Zealscape program to another setting, but in the end, her subconscious is too tied to Greenview House and everything that happened here.

She opens the door to the room where she last saw the young girl and the doctor she knows from earlier nightmares. They are nowhere to be seen.

"Anyone here?" she calls. "Come out, come out, wherever you are!"

Silence.

Carina turns away. Needing her fix, she creates her first victim, bringing him to life on a table before her, prepped just as she wishes. Half the fun is the hunt, but when she first plugs in, there's never the patience for it. It's an appetizer of violence before the more leisurely meal.

Carina has a very specific type, here in the Zealscape. She kills criminals, perpetrators of terrible, fictional crimes. They are usually men, middle-aged, cocky in their assurance that they are getting away with their wrongdoings. She has killed women, for a bit of variety, often "angel of death" types. Never children or teenagers—which is why the vision of the girl was so damn jarring.

Where had that come from?

The Zealscape is where Carina lets it all out so that those people out in the real world, those strangers who seem as insubstantial as her dream creations, are safe from her. She has killed hundreds of figments within these walls over the last six months. Used almost every weapon. Killed quickly. And slowly. The one constant is that she never tires of it.

The man pushes against his bonds, the whites of his eyes showing. Carina has created him a serial killer, like her, but he preys on the innocent. He buries young boys beneath his house, like John Wayne Gacy. He's not real, but he deserves death.

Her fingers itch and she moves closer. His chains rattle as his struggles grow more frantic. A desperate, delicious gurgling bubbles from his throat. Her fingers tingle in anticipation, and her heartbeat quickens.

Carina doesn't speak to her victims. She did in the beginning, trying to make these fabrications of her imagination understand what she was about to do to them. It grew dull, unlike the act of killing.

Carina sometimes finds her situation amusing, when she's coherent enough for amusement. The government doles out unlimited Zeal to keep criminals off the streets, yet offers them an unlimited playground to hone their criminal skills. With chronic Zealot mortality rates as high as eighty percent, however, the government doesn't have much to fear.

Closing her eyes to concentrate, she opens them to a long, thin knife resting in her hands. There are some weapons she prefers—the knife is particularly instinctual, personal, whereas the gun is too distant, even if the kickback and the *crack* are satisfying.

Carina hefts the knife.

The man below her is in his physical prime, muscled as a wrestler. He's strong, the chains binding him straining with each pull. Her usual type is older, paunchier. Though she still buzzes with the need to kill, she forces herself to slow down, at least a little. She runs the knife tip along his skin next to the bonds. A tear slides down his cheek. She wipes it away with her thumb, then brings her fingertip to her mouth, tasting the salt. It feels real. Real enough.

His pain and fear feeds her, as if she grows larger from it. Only here, when the blood runs onto the white floor, does she feel alive any more. Carina is not that wreck of a woman strapped to a Chair in the Zealot room, suffering from mouth sores and malnutrition. That woman is the ghost.

The man whimpers again. Carina relishes the sound for a moment, then stands and thrusts the knife into his throat. Blood spurts from the punctured artery, painting her face red. She leans her head back, holding the hilt tighter, pressing down hard. All too soon the gurgles stop. She has not given this man a name, or imagined what life he might have lived outside his crimes. His eyes are wide, his mouth open in shock. She takes her hands away from the hilt. Her hands stop shaking. Carina sits next to the body, closing her eyes, breathing in the iron tang of blood.

She's euphoric after the kill, and these brief moments before the craving returns are the only times she feels even remotely like her pre-Zeal self. Guilt bleeds in around the edges, even if she can't regret that glee of the kill.

A few years ago, Carina had this under control. An occasional impulse she could push back and ignore. Nothing bubbled to the surface; it hadn't since she was a teenager. She'd seemed like a perfectly functioning member of society. A great career, a promising future. And then, slowly but surely, it had all unraveled. A Zeal trip here or there. Once a month. Then twice a month. Weekly. By the time she'd left Sudice, it'd been every other day.

Now, she rarely leaves. She doesn't trust herself out there. A wolf among sheep who'd never see her coming.

When she opens her eyes, the body is gone. A benefit of dream worlds: no cleanup. No fear of being discovered dumping the body. No fear of discovery at all.

Dealing with the orderly's accusing eyes is the only judgment she faces, and one she never fears.

She holds onto her sense of self, staying calm and collected. Replete. The mind of the scientist is back. She wanders the imaginary halls of her childhood home, peeking through the doors: the old home gym, her mother's bedroom, preserved just as it was the last time she left it and never returned. Her teenage room, with its holographic band posters and unmade bed, reeking of a desperate attempt at normalcy.

All too soon, that buzz returns. Her fingers twitch. That delicious expectation of following her victim and their moves: where they'll be, how she'll take them and make them hers. Her thoughts turn only to blood and flayed muscles. Of taking out organs and hefting them in her hands, arranging them just so.

Here in the Zealscape, she can lose herself in the hunt as much as she wants. Here, she hurts only herself, as more and more of her body wastes away, strapped in the Chair in the Zeal lounge. Her body warms, thrums with excitement. She whispers Zeal's newest catchphrase to herself: "More real than reality."

Carina enters another room. In the real Greenview House, it was a guest bedroom and study, but now it is her planning room. One wall is blank, and she can visualize and design her next victim. She decides to go back to her roots: a distorted echo of her first target. Carina builds the man from scratch. Early fifties, a beer gut, hair and beard of graying brown. Hard eyes, an unhappy slash of a mouth. Large hands that make blocky fists. He is different enough that the sight of his face doesn't make her shudder. She feels awareness sharpening. She's growing closer. Her fingers twitch.

After creating him, she sends him away. She spends a few minutes programming his background—his job, his friends, sketches of his wife and family. This criminal has a penchant for child porn. She can again pretend it's vengeance, not pure, selfish pleasure. Most Zealots don't have such control over their drug-fueled dreams. Then again, most people don't have PhDs in neuroprogramming.

She can't wait any more. Her skin is hot with need.

Carina walks through a door on the far side of the room and steps into a hallway that transitions seamlessly into a street. She follows her prey at a distance, watching the graying head bob as he walks. Her jaw is clenched tight. She barely blinks. The other people on the street are only vaguely human-shaped, with blurred ovals for faces. Nightmares for anyone else, but for her, just stand-ins.

Carina grasps a Stunner she conjured in her pocket. Sometimes she'll stretch out the hunt—stalk them for longer, make their lives more detailed, lose herself in the fantasy— but she can't today. Her breath catches in her throat. Her eyes in the Chair, back in reality, dilate behind closed eyelids. Almost time. Almost time to feel alive again, for a little while.

She's just taken out the Stunner in a quivering hand when it happens.

The street disappears, along with her quarry. Just gone, as if someone has hit a switch. The whole room turns black. No, darker—that blackness of the space between stars. There have been glitches in the system before, but Carina knows, with a deep certainty, that this is something more.

She's lost the sense that she has a body. Her mind seems to float in the darker-than-darkness. Then light explodes back into her world.

Numbers, sounds, flashes of brightness, the feel of fingernails against her skin, of bubbles on her tongue. All her senses fragment and blur. Between the overloads is a snapshot of cohesive thought.

I'm dying. This is what dying must feel like.

The noise and the chaos begin to crystallize. Five images, over and over: A bee, buzzing, its wings flapping frantically, its antennae twitching. A rose, in full bloom; brilliantly, impossibly red, a drop of dew on one petal. A thorn, from the rose, its point curved and wicked. A drop of blood, welling on a fingertip. And eyes, staring right at her, wide and fathomless. Heterochromic—one green, one blue. They play, over and over and over again, telling a narrative she cannot hope to understand.

And then they stop, though she can still sense them, as though the images are flashing just out of sight.

The last image, the mismatched eyes, takes over her entire vision. It zooms out, until Carina sees the rest of the face, and then a body on a Chair in that lab she recognizes all too well. The last vision had been through the girl's viewpoint, but Carina is sure this is her. She's young—fifteen, sixteen at a push. She's all doe-eyed innocence, spindly, coltish legs, her hair half an inch long. She reminds Carina a little too much of herself as a teenager. The girl is dead.

Part of her short hair has been shaved away. Dr. Roz Elliot has opened up her skull, poked about in the contents, and sewn it back up, yet dead flesh does not knit. Her tanned skin is pale and chalky, legs akimbo.

"What did you do, Roz?" Carina asks the darkness.

The dead girl does not answer. Her eyes are open and staring. One blue, one green.

As if Carina blinks, the image is gone, and all is darker than black once again.

•

Carina awakens again into the grimy Zealot room, her mouth dry. An alarm again blares through the room.

There's no attendant. Carina twists her real, hurting body on the Chair, the wires tugging at her skin. The beeping doesn't stop, pulsing with the throbbing of her temples. Far away, she hears frantic footsteps and concerned voices calling out to each other.

"Where's the fucking orderly?" Carina yells. Her head still spins with the images.

The orderly who put her back in the dream enters the room. Stops, stares.

"You're not dead," he says.

"Should I be?"

"Everyone else is."

•

Carina stumbles home, clutching her coat around her thin shoulders.

The police who came to the Green Star Lounge wanted to interview her about what had happened, but she put on the "I'm-an-unhinged-Zealot" act, flying spittle and all, and they left her alone pretty quickly.

They decided she was lucky to be the only survivor. They let her go. One drug-addled woman is clearly not the cause of the malfunction of the Zeal lounge. It'd been a slow day, but thirteen Zealots are now dead. Who will mourn them?

The images play in her mind as Carina totters on unsteady feet. The bee. The rose. The thorn. The blood. The eyes. And then the dead girl with the same mismatched eyes. Carina knows her Zealscape intimately. Every corner. Every seam. Every brick. She's built it so carefully over the last six months.

This is something else.

She reaches her apartment, tucked into the Chesterfield Square neighborhood of South Los Angeles. Once, these few blocks had one of the highest crime rates in the world. Now, most of the inhabitants are Zealots plugged into their dreams. It is a ghost town.

The entrance to the apartment building senses her VeriChip and she sends the passcode from her eye implants to the door. The metal grate scrapes open. She makes her slow progress up the stairs, pausing to catch her breath every few steps, her knees shaking. This apartment was cheaper than one with an elevator. She underestimated how quickly her health would start to deteriorate. Falling against her front door, she sends the next passcode to the lock.

Once Carina was tidy, but now her clothes are scattered around the apartment, and she hasn't even bothered sending the bots around to clean. She tends to throw away clothes when they're too dirty to wear, buying cheap new ones from the replicator. The sweat-stained sheets on her bed need changing. This is the place where she has a few hours of fitful sleep or eats some tasteless, vaguely nutritious food before going back to the Green Star Lounge.

This is the place where she looks at the scan of her brain, trying to find out why it's broken and she now wants to kill everyone she comes across. Setting the program to load, she goes to the bathroom.

Her tooth is still there, the eroded root crusted with dried blood. She washes her hands, and the tooth disappears down into the pipes. She tongues the empty space in her mouth where it used to be, wincing at her sore gums. It could be fixed, but it'd mean more time out of the Zealscape or away from the project.

Then it hits her: the lounge will almost certainly be closed tomorrow and she doesn't know how she will get her dose of Zeal.

She should care more about the people who died. She should worry that going back to the same lounge, or another one, means it could happen again, and she might not be so lucky if it does. But she can't care about anything except finding that next hit.

Carina collapses on the sagging couch. The wallscreens are always turned off. The kitchen cupboards are empty, so if she wants to eat, she'll have to order NutriPaste from the replicator, as that's all she can afford. The thought of its chalky texture turns her stomach. So she sits. *Bee. Rose. Thorn. Blood. Eyes, one green, one blue.*

What do they mean? Is it gibberish, some strange side effect from a virus let loose in the Zeal program subsystem? The bit of her that was once a neuroprogrammer is curious, but that part is mostly swallowed up by Zeal apathy. She can only care about her main project.

Her brain scan has loaded. It floats in the middle of the living room, taking up most of the space. Her implants are old and need refreshing, but they work well enough for the Zeal, and that's all she cares about.

Carina can find nothing physical to explain the gradual unraveling of her mind. Her prefrontal cortex seems normal. Her ventromedial cortex is not shrunken, so decision-making should also still be fine. Her dopamine receptors are shot, but that's more thanks to the Zeal than any existing precondition. The way she processes emotion and empathy is different, but she's been like that since she was a teen and it doesn't really show on her brain. Once, her emotions had been entirely walled away. For years, nothing had touched her.

It was only once she started feeling again that she also started wanting to kill.

She's been trying to get back to how she was five years ago. She might have created a somewhat workable code, but she doesn't have the proper equipment, nor a lab. Once, she toyed with going back to Sudice for access to the Los Angeles lab. It would have meant Roz would find out her address, but Carina thought enough time had passed that it might be all right. Her recent Zealscape vision, if it's true, kills that plan.

She sends her brain scan away, too tired to try and puzzle over the code any more. She hasn't made any real progress in months, anyway. Her concentration is shot, and she's lost her touch. Somewhere deep inside her, she wonders if she's too far gone ever to find some semblance of normalcy. Or if she even cares.

Carina turns on her implants and brings up photos of the old team at Sudice. There's Dr. Mark Teague, smiling and waving at the camera, his tanned skin glowing, silver hair glinting in the overhead lighting of the lab. There's Dr. Aliyah Zahedi, with her enigmatic smile, dark skin, orange hair a little mussed from running frustrated fingers through it all day while running her trials. She'd been the quietest of the bunch, but with a wicked sense of humor. And there's Dr. Kim Mata—part-Japanese, hair just starting to gray and cut into a short bob. Even though Mark is twice her age, Kim looks older, as she's one of the few people in Pacifica not obsessed with flesh parlors. Carina hasn't thought of Kim, her constant nicknames, her wheedling jokes, in months.

Dr. Roz Elliot is not in the picture.

Carina hasn't thought about any of them much in the last few months. When she left Sudice eight months ago, they were often in her thoughts. Then the Zeal took over. She'd befriended them, as much as Carina could be friends with anyone. She'd grown used to them, admired their minds enough that they became real to her. Even when she started wanting to kill everyone around her, Mark, Kim and Aliyah were safe. Fundamentally, they were good people, and Carina only kills criminals—at least, so far, though she fears her control weakening.

Carina opens the staff image of Dr. Elliot and narrows her eyes as she takes in the perfect dark-blonde bob, the bland smile for the camera. There's a criminal. There's someone Carina wouldn't mind hurting.

Carina has no recording of that vision in the Zealscape. If she had, she could send it to the authorities, let them deal with whatever Roz has done. No proof, no crime.

Opening up the other staff photos, her gaze lingers on Kim. She's a head and a half shorter than anyone else on the team. Flyaway hair always escaping her bun and framing her face. Kim could probably tell her something about what happened today, but Carina doesn't want Kim to know just how far she has fallen. She looks at Kim's wide smile as she displays one of her precious collectible figurines, proudly balancing it on one palm, its tuft of pink hair almost tickling her nose. Kim looks goofy and playful, and not at all like one of the best neuroprogrammers in Pacifica; not like a woman traumatized by the murder of her wife. Carina turns off her implants.

She sits and stares at the blank wall for hours, blinking slowly. At some point past midnight, basic human survival instinct kicks in. Mechanically she goes to the bathroom, then the kitchen to order some NutriPaste from the replicator, grimacing at the taste and drinking water to wash it down.

Zeal withdrawal is already kicking in. Her limbs twitch as though they've been electrocuted. Her mouth is dry no matter how much water she drinks. The synapses in her brain aren't firing quite right—thoughts spiral into nothingness. There are no urges to harm anyone in this plane of reality. They are safe, as long as she has her dose.

The images are still loud and clear. The dead girl's face, staring ahead, accusatory.

22

"I didn't kill you," Carina says out loud to the blank wall. "Get out of my head."

The girl doesn't answer. She can't. Carina bashes her fist against the wall. It hurts, but even the pain is distant.

She isn't sure whether she wishes she'd died tonight or not. Admitting that uncertainty only cements the fear lingering in her fractured thoughts. Sometimes Carina wants to fix whatever's wrong with her and find a way back to life. Other times she wants nothing more than, if not to die, then to cease to exist. A subtle difference. That feeling is growing stronger as more of her is consumed by Zeal.

Carina doesn't sleep. She waits for morning, where she'll find another Zeal lounge and plug back in.

FOUR

DAX

*An abandoned warehouse, Los Angeles,
California, Pacifica*

<We're in!> Raf sends to the Trust through his implants.

<You sure about that?> Charlie asks. <You said that an hour ago.>

<I'm sure. We're definitely behind the firewall, and no one's any the wiser.>

Raf rambles on about how he did it in a litany of technobabble that Dax immediately tunes out. Raf's almost dancing in place with excitement. Their avatars all look like they do in real life, so he's still the shortest of all of them, a Mexican-American man with a tidy beard and hair in desperate need of a trim.

Raf's VR world is as black as the night sky. His code orbits the group in a corona of green, blue and dark purple. The edges of Dax's, Raf's and Charlie's avatars glow softly, like angels in darkness. Everything feels removed. Physical sensations in the VR are muted and brittle.

Dax tried to figure out how it all worked when he first joined the Trust, but anything more than the basics of coding continue to elude him. All he knows is that Raf has somehow slipped them behind the complicated security system of Sudice, Incorporated. They're in the outer DMZ levels—not close enough to do any real harm, not yet, but it's still further than they've been in a long time. And the first real progress they've made since they lost Tam. He tries not to think of his twin sister. Tries not to look at the spot in their circle where she would have stood.

<The virus?> Charlie asks. The leader of their ragtag gang floats in the darkness with them, scarlet-red hair particularly spiky in her VR avatar.

Raf nods and, with delicate dancing of fingers, slips it behind the firewall. With his usual artistic flare, Raf has crafted the virus in the form of a snake. It will sit behind the firewalls, spreading out its tail, catching information, but do nothing else. Not at first. Raf has spent months on it, probing the outer firewalls and security for weaknesses. And Dax, Charlie's right-hand man, has overseen logistics and planning, fretting over each detail, certain that at any moment they'll be caught.

If they are captured, there will be no trial. Their bodies will not be frozen and put in stasis with other Pacifica criminals. Sudice will not let them fall into the government's hands. They'll be killed by the company—quickly, if they're lucky—and then incinerated, rolled back into a replicator, and churned out as plastic Tupperware for leftover dinner.

<OK, good. That's enough for now. Let's get out now,> Charlie says, terse.

<Already?> Raf pouts. <We haven't done anything.>

<We've been through this about twenty times, Raf. We plant it. We get out. Now.> Charlie's tone brooks no argument. <We've got a matter of seconds before the Wasps sting our asses. Pull the plug, Raf.>

A second later, the code vanishes. The virtual reality simulation powers down. The Trust are merely three people standing in an abandoned warehouse in east Los Angeles. The switch back to reality is always jarring. The real world doesn't have the hypersaturated colors or heightened emotions of the Zealscape, nor the crisp yet distant edges of virtual reality. Reality is messy. The warehouse smells of the rotten rodent corpses that are moldering in its corners.

"Did they track us?" Charlie asks as they all take the small electrodes off their temples.

Dax checks the VR specs on his implants. "No buzzing of security Wasps out there, and no one within a hundred feet of us in either direction. I think we're good."

"Glad to hear it."

They take a moment to stretch out the cramps in their muscles. Charlie shows off and does a few slow flips around the warehouse, then tugs her leather jacket straight. Raf applauds, and Charlie gives him a little sardonic bow.

They pack up their kit. It's all custom-made by Raf, with some hardware and firmware thrown in by Charlie. Almost nine months after joining the Trust, Dax is still a little amazed Raf is walking free. If the government and Sudice had their way, Rafael Hernandez would be in custody. Then again, the man could probably hack his way out of stasis. Raf rolls his shoulders. His dark hair is messy.

"You gonna help me pack up, or are you just gonna stare at my pretty face some more?" Raf asks Dax.

Dax rolls his eyes and hefts a backpack. One by one, they slip out of the warehouse, through the blind alley where the surveillance drones don't fly. Charlie leaves first, her scarlet pixie cut hidden by a hood, only her blue eyes flashing in the darkness. Raf lifts his own pack and follows her.

Dax goes last, and can't help but glance behind him. He wishes Tam were here, able to slink out right next to him like always. He can just picture her, with her features an echo of his own—they'd be mirror images if he hadn't had his testosterone implant fitted and started visiting flesh parlors at puberty. He can almost see the smile she reserved only for him, and hear her teasing words: *Hey asshole, I know you. We shared a womb and you hogged all the extra space.*

Tam's not there. She's gone, somewhere he can't follow, and he doesn't know if he will ever get her back.

Dax throws a DNA scrub grenade over his shoulder as he leaves. The ball hisses as it hits the floor, the tiniest nanobots floating through the air to eat every dead skin cell and piece of hair they left behind before self-combusting. Not so much as a strand of rat hair will be left when they're done.

Maybe it'll even improve the smell.

The three of them take different routes. Dax walks alone through the abandoned streets, the dark night lit up with neon signs. Holographic advertisements dance along brick and concrete walls. A beautiful woman with lavender hair winks at him, pursing her lips to showcase her red lipstick. Athletic men and women flex their muscles, advertising the latest and greatest in nanobots that can repair—and build new—muscle faster than the human body ever could. A couple dancing, promoting a new brainloading program that enables anyone to move as gracefully as they do. The late spring humidity is stifling, the air close and scented with frying oil, ginger and onions from a nearby takeout joint for when people want a non-replicated meal. In one of the apartments above him, someone practices the saxophone, jazz music drifting down over the hush of the street.

The Trust meet again at an unmarked hovercar. Dax is the

last one to enter. It takes off and heads back to headquarters, which Raf has affectionately named the Technodrome. The others speak among themselves, but Dax is silent. He looks out the window at the untidy sprawl of Los Angeles, the endless sea of lights. Tall skyscrapers merge with the smaller, floating buildings between them, connected by thin, flexible bridges. They are the most recent additions to the city, and work so well with the frequent earthquakes that the city will probably make most new buildings float. It'd mean the ground could go back to being green to combat the still-lingering smog. Or that's the plan. Dax thinks it would look beautiful.

Other hovercars whoosh past the window. Dax should feel triumphant. They've planted the virus. It'll lie low within Sudice's systems for a few days as Raf tinkers with processes and creates modified backdoors. The program will amass data and split it up into small packets, exfiltrating it over time encoded as normal corporate traffic. The Viper is in part an AI, making sure all information leaving doesn't trigger anomalies and bring in Wasps, Sudice's security AI bots. In all likelihood, the Trust won't find anything terribly useful. But if the Viper can stay undetected and disappear, then that's a weapon to use for a bigger exploit.

The rest of the Trust are smug. Even Charlie is smiling, looking out the window over the City of Angels. None of them mention Tam. His sister as good as died for them all. Her body is alive, well hidden, but they can't reach her mind.

Dax knows the others wonder if Tam betrayed them, though they know better than to say that to him. His hand snakes up to his neck to clutch the Shoshone bead necklace his sister made for them at their home in Timbisha, in Death Valley, back before they left home and plunged headfirst into danger. They should have stayed on the reservation. Tam's injury four months ago nearly drove the Trust apart. Maybe it should have stayed broken.

Even if everything works perfectly with the Viper, it's highly unlikely that they'll all come through this unscathed. Dax sighs, fingers running over the beads for comfort. The only other option is to do nothing, to let Tam's injury be in vain. That's not an option. For Dax, or for any of the others.

FIVE

CARINA

Chesterfield Square, Los Angeles,
California, Pacifica

The next day, the Green Star Lounge is still closed.

Carina stares at its darkened entrance and curses. The nearest Zeal lounge is about a mile away, she has no money for a hovercab, and the withdrawal is kicking in hard.

She starts walking, wrapping her arms around herself to stop shaking so badly. Every half block she pauses, bent over, wheezing. If she was healthy, it'd take her about fifteen, twenty minutes, tops, to reach the next Zeal lounge. It takes her forty-five instead. Forty-five long, agonizing minutes. She retches onto a potted tree on the sidewalk, but all that comes up is bile.

People's eyes glaze and slide away from Carina. They're embarrassed for her—a Zealot out in public, suffering from the drug that most can take with no ill effects. A physical reminder that Pacifica isn't as perfect as it pretends to be.

Zeal is integral to so many aspects of Pacifica. It's a neuroware component of brainloading information directly into their implants, or it can be used to assist with therapy. For nearly all of the population, if they have a bad day, they can go to a Zeal lounge on their way home. Normal citizens frustrated by office politics, or their relationship, or a friendship gone sour, go to the slick Zeal lounges in the better parts of town, where the addicts don't go. They take a hit, plug in and imagine killing their boss, or maybe they have really good, angry sex with someone—either another person plugged in to the same Zealscape, or an imagined figment—or they have a proper blow-out screaming fight with their friend. Then they unplug, go home. Zeal is but a temporary catharsis, more vivid than the virtual reality feeds you can order off your wallscreen. Only the defective ones grow addicted. The ones with brains wired for violence, the ones in high danger of becoming criminals.

Carina hasn't always been like this, though she's always dreamed of murder. At sixteen, everyone takes their first hit of Zeal. She took it along with everyone else, and killed the man in her imagination she'd dreamed of killing every day of her life since she could remember. Everything she'd ever experienced paled in comparison to that sensation of ripping into flesh, or making someone else scream in pain until they could scream no more.

She came out to face a very unnerved orderly, but Zeal had done its job. She felt freed, sedated, but she didn't crave another hit. She still avoided the drug, afraid of how much she'd enjoyed it. Until a few years ago, when the urges to kill grew stronger, until they threatened to consume her entirely.

Carina finally reaches the Zealot lounge called Vellocet. It's flashier than her old haunt, which looked like a hospital ward. That had actually been comforting. This one, with its purple lights and 1960s-inspired furniture, makes her lip curl.

She trudges in. Beggars can't be choosers.

Thrusting her credits at the receptionist, who looks at her as though she's trash, Carina writes down her identification number for them to call out. In the nicer lounges, people scan their VeriChips, but here in the Zealot shitholes, no one wants the government to know. There's the fear that the government will watch, see how deranged their dreams are, and they'll disappear, frozen into stasis without a trace. These lounges aren't meant to record trips. Carina's fairly sure the government watches them anyway. They could crack down on Zealot lounges, but they choose to let the addicts take care of themselves, one failed body at a time.

The paradise of Pacifica.

Carina shuffles, her legs giving out just in time for her to collapse into an empty chair. She's thirsty, but there's no water. Her lips are dry and cracked, her breath stinks and her hair is stringy with sweat.

The lobby is busy, and she recognizes a few faces from the Green Star Lounge. Lucky souls who weren't there yesterday. She waits, the shakes growing worse, her patience wearing thin.

Finally: "700628."

The orderly barely gives her a second glance as she leads her down the hall. Old music plays. Carina knows this band: The Beatles. Her father played a lot of their songs, their voices echoing through Greenview House those few times *he* was in his good moods. The Beatles sing about an octopus.

The orderly plugs Carina into a Chair while whistling along with the music. It puts her on edge, but she resists the urge to lash out, not wanting to risk being thrown out. She wouldn't last long enough to make it to the next Zealot lounge a mile away.

"Sweet dreams," the orderly says, as monotone as all the others who have said it to Carina over the last few months.

As the drug takes hold, she can't help but feel a thrill of fear. What if whatever happened to her before comes again?

What if she joins all those souls who died yesterday? What if she finally disappears?

Carina smiles as she falls back into dreamland.

•

At first, nothing seems to have changed. Carina is back in Green-view House. She appears in the dining room, and makes the dining table, chairs and china cabinet disappear with a blink. She burns with the desire to kill someone; it itches like anxiety.

The same muscled criminal she created yesterday appears. She cuts corners—the figure's vague and barely sketched. Wrapping her fingers around his throat, she squeezes, feeling the pulse jump beneath her fingers. She's about to break his neck when his features shift, becoming the teenager with the mismatched eyes.

Carina lets go. The girl staggers back, staring at her. One green eye. One blue. Even as Carina watches, the simulacrum becomes more detailed, until she's a perfect replica of the murdered girl from the earlier vision. The girl falls to the ground, pale as though she's been dead for over a day, even though scant seconds ago Carina could feel the pulse in her neck.

After the first rush of adrenaline, Carina feels strangely calm. It's happening again. Whatever virus was in the Green Star Lounge has come here. She won't be able to escape her fate a second time. It's almost a relief.

"Find out who killed me," the girl says. Black blood dribbles from the corner of her chapped lips. The cut on the side of her head is almost a terrible smile, the metal sutures like ragged teeth.

"No," Carina says. "I don't care who killed you."

"You should. You will." The girl disappears.

Carina presses the heels of her palms against her eyes,

steadying her breath. When she takes her hands away, Dr. Mark Teague stands before her. Boyish good looks, light-brown skin, a shock of incongruous gray hair. He gives her that signature crooked half-smile. One that melted most people's hearts like butter, but only softened hers ever so slightly.

Carina's old colleague has never appeared in her Zealscapes. Before she left it all, he, Kim and Aliyah were among the few people she trusted. Her three fellow scientists, pitted against their boss, against Sudice's true plans for their research—against the world, it seemed sometimes. Despite all the people she's harmed in her dreams, she's never created those three.

"If you're seeing this, Carina, then I'm dead," Mark says.

Carina says nothing. It doesn't feel true; he can't be real. Mark flickers—some feedback—and Carina immediately recognizes it as a glitch, not part of the Zeal dreamscape.

It's foreign.

She suspected this when her Zealscapes shifted so strangely, but it's supposed to be impossible. Shared visions, sure, if people are plugged into the same room and network. But not this.

"What happened?" she asks.

"I do not know. This is pre-recorded, set to send once my life vitals end." He does not look particularly sad, but then she supposes when he created this, however long ago, it was only a precaution. He looks the same as ever, but Carina knows he was close to seventy when they worked together, even though he looked like a prematurely graying twenty-five-year-old. Good flesh parlors and gene therapy.

"I recently changed this recording to be sent only to Carina Kearney upon my death. You will already have received other messages from me."

Carina swallows. "The images? The murdered girl?"

A pause as the program takes in her response. "Those images have been specially chosen. The bee. The rose. The thorn. The drop of blood. The mismatched eyes. They're more than images. They each contain encrypted information, which has now been downloaded deep into the frontal lobe of your cerebral cortex. I've tried to make this as secure as possible because I feared this message could be intercepted during transmission to you; or I could still be caught, and then the information could be used against you."

"What have you done? Why?" Her voice rises. This is the most emotional she's felt outside of a kill for months.

Another delay as Mark's AI program processes her words. "I'm sorry to do this to you. The images are inconvenient, but it was the only way I could move it off their servers without detection. You can help finish this. You are the natural choice."

"I'm not. I left Sudice. I want nothing to do with this. You know where I am, and what I've become."

His face creases in sadness. "I do know. You should have come to me, when you found out what Roz was really doing. We could have worked together." His eyes grow haunted. "Maybe we could have prevented what happened next."

"Maybe I should have," she concedes. She'd run away from everything, from everyone, without even a look over her shoulder. "Who's the girl, Mark?"

"You'll find out. It's all in your head now. Will you help me?"

"Help you do what?"

"Destroy Sudice."

Carina can't help but laugh. "Destroy Sudice. Are you absolutely cracked, Mark? I'm not even doing a very good job of helping myself. I don't know how the hell you expect me to be able to help you."

Another pause. Carina isn't sure how the AI will respond to her outburst, but she knows whatever AI program he's installed over the messages is good. He must have spent months on it, making sure the AI could have some sort of response, no matter the question.

"You can help me. And you have more reason than most to hate Sudice and want to take them down. Such a brilliant mind. What they did to you was just as much of a crime."

Carina feels trapped, as though she's being backed into a corner. "What are you talking about, Mark?"

Mark smiles sadly at her. No. This isn't him. Dr. Teague is dead. She is speaking to a clever echo of him. A ghost is asking her for help, and she wants nothing more than to turn him down.

"You were the only one I could send the images to," he says, voice still blandly pleasant, "because your memories are in the Sudice database. The bee, the rose—all the images are tied to specific memories from your past."

It takes her a few moments. "From phase one of the Syn-Maps project? Those would be old memories, from when I was sixteen."

"Roz kept all of them."

Carina suppresses a shiver. "Why? That experiment didn't work properly."

The AI's face falls. "I feared this."

"Mark?" She's finally feeling afraid. It spreads through her stomach, the sensation enhanced in the Zealscape. She wants to run.

Mark's ghost reaches out and touches Carina on the fore-head. "I'm sorry."

Something deep within her shifts, clicks back into place. Something she never even knew was out of alignment.

"Roz blocked you," Mark says. "I found it, when I was trying to see if this plan would work."

Memories swirl through her mind. Roz leaning over Carina strapped into a Chair. Just like the teenage girl. Having her look at Rorschach tests; endless hours of questioning and experiments. Pain, so much pain.

"SynMaps didn't work," Carina whispers.

"That's what she wanted you to think," Mark says softly. He comes closer, rests his forehead against hers. She can't feel it. Pushing away a memory of Mark laughing in the lab, she knows he's not real and is only a clever program, but it's comforting just the same as her world falls apart.

Whatever Roz did to her has suppressed her memory. It's there, but she never thinks of that time in the lab, of what really happened to her when she was a teen.

"She did this to me." It's hard to say the words aloud.

"She transformed you under phase one of SynMaps, took you under her wing, and kept monitoring you under phase two. I found out after you left."

The girl Roz killed knew Mark. "Roz had you work on the real reason behind brain recording."

"God help me, I did. And I know that I regretted it to the end of my days."

Carina's still trying to come to terms with her world tilting on its axis.

"You have to unlock the images, Carina. They'll come to you, in the right order. You will be guided into remembering them. They . . . are strong memories."

Carina should say something, but the words die on her tongue. She can't stop thinking about Dr. Roz Elliot, leaning over her, taking her memories and examining them from every direction. Finding out what made her tick. Molding her. Until she was someone different. Cold. Unbothered by ethics, if the end result was worth it. Someone more like Roz Elliot.

Until it fell apart.

"Roz is why I'm like this," Carina whispers, gesturing to the walls of Greenview House. "Why I'm here."

"Her programming broke down. Your urge to kill is the side effect."

"Could you have fixed it?"

"I don't know. Have you been trying?"

"And failing. I don't have the equipment."

Mark's ghost's lips purse. "Together, we could have done it, especially if Kim and Aliyah helped. Unfortunately, though, even if you gain access to equipment, I must ask you not to run any additional programming on your brain until all the information I sent has been unlocked."

Carina swallows. "It'd delete?"

"Almost certainly. Also, it'd fry your brain."

"What the fuck, Mark."

"I know. I'm sorry. As soon as it's all out, though, you're in the clear."

Her hands ball into fists. Even if she walked into a perfect lab tomorrow, she wouldn't be able to use her code. Never mind that she's a long way out from solving the problem of her own brain—that vague hope of figuring it out is one of the few things she has left.

"What Roz did to you is unforgivable," Mark says. "This is why I've had to involve you. I didn't want to, but you know what they're capable of. It didn't stop with you. It didn't stop with the girl." His voice closes. "Sudice won't stop unless we make it. So I ask you again: will you help me?"

Carina takes in a shaking breath. "Yes. Yes, Mark. I'll help you. I don't have much choice."

Mark leans back and rests a hand on her shoulder that she still can't feel.

"To release the first image, you must be out of the Zeal-scape," the AI says. "Focus on your earliest memory, but doing it here will not work."

"OK." Greenview House looms in her mind, but he's right. Her first memory does nothing here.

"That will start the process. From there, it's up to you. At some point, they will probably come after you. You will outsmart them."

"I doubt that." She looks at him. "How many of my memories have you seen?"

"Enough." A pause. "Trauma shows on the brain, and you've had more than your share." He pauses, and something like pity crosses his features. She's embarrassed, guilty—it flares into another violent urge. She wants to stab him, kill him herself, even though he's already dead. Her hands clench.

"Fuck you, Mark."

He doesn't flinch. "I'm sorry, Carina. I had no choice."

"There's always a choice."

Again, that haunted look. "That's true enough."

"If you found my memories, it's only a matter of time before Roz brings them up again."

"I deleted them. And their backups. Your memories are dead and gone from Sudice's servers. Nothing can bring them back."

Carina swallows. "She'll have her own backups, Mark. I hate what you did. I absolutely hate it. But I hate what she did so much more."

"That is precisely what I was counting on. This is the right thing to do."

"You know I've never cared about doing the right thing."

"You did, though, Carrie." Carina flinches at that old nick-name. "A harsh sense of justice at times, yes, but that means I know you can do what needs to be done."

His outline fades, pixellates. The AI is terminating.

"Mark!" Carina calls, voice shrill. She's still angry at him, dead or not, but she doesn't want him to disappear. That will mean he's really gone. "Mark! Does Sudice know that you sent me this?"

"Not at the time of recording. But who knows what could have happened after? I would count on them coming after you sooner rather than later."

He disappears.

"Motherfucker," Carina spits. "Mark Teague is going to get me killed."

The Zealscape begins to shimmer. Either Mark's ghost has triggered something, or security Wasps have sensed the disturbance of his coding. Wasps are owned and patented by Sudice and licensed out to Pacifica. Mark's ghost was right; it didn't take long for them to find her.

"Zeal program! Wake me up."

SIX

CARINA

Vellocet Lounge, Los Angeles,
California, Pacifica

Carina comes out of the trip, but this time there are no alarms except the local one to say she's awake too soon.

The orderly was sloppy—Carina's restraints are loose enough to slip over her wrists. Unplugging the alarm, she tears the needle out of her skin, though it hurts. She keeps it, just in case. She likes needles. Carina staggers upright, her underused muscles protesting. Wrapping her coat around herself, she shuffles into the hallway.

Bad luck: a white-clad orderly is in the hallway. "Hey," he says. "700628, you're not supposed to be up for another six hours."

She ignores him and keeps moving.

"Wait!"

She breaks into a shuffling run, reaching one of the side entrances. The orderly does not follow. She doesn't have a plan, but she'll figure something out. If Sudice is actually after her, there's about five minutes before they swarm the place. If she's lucky.

Carina exits the Zeal lounge to the side alley, squinting in the afternoon sunlight. Her lungs burn, but she can't stop. She darts toward the entrance of the alley, but a man steps forward to block her path.

He's wearing all black, which is concerning, but he's wearing a scrambler mask over his face, which is even more worrying. Every few seconds, his features change—it's always a generic face, enough that if it's captured by the camera drones, he can't be linked to a specific identity. No one good ever wears them.

Carina doesn't hesitate, because that's her only advantage. He's twice as big as her, and he only has to look at her to know she's a Zealot. She rushes and ducks under him. He grabs her shoulder, but she manages to twist from his grip, though her muscles scream. Sprinting down the alley, she tries to get to the well-lit West 54th Street, where she has a slim shot of finding someone to help her.

Footsteps follow. More than one set. She speeds up, though her battered body protests and her heart hammers.

She accesses her implants but doesn't call the police. It'd be useless—Sudice have everyone in their pocket, and they've probably already blocked her emergency calls. But she knows a subfrequency.

Sending out a quick blast of "HELP!" and her location, Carina prays it actually goes through to one of the few people who can find her.

They hit her from behind with a Stunner.

Her muscles go limp. She falls, sprawling face down on the pavement. All the wind rushes from her lungs, all thought flees her mind.

Hands haul her up. She sags. The man clutches her under the arms. He smells of spearmint. She wonders what her bounty is, what his cut will be. What he'll buy with his blood money.

Carina tries to lift her head. She's on one of the upper street levels, quiet and empty. Hovercars stream past on the 110 airway, but even if she waves frantically for help, they're moving too quickly. The other set of footsteps grows closer. Slow, considered. Carina gasps in a breath of air. Spots dance along her vision.

The person pauses in front of her. Dr. Rosalind Elliot.

The woman who took her in as a grieving teen, with promises of putting her back together again. Her first employer. A woman she at one point trusted implicitly, almost considered a friend and mentor. Was that real, or was it engineered? Roz experimented on her like all the rest. The same anger Carina felt in the Zealscape blooms within her. She holds it close, like a coal, as she's limp in the black-clad man's muscled arms.

"Roz," she manages to say.

"Hello, Carina," Roz responds, smiling. She looks exactly the same. Her razor-straight dark-blonde hair is a little longer, resting on her shoulders. She's not wearing the sleek dresses and heels from her lab days, but all-black clothing, like the muscled goon who still pins Carina tight. Roz has added bright red lipstick to look more *agent provocateur*. It's like her to show a little flair for the dramatic.

It's strange she's actually here, rather than sending someone instead. But then, Roz never trusted others to do things properly.

The Stunner has hit Carina off-center. She can just barely move her right arm and leg. In her right hand, she holds the needle hidden between her fingers. By some miracle, she hasn't stabbed herself with it. She'll have one chance. Perhaps she can get some answers, first.

"What are you doing here? What's going on?" she asks, voice still slurred from the Stunner. She wriggles her toes, willing more feeling to return.

"You're cute when you play stupid, Carrie." Mark, Aliyah

and Kim were the only ones she tolerated to use that nickname. Roz steps closer. "You know exactly why we're here. You've always had a way of finding out just a little more than is good for you." She tuts. "Dr. Teague went and did something very naughty, and now you're implicated in it. Thought you could slip away from me, but I always knew you'd come back." Roz rests a gloved hand on Carina's cheek, almost tender and maternal. Carina wants to turn her head to the side and bite her fingers, draw blood, taste the iron, but then she'd reveal that she's able to move.

"I have no idea what Mark is up to." Carina deliberately uses the present tense.

"Oh, Carrie. Mark is dead. I killed him myself."

It gives Carina a jolt to hear Roz say that. It's a pity brain recording never ended up working (as far as she knew). Carina would have set it up as soon as she saw her, and kept that confession to use as a weapon. A memory no one could refute in court. But the thrill goes deeper than that: she always knew Roz was like her in a way. Capable of killing. The girl. Mark. Who else?

"But then, you know a little bit about death, don't you, Carina?" Roz smiles again.

"I know what you did to me," Carina says, keeping her voice low. "The block is gone. I remember all of it. Every twist of pain. Every scream."

Roz's smugness falters, just a little. "Little present from Mark, then?"

"Fuck you." She packs all her anger into those two words, throwing them like knives.

Roz recoils. She's still close, her cold blue eyes unblinking. It's been a long time since Carina has felt fear in the real world, but there it is, spreading through her, insidious and cold.

"I have nothing to do with whatever Mark was up to." Carina ignores the dig about death.

"Of course you do. He sent you a parting gift, after all. It was the last thing he ever did." Roz's gloved hand comes close again, rests on Carina's left temple.

She swallows. "He hasn't sent me anything."

"Liar." Roz's lip curls. "I'm tired of this game." She looks past Carina, to the man behind her. "We're taking her in." Her sharp gaze returns. "I have to say, I'm looking forward to slipping back into your mind."

Carina's panic bubbles over. Her chest is tight, her breathing shallow. She can't face that pain again. She won't.

<Coming for you,> the voice in her implant says on the subfrequency. <Get to the edge of the pavement in ten seconds exactly.>

The Stunner's effects have worn off a little more. She can only hope it's enough.

One.

Two. Carina lets all her muscles relax. *Three.* She flicks the needle down from between her fingers and jabs it into the man's thigh. *Four.* He flinches, releasing her, and she turns and sticks it into his neck. *Five.* He's wearing a Kalar vest, but there's a gap between the collar and the scrambler mask. *Six.* . She strikes out at Roz, the needle slashing her cheek. *Seven.* Roz doesn't even have time to cry out before Carina shuffles to the edge of the dark road. *Eight.* A hovercar stops in front of her, the door opens. *Nine.* Carina jumps in and turns around in time to see Roz shriek as the door closes. *Ten.*

Carina collapses in the hovercar, adrenaline coursing through her bloodstream. Almost as good as Zeal. The unmanned hovercar hurtles away, heading for the densest parts of traffic to lose whoever may pursue.

"Oh, thank Curie, it worked," Dr. Kim Mata sends Carina through her implants.

"Kim. I didn't know if you'd get it. Or if you'd want to help me." It's strange to be speaking to Kim again. Just yesterday, she'd debated pinging her, and then had wimped out at the last minute, too ashamed of her own weakness. What if Mark told her about the memories he'd found? What if Kim and the others know what she's done?

Kim's face appears on one of the blank walls of the hovercar. She's unchanged. And there's a hint of apprehension in her expression. A hint of fear. "What in the world is going on down there?" she asks.

"Is this hovercar secure? Is the line secure?"

"Yeah, it's all untraceable."

"Even from Sudice?"

"Yes, even from . . ." she trails off. "Oh, God. Sudice is after you?"

"Asking you for help was dangerous, and I'm sorry. I've turned you on your employer, but I couldn't think of what else to do. Mark got me into this mess."

"Slow down. I'm really confused. Mark is involved?" Kim's forehead wrinkles. "He left the company a month ago. Poor health—has some sort of lung disease they're trying to blast with gene therapy, but it's stubborn. He refused mechanical lungs."

Roz must have given Mark that disease. "Mark is dead."

A pause. "What?"

"Roz killed him."

"What?"

"It's true."

The hovercar speeds over LA, bright lights blurring together. Carina looks at Kim's face. Her features have fallen and tears are rolling freely down her face. Carina still finds it vaguely interesting when people cry. Even when whatever Roz did to her started faltering, Carina never cried.

"What did Mark do?" Kim asks, wiping her face with the back of her hands.

"Evidently he's sent a bunch of encrypted information into my head. He told me how to release the first one—"

Carina stops as her first memory smashes into her. Like when you're told to think of anything other than a pink elephant, and a hot pink elephant is the only thing you can imagine.

Her first memory was of fire.

Her dad made a giant bonfire in the backyard, burning all the autumn leaves. Her mom stood upwind, smoking a real cigarette, goggles on to protect her eyes from the smoke. Carina took off her own. She was four, bundled up in a small parka, scarved and hatted and mittened. That winter was freezing, by California standards.

Carina remembered the smell of the smoke, so sharp, and the way her eyes stung, water running down her cheeks. Hidden in the dead leaves was the body of her childhood cat.

He had died a few days earlier. Her father said he would have a proper Viking send-off. It was only years later that Carina learned that made no sense—Vikings were burned, but poor Amoy was never set off on a floating pyre. They were in the clearing where Carina played by herself most afternoons. Behind them, Greenview House rose in the distance, as if watching over them. It was a grand house, with its white paint and dark green shutters, nestled into the forest. So secluded. So silent.

Carina turned to her mother and held out her arms. Her mother stubbed out the cigarette—a real, contraband cigarette—and came over, picked her up. They turned and watched the flames, and Carina snuggled closer to her mother. She always smelled of tobacco and peppermint.

The memory ends, and the first image unlocks.

The bee rises in her mind's eye. Large. The small head dominated by the huge, multifaceted, dark liquid eyes, the antennae twitching. The bulbous, fuzzy, segmented body banded yellow and black. The six limbs, curled up in flight. The wings moving so fast as to be almost invisible. The buzzing.

"Carina?" she hears from far away. She is too far gone to answer.

It feels almost like brainloading, the process of cramming as much information and data into your brain as you can while you sleep. Images flash in her mind's eye. Documents full of information settle into her memory, as if she's speed-reading impossibly fast.

Carina had brainloaded as much data as she could tolerate as a teenager, blasting through her PhD so she could take the shiny position at Sudice that Roz dangled in front of her. Night after night she'd brainloaded, until her professors warned her that if she didn't reduce the quantity of information blasting into her brain, she'd have a seizure or an aneurysm.

This time, though, there's no need of a Chair, no small dose of Zeal to lubricate the transfer. Yet again, Mark has found a way to do something she'd have said couldn't happen. The information unfurls in her brain, opening and settling into her mind. The pain and pressure is so intense she feels as though her head will burst.

It all centers around a group called the Trust. A small team of hackers—a little annoyance to Sudice, to be swatted away. Most of their stunts have done little apart from leaking some information, quickly superseded. A few things they found were useful—hurt the company's stocks, led to some awkward, somewhat embarrassing questions from the government or shareholders. Their last attack went awry and they were meant to have scattered, but recent information from the inside suggests the Trust have re-formed. Names: Charlie, Rafael, Dax and Tam. The information still slams into Carina's cortex, like endless fireworks.

"Carina," Kim says, insistently. "Carina?"

"Yeah," she replies. "I'm here. I think."

Sitting up, she brings a shaking hand to her temple. "I feel like I've been hit by a hovercar."

"What happened? Are you OK, sweetpea?"

"Mark's first image. Encrypted information just . . . exploded into my head. I have a bitch of a headache."

"How did he manage that?"

"Your guess is as good as mine. Must have developed a few tricks."

"Bastard. He could've at least shared." Kim's face goes slack. "I'm a terrible person. He's not even cold in the ground and I'm insulting him."

Carina is not sure what to say. Comforting people has not been her strong suit for a very long time. She settles for: "I'm sure he wouldn't mind. You called him a bastard enough times when he was alive."

A weak laugh. "So what is the plan now?" Kim asks.

Carina hates it, but her first thought is suspicion. She thought of Kim as her friend when she worked at Sudice. Kim still works for them.

"I—" Carina begins.

"No. Actually, don't tell me. I'm about 99.99 percent sure this line is secure, but you never know. Is it useful?"

"I think so." She sifts through the information, but Sudice doesn't know where the Trust are located, where their headquarters are, and Mark has not provided that detail. How helpful.

It's difficult to concentrate. Carina had been plugged into the Zealscape for a few hours at the Vellocet Lounge, even though it felt like minutes. Time is strange in the Zealscape. It hasn't been enough of a hit, and already her body is protesting at the lack of drugs in her system. It won't be long until she's in withdrawal again.

She looks uneasily out the hovercar window. "Why aren't they following us?"

"I took the liberty of putting a temporary block on your VeriChip and your implants."

"Thanks."

"Won't last long, though. They'll be trying to find ways around it. Might even ask me to do it, which would be best. I can stall at least a little while that way."

"Should I go to the police? Ask to be put in protective custody?" Carina already knows the answer to this question, but feels she should at least go through the motions.

"Would be nice if you could, wouldn't it?" Kim sighs. "LA cops are just as much in Sudice's pocket as the SF ones. I know a detective I'd trust to take you in, off the radar. He helped with the Ratel and Verve shit that went down." She looks sad. "I lied to him, when I told him SynMaps was over."

Gaining access to Verve a few months before Carina left had been a huge step in their research. Kim had watched the Ratel, San Francisco's underground mob, go under, knowing she'd helped it happen. Her wife had been a detective in the SFPD, killed in the line of duty, probably thanks to the Ratel.

"Sudice makes liars of us all," Carina says.

"This is true," she concedes. "Unfortunately, we can't use him. He's fucked off to China again for a few months with his girlfriend. I can try to ping him, see if he'd come back, but he wouldn't arrive for a few days."

"Don't bother. One off-the-radar detective won't be enough to protect me anyway. I think what Mark just gave me is the only safe place I can go. The problem is, he didn't tell me where."

Kim's wearing her problem-solving face. Carina knows it well. How many times did she see it in the lab during her time at Sudice? "Worry about that later. You're going to need to get yourself down to a chop shop and get your VeriChip swapped."

"I could do it myself. If I could get another chip."

Kim looks at her with a critical eye. "No, you can't. Not with the shakes you're having."

Carina looks away, ashamed.

"I don't blame you, Carina. You've been dealt a rough hand."

How much does Kim know? It's a horrible feeling, to suspect Carina's secrets are not her own. If Mark wasn't already dead, she'd kill him herself. She sighs. "You're a rotten liar, Kim. It's only easy to get addicted if you crave violence."

"Well, fine. But I still don't blame you. We've all got our issues."

Carina gives something akin to a laugh, though it sounds more like a cough and a hiccup mixed into one.

"OK, I'm going to drop you off at a chop shop I know down there. I've just messaged my contact on a secure line. He'll take your chip and refresh your implants. When that's over, you should go to this flesh parlor—" Kim sends her the location— "and get your face changed. That together will buy you some time. I know Mark. *Knew* Mark." She falters. "He'll have put this together elegantly. I have faith in you."

Her earnestness is difficult for Carina to take. She doesn't know what to do in the face of naked emotion. Usually she reacts inappropriately, offending people. She tries to make the correct response. "Thank you, Kim. For all of your help. I appreciate it and hope your faith in me isn't misplaced." There. Carina sounds like a robot, but Kim beams in response, her eyes watery.

The hovercar begins to descend. Carina stares at her wrist, the VeriChip hidden beneath her skin.

"The chop shop guy looks like a mean bastard, but he's good. If a little illegal."

"More than a little," Carina says, looking at the chop shop disguised as a Chinese-Greek fusion restaurant. She takes a moment to wonder how exactly that would work. Dolmas or egg rolls? Not that anyone ever ate there, anyway. The CLOSED sign across the front looks permanent; one of many restaurants that couldn't compete with replicators in every home.

"I've credited him more than enough money, so if he tries to charge you up-front, don't give the greedy bastard another credit, but offer him a bonus after as some extra incentive," Kim says.

"Yeah, I will." Carina has some money, but a bonus will probably take up most of what she has left. Foreboding rises within her. Some illegal backwater chop-shop surgeon is about to cut into her, to buy her enough time so Sudice doesn't find and kill her for the information locked away in her head.

"OK. I'll leave you for now, but I'll see what I can do from up here. But don't tell me anything, right? I don't want to be any more culpable than I already am. And I wouldn't put it past them to send you a dummy version of me." Kim takes a deep breath. "I've missed you, you know. Worried about you."

Carina can't bring herself to tell her that Kim and the others haven't crossed her mind much at all. She doesn't have to say it. Kim knows—it's written all over her body and face.

"Good luck, sweetpea," Kim says with a sad smile.

She tolerates the endearment. "I'll need it. Thanks again, Kim. I owe you about half a million favors now."

"Take down Sudice and we'll call it even." How has it been for Kim, Carina wonders, forced to keep working for a company she knows has committed every crime in the book?

"Everyone seems to think I can do that except me." The hovercar door slides open just as the door to the shop does. A hand waves, beckoning her closer.

Carina jumps out and runs inside.

SEVEN

CARINA

The chop shop, Los Angeles,
California, Pacifica

Kim is right. The man looks pretty terrifying.

In a world where people pride themselves on looking as perfect as possible—erasing scars and moles, re-proportioning their bodies as desired—plenty of people push themselves in the other direction. Some deliberately scar themselves, keep a blemish or later re-create it in open defiance of flesh-parlor and gene therapy culture. Others see just how far they can take their appearances away from the naturally human look.

This man is one of the latter.

The whites of his eyes are tattooed bright green, and he's brightened the irises a brilliant cobalt and purple. His skin is a medium brown, but the texture is pebbled like a lizard's. Horns sprout from his forehead, and more mini horns line where his eyebrows used to be. His hair has been swapped for tentacle-like strings that move softly of their own accord, like Medusa's snakes. His lips are dark blue, his body large and muscled, tattoos of swirling designs dancing beneath the textured skin.

But none of that is the strangest change he's made to his body.

That would be the third arm.

It erupts from the middle of his chest, a perfect match to the others, the elbow double-jointed. The nails on all three hands are black, pointed talons.

Carina blinks at his appearance, but otherwise she does not let her surprise show on her face. "You know why I'm here," she says.

She doesn't introduce herself, and he likewise doesn't supply his name. She decides she'll call him Chopper in her head. Not creative, but it'll do.

"Twenty K credits." His voice is low and gruff.

"You've already been paid. Don't pretend otherwise."

He grunts.

"I'll give you a bonus if I'm happy with your work. After."

He considers her. She stands tall, staring him down. A ghost of a smile flits across his lizard-like features and then he motions her to come deeper into the store. No one else is here. Carina is jumpy, and not just from the withdrawal. This man is a total stranger. She's reasonably sure she can trust Kim, but not entirely. She'd mentioned a dummy—what if Roz has already killed Kim, and sent a virtual simulacrum to sniff information from her? They could be on their way now. And what's to stop Chopper from bashing her over the head, taking Kim's money and turning her over to the authorities anyway? He's not an idiot; he knows she's wanted for something.

Carina likes to control everything. She is not spontaneous. Even becoming addicted to Zeal was not an accident but a calculated decision. At the moment, with no plan and a VeriChip that will soon broadcast her location to Sudice, she has no choice but to try and believe in the goodness of people, which almost makes her choke with laughter. She's never had much faith in humanity. They're all too selfish to be good.

The room at the back looks a lot nicer and more modern than she'd anticipated, compared to the dingy exterior. It's not a patch on her old lab at Sudice, but everything is clean and the equipment seems to be in good condition. One of the wallscreens is entirely made up of feeds from the microscopic security cameras positioned in dozens of places around the building. It would be hard to sneak up on the man in front of her.

"So who do you wanna be?" the lizard man asks, motioning her to a Chair with his extra arm.

"Excuse me?"

"I can give you plenty of identities. Got a preference?"

"Uh." She didn't expect to be given a choice. She thought he'd just stick a chip in her arm and she'd be whoever he thought fit. "I guess I don't really know."

He shrugs. "OK." He starts rifling through a drawer.

She wants to ask him about the extra arm, but everyone must, so she squashes the urge. But then, how many people do the same thing—afraid to anger him by pointing out the obvious? The question rests on the tip of her tongue before she abandons it. She can't really find it in herself to care. She has bigger concerns than a lizard man with a third arm.

He reaches out and takes her wrist, running the pebbly pad of his finger over the skin, finding the little hard spot of the chip. Strange. That chip has been in her arm almost since birth, and now it's about to be removed. It has everything—her biometric data since she was a newborn, records of food eaten and health levels, steps taken, hours slept, miles run in brief attempts at fitness before she caved like every other person and got muscle mods. Her mods stopped working once she became underweight. So much data about her life is hidden in that tiny chip. He'll have to destroy it to keep his nose clean. She assumes it must all be backed up somewhere, to be picked over by algorithms for advertising or some such. Will she ever be in a position to wear her own identity on her wrist again, or will she die being whoever she's about to become?

Shaking her head, she banishes the useless questions.

He considers her again, a long, searching look made more unnerving by his green, blue and purple eyes. "I've decided you're going to be a teacher. You look like you could be one. Though you're probably gonna go change your face after this, huh?"

She nods, guardedly.

"Choose a face that looks like a teacher." He smiles. His teeth are pointed and serrated, like a shark's.

She might not ask about the arm, but she has to ask about the teeth. "Don't those cut the inside of your mouth?"

He shakes his head, grins wider. "Look closer."

She does. The little serrated edges retreat back and forth. "Automatically fold down when I close my mouth."

"Ah. Clever." This is a surreal conversation. It's been a very strange day.

"OK, we're ready to go."

He smooths a local anesthetic over her wrist.

"You gonna look away? Most people do. Don't like blood, you know."

"I don't mind the sight of blood." A flash of a memory from the Zealscape, her knife slicing through live flesh, blood welling then dripping down the sides of the torso.

He takes up the scalpel and makes a little incision. His two hands press down the skin and his third arm does the actual surgery. He finds the little chip easily, drawing it out. A relief—Carina didn't particularly want him digging around her wrist to find it. VeriChips can be cleared and wiped remotely, with a new personality added in, but that won't change the serial number on the chip. She could still be tracked if someone was truly determined. So now she'll have a new one, a VeriChip of a fake, virtual girl, every detail of her life constructed from the moment of her false birth. But the actual chip, with its serial number and make, probably belongs to a dead person.

Waste not, want not.

Taking away one of his hands, the Chopper opens up the code of the chip, projecting it from his implants onto a white screen, letting her see it. He activates the files, scrolling through all her new history. Her new fake name is Althea Bryant. She oversees the brainloading of seven-year-olds, and then coordinates their activities during downtime. That's really all teachers do these days.

"The chip's good, yeah." He sprays some Amrital on the wound, which stops bleeding and scabs over immediately. Within a few hours, it'll be like it never happened.

Time for the next step. "This is probably unorthodox, but I'd like to amend the implants myself." She really doesn't want anyone else poking around in her head.

"You got the knowledge?" he asks, skeptical, taking in her malnourished body, her stringy hair, her shaking hands.

"I'm a neuroprogrammer. Or I was." She probably shouldn't tell him that. But she doesn't like the thought of someone else writing the code for her implants, doesn't trust anyone else to do it just right. "I have something on my implants I have to back up physically, too."

She needs to keep the code she's been working on for months. The implications of it hit her. It could possibly hold, and Chopper has the equipment she needs.

If it weren't for Mark's booby trap, she could run the code

right here—hope that even though it's not finished, it helps her piece herself together again.

Reality kicks in, harsh and heavy. Even if Mark hadn't said messing with her neuroprogramming would likely short her brain, the code is raw, and could kill her as easily as cure her. Mark's dying wish was for her to help him finish what he started. She's trapped on this path and has to see it through. She doesn't have to like it.

He pauses. "How 'bout you get everything started, prep it all, but I do the actual last bit, look it over and activate the code. Hard enough to operate on yourself at the best of times, and your health is bad, girl."

Carina gives an embarrassed cough. It's been weeks since she's had to stay for any length of time in this crumbling body, acknowledge how it's beginning to fail, face the fact that everyone can see she's a Zealot.

"OK. That's a good compromise. I appreciate it." She's warming to Chopper. His no-nonsense attitude, the fact that he so obviously doesn't give a flying fuck what other people think, that he'll give himself an extra appendage just because he wants to and it's more convenient for his work.

He backs away from the screen, gestures for her to come forward. It's difficult to concentrate—the Zeal withdrawal has turned up from a low hum of physical annoyance to a constant throbbing of need.

Chopper's interface is a bit different to what she's used to. The whole shop has been shielded, her implants cut off from external data. At least neuron dust doesn't have serial numbers, and as far as she knows, they can't track her from the actual nanobots themselves. The extra security should be enough. *Should.* Another thing out of her control that she has to hope doesn't come back to bite her in the ass.

Another tremor shakes her muscles.

"Here." Chopper passes her a pill. She eyes it mistrustfully. "What is it?"

"It'll help the shakes."

She still hesitates.

"If I was gonna kill you, you'd be dead. If I was gonna turn you in, you'd be turned in. Whatever you're up to, it's your business. Though I still want that bonus." Another sharp-toothed smile.

With a little mental shrug, she swallows the pill dry. It takes about a minute to kick in. Her withdrawal is still there, that gnawing emptiness wanting to swallow her whole, but her hands don't shake quite as badly. Her head is a little clearer.

"Thanks. What is it?"

"Modified beta blocker, mainly. Here." He tosses her the rest of the bottle. She thanks him and the bottle disappears into her pocket.

"That'll cost extra." More teeth.

"Yeah, yeah. You'll get your bonus." Her voice has taken on that far-off timbre it gets as she concentrates. Soon, Chopper and everything else falls away. The program runs through her, mapping every nook and cranny of her brain. How many times has she mapped her brain? Both to compare against the subjects at Sudice and since she left, to try and figure how it's changed. She's looked at her own brain more than at any other.

It still hurts to see how the Zeal has changed so much already. The dopamine receptors. Her memory and motor functions are affected, but it's one thing to know she's an addict and another to see it right in front of her, in her very brain.

Deep within those swirls is a more serious flaw, the reason she's like this in the first place, and she can't figure out how to bring herself back to how she used to be.

Chopper looks at the map, and it makes her feel more exposed than being naked ever could. Mark's ghost has already told her he rifled through memories she thought long deleted, and now a stranger sees right through her.

Carina's hands dance through the air, fingertips manipulating the programming on her neural dust, the hundreds of nanobots scattered throughout her brain—the occipital and auditory lobes, a few others to help memory, not that they did much any more. Taking out all the data stored within, flushing the cache, refreshing the microscopic servers. It won't protect her completely, and she plans to stay off external data as much as possible. They'll be out there. Waiting, watching, hoping for her to mess up.

Her fingertips pause as she looks at the various parts of her brain that store memory. Locked somewhere in there is all the information Mark sent her. All the many secrets linked to her memories. If only they lit up like beacons, and pointed the way. No such luck.

"Why not treat it?" Chopper asks, breaking her concentration. "They can do that pretty easy these days."

"The Zeal addiction?"

"Yeah. I watched all those ethics debates." Carina had already started growing addicted, but she'd watched a few and remembers half-read bits of news articles. It's a recent pushback. People pointing out that just because your brain is wired for violence doesn't mean you'll actually commit it. Certain factions are leaning on the government to fix the Zealot problem rather than let a percentage of the population slowly kill themselves. Too few people care. Zeal's been part of the fabric of Pacifica for so long now that people close their eyes to the violence, just like people before the Great Upheaval used to avoid thinking about the abattoirs that supplied their bacon.

"I don't know," Carina says. "It's complicated." For a second, she wants to confide in him. *I want to kill people when I'm out of the Zealscape. Everyone I come across. All the time. So I hide in the dreams and conjure up criminals, so I can pretend I'm not as twisted as I am.* She imagines his eyes widening as she backs away, wondering if she'd take a swing at him. She wants to. She'd take one of the scalpels on the side bench, launch herself up, slip the blade into his neck, so sweetly. He is a criminal, after all . . .

She swallows. Hard.

The lizard man shakes his head. "Whatever. Your business. You done yet?"

Carina turns back to the code, forces herself to rid her mind of anything except the characters and numbers before her. She makes a last swish with her fingertip. "Yeah, think it's pretty much ready."

He looks over her amendments. "Not bad."

She feels a little flush of pride. "Thanks."

"OK, lie back."

She settles back into the Chair.

Chopper comes forward to give her the anesthetic, but she motions him back. "I should stay awake. Whatever you give me will take a little bit of time to wear off, and I've got to jet as soon as I'm able."

"Your call. It'll hurt like a bitch, though."

"I know."

He makes the last little changes, shows her what he's amended for her approval, and then starts to run the updates.

This is the hard part.

Carina's eyes bulge as she stares up at the ceiling. Her fingernails dig grooves into the side of her Chair. The pain is everywhere, and everything—a presence running out all other thought. She can't worry about Sudice, her desire for Zeal or her failing body. She can't fear that Chopper or Kim will turn her in. She can't focus on the fact that, at any moment, men wearing black Kalar suits and scrambler masks could find her and take her away while Roz watches, self-satisfied smile on her face. She can't worry that she's rusty, coded something wrong, and the lizard man hasn't caught it. If that happens, her implants could fry, taking her brain along with it. She can't worry. There is only pain.

Perhaps pain is a better drug than Zeal. In some respects.

Carina loses sense of time, but eventually the pain ends. She gasps in the Chair.

Chopper looks over her biometrics. "You're doing as well as can be expected. If you can, try and get a good long night's sleep, let the new code settle a bit."

She rubs her forehead. "I have a feeling there's not a lot of sleep in my immediate future."

"Probably not."

He holds out his hand. Nestled in his palm is a tiny silver datapod, twisted like a seashell. "Your backup."

"Thanks." She slips it into her ear, but doesn't re-download the information yet. "Here's half of your bonus," Carina says, digging in her pocket for her last credits. It's all she has on her, and she can't access her bank account. "My associate will give you the rest." She hopes Kim won't be too angry at her for volunteering more of her money.

"I'll show you the way out. Duck through the streets, there's a Metro stop in about 500 meters. Do you know where to go after that?"

She shakes her head. "I'll figure something out."

He sends her an address and a location through her amended implants, storing it in her address book. "That's a good flesh parlor I know, if you decide to change your face."

"OK." It could be the best flesh parlor in the world, but she won't go to it any sooner than she'll go to the one Kim recommended. If Sudice find this man, it'll be too clean a link to her next steps.

She stands up. Even with Chopper's magic pill in her system, she still feels like a wreck. And now she has to dash through Los Angeles, find a hideout and come up with a plan before her body completely gives out on her. Great.

Chopper walks her to the door, and she caves and turns to him: "OK, I swore I wouldn't ask, but I have to. Why the third arm?"

He smiles and holds open the door. The serrated edges of his shark teeth glint in the light of the street lamp.

He grins, a little wickedly. "So I can type and jack off at the same time, if I want to."

That startles her into a laugh. "Fair enough. Thanks again. You've probably saved my life."

"Don't lose it, then."

"No promises."

She runs into the darkness on shaking legs.

EIGHT

ROZ

Highway 110, Los Angeles,
California, Pacifica

Roz swears. The hovercar that she's ordered has arrived, but far too late. *Useless. Useless.* She gets in, falls into a seat and rests her head on her hands.

"We can't track them, can we?"

Her hired muscle takes off his scrambler mask and pauses as he accesses his implants. "Her signal's blocked."

"Of course it is." Carina has probably found a way to do it herself. But Roz blocked her implants. So how did she hail a hovercar? A subfrequency? It niggles at her.

"They'd better be able to unblock it in the next ten minutes."

"It's in progress, Dr. Elliot."

Roz leans back in her chair. She accesses her neuroware and has her implants release serotonin to dispel the headache lurking in her temples.

"I have to make a call," she tells her bodyguard. The muscled man nods and accesses his own implants, face slack and eyes glazed. His neck is still bleeding from Carina's needle.

Roz uses the private line. Mr. Mantel accepts almost

immediately, and his face looms in her vision. His features are severe, his dark hair perfectly combed and gelled.

"Carina Kearney got away," she says, starting with the bad news.

"That's . . . deeply disappointing, Roz." His mouth turns down in disapproval.

"I am aware. We're containing it. I told you I needed more backup." He only gave her the budget for one.

"You said she was a Zealot."

"Yes, but she's still what I made her, even if she's let herself go around the seams."

Mr. Mantel raises an eyebrow. "Your shining example is now a sickly drug addict."

Roz keeps her face blank, though she grinds her teeth. "She was a prototype. You know the next version is more than adequate."

"I do, and that's all well under way." He smiles tightly, his eyes nearly turning into credit signs. Born rich as sin, and still greedy for more. "You made the mistake of growing too close to her, though. Taking her under your wing like that."

"Long-term observation, nothing more. I couldn't let a mind like that go to waste." The girl made several breakthroughs in SynMaps. Roz doesn't regret what she did. "Carina won't be able to evade us for long, Mantel, never fear. She's in bad shape. Get the bots to sweep the chop shops. If she's masking her steps, that'll be what she does next. Get rid of the VeriChip before we find it, alter implant programming."

"We're on it," Mantel says, and Roz knows he bristles at her ordering him about. Good. He should get used to it.

"Dr. Teague will have told her where to go next. We figure that out, then I can find her and rip that information out of her head before she can make a nuisance of herself."

"Find her." He pauses. "I cleaned up your mess with Dr. Teague."

Again, Roz keeps her face blank. She remembers the feel of pulling the trigger and watching him fall.

"Let others do the dirty work, Roz."

"Of course, Mantel." He gives her a curt nod and the line goes dead.

Roz imagines finding Carina, hacking her implants and dragging everything from her. The information Mark sent, but more. What made her leave Sudice when she'd been so promising. Carina had always been an enigma. As if no matter how much Roz delved into that brain, another secret was lurking, just out of reach.

Roz will siphon everything from that shattered mind until nothing is left.

NINE

ROZ

THREE YEARS AGO

Sudice headquarters, San Francisco,
California, Pacifica

Roz hasn't seen Carina in seven years.

"Welcome back to Sudice," she says with a smile.

Carina now looks like a woman rather than a girl, dressed professionally in a sheath dress and comfortable heels. Blonde hair pulled back from a face brushed with understated makeup. Roz remembers meeting her for the first time as a quiet thirteen-year-old. A perfectly normal teenager, but for her overbearing father and the trauma of losing her mother. She seemed fragile. After Roz's sessions she was forged into a cool, collected, brilliant young woman, meant for great things.

Now she's come home.

Carina meets her eyes, nodding. How much does she remember? How well does that mental block Roz installed make Carina not think about the . . . less savory parts of the first SynMaps experiment?

Roz shakes her hand. Carina barely touches her fingertips, lets go immediately.

"The rest of the team has already arrived. Why don't we go meet them?"

Carina smiles, nods. She's still cool as a cucumber. She follows Roz to the elevator, a polite half-step behind. The robotic secretary's smooth silver head turns, watching them go, before turning back to greet the next customer.

They take the elevator to the top floor. Carina stands, perfectly safe, perfectly collected.

They arrive at the top level. Carina pauses at the floor-to-ceiling windows, looking out over San Francisco Bay.

"I missed this view," she says.

Roz never tires of it. Sudice's building looks out over the Embarcadero, toward the bay, the Bay Bridge standing tall even though hardly any vehicles travel by land any more. Sailboats take advantage of the morning sunshine, the larger boats for tourists setting out to circle the now-condemned Alcatraz or sail under the bridges. Hovercars fly past, smooth as stingrays, light reflecting off their metal hulls. Skyscrapers rise from the sloping hills. By day, the bay is the same steel-gray it always is, but by the time they leave work, the view will be transformed. The buildings will be illuminated from within. The bay will glow green from the algae farms that give the city energy and a food supply. The entrances to the underground MUNI tunnels will shine the same emerald.

Roz shows Carina her new office on the way to the lab. Carina takes off her jacket, sets down her bag and puts on the waiting lab coat. She compliments the office, with its spacious desk, the white wallscreen where she can project things from her ocular implants.

Roz's virtual assistant, Vera, has ordered a potted orchid from the replicator, which is a nice touch.

"Come," Roz says. "Let's meet the others."

"Of course," Carina replies.

At the door to the laboratory Carina falters just for a moment, her brow furrowing. She swallows hard and then her face smooths back into her mask. Roz's pulse spikes. Does she remember?

But Carina walks right into the lab ahead of her, as if nothing is the matter. It looks different than it did seven years ago. No expense has been spared, every state-of-the-art piece of equipment kept immaculate.

Roz gestures to her colleagues clustered in one corner of the lab, waiting for them. "You met at the interview, but here are your new colleagues, Carina: Dr. Kim Mata, Dr. Mark Teague and Dr. Aliyah Zahedi." Carina takes them all in. Kim Mata, wearing a bright turquoise and yellow striped dress. Mark Teague, his smooth baby face contrasting with his silver hair and slick dark purple button-down shirt. Aliyah Zahedi with her deep brown eyes and vermilion hair in an asymmetric bob, wearing a dress not unlike Carina's. They are a complete team of scientists, each with their own virtual assistants. A tingle goes down her spine. The work they will do here could be revolutionary.

Carina says her hellos with that same cool but polite detachment.

"We've stuck to our schedule," Roz tells them. "Trials will start in a month. That will give you all enough time to catch up with our preliminary research and studies."

"You've been a little vague on what we'll actually be doing here, Dr. Elliot." Carina's voice is flat and expressionless. "I understand the need for confidentiality, of course, but . . ." She trails off. Her eyes have snagged on the title of one of the articles: "Lessening Fatalities with Deep Brain Tissue Mapping."

"You will be fully briefed," Roz continues. "But I'm sure you've figured out what we do here by now."

Carina says nothing.

"You were the natural candidate, with your extensive re-search on memory in your doctoral work. We're aiming for the impossible here," Dr. Teague says, smiling brightly. Roz tilts her head, observing Carina. The newest employee's eyes narrow.

"I have guesses. Do you wish to hear my hypothesis?" she speaks clearly, elocution perfect.

Roz holds out a palm, inviting her to proceed.

"You want to figure out how to record memory. Completely. Everything someone sees, smells, their impressions, the thoughts in their mind. More than simply what ocular implants see and auditory implants hear . . . More than a virtual reality re-creation of events. Memories fade; wetware can only do so much. These recordings wouldn't. We could essentially time travel back to any moment in people's lives and see what they've missed the first time or forgotten. So that others could tap into these mem-ories, too, if needed," Carina says. "Living history, accessed at any time."

"Would that make people immortal?" Mark asks.

"Let's not get ahead of ourselves," Roz says. "At the moment, we're only looking at brain recording."

The other scientists nod at Carina, pleased that she's found the kernel of the research so quickly. Roz's eyes narrow in cat-like satisfaction. This will work. She can feel it in her bones. Her head moves, her hair swinging.

"Yes," Roz says. "We wish to create a perfect re-creation of a memory. As if you become that person, experience it as that person. And we'll find a way to do it where they don't almost all die."

TEN

DAX

"I don't see the point," Dax says. "We haven't found anything. All that work, all that risk, and it's turned up nothing."

"It's only been a few days," Charlie replies. "Patience is a virtue."

They're in the living room of their underground compound— the Technodrome, as Raf still calls it, despite the others' eye-rolls. They sip their coffee, still waking up. Charlie's bright red hair sticks up from her head at all angles, the artificial light from the false window illuminating it like a halo. Raf has some code circling his head. The Viper they planted the other day in Sudice's system has deleted itself and transmitted the results. Raf's initial diagnosis is that they haven't found anything concrete they can use against Sudice. A few lists of minor staff; a day's record of the door entry to the lobby, which is slightly more useful.

Dax finishes his coffee and stretches. "Our source has gone totally quiet. I think they've been compromised." He pauses, looks around at the faces of the Trust, decides to jump in with what's been bothering him. "I can't help but feel it might be time to pack it in, while we're still able to."

He lets the words hang in the air. Raf and Charlie don't meet his eyes. He knows they're thinking of Dax's sister. They'd all plugged into virtual reality, the one Raf created using the Zealscape as a template. The Wasps showed up just after they breached the firewall. Wasps are designed to sense any anomaly within their environment. Anything that looks or smells different from normal traffic is inspected further. If it's determined to be a threat, it is eliminated. Raf was meant to have tunneled all the Trust's activity into things it would expect to see, but somewhere, they were sloppy.

Everyone else disconnected fast enough. Not Tam. The Wasps severed the connection with her still inside it. It fried her implants, and they couldn't recover her consciousness. Tam's body is with Raf's boyfriend, Kivon, and he looks after her. She's still in a coma, in an illegal stasis pod in Kivon's storage unit outside of town.

The guilt slams into Dax five seconds after he wakes up each morning. He hasn't told their parents. They deserve to know, but if they started asking too many questions, Sudice might realize she's still alive, in body at least. Though it was Tam's idea to join the Trust, his parents would be so disappointed that Dax hadn't talked her out of it. Kept her safe. He's failed them. He hates Sudice, what they took from him, but he's been thinking about it constantly over the last few days. He doesn't want to lose anyone else, either. Maybe that's selfish. Dax can't help it. Maybe Sudice is too big to fight.

"We can't just give up," Raf says, turning off the code, his tongue darting over his lips. "I can't believe you'd suggest it."

Dax rubs his face with his hands. He forces himself not to think about Tam. "I can't be the only one with doubts. I'm not, am I? You're both worried our source is gone or compromised."

Charlie shrugs. "It is weird they've gone silent. Maybe there's been some heat and they're just waiting until the coast is clear."

"Something's gone wrong," Dax tries again. "Maybe we shouldn't pack it in completely, but maybe we should take a break, too."

"I'm leaning more toward Raf," Charlie says. "We'll never get anywhere if we give up. Then they win."

Dax sighs. "I'm beginning to think they're going to win everything, and we're going to lose our lives. It's David and Goliath."

Raf bristles. "David beat Goliath in the story, so that's a shit analogy. And no one's making you stay, you know."

Charlie's mouth opens, but she snaps it shut and shakes her head. "Calm down, Raf. It's too early for a fight." She runs her fingers through her short hair. "I agree this plant doesn't seem to be giving us any real results, which is disappointing. Still, though, we've proved it's a potential way in—that's not useless. We'll put our heads together, try and figure out what to do next. And yes, we'll make it as safe as possible. I don't want anyone else getting hurt, either."

A pause. All the words they could say float in the air, unspoken.

Charlie pushes on. "Raf, any ideas you've been cooking?"

Raf flicks the code on again, obscuring his features. Dax knows he uses it as a shield when he's upset. "Been toying with a few things. I can run them with you this afternoon and I'm sure we can come up with something. We need to focus on people, not machines. It's the best way. There's no patch for human stupidity."

"So you keep saying. We'll take a short break, as a compromise. Tensions are high, and this is our first job since Tam . . ." Charlie's voice chokes. She clears her throat and continues. "It was never going to be easy. But you believe in the Trust too, Dax. I know you do. You know just as much as any of us how much Sudice need to be taken down. And I'd personally give my life up for it. I've already thrown a lot of it away for this cause, and you damn well know it."

"We all have."

Charlie is the reason the Trust exists, and the main reason it's survived as long as it has, compared to all the other would-be revolutionary groups. Charlie's last name is Mantel: she's part of the Mantel dynasty that owns Sudice, and is second cousin to Gregory Mantel, the president. Or she was. Charlie's renounced all ties with her family. Changed her name. Changed her face. Cut off contact. She says she regrets that sometimes. It would have been easier to stay in the family, work from within; but while Charlie has many skills, lying is not one of them. She'd have been caught by now, and silently dealt with by the family. Better to be on the outskirts, with a new life, and use the many secrets she gleaned through the first twenty-four years she spent with them to chip at their defenses from the outside. Dax has never found out what actually spurred Charlie to leave.

Raf turns his back on Dax, going to his room. Dax watches him go. Charlie sighs and drains her coffee.

"We need to stand together if we're going to have any chance in hell of pulling this off, Dax."

"Yeah."

"You know Raf gets upset by the thought of quitting or dissent within the group. If you have concerns, come to me first."

"We're only three people now—does that constitute a group? Or are we just a trio?"

"We are a small group."

"OK. Sorry." Dax has so much more to say, but why fight? He's said his piece, and deep down, he's afraid to continue, and he's afraid to quit.

There's a knock on the door.

Charlie and Dax startle. Raf pokes his head out of his room. No one is meant to get close enough to knock. About three alarms should have sounded by now.

"Shit," Charlie says. They stay still, perfectly poised in a frozen tableau.

"Guess we better see who it is," Dax says.

ELEVEN

CARINA

The Golden Line, Los Angeles,
California, Pacifica

Carina runs toward the Metro stop and jumps on the first train that arrives. She wants distance between her and the chop shop. When she has a chance, she'll wipe her new VeriChip and give herself another identity. Still won't help much if Sudice find Chopper and access her new serial number, but it's better than nothing. Maybe later on she can get yet another chip—somehow—and confuse the trail further.

As Carina collapses on the train seat, her vision tunnels. The pill Chopper gave her has already worn off. Zeal withdrawal is in full, horrific effect. With fumbling fingers, she finds the bottle in her pocket, but her fingers are too weak to twist the top. It drops and rolls away down the train car. The strangers' eyes follow the bottle, then glance at her. Some of the eyes are filled with pity. Some derision. Most slide away as soon as possible, pretending they never saw her at all.

One man moves, picking up the bottle as it rolls past and walking up to pass it to her. He takes care that his fingers do not touch hers.

Carina gives up on opening the bottle, shoving it back in her pocket. It won't do much at this point, anyway. She leans back against the seat, sifting through all the information that just added itself to her brain. She can theoretically see how Mark managed it, but the pure sophistication still astounds her. The information must have scattered into the neural dust in her long-term memory, and the brainloading implant will only accept the information once the required memory was accessed. But still—how is she supposed to know which memory ties to what? She has no perfect catalog of her life in her head. Just the normal untidy memory—half-remembered images and impressions that fit nowhere else, half-forgotten moments in time, and many that she could never remember at all.

That was another difficulty with the trials back when she was at Sudice, both times. Humans' filing cabinets of memory are intrinsically messy. Connections run through memories that have nothing to do with chronology. Smells or sounds link just as easily. Dreams are inspired by real-world events. Only fragments remain of most memories, as the brain naturally sheds excess information.

Even if Carina and the other scientists at Sudice could have figured out how to brain record perfectly, with no negative side effects, it couldn't have retroactively brought the memories to life as much as they'd once hoped—once they'd cracked it, new memories would have been perfect, but not older ones.

The second phase of those SynMaps experiments went more smoothly once they had access to Verve, the Ratel's twist on Zeal. It would have been a disaster in Pacifica if the Ratel had managed to roll it out, large-scale, as they'd planned. The drug worked like Zeal, creating dream fantasies often tied to real memories—gaps filled in, until the fantasy felt better than the true memory. For brain recording subjects, it could help jog other details, but true facts versus Verve replacements were difficult to determine.

Carina thinks of the girl and her mismatched eyes. Roz had injected the girl with Verve before operating on her.

What else was Roz doing with the drug? Carina has stayed far away from Verve since the one and only time she tried it. It doesn't have that convenient perk of dampening violent urges in the real world that Zeal does; it does the opposite, making people more prone to violence. The Ratel had been slowly swapping Zeal with Verve in dingy Zeal lounges, hoping to create so much chaos that they could step in and pluck power from the government. That ploy failed. Badly.

Brain recording would happen one day, though. Then every brain would be a perfect archive of memory. Every moment kept forever, whether you wanted to remember or not.

Carina thinks back to her first memory again. The fire. The leaves. The smell of smoke. How did Mark even know to attach it to that memory in particular? She can't remember if Roz ever mapped that one at the lab. And how would he know Carina could find them all, and in the right order? The bastard has hidden a scavenger hunt in her brain, and she can't trust that it will all actually work out.

Ah. One puzzle piece falls into place. This is possibly what he searched for first, when he found the memories. To prove they were hers.

She remembers her first Christmas party at Sudice labs. The first time she tried Verve.

They had the party in the lab after hours. Roz elected to go home. Kim went full Christmas spirit. One of her old girlfriends had been English, and she'd sought out the paper crowns and Christmas crackers you pulled apart with a *pop!* and a whiff of smoke. Everyone wore their paper crowns, most of them askew.

Mark had made his own gin, so everyone forwent the synth stuff and drank the moonshine out of sterilized beakers. Faux-turkey and cranberry sandwiches lay on a platter before them.

They were sitting on the floor, shoes kicked off but lab coats on, and it was all merry and festive. Carina was not one for parties, but she remembers thinking that if she hadn't been there, she'd have been sitting in her grand apartment all on her own, eating a Christmas dinner ordered from the replicator. It was almost as though they were friends, and that tightness wound within her chest loosened minutely.

The party devolved into drinking games. They asked each other questions about themselves, and they had to either answer or take a drink. Or answer and take a drink. By that point, the rules had grown fuzzy.

"What's your earliest memory?" Mark asked Aliyah.

She paused, thinking, twirling the moonshine gin and tonic in her beaker. "I'm not sure if it's my first memory. It's a very clear view of my mother's face. I think it is a memory—she looks so young compared to how I remember."

Mark nodded. "Good one. Think lots of people's first memories are their mother or father's faces. What's yours, Kim?"

"Some asshole kid throwing a rock at me when I was playing at the playground. Must have been around three or four. My mom went up and screamed at the kid and then screamed at his parents. So from the get-go I knew not to mess with my mom." She grinned and took a swig. "Afterward she took me to Santa Monica Pier for ice cream, then we rode the Ferris wheel." Her smile faltered. "One of the few nice memories with my mom. She could be pretty cold."

Mark raised his glass to her. "I know all about cold parents, too. You, Carrie?"

Though normally nicknames annoyed her, she had let it

continue. It showed they were comfortable with her, which was good.

Carina told them the story of her first memory, with the burning bonfire, her mother smoking, the meadow near Greenview House. Mark was very interested in the house, thinking the whole image very quaint.

"Can we map it?" he asked me, excitedly.

Carina frowned. "You mean, use Verve stuff? Not sure I feel like being your human guinea pig, Mark." They'd only just been granted access to Verve, but weren't yet allowed to use it for their sessions.

Mark made puppy eyes at her. "I've been studying it a lot lately. I think we could make a really detailed view of Greenview House, and it'd be cool. C'mon, please?" He was the oldest of their group, but still as excited as a child about his research. "Don't pretend you're not interested in seeing what Verve would do to a memoryscape."

Carina sighed and drained her glass. This was a terrible idea. But she was just drunk enough to decide to throw all caution to the wind. It wouldn't be the first time that memory had been mapped. "Fine."

Mark administered the drug and plugged her into the Chair. Kim and Aliyah clustered around her.

It worked. Mark entered the dream with her, and between them they were able to make a pretty good rendering of Greenview House and the burning leaves. Memories are fuzzy things. But Verve managed to fill in details and bring it to life. The sky was brighter than it might have been that day, the forest denser. Yet it felt . . . complete. Real enough to touch.

Carina stood and gazed at the house. In this memory, that house was brand new. All the horrible events hadn't happened yet in it. Some had, though. Enough. She turned to look at the burning leaves. Bile burned her throat. She made the signal, and Mark took her out.

He was looking at the map of her brain on another screen, his body blocking her view. "Hmm," he said.

"What?" she asked.

"Nothing. It's just a complicated memory, that's all. More gin?"

Carina comes out of the memory of the Christmas party. Had that been what gave Mark the initial idea for this? He couldn't have known that memory had been recorded before by Roz, years before he'd ever seen it.

She found the Verve experience terrifying. When she woke up in that lab with Mark leaning over her, she wanted to hurt him. He might have seen that—he backed away from her. She held back, just, but she went to a Zeal lounge first thing the next morning, before work. She stayed as far away from Verve after that as she could.

The train is quieter now. There are empty seats to either side of her. Something about the Christmas party niggles at her. She'd forgotten all about it. What did Mark see?

Oh.

A few months later, Mark moved a conversation around to repressed memories. When he discovered Carina's memories, he would obviously have discovered the block Roz installed. Did he find other curbed memories, too?

"Oh, Mark, you clever, sneaky little bastard," she says out loud, and the other people on the train give her nervous sideways looks.

The rest of her memory unlocks. She doesn't remember this, can't be sure if she ever really remembered it before, but she knows it's real.

She was small again, wearing her parka against the cold. The leaves were burning, limned in red and orange. Some swirled away in the wind, revealing the half-burned corpse of her childhood cat.

"Amoy," she wailed, moving closer to her mother.

Carina's father touched her arm, and Carina's mother set her down. He urged her closer to the dead cat. She struggled, trying to get away, but he only gripped her tighter, not quite hard enough to hurt.

"Listen to me. Everything dies, Carina," he said. His voice was deep and pensive. "And everything goes away. Nothing is permanent. The sooner you know this, the better. You do not have to fear what is natural."

She wants to listen to him. At that age, her father was her whole world. She worshipped him. Part of the cat's skin had disappeared from her face, showing her blackened skull. Carina remembered petting that skull, when it had been alive and covered with soft fur and warm ears. She sniffled, but she didn't cry.

Her mother inched closer, wanting to take Carina away from the flames. He held out his hand and, with a look, stopped her in her tracks. She stumbled, too close, and the edge of her coat caught fire. Her mother swatted at it, frantic, and the smell of burned goose feathers joined the smoke.

Carina looked up at her father, holding his hand tighter.

There's more, she's sure there's more. Why has she forgotten it? Her first view of death was too much for her. Little did she know what would come after.

It's enough.

The Bee rises in her vision again. The sting in the tail.

At the next stop, she leaves the train, staggering out as

the information takes hold. She finds an unoccupied corner in the station and falls down against the walls. All the intel she needed before streams into her: who the Trust are, where they're located. This is what Sudice never had. They had only those blank monikers and scattered rumors.

Mark has everything. Or he did, before he sent it to her.

He was their source on the inside for over a year, giving them what information he could. He knew that he wouldn't be able to do that much longer. And he knew this information had to be even better hidden. If Carina had been caught right away, someone might have gotten the first level of encryption, but not the second, unless they knew to look for it. And how would they know to search for a repressed section of her first memory, when even Carina herself hadn't remembered it?

Mark took a risk, and it's paid off.

When it's all over, she looks up blearily. She's still attracting stares from people moving past her to the train platform. Not that long ago, homeless people might have slumped here, a hat or a battered cup held out for change. Now there are no homeless, so the sight of a dirty, unhealthy woman on the ground is not quite so easily ignored.

She stands up, feeling worse than ever. Her body won't last much longer. She'll lose consciousness or have a seizure. With all the brainloading, she's surprised she hasn't had one already. With burning eyes, she looks at a map on her implants and figures out where she needs to go.

•

The Trust headquarters looks like a normal, boring office building. It's downtown, which is surprising. But then, there's so much traffic and code floating around that it's probably easier to hide what they're doing here than if they'd chosen a hidden, out-of-the-way warehouse, where if the same people kept coming and going, it'd flag the camera drones.

It lacks drama, though, this small, unremarkable building of white concrete and black glass, flanked by palm trees on either side. A sign out front says it belongs to the DeMille Corporation. A small building, only a few stories high, wedged between two giant skyscrapers. Someone walks past and their eyes automatically slide from one skyscraper to the other. Many people come and go on the sidewalk, and hovercars zip overhead.

The sun beats down on Carina as she stands outside the building. She needs to get out of sight before someone calls the cops on the obvious Zealot loitering outside a nice office building on Grand Avenue. She enters the security code Mark gave her in the second part of the Bee information, and the door whooshes open.

Inside it's air-conditioned and quiet. Carina feels incredibly out of place. She's stumbling, and she can smell her own body odor. Her breath stinks and she really wouldn't mind a shower.

She passes some empty offices. Everything is clean and tidy, no clutter. No one actually works here. The building is listed as extra offices in case of overflow for the bigger branch a few blocks down, which is a real, bustling office. This is used for storage and for secrets.

The inner door is at the back, and leads down to the basement. Once it was underground parking, but they've converted it to living quarters, heavily shielded and encrypted. It's where all the planning happens, but little of the actual hacking occurs, for fear it could be traced. She opens the second door with the code and stumbles down the stairs. One last corridor. One last door.

Barging in on them might be a bad idea, but they change the code here every twenty-four hours. Mark doesn't have the next one because he's gone. She rings the bell. They don't answer, but they have to be there. Unless somehow they know Mark is dead, and they've flown the coop. Carina has only the vaguest idea of the people who are behind this door. All she knows for sure is that they must hate Sudice as much as she does.

Ringing the doorbell again, she falls. She's reached the end of her strength, and focuses her fading eyesight on the camera lens over the entrance.

"I know you're the Trust. The source sent me. I have the information you need to take down Sudice."

She faints.

TWELVE

ROZ

The Luxe Hotel, Los Angeles,
California, Pacifica

Roz has no idea where Carina fucking Kearney has disappeared to.

She hasn't slept in eighteen hours. An entire team helps her, though Roz has very deliberately left Kim and Aliyah out of it. She's been monitoring their implants, and so far neither of them appears to have reached out to Carina, but that doesn't mean they won't.

How is it that Carina has disappeared without a trace, when she looked so tragic and frail on the street? It's embarrassing.

She must have found a new identity, and it'd only take her putting her matted hair over her face to stop the cameras from identifying her features, if she hasn't already gone to a flesh parlor.

Roz switches the code circling her head like a swarm of insects, rubs her temples and releases more painkillers into her system. She'll have to sleep and come back to it in the morning.

It feels like defeat.

Sitting down on the bed, Roz takes off her heels, peels off her clothes and lies back on the covers in her underwear, staring up at the ceiling.

She found a little information in Mark's files after she killed him. She pushes away the image of his lifeless eyes staring up at her as she rifled through his code and files. There's no time for regret, even if Mark was once a good employee. A nice person. Too nice, in the end. Too concerned with morals, in a business where morals must be left at the door.

She suspects Mark set the information up to dole out at different times, because doing it all at once would kill Carina. If Sudice catches her before it all releases, it'll be much harder for Roz to extract. Very clever.

Damn Mark Teague.

He's linked the five parts to Carina's memories, and Roz thinks he's used the same images she used in her own work. An extra little jab. She's told Sudice to monitor implant data levels throughout Los Angeles. A spike in brainloading activity that high might show up on their systems. By now, though, Carina's probably amended her implant code, rerouted it to ping from a different location.

Idly, Roz draws up her files on Carina again. Opens her brain scans. Looks at all the dips and crevices of the woman's brain. She remembers first studying it, back when Carina was only thirteen, young but not innocent. When Roz started seeing what memories the girl had lived already, she knew she could change Carina into someone stronger. Erase the pain the girl had internalized, protect her from more. Though the project had a different focus, in a weird way, she'd wanted to protect Carina, back then.

How things change. Now all she wants to do is kill her.

THIRTEEN

ROZ

THREE YEARS AGO

Sudice headquarters, San Francisco,
California, Pacifica

Brain recording trials are about to begin. Project SynMaps has been resurrected.

Roz feels a flutter of excitement, like a child on the first day of school. They've been preparing for this. Roz has worked so much overtime that HR keep threatening to lock her out of the building after 8 p.m. She hasn't slept more than four hours a night, and most of that has been spent brainloading medical journals by the volume. She hasn't gone on a single date, though she'd promised herself that this year she'd put herself out there more. Her entire life has been about these trials.

She *needs* brain recording to work. It's only the beginning, though the others don't know that. If she can pull off her next goal, then her career is set. If anything goes wrong, she's through.

They all know what the SynMaps trials will be like. It won't be easy, but they can't flinch.

The first round of volunteers is brought in. They have all

signed the waiver forms. Roz and the others are not liable for anything that happens. Not that anyone would know—these people are as good as invisible.

Roz can't help but feel a little nervous. It won't be pleasant, but her team shouldn't be doing anything unduly dangerous, at least to start. There's only so much that can be learned from AI humanoids. No matter how lifelike you make them, they're not flesh and bone. They can never be as intricate a biomachine as the real thing. Cloning was outlawed long ago, and although Roz tried, Sudice has not been granted special dispensation in this case. So she found the next best thing. Risk using real humans and the government gives its blessing, if the people are deemed unimportant enough. Typical.

There are four subjects to start with—one for each scientist. They each have a robot to assist them, and even though there's one down in the lobby, Roz can't get used to their blank, metallic faces and silver eyes. They are useful bodies for everyone's virtual assistants to use. Roz was able to pull some strings from Sudice's headquarters in China and convince them to send all the scientists the latest virtual assistants. The AIs are widespread in Asia but haven't made it over here, though it's only a matter of time. They have more personalities than the operating systems run in the rudimentary robots here in Pacifica; Roz is growing to like Vera. Virtual assistants will make perfect helpers, she predicts. They don't bicker. They don't flirt. They organize your schedule, help point out your mistakes before you make them. Roz has no plans to give Vera up when SynMaps is over.

The subjects—two men and two women—seem nervous and subdued. All are in peak physical health, ages ranging from twenty-five to thirty-four; a range of backgrounds; raised in different parts of Pacifica, with different income brackets.

Today will be easy. They will map each of the subjects' brains in even more depth than was done for the initial screenings. These will be the blueprints for her team. Soon they'll know these people's brains better than they know the palms of their own hands.

It's a long day. The subjects are antsy. Roz does not encourage the other scientists to use their real names. She doesn't want them to bond—it could impact the data. They are called Subjects A, B, C and D. At some point she's sure they'll evolve nicknames, and she supposes she'll allow it. Carina will stick by the rules, treating her subject like a chimp or a rat. It is her way.

They'll start simple: only recording a tiny aspect of the present memory in the laboratory, using a similar process to brainloading. Though people can take in hours of facts as they sleep, the information trickles in in such a way that not all of it is absorbed. Then the same information is sent over a few days, and gradually the brain takes in the information piecemeal. If the information was summarily brainloaded all at once, it could overwhelm the brain and cause seizures or aneurysms. It's the same with memory recording, though at a much lower threshold.

It's like the brain only wants to remember so much, or only has so much bandwidth. Even those with eidetic or photographic memory can't recall everything in as much detail as Sudice is trying to patent. This stage will prove useful. People never forgetting a moment. An eyewitness testimony infallible in court. No criminal able to escape their own memory.

It's still only the beginning.

She watches her team perform their perfect ballet. The mapped brains float above the subjects' heads, the neural dust scattered throughout their cortexes showing up as bright lights, like stars. All of them, except the robots, look up in wonder.

•

The first day has gone well.

Roz invites Carina for a drink. A chance to catch up out of the office. Carina agrees.

They go to the exclusive Zenith club at the top of the TransAm Pyramid. Roz has been once before, just after she first moved to San Francisco, and enjoyed it. She's always meant to go back, but there has never been time.

The nice thing about hostess clubs is, yes, they're more expensive, but you end up having a much better experience. The hosts and hostesses know that you either do not have friends or aren't in the mood to interact with them that night. Sometimes you want guaranteed fun, to be coddled and pampered by strangers, and you're willing to pay for it.

Roz's bonus has entered her account, and Carina has been working the same long, strenuous hours. She's never mentioned other friends like former students from university. As far as Roz knows, Carina goes to the lab, goes home and comes back. They're two peas in a pod.

Carina and Roz part ways briefly. It's been months since Roz has dolled herself up to go out, and she takes her time, choosing a red dress and applying her makeup with care, smoothing extra serum to erase the circles under her eyes, putting on ridiculously high heels she'll regret halfway through the night. She examines herself critically. She could do with another trip to the flesh parlor once the trials are under way. The skin on her jaw is softening a little more than she'd like. But her eyes and forehead are still free of wrinkles, as smooth as a seventeen-year-old's.

Roz arrives at Zenith early, taking a table near the window, hiring a few hostesses for the evening to appear at their table once Carina arrives. Though this is pleasure, it's business, too.

This is an informal diagnostic, with hostesses around them to lessen the suspicion. She plans to probe Carina gently, see if there are any emotions breaking through from her own time as a subject in the lab. The faltering expression Carina wore just before she entered the lab the first time worries Roz. There shouldn't have been any hesitation. Also, a week ago, Carina deviated from her home-lab-home routine and went to a Zeal lounge. That is also curious. She shouldn't feel any desire for the drug.

Roz was Carina's mentor for years, and she made sure that aspects of the bond would stay strong in the girl's memories. If anything goes wrong, Carina should hopefully come to Roz before anyone else at Sudice.

The view from the sixty-eighth floor of the TransAm Pyramid is almost as good as the one from Sudice's lab. The original TransAmerica building, the one that crumbled in the Great Quake of 2055, was only forty-eight floors, with the top floor a boring conference room, but since then they've rebuilt the iconic building larger and with modern materials. Before, the Crown Jewel of the TransAmerica Pyramid was blocked off, but now it's suspended at the top of the steepled building, its harsh glare filtered through red-paned, unbreakable glass. The crimson gives the entire bar a warm, flattering glow.

Roz stands holding her drink and looks down at San Francisco. The San Bruno Mountains, Treasure Island, the piers jutting into the glowing green water of the bay. The tops of the skyscrapers near the TransAm look almost dainty, their roofs topped with gardens, ponds in the middle glowing with algae. Several of them are greenhouse skyscrapers, filled with fruit trees, a different kind on each level, or loamy vegetable gardens, windows always cracked to release extra oxygen into the atmosphere. Sometimes, she can't believe what a beautiful city San Francisco is.

"Good evening," says a voice behind her.

Roz turns to see Carina, dressed in a smart blue suit, the blazer unbuttoned, wearing a flowing, geometrically printed blouse and heels. Her hair is down in soft, blonde curls, and she looks utterly transformed from the focused, unsmiling scientist Roz sees every day.

"You look great," Roz says.

"Thank you. As do you." Carina produces a smile, and the smile is just as plastic as the ones she tries on in the lab from time to time.

Carina and Roz take their seats and the two hostesses arrive, glittering and model-perfect. They ask what Roz and Carina want and they scroll through the drinks menu on their implants. They both choose old-fashioned cocktails, made with synth alcohol. Roz goes for a Nikolaschka, with ersatz cognac, lemon, coffee and sugar. Carina chooses a Twentieth Century, with false gin, Kina Lillet, crème de cacao and lemon juice. The drinks arrive promptly, the hostesses delivering them with a smile. The hostesses access Roz's and Carina's public profiles, creating conversations from the interests they have listed upon arrival. Roz admires hostesses. They know so much about so many things, from hours and hours of speaking to people they might not necessarily find interesting. Yet you'd never know.

If the government ever needs to recruit spies, they could do worse than looking right here at Zenith.

Roz and Carina play along. Carina appears to be enjoying herself, and before long, they're three cocktails in. But soon Roz sends the hostesses away with a generous tip. The ice has been cracked.

As soon as the hostesses leave, Carina goes silent, looking down over San Francisco. Her face is still carefully blank, but

Roz senses things going on beneath the surface. Roz hasn't seen Carina in years before this project, and somehow she thought the girl would be . . . different. She can't pinpoint how, but she has a strange sense of disappointment. It's not an emotion she lets herself feel often.

"Is anything wrong?" Roz asks.

Carina gives her that empty smile. "Of course not. This is a lovely evening. Thank you for inviting me." Roz stops herself from tutting. Too robotic. She's meant to be more convincing than that.

"It's nice to be away from the lab for an evening, sure enough," Roz says, taking another sip of her drink.

"We're on the cusp." Carina's voice is distant.

"Come again?"

"This is right before the project properly starts. We are about to pass the point of no return." Carina looks at her. She's not blinking regularly enough. Another flaw—it makes other people nervous. Roz frowns. She'd noticed that when Carina was a teen, and thought she'd fixed it.

Roz says nothing.

"Does it bother you, what we're likely to do to these subjects when we're trying to find out how to record their memories? Do they really know what they're in for?" Carina's head turns toward the bay as she takes a drink.

She's remembering, Roz thinks. She has to be.

"It is regrettable that some aspects of the trials will be painful, but they have been well-briefed in what this will entail. They agreed." Roz pauses. "Does it bother you?"

"No. Not at all. I feel like it should."

The first phase of SynMaps drifts between them, Roz remembering everything, Carina hopefully never thinking about it at all.

"I'm grateful," Carina says, before Roz can come up with a response. "It'll make it easier for me than, say, Dr. Mata."

"That's true," Roz says carefully. "I think for some of our team it'll be difficult to treat the subjects objectively, especially as we spend more time with them. We've put measures in place so the others aren't at risk of growing attached to their subjects." Another little pause. "I don't expect it'll be a problem for you."

Carina laughs and finishes her drink. "Yes. I've never suffered from an overabundance of interpersonal connections." She does not sound self-pitying. Simply factual.

Dread is still rising in Roz, as inevitable as the small waves on the shore of the bay. "Well, I can't say I have, either. It comes with the territory. Sudice takes everything and doesn't leave you much in return." Roz, by contrast, hears the bitterness in her own voice. It surprises her.

"When you're driven," Roz continues, "you see only the end goal. Everything else falls by the wayside. And good riddance to some of it."

Carina folds her face into the closest thing to a genuine smile Roz has seen since she returned to Sudice. "Another drink?"

Roz motions for a hostess. They keep to lighter subjects for the rest of the night. The conversation flows more easily, veering from politics to favorite recipes from the replicator. Later, when Roz is back in her empty apartment, wiping off her makeup, she knows Carina was only playing the part Roz most wanted her to play.

Worst of all is that, in Roz's professional opinion, the code she so carefully laid down in Carina's neurons during the first phase of SynMaps is breaking down. Before phase two can properly begin, she'll have to find out why, and fix it.

FOURTEEN

DAX

The Trust headquarters, Los Angeles,
California, Pacifica

Dax is tasked with bringing the mystery woman back to some
semblance of health.

It won't be easy. In fact, he's amazed she's made it all the
way to their door in her current state. Pure willpower alone must
have done it. He can tell she's not a long-term addict, but the
recent downturn in her health is acute. Her vitals are poor.
Her blood pressure's a wreck, immune system shot, liver already showing early signs of cirrhosis, organs overworked and
strained. Her brain is in overdrive, trying to come to terms with
all the information processed through her implants over the
past day. What has she been downloading, and why?

Dax puts her on fluids and nutrition, and floods her system
with antibiotics using her implants. So many Zealots have the
ability to make themselves feel better hiding right in their
bodies, but they grow so apathetic they can't even be bothered,
or they forget how to do it.

This is the sort of shit that made him stop being a doctor.

He was once a waxworker, a plastic surgeon, working in a
flesh parlor for eight years. Giving people new faces all day,

every day. Smoothing this, shrinking that, growing something else. He'd decided to go into medicine when he'd seen the magic his own surgeon had wrought after Dax's hormone therapy. He'd been amazed at how the body could change to fit his interior sense of himself. He wanted to create that same magic for others.

As a waxworker, he was jaded by the endless tucking and smoothing away of flaws that not even the best gene therapy could totally eliminate. No one is ever content with who they are. More than that, Dax came to understand how the greater health industry operates. Supposedly there is free health care for all, but the government doesn't actively go after those who fall through the cracks, like Zealots, and urge them to have regular checkups. Why bother? If they stay healthy and on the streets, they might become criminals, and that would harm the crime statistics. They're regarded as best forgotten, until they wither away.

He helped one or two Zealots who had managed to break free of the drug and come to see him afterward to undo as much physical damage as possible. They went on to recover, and Dax keeps subtle tabs on a few of them even now. None of them have become criminals, as far as he can tell. So Zealots are not hopeless cases. Not all of them.

He launched petitions, spoke to the government, participated in the ethics debates, trying to see if there was any way to change current policies relating to Zealots. It resulted in nothing but frustration—and veiled threats for challenging the status quo.

For the Pacifica government, it's eugenics. Dax looks down at the unconscious woman whose name, he's sure, is not Althea Bryant. The government knows that soon she'll die if left to her own devices on Zeal. They don't care.

The woman came around, very briefly, late in the night.

Charlie helped her bathe, as she couldn't stand. Her stringy, matted hair is now washed and brushed, transformed from murky brown to a pale blonde. Once this woman might have been pretty, like everyone in Pacifica, but Zeal has ravaged her beauty. Several of her teeth are missing, others rotten. He can fix that, but he'll wait until she wakes up to give consent. Her skin has broken out in painful acne across her sunken cheeks, scarred pockmarks the remnants of past pustules. Her cheekbones are stark against her skin, temples appearing too wide in her shrunken face. She has more sores on her skin and in her mouth. Dax can't help but feel pity.

He sighs. He's stabilized and injected her with extra nanobots to go in and knit together broken tissue, build up the blood cell count, help her on the path back to health. It won't happen overnight, but within a few days the worst of the physical addiction will be gone, most of the toxins flushed out.

He's keeping her sedated for the moment, but the next week won't be much fun for their mystery woman. Dax can't do anything for mental addiction.

That will be something she'll have to overcome all on her own.

FIFTEEN

CARINA

The Trust headquarters, Los Angeles,
California, Pacifica

Carina wishes she would die already.

She feels like she's drowning. Her lungs have filled with liquid. The veins in her eyes have exploded, the whites stained red. Her body convulses, gasping for air.

If there were any sort of weapon around her, she'd use it to stab herself. Shoot herself. Bleed out onto the floor.

Anything is better than this.

It's not physical. By now her body has expelled most of the carnal need for the drug. Short but severe. She drooled. She spasmed. She threw up, retching into a basin as someone held her hair back. But that's over. Her body is the healthiest it's been in almost a year. But her mind . . . her mind is screaming. Even kicking Verve after Max's Christmas experiment was nothing compared to this. Her system has been so saturated in Zeal for so long.

Carina wants to kill. She wants to stalk, to capture, to murder. She's done it over and over for most of her waking-sleeping life the last year. They weren't real, her victims. But they felt real. Her mental pathways yearn for that same broken, beautiful release.

She can't have it.

She'd kill herself to at least kill something.

Carina misses the Zealscape Greenview House, that twisted, horrible echo of her childhood home. Hiding away from the real world and being able to control every aspect of her surroundings. Tweaking people's faces with a mental flutter. Making buildings rise and fall in the limitless rooms of the house. She was a god, feared by those in her clasp as she exacted her judgment on them for her own pleasure.

Now, she is irrevocably human, trapped on one plane of existence.

How is it that everyone isn't addicted to Zeal? Plenty spend most of their lives staring at wallscreens, in virtual reality. Plenty plug into the Zealscape for the more visceral experience for an hour or so a few times a week. Why is it only this way for those they deem will become criminals?

Deep down, in the part of her not screaming in mental pain and confusion, she has a pretty good guess as to the answer: because the government doesn't want law-abiding citizens to become addicts. They aren't dangerous like she is. Not in the same way. Let them play in virtual reality, which is cheaper, less addictive. Let those people be active members of society.

Hidden in her mind are memories that will unlock whatever else Mark put in there. Somewhere in her broken brain are the answers. If only he'd chosen someone else. Anyone else. She won't be able to help. She's only a drug addict wanting to hide away from her own memories. Her own twisted atonement for what she did, all those years ago and in Sudice. For what she'd do, if unleashed out there in the real world.

She wants to keep her memories walled up and locked away. Mark will have linked information to the darkest corners of her mind.

They must have made more breakthroughs in brain recording after she left for Mark to do what he did, even though she knows that the SynMaps project closed down again. Or at least, it was meant to. Kim had sent her a message she hadn't responded to, a month or so after she left.

A small percentage of people, about five percent, will die attempting brain recording, right out of the gate. For most people, it can work for a short period of time relatively safely, for undercover operations and the like. As far as Carina knows, only a few people can take the processing speed of proper brain recording. It wouldn't be profitable enough to roll out on a large scale—too many legal pitfalls and too much red tape—so Sudice scrapped it.

Carina doesn't know how to unlock what Mark sent her. Should she sit here and try to run through every memory in her skull? All memories, senses and thoughts are scrambled as her brain yearns for more Zeal and more escape. Those burning leaves of her first memory again, the red veins fading to black, the spent skeleton of a leaf crumbling to ash and blowing away. Her first day at school, the way the patent-leather Mary Janes gave her blisters. Her first kiss and how she thought she would have felt . . . more. Yet when he pulled away and smiled at her, she couldn't find it in herself to smile in return. He didn't kiss her again. The friends she'd tried to make and then discarded once her emotions bled away, without her even realizing what was happening. Hours and hours spent in Greenview House.

Greenview House. She feels herself being drawn to a memory. Her thoughts slow and snag. Is this Mark's work? She falls into it, as inevitable as a Zeal trip.

Carina was fifteen when it all changed.

For years, she had woken to the smell of toast. The warm,

nutty scent stil reminds her of the few good parts of Greenview House. Her mother didn't go in for full, bacon-and-egg-laden breakfasts. Every morning, she and her mother would sit at the table and eat toast. Her father never ate breakfast at all in the house, usually going to work as soon as the sun crested the hills.

That morning, there was no smell of toast.

Carina got up at her usual time. Put on clothes. Brushed her teeth. Then she couldn't take it any more. That absence of smell.

Had her mother slept in? She went down the hallway to her mother's room. Her parents had had different bedrooms on opposite sides of the house for as long as she could remember.

It was empty. The bed was not made. That was strange. Her mother always made the bed. Not with military precision, but she pulled the covers up. Her mother liked things to be pretty but not perfect.

The room had the strange sense of being unoccupied. Carina felt cold, her fingertips numb.

It wasn't like her mother to just leave her. Had her mother gone out on an early morning errand? Out for a jog? No one in her family had nano muscle inserts. Her father didn't allow it. Some technology in their life was fine, but anything directly in their body was still considered the ultimate taboo.

But would her mother go before toast?

The kitchen was also empty. Her father had left for work.

Carina spent the whole day alone. She didn't go to school. She kept pinging her mother and getting no answer. She tried to find her mother's location on the wallscreen, but it was blocked. Her father was at his desk, but he was closed to all calls while he worked, raking in accolades for his environmental work. He'd won awards, the fancy ones where she'd had to tag along to elaborate dinners while wearing uncomfortable frilly dresses.

Her father returned at half past seven that evening, his mood a storm cloud. He asked her why she hadn't gone to school. She said, as calmly as she could manage, that it was because her mother was missing.

He paused as he accessed his implants, trying to ping her mother. Like her, he received no answer.

"You're sure she's not here?"

"I'm sure." She was on the verge of tears, but tried to keep them back. Her father couldn't stand crying. A tear fell down her cheek anyway.

Her father slapped her. Carina didn't bother bringing a hand to her face. She was no longer surprised by the violence.

Her father dithered for an hour before finally calling the police.

They arrived in their hovercar and asked their perfunctory questions:

"Would she have any reason to leave?"

No hesitation. He plays the part of Concerned Husband, even though he never spoke to his wife except to scream at her, never touched her except to hit her, too.

"No, I don't think so. We have a pretty good life out here." A rueful smile. The police ate it up, offered sympathetic smiles in return. "Don't we, honey?" he asked, looking at his daughter. The warning in his eyes.

"Pretty boring and uneventful," she said, choking on the words.

•

A flash of a petal in her mind's eye, a twist of information, and then Carina tumbles into another memory.

•

The police never found the body.

After a few months, her father threw a memorial in San Francisco. Everyone came. Carina stayed stiff and silent. She'd cried so many tears behind closed doors, it was a wonder she hadn't drowned in them. Dr. Roz Elliot was at the funeral. She offered Carina a piece of candy, as though she were a child, and Carina sucked on it quietly during the ceremony. Sour, sour apple.

She wanted to run away, into those twining streets of San Francisco. Hide where her father could never find her.

Yet she climbed into the hovercar after the funeral with no protest, staring silently out the window as they flew back to Woodside and Greenview House.

•

Another petal falls, draws her to a few years later.

•

After four months of therapy, her father pulled the plug.

"No!" Carina protested when he told her. "It hasn't been long enough."

"You're too dependent on her. You tell her too much."

"I don't!" She'd never told her therapist her father hit her. The therapist was a woman nearing retirement, with beetle-black eyes and a harsh slash of a mouth that never said unkind words. Her father didn't strike her often, maybe once every other month, and he made apologetic noises each time, bought her something she didn't need. She'd been working her way up to telling the therapist, and perhaps he knew this. Carina did tell her about the manipulation, about how she walked around her house as though she were on eggshells. About how he never let her wear makeup because of his upbringing and beliefs, and she rarely saw friends outside of school. She'd scattered the details into their conversations. Her therapist was smart. She was piecing it together.

"I'm tired of your weakness," her father said.

Grief isn't weakness, she wanted to say. Existing despite you is strength. It was something she'd learned in therapy. She kept the words locked behind her lips, but she said them in her head as loud as she could.

"I've found a better course of action for you," he said.

Her stomach knotted with dread. "What?"

"Grab your coat. Let's go."

He took her to Dr. Roz Elliot. She shook Carina's hand, which was freezing cold. Dr. Elliot said they'd do great work together.

"What are you planning to do, exactly?" Carina asked. "My father didn't say."

"Nothing drastic, I promise." Dr. Elliot gave a small laugh that did nothing to reassure Carina. "It's a new procedure to help people with trauma and PTSD. Helps them cope better. Your father says you're still having trouble with the loss of your mother."

Carina couldn't help but be a little curious. There'd been a hole in her since her mother left. She wouldn't mind waking up without that heaviness of absence in her chest. It weighed her down so much she couldn't do anything most days, not even work toward what she wanted the most: answers.

They thought her mother had jumped off the Golden Gate Bridge, her body washed out to sea.

Carina doesn't believe that. Her mother wouldn't simply disappear. They showed her a still from a camera drone: a woman in a pink coat like her mother's on the Golden Gate Bridge. Evidently her VeriChip signal went dark within the city. She didn't believe it was her mother, and she couldn't see her face.

"I'm pretty sure this is too experimental to roll out on a traumatized teen," Carina said. "I should probably stick with therapy and antidepressants."

"Let me perform one treatment, and see how you feel afterward. If you don't feel it's helping, we can stop. I promise."

Carina paused, sizing up the scientist. She seemed so collected and assured. So confident. Carina wanted to trust her.

She agreed to one treatment. Dr. Elliot hooked her up to a Chair, walked her through a few images. Her own brain scan hovered in the middle of the lab, dark as a thundercloud. Nothing much seemed to happen, though at one point, Dr. Elliot gave her a small dose of something. She claimed it was only Zeal, to make the brain scan clearer.

Though Carina was entirely sure she'd stop after one treatment, at the end of the session, she found herself agreeing to a second session. As if all her opinions about receiving the treatment had been erased. She returned home.

There were roses in the front garden at Greenview House.

•

They were separate memories, not just one, but all linked together through associations in her mind. A rose unfurls before Carina in her mind's eye, the petals wet with dew. The heady perfume reaches her. Carina bends forward, until she's close enough to kiss the velvet petals. The bloom shakes, as if battered by the wind, and then breaks apart into pixels and long strings of code. They settle into her brain.

Like the Bee, it's too much information to process at once. Carina lets her exhausted, wrung-out mind take it all in. She knows she has struck gold.

When the last of the Rose information has downloaded, her brain feels calmer. It still wants Zeal, but she no longer feels as though she's drowning with that need.

Someone comes into the room. The light is dimmed to spare her sore eyes. She's not sure who it is; she didn't have a chance to see any of their faces before she lost consciousness. She has to have come to the right place. So who's standing before her in the dark? Is it Charlie? Raf or Dax? What are they like?

"Who are you?" she asks.

"I'm the person treating you."

"Ah. You must be Dax, then. The former physician. Should have guessed." Her voice is raspy, but she's pleased at how coherent she sounds. Inside her head, it's still a chaos of desire, memories and encrypted information, but she's managed to hold onto a little bit of Carina Kearney. Perhaps it will be enough to see her through.

A swift inhale of breath. He didn't expect her to know his name. She smiles in the darkness. She can frighten him further.

"Then there's your sister, Tam. It's a shame, what happened to her."

For a second, she thinks he'll tackle her. Push her to the floor, put his hands around her neck. Neutralize the threat. Instead he stares at her, shoulder muscles wound tight.

"Relax," she says, keeping her voice mild. "Obviously, if I wanted to turn you in, I would have done so."

"Maybe you will when you're recovered. Or maybe you're a spy. Maybe I should just kill you right here, and tell the others I couldn't save you from your addiction."

She takes a moment to consider it. He probably has a poison on him. Maybe in his left pocket. Her reflexes aren't as bad as they could be—she did surprise Roz's guard—but unlike that man, Dax won't underestimate her. She shrugs. "That'd be your mistake. Mark wanted me to find you. I have information you need."

He shifts, and she can finally have a good look at him. Long dark hair hangs past his shoulders. He has a thin face, full lips, high cheekbones and a small cleft in his chin. From the information that just unlocked, she knows he's Native American, of the Timbisha Shoshone, and grew up in Death Valley. He is trans. He's about the same height as Carina, slim but broadshouldered, and toned in a way that suggests he either has very good muscle mods or actually works out. Good-looking. It's been a long time since she's been with it enough to even recognize someone as attractive.

Carina slides the IV needle from the crook of her arm and sits up. Her neck hurts. The rest of her hurts . . . a lot less. Her arms are healed; the many bruises from countless Zeal needles gone. The scars are still there, but the veins under her skin aren't quite so stark. Even her torn and bloody cuticles are a bit better.

Dax passes her a mirror. She hasn't liked looking in them these last six months. She closes her eyes and steels herself.

It's still bad. Her hair has thinned enough that she can see her dry scalp through the fair strands. The bags under her eyes are just as dark as before. She's so thin.

"I didn't do anything except fix the really dangerous risks to your health. I could fix your teeth and plenty more, but I concentrated on the essentials. You came close to dying."

Carina probes her mouth with her tongue. How had she not realized she'd lost four teeth? Most of the others are gray with decay. She hesitates, then decides. "I'd like it if you could fix them. In fact, I wonder if you could do one better." She looks up at him. "Can you give me a new face entirely?"

Dax blinks. "I can. But I want to know who you are, and why you're on the run. Why you're really here. No bullshit."

Carina considers him. His mouth is set in a stubborn line. A few strands of hair have escaped the loose ponytail and frame his face. The information she's downloaded on the Trust has a personality profile for Dax, which is useful. It says he has a strong moral compass. That he's trustworthy, if he thinks the person is worthy of that trust.

"My name is Carina Kearney," she says, electing to tell the truth. "I used to work for Sudice. With Mark . . ."

"Who's Mark?"

"Your source."

Dax swallows. "He hasn't told us his name."

"He was Dr. Mark Teague. I worked with him on the Syn-Maps memory trials, starting around three years ago."

He starts. "SynMaps? The experiments that tortured people?"

She doesn't blink. "Yes. Those. I quit and left when I didn't agree with how they were conducting those experiments." It's more complicated than that, but she doesn't feel like going into the nuances. "Mark is dead."

Dax leans back into the darkness again. She can't see his face, but his hands clench.

"I didn't know anything about what Mark was up to," she continues. "I didn't even know he'd left the company. Then, yesterday, I was . . . plugged in as usual—" Carina hates how her voice flickers—"and he sent me all this information. It's hidden in my head. I have information on your group. A lot of it. But I have the potential for more. I managed to unlock a second lot of information on Sudice. I can guarantee you, it'll have things you can use to hurt them."

"Like what?"

She mentally rifles through it. "Accurate, up-to-date personality profiles on every employee. Meaning you can sift through and pinpoint which employees are susceptible to bribery through money, sex or patriotism. There are a lot of people in there who aren't happy. They just need to be pushed in the right direction, with the right amount of pressure."

She pings three profiles to his implants as an example.

Dax stays silent, turning around the information she's given him. "Interesting."

"And that's just the tip of the iceberg. So: you need me. I need protection until I get the rest of the information out of my head. I'll give it all to you. Then I can walk away and not have to deal with this."

"This is still weird. Why didn't he just send it to us? Why you, especially in your physical state?"

Harsh, but fair. "He was afraid it'd be traced, I think. He said I was the only person he trusted, and he clearly wanted me to bring this to you. He knew my brain well enough from when we worked together to be able to pull this off." Again, she's skipping over a lot of details, but this Dax doesn't need to know everything. "I have my reasons for hating Sudice, too."

Dax considers this. Carina knows he takes care of logistics along with Charlie, and already he's trying to formulate a plan with the limited knowledge she has given him. He sighs, meets her eyes.

"OK. What do you want to look like, Carina?"

•

Carina wakes up from the medical coma and the first thing she does is run her tongue along her new, whole teeth.

Dax hovers above her, lit from behind. He helps her sit up.

Carina feels vulnerable. This man she barely knows has put

her unconscious and changed her body and face into something else. It's a different, strange sort of intimacy. This total stranger has now seen underneath her very skin.

She's not new to flesh parlors, though she hasn't gone as often as a few people she knew in San Francisco. Mark, for instance, seemed to go every week. She hasn't been to one since quitting Sudice, and when she worked at the lab she was still in her early twenties; so what with a combination of decent genetics, even better gene therapy, and the elasticity of youth, she'd only made minor changes to her body.

After she'd left Woodside, she had wanted to change herself entirely. Rewrite her face into a new start. In the end, she'd held onto her face, to have something familiar when everything else had changed so completely.

She can't look in the mirror just yet and acknowledge the fact that yes, after twenty-four years, she's changed her features into a stranger's. The blonde locks, the once-full cheeks and pointed chin had worked well for her. People never expected the true devil hidden behind the sweet face. In recent months, the Zeal had burned away any softness, left her forged yet fragile.

Dax had left her alone with the implant program to design herself before the surgery. It was strange. She had scanned her body, wincing at the ruined echo staring back at her. The app was encrypted, and everything within the Trust's headquarters was triple-encrypted on top of that.

So for a few hours, she tweaked everything about herself. She narrowed and widened her nose, eyes, lips, chin and cheekbones. Carina strayed from anything that would require changing the actual shape of her skull. Longer recovery time, and the thought of it made her squirm.

People don't often change as much about themselves as one

might think. In general, everyone tries to look like the best possible versions of themselves. They want to look younger, slimmer, healthier, happier. It means that everyone looks like real-life models, airbrushed to perfection. Yet so much perfection lends everyone a certain sameness, and so people love to peacock themselves. There are also plenty like Chopper, who change themselves until they are completely unrecognizable.

Eventually, Carina decided on a face.

In the bed, still groggy with the medicine, she prepares herself and opens her eyes.

The new face stares back at her.

She's gone for dark purple hair, as it's especially in fashion in Los Angeles this season (so ubiquitous that even she has noticed it's a fad) and means she won't stand out. She doesn't have to worry about roots; her hair will grow from her head that dark violet, the pigment written into her very DNA. It's thicker and lusher already, though some strands are shorter than others. Her skin is as pale as before, but the scars and acne have disappeared, and against the dark purple her skin seems to glow, looking better than before she ever touched Zeal. The circles around her eyes are gone, and her irises have darkened from light blue to a deep indigo. Her eyelashes are longer, her eyebrows the same shade as her hair. Her lips are not fuller exactly, but a different shape. Her sunken cheeks have filled out, her chin stronger, less pointed.

It's a beautiful face. It doesn't feel like hers.

Dax understands her stunned silence and leaves so she may investigate her body on her own. She appreciates the gesture, though it's not as if he hasn't seen what's under her nightgown. He created it.

Carina has been asleep for a few days to speed up healing. She's no longer emaciated, is even a little plumper than she was before she threw herself into Zeal lounges, so that the new nanobots have energy to rebuild her wasted muscles. She didn't want to change her body too much. She didn't wish to grow taller and change her center of gravity. Her breasts look like they used to before she'd lost so much weight they'd deflated. Identifying moles have been removed or moved somewhere else. She raises her arms above her head and turns around in front of the mirror. It's remarkable.

"You're good," Carina says when Dax returns. "Surprising, really, that you gave up your career for a life of crime. You worked in one of the top parlors. Right?" She knows he did. It's in his file.

The muscles in his jaw tighten. "It wasn't the life for me."

Carina shrugs. "Just seems a shame to waste this talent, is all I'm saying."

Carina can't stop looking at herself in the mirror. Her old face is gone forever. Even if she ever goes back to a flesh parlor and has them change it back from the biometric snapshot Dax took before he put her under, it won't be quite the same.

Humans change all the time, she reminds herself. Every seven years, all cells are replaced. Is this so very different?

"I took the liberty of swapping out your VeriChip and destroying the old one."

"I'd only put that in yesterday," she admits.

"Four days ago. You've been asleep, remember. You went to a chop shop?"

"I did."

"Sudice are good. At some point, they'll figure out where you went and whoever swapped it for you will give up the serial number to save their own skin. So that breaks the trail."

She hopes Chopper will be smart enough to evade Sudice. "So I'm no longer Althea Bryant?"

"No. I haven't turned it on yet, so you can come up with your own identity."

Althea Bryant was a mayfly. Lived and died over the course of a few days.

How did he have a spare VeriChip? They're carefully sanctioned by the government. She still doesn't know who to be next. He leaves her with the programs again. At the door, he turns back.

"Charlie and Raf are going to want to meet you soon."

He closes the door. Carina's pulse spikes with the slightest hint of nerves. A few years ago, she wouldn't have felt that. Charlie and Raf are dangerous. Their goals should align, in theory, but she can guarantee they won't like her.

No one ever truly likes her. They all sense that, deep down, she's broken.

SIXTEEN

ROZ

Three years ago

Sudice headquarters, San Francisco, California, Pacifica

Roz should have known SynMaps was going too smoothly.

The day starts out well enough. The subjects arrive on schedule, as usual. The fourth week of the trials has begun. The team has finished mapping their subjects' brains in detail and are starting to integrate Verve into their initial experiments, chronicling important memories and filling in the blanks. It doesn't require as much brainpower as full brain recording, and has fewer side effects. All the subjects are strapped into Chairs, their fingertips and eyelids twitching as they experience their dreamscapes.

All morning Carina has been frowning, a line forming between her eyes. It's so unlike her usual blank mask, Roz is curious. She leaves her own subject, a woman locked in the memory of when she lost her virginity. Roz is all too grateful to have an excuse not to watch that awkward, saccharine-sweet moment. Her own first time was not so shy and exploring. Not unpleasant or cruel by any stretch; but seeing her subject's

116

memory reminds Roz that she didn't lose her virginity with someone she loved, or even particularly liked.

Scientists, subjects and robots are all in the same room, but each scientist has a force field around them and their subject, like bubbles, so that conversation will not leak through. It gives a semblance of privacy but also a sense of camaraderie. Roz doesn't want everyone separated, in little solo cells. It's too remote, removed, and there's too much scope for secrets.

Mark and Aliyah are both hyper-focused on their own trials. Aliyah has made great strides. She's already mapped over a dozen memories enhanced by Verve and is extrapolating what types of details are most remembered, and which have to be artificially re-created, and whether any of the memories are becoming clearer thanks to the drug.

Thank you, Ratel, Roz thinks. *Your new drug might just help us crack this.*

Carina, surprisingly, is the furthest behind. Roz does not want the scientists growing close to their subjects, but Carina has formed no relationship with Subject B at all. He is actively nervous around her. There has to be at least some modicum of trust between them for this to work. Especially when things don't go smoothly.

"Carina," Roz says. "May I speak to you for a moment?"

Carina looks up from the code circling her head that she's been amending before she sends Subject B back into dreamland. She nods, curtly, powering the halo down.

"Take a break, Subject B," Roz says. The subject looks grateful as Carina unplugs the needles from his arms, though he shies away from her touch. He leaves the room, saying he's making for the cafeteria for some coffee. There's a replicator in the next room—why go all the way down there, wonders Roz? Then she realizes it's because he wants to be further away from Carina.

He's not just uncomfortable around her. He's afraid.

Roz takes Carina into her own office, a sumptuous corner room overlooking the bay. Carina doesn't seem nervous, but then again, it's hard to tell with her. It shouldn't be. It didn't used to be.

"You and Subject B don't seem to be getting along as well as the other pairs, it pains me to see."

"I am finding him moderately difficult to work with, yes," she agrees easily enough.

"Would you like me to terminate him and find a new subject?"

"No!" Roz is startled by the force of Carina's outburst. "I don't particularly care for him, but if an entirely new subject is brought in, I'll have to start mapping the brain and testing memories with Verve all over again. I'll fall too far behind. The SynMaps trials are meant to go in tandem, correct?"

"They are. Why don't you tell me about the trouble you've been having with Subject B, and we can work through it?"

Carina pauses, as if weighing up whether to speak.

"Go on," Roz urges.

"When were you going to tell us that all of the subjects were criminals meant to be in stasis?"

Roz blinks. She chooses her own words carefully. "I was going to, but I wanted you to become acclimated to them first." The truth is, she didn't know how to tell them. Criminals were the easiest human subjects to procure. They were grateful for a stay of execution, as it were. All their brains were more or less fully functional.

Carina has the gall to scoff. "That's a terrible scientific approach. We should be fully informed. Some of them may have subtly different brain structures. Some serial killers have smaller prefrontal cortexes, reduced empathy, varying responses in the amygdala." She sighs, pursing her lips. "The main thing that's bothering me is, they've signed disclosures, haven't they? If we find any evidence of wrongdoing in their brains, we can't hold them accountable for it."

"Ye-es." Roz had convinced Mantel to put it in. A little extra incentive for stasis candidates to sign up.

"Well. I've tried not to let it color my interactions with him, but my subject is a criminal, and I think he came forward for these trials specifically to be able to share his crimes with his scientist and know he can't be brought down for them."

Roz knows what crimes Subject B has committed.

"You gave me a serial rapist for a subject, Dr. Elliot."

Roz knows she should feel guilty. She can't, though, because she did it deliberately. Ever since she saw that flicker. There are other hints. The way Carina acted that night at Zenith, and the way she is actually bonding with the other scientists when she should be keeping herself separated, focused on the work. Roz created Carina to work hard, to be unbothered by ethics: how would she react when faced with an ethical dilemma in her work like this?

Horrific, yes. Twisted, yes. Interesting data for Roz's hypothesis? Undoubtedly.

"I've seen his memories many times now," Carina says, her voice even. "Over and over. Always women. Subject B is particularly happy he has a female scientist. You've noticed he doesn't like Mark. I think if that's who he'd been assigned, he'd have quit right out."

"Do his memories bother you?" Roz asks, choosing her words carefully.

Carina gives her a strange look. "Of course they bother me.

I'm more equipped to deal with him than the other members of the team. Especially Mark. He cries at commercials. Never met a bigger bleeding heart."

"Do you feel at risk?" Roz asks. She's watching Carina's pupil size, her body mannerisms. Carina's head twitches to the side, just once. A little glitch.

"No. He's chemically castrated."

"Yes." Roz had ensured that. She isn't a total monster.

"That will affect results, too. If you'd properly briefed me, I wouldn't be so far behind the others." One aspect of her programming that's holding strong. Carina cannot abide failure. She'll do anything to succeed. Being last has gotten under her skin in a way few other things could.

They stare at each other, at an impasse. Carina's blue eyes and baby face contrast with her serious expression and harsh words.

"You're right," Roz says. "I apologize. It's a tricky situation."

"Yes. What you are doing with Sudice's blessing is not legal. I've checked."

Roz says nothing.

"I understand your approach, even if I think it's a poor one."

Roz narrows her eyes at her, then smooths her face into her own mask. "This is only step one. To ensure it's safe enough for non-criminals."

"What have the other subjects done?" Carina asks.

"I'll send you their files."

"You're gambling with their lives."

"Do you really think they're in danger?" Roz counters.

Carina falls silent as she thinks this through. "I'm not sure. None of us are."

"That's true," Roz concedes. Carina's head jerks again, as if flinching from a fly. "I appreciate you coming to me, and your honesty. I want you to always feel that you can trust me."

"That would be easier if you did not withhold vital information."

Roz bites down on a sharp retort. "That's fair. But I want you to know I have your best interests at heart." She steps closer to Carina. Hesitates, and then sets a hand on Carina's shoulder and squeezes. Carina doesn't flinch, but she tolerates the gesture more than appreciates it. Roz drops her hand, and wishes she hadn't done it.

"I do. If you don't mind, I'd like to get back to my subject. I have a lot of work to do." She turns to leave the office.

Roz can't help it. "Why is Subject B afraid of you?"

Carina rests a hand on the door as she turns back. "I give him nothing. He tries to goad me into a reaction, and I look at him as if he's no more interesting than a piece of furniture. I am very clearly asserting I am stronger than him. In his castrated state, he feels extra vulnerable. It keeps him cowed."

Roz nods. "Right."

Carina's eyes blink rapidly, one eye faster than the other. Another glitch? Roz should demand another brain scan, reset her code now, but before she can say another word, Carina leaves.

Roz stays in her office for a few moments, composing herself, before she returns to Subject D. Carina is working with Subject B again. He doesn't look like a serial rapist, but then very few actually do, especially these days. He's handsome, sculpted in flesh parlors to look like an old actor from the 1930s. That sort of reassuring, confident, strong-but-not-threatening look. Roz's eyes slide away from him.

She finishes with her own Subject D. Thankfully, the woman is still thinking about her teenage years, though even that is hard to stomach knowing a serial rapist is in the same room.

Roz delves into some of the woman's other crimes. She stole government secrets. Pacifica found out, arrested her before the journalist drones could even sniff the story. She hopes that once these trials are over, there will be a pardon. All four subjects will be packed off to stasis, to disappear onto ice like all the others.

At the end of the work day, after the subjects have gone back to their apartments, Roz gathers the team together and tells them that the subjects are stasis criminals. No one is entirely surprised, but all are deeply annoyed at her for withholding the information. This is fair, she says to them, as she did with Carina. She didn't tell them at first, for fear that they'd pull out and they'd have to delay starting the project while they found replacements. Now they are in too deep, all interested enough by the science to overlook the murky legality. At least, she hopes so, and they've all signed ironclad nondisclosures.

Everyone goes home. Roz stays, working on her side project. Her true project.

Before she can make proper headway, she has to fix phase one of SynMaps: Carina.

SEVENTEEN

CARINA

The Trust headquarters, Los Angeles,
California, Pacifica

Carina is finally ready to meet the Trust.

She's spent the morning going over their profiles again, closing her eyes as the facts come up. She can sense the information is planted and not her own, just like a brainload, so it's easier to draw on. Crisper.

Someone has given her clothes, since the ones she arrived in were torn, a little bloody and none too clean in the first place. Underwear. Plain dark trousers and a blue T-shirt. New boots that need to be broken in before they will be comfortable. Serviceable, but somehow completely different from what she would have chosen herself. Combined with her new face, it makes her feel even more alien.

The door to her room is locked from the outside. The Trust are talking as they eat, cutlery clinking. She buzzes them impatiently from the panel on the wall. Their voices trail away.

Dax opens the door and leads her to the kitchen, almost like she's a prisoner. Hesitating at first, she pushes on. She doesn't like meeting new people, even if, in this case, she knows a lot more about them than they do about her. Carina used to meet strangers with total detachment. She pretended to find them interesting, but never did. Facts, projects, *science* were the only things that truly fascinated her. She faked her way through the proper social etiquette. After so many months in the Zealscape, she's not sure how she'll react to outright aggression or hostility. Will she strike back and kill someone before even realizing what she's doing?

That wouldn't exactly make the best first impression.

She enters the kitchen, which looks surprisingly homey considering it's in a converted hovercar park basement. The two unfamiliar members of the Trust stop eating and look at her. Carina stands stiff and straight, meeting their gazes. She'll make the first parry.

"Good morning, Charlie, Dax and Raf," she says, greeting them by name and nodding at each in turn.

"Well, you look a lot better than you did the other day, I'll give you that. But who the hell are you?" Raf asks.

"I'm Carina. You're Raf. The hacker. Former government. You sold information. Pacifica was pissed. You went into hiding, stayed there. Pacifica thinks you're dead or abroad. You never told the others what exactly you stole, or what made you decide to turn against your employer. Raf isn't the greatest alias considering your name is Rafael Hernandez."

She tilts her head up. Perfect little threat at the end.

Raf shrugs. "They already know my name. Sudice can't find me anyway."

"You should all know better than to underestimate Sudice." She turns to the woman with the short, red hair. She's staring at Carina, arms crossed, an eyebrow raised.

"Charlie, formerly of the Mantel family. Born in New York. Second cousin to good old Mr. Mantel himself. Studied engineering and psychology, primarily, though you're a decent hacker. Also a talented painter, though you haven't lifted a brush since you left home. Creator and ringleader of the Trust."

"I didn't know you painted," Raf says, surprised.

"I wasn't that great." Charlie's mouth twists. "Are you saying Sudice know I'm in the Trust?"

Carina taps her temple. "I'm not sure. Don't think so. This bit is all Mark's intel." She turns to the man who brought her back from the brink. "Dax. I already know all about you." She flashes him a smile, showing too many of her teeth. It unnerves him. Good.

"And then there's the member who's not here. Tamaya. Or Tam. Dax's twin sister. Grew up with him in Timbisha. Studied software engineering, was Raf's mentee. Attacked by AI Wasps, which are nasty. Pacifica don't know what became of her after that. Where is she?"

Dax's hands have clenched into fists. "We're not on close enough terms to discuss my sister."

Yes, that's definitely a sore spot. She files that away.

"Sudice have their suspicions about who you are, and they're not far off. They think you've disbanded, but there are rumors you've regrouped. If they find out you definitely have, they'll squash you like flies."

"They can try," Raf says, all bravado.

She's unnerved them enough with what she knows. Now to placate them. "So. Dax will have told you I am Carina Kearney. Then I was Althea Bryant for a brief moment, and who knows who I'll be next. I used to work for Sudice but left as soon as I saw too much, and then your source stuck everything he knew in my head, but I haven't figured out how to access it all yet."

"Yes, we know that," Charlie says. "But we still don't know what your true alliances are."

Carina shrugs. "Guess not, though you can map my brain

to see if I'm telling the truth, if that'll make you feel better. I don't have *any* alliances. That's why Mark chose me. I was well on my way to dying until he went and interrupted it. Can I have some coffee?"

Charlie gestures to the replicator. "Help yourself." She stands, holds out her hand. "Sorry for the frigid welcome. We might be called the Trust, but you might have gathered we're not exactly the most trusting people."

Carina takes her hand, shakes it. Not too hard. "Thanks. And I get it. I've got plenty of trust issues of my own, believe me." She orders coffee from the replicator. Black and bitter. She's starving, so she orders some eggs and toast as well without asking.

She sits down, sipping her coffee. "So, I know all that you've been up to, except for the last week or so. Mark's records stop with his death."

Charlie's face falls. She has the kind of face that's clear as glass, showing all emotion underneath. "I never knew who our source was. I had suspected Mark, but . . . never really thought he'd be brave enough to turn on Sudice."

"You and me both," Carina replies. Mark had never seemed to have a problem with authority. He loved the science, the data. He was not her first thought when thinking of who might sell out Sudice's secrets.

That's probably the reason he went undetected for as long as he did.

Carina takes a bite of egg, chews and swallows before continuing. "Mark wasn't able to feed you much intel because he couldn't get it to you safely enough. So I'm basically your delivery service, even though he didn't ask me what I thought about it. Or his AI didn't, anyway. I'm not a strategist. So I'll tell you what I know, and we can at least hurt them a little with what I have. Hopefully I can figure out how to unlock the rest."

Carina acts brusque and ever so slightly irreverent, knowing it's what they'll respond to, though they'll bristle a little at her being a new authority in the group. Let them. Carina knows her worth; she's vital to them. They'll listen.

As she finishes her rubbery synthetic eggs, they begin, cautiously, to share information with each other. It's not comfortable. Both sides feel like they're giving away secrets, eroding ground. But the more time they spend posturing defensively against each other, the less time they have.

"We've been looking at ways to target people within Sudice, but the main problem is that most of the personnel records are well-sealed. I haven't been able to get in," Raf says.

"Well, I've got you covered there." Carina projects the personnel files from her eye implants onto a nearby white wall. The Trust stare at the faces and information scrolling past.

"Wow. So you weren't lying to Dax," Raf says, his eyes lighting up with glee before they dim in suspicion. "And you'll just hand this over to us? No hesitations?"

"I don't know what to do with it on my own. I'm a neurohacker. I can't do much with actual servers that are outside the human brain." She pauses. "And I promised Mark I'd help."

"He spoke to you before he was killed? Do you know who did it?" Charlie asks.

"No, in a weird way . . . he spoke to me after he died." She presses the wireless electrodes to her head, sending the information to the Trust. She tells them about the AI ghost that came into the Zealscape, explained what she had to do. She doesn't mention the true reason he knew she'd help. They don't need to know her mind was reworked like putty by the woman who's leading the search against them.

"Jesus. I'd kill to get my hands on that code," Raf says. He winces. "Rephrase that to be less insensitive." A halo of code

127

pops up as he goes through the information he's just received. She only sent intel from the Bee and the Rose, and the Rose includes a lot of information on the Trust. She wonders if they all know each other's secrets. If not, that'll be interesting.

"There it is. Come up with a plan and let me know what it is. I'm still not at my best." She tears the electrodes from her temples. Understatement. Now that she's eaten, she's flagging terribly, even with the coffee.

The Zeal addiction may be broken, physically and mentally (for the most part), but she also isn't used to being conscious for long periods at a time. She needs a nap. Carina drains her cup and leaves them to it. She's done her part.

In her small room, she falls asleep and dreams of killing people. Slowly. Meticulously. As she has so many times before. The man she conjures up is an aggregate of Subject B, the man she studied in Sudice. She cuts him open and takes out his organs one by one. He's still alive and screaming as she does it. Eventually, she stabs him in the throat to shut him up. But all the details blur together. Her form seems to shimmer and teleport from one side of the room where she does her gruesome deed to the other. She can't control the hunt. Even the killing feels false. There's no way to heft the weight of the body parts in her hand. It all dissolves into darkness.

When she wakes up, a dry sob catches in her throat.

Dreams aren't a patch on the Zealscape.

She yearns for more.

EIGHTEEN

DAX

The Trust headquarters, Los Angeles,
California, Pacifica

After Carina leaves, Raf wastes no time rifling through the information. The Trust gaze at the white wall, not even looking away for a sip of coffee. There's so much here. Personnel files of the important members of Sudice, with the notable exception of Mr. Mantel himself. Dax supposes even Mark had his limits. The potential weaknesses are already highlighted for them. Some are greedy. Some are already doing little jobs on the side for more money, not content with their lavish salaries. There are copies of their work diaries. Perhaps no longer up to date, but quite a lot of these events and meetings won't change. Sudice runs like clockwork.

There are no passwords, but there's enough information that Raf will be able to find a way in. There are corporate Sudice working practices and standards, highly encrypted, sensitive information Mark has somehow spirited out of the servers.

There's material on the types of things Sudice does to remain such a powerful corporation. They perform plenty—plenty—of espionage on their own. They monitor their employees' implants. If they think an employee is doing something they shouldn't, Sudice set the ocular implants to take a photograph every time they blink. They'll record the sounds that come through on auditory implants. The websites they visit, whether at work or at home, the music they choose to stream, the shows they watch, and their choices of pornography.

Sudice monitors it all, and employees don't realize their privacy is being violated every day. Yet, hidden in their monumental personnel contracts, everyone who works there gave Sudice permission. Going public with just this won't do much at all.

Dax is able to draw up Carina's old personnel file. It's fairly sparse, with obvious gaps. Someone's tampered with it. Carina herself, or someone she used to work for? What remains shows Carina didn't watch or listen to anything unusual in her time there. Her reason for leaving is listed as "laid off." That smells bogus.

Carina's implants were already blocked when she crashed on their doorstep, thankfully, and well enough that Raf was satisfied when he checked them. Either she did it herself or got someone to do it for her. He should check into that, Dax thinks. Who else has she been in contact with since Mark sent her the information?

Dax focuses again on the intel, annoyed at his wandering attention. Sudice has fingers in many other companies' pies, but hidden: masked share prices, bought-off employees. Sudice covers its tracks well, but Charlie asks Raf to look through the data and see if they have been sloppy. There might be splinters of data they can collect and add to the incriminating bomb of information they eventually hope to ignite. Something that stockholders can't ignore. That the government can't ignore. That the people of Pacifica and the rest of the world can't ignore.

The Trust's goal has always been to wake everyone else up. Shake them from their virtual reality or their Zeal-fueled slumber. Make them see the ugliness of the corruption as it truly is around them, beneath the veneer of plastic surgery, glittering clothes and flashing advertisements.

"There's a lot we can do with this," Raf says. "It's a big break. We have a chance of hurting them. All the Vipers in the outer levels wouldn't have been able to collect even a fraction of this information." His face splits into a grin.

"It's not enough, though," Charlie says. "Not yet."

"I agree," Dax says. "They'd be able to weasel out of this. It's a start, but only that."

Raf narrows his eyes. "Stop killing my buzz."

Dax shrugs. "Buzz away."

Raf throws up a middle finger as an answer. Dax rolls his eyes.

"Stop bickering," Charlie says. Her fingertips are raised, scrolling through the information, her eyes speed-reading, lips pressed together. Charlie pauses. She flicks forward.

"Charlie, go back," Dax says.

She takes a breath, then does. Dax and Raf read. Their eyes dart to her and then back to the information on the screen.

"Charlie," Dax says, slowly. "Why didn't you tell us the reason you left the Mantel family was because you stole over a trillion credits from them and therefore Sudice?"

"Wow. You're like another step removed from the black sheep of that family," Raf says, giving a low whistle and leaning back. "You're the freaking wolf."

"I knew you had money," Dax says. "That's . . . a lot of money."

"Touching you haven't hacked into my bank accounts, I guess, Raf. I had to fund the Trust somehow." She gazes up at the file, licking her lips. "I thought I'd covered my tracks. I thought they didn't know it was me." Her voice has gone low and flat with fear. Dax wonders what it has been like for her to grow up under the shadow of that family. To be raised around so much money that a million credits feels like pocket change. To be that far removed from how actual people live.

Dax toys with the ends of his hair. "God, way too much money, Charlie. They knew the minute you left. They don't know how, and they covered it up. Didn't want anyone else getting ideas."

"Think what the media bots would do if they found out," Raf says. "It'd be carnage."

Charlie shrugs. "Whatever. The media bots haven't found a thing. And they won't. Congratulations, you now know why I left."

Dax has never heard such bitterness in her voice. "Not really," he says. "We know you stole money and can't go back. We still don't really know what turned you against your own family."

She glances up at the wallscreen again. Her face is a blank mask. "It wasn't any one thing. All the titbits that trickled down to me over the years. I was nineteen when I realized the company my family owned was responsible for far too many deaths. That they had a hand in every war during the Great Upheaval, provided all the weapons. There's so many secrets stuffed within that company, and they're literally getting away with murder and then some. You all know this as well as I do. There was not just *one* thing. There were *thousands*."

Raf flicks to the next file. It's his. There's not much on Raf that the group doesn't know about already. For someone who is very good at hiding the secrets of his past from the internet, the government and the police, he is very honest to the Trust about his past. He's told them how he stumbled into hacking as a kid and became good enough that, when he was twelve, the FBI knocked on his mother's door and nearly gave her a heart attack. They had recruited him to work for them by the time he was sixteen, and he was one of the pivotal inventors of Wasps, which he regrets. Security AI Waspbots, strong enough to kill someone if they're using a virtual reality interface to go somewhere online they shouldn't be. He invented the very thing that hurt Tam. Dax tries not to resent him for that. Some days that's easier than others. He reaches up to toy with his sister's necklace.

The government's choice to put Raf close to all those state and federal secrets proved to be a mistake. Raf grew close to another hacker named Aster—Dax only learned about him from Charlie—and that name isn't in the file. Aster found out something, planned to go public. Instead, he disappeared. Dead, put in stasis—the same thing, really. It was Raf's turning point. He rifled through all their secrets, and then found out a lot about other corporations.

Raf had a hand in the downfall of one of Sudice's subsidiaries, Truglio, and when the government realized one of their own hackers was the one behind it, he had to leave, and fast. He went deep underground but still kept an eye on things.

Raf and Charlie had been childhood friends, though neither of them ever went into the details of where and how they met. They'd grown apart, but Raf always made sure to leave small, encrypted breadcrumbs so Charlie could find him. When she was kicked out by her family, she definitely needed him. He took her in and gave her a new identity.

At first, they hoped that they could take down Sudice on their own, but they soon realized they would need at least a little more help, if there was any chance of actually doing the impossible. They began recruiting.

Raf found Tam. She had always been wary of large corporations, and had little faith in Pacifica's commitment to due process. Dax and Tam had grown up away from the rampant obsession with perfection, in a place where tech was not integrated into every experience. All through her youth, Tam had been an activist outside the Timbisha reservation, trying to make a difference. She'd been arrested and fined dozens of times, Dax always bailing her out. Tam had studied law, hoping to make a difference the legal way, but she'd been stopped at every turn by the government or Sudice. So she'd learned to hack, and had become good enough that Raf noticed. She wasn't as adept at covering her tracks as she thought she was, and if Raf hadn't stepped in, she would have been discovered. Raf probably saved her life.

Dax's own backstory is rather boring in comparison. He grew up with Tam in Timbisha, close to his family. He told them he was trans at age eight, and changed his name and clothing immediately. At puberty, the tribe supported his transition, and he took puberty blockers for a few years, then hormones, and visited a flesh parlor in Los Angeles. He left the reservation reluctantly when Tam went to university, and decided to study plastic surgery. By the time Tam joined the Trust, Dax was already disillusioned with being a waxworker, so he came too, his medical skills proving useful. The Trust had been completed.

They were a unit. Wherever Tam was, so was Dax. Until now. He's been searching for ways to help her, to try and wake her up, but it's all neurological, and he's no brain surgeon.

It hits him then: Carina is.

Hope digs its talons into him. Would she help?

Tam's information comes up on the screen. He looks away. *Has it already been six months?* Dax wonders. Grief is a strange thing. It can fade into the background and then flare up at a moment's notice, almost choking in its intensity.

The Trust had been plugged into a virtual reality interface, sneaking around the outskirts of Sudice's security, when Raf sensed someone tampering. Wasps converged on them, and Raf couldn't shut them down quickly enough. Dax knew they were nothing more than code, but in virtual reality they looked like monstrous insects.

He remembers the phantom feel of the wind of their wings. Looking into those fractured eyes, thinking: *this is it. This is the end.*

That unchangeable moment in time: a Wasp stinging Tam's avatar. Her high, pure scream. The sight of her disintegrating before his eyes. Raf frantically trying to evade his own attackers while starting emergency exit procedures. Waking up in a warehouse, looking over at Tam, and all too soon knowing her body was only a shell. Tam was gone, and no one knew if she was trapped in a corner of her mind, or if she had fled completely.

Dax knows what Raf suspects: not that Tam was an intentional spy, but that someone had tricked her into giving away information that compromised them. If it's true, she marked her own downfall.

Dax has to believe—he has to—that she wasn't a traitor, even accidentally.

The Trust comb through the information while Dax stares at the tabletop, trying and failing to keep his emotions under control.

"Well?" he asks, still looking down.

"She didn't give them anything," Charlie says softly. "Not that we can see."

Dax's shoulders droop. It has been a heavy weight. "How did they know where we'd be?"

"Unclear. Just found a trail and followed it," Raf said. "I'm sorry for thinking it might have been her. I guess it was easier than thinking I'd been careless."

Dax thought he'd be angry, lash out at Raf, but he is only tired. His eyes run over the information. Tam didn't give them up. If he can convince Carina to help, if Tam can come back . . . he could have his sister again. Maybe. The chance is still microscopic, but it's a chance.

Dax stands, the chair screeching. Let the others sort through all the information. Let them decide what to do. With Carina. With Sudice. With all of it.

He's had enough of secrets for one day.

NINETEEN

ROZ

Sixteen months ago

Sudice headquarters, San Francisco,
California, Pacifica

The SynMaps trials are progressing beautifully, but Roz is still uneasy and frustrated.

The scientists have taken the news that their subjects were criminals better than she expected. Then again, all the scientists—except for Carina—had already been exposed to the twisted ethics of corporate science. How you fit the data to support your hypothesis, so the company makes its bottom line and the product can be released. Even if it's still flawed, still bugged. Still dangerous.

It's business.

So they continue. Carina's subject is by far the worst of the group. The other crimes are less severe. Roz's subject has committed fraud, hacking into banks and siphoning funds. Aliyah's subject is an arsonist, notably having burned down a hospital, though luckily for him, everyone was able to evacuate safely. He reacted so poorly to Zeal therapy that after his third large-scale fire, it was the stasis ice-tray for him. Mark has

137

another one whose memories are not terribly fun to peruse. This subject, based out of Hollywood, hacked into feeds and implants for celebrities, leaking personal information to the hungry masses. No celebrity was off limits. He'd find whatever he could on them. Nude pictures, sex tapes, celebrities complaining to trusted friends about other celebrities. He made millions off it, but that's all been confiscated now that he's been caught. Mark says he isn't repentant. The famous people had the best security money could buy, but from the subject's point of view, they were asking for it. All the combined lawsuits meant he would have ended up in stasis without a doubt, but he's weaseled his way into this instead.

Roz has no doubt that, were all these subjects released, they'd return to their crimes. Roz can find no hint of remorse in any of their brains. Roz, therefore, in turn has no guilt of her own.

Carina is handling Subject B well. She has a specifically blank look when she works with him; she'll speak calmly, but stare through him as if he's not worth seeing. Subject B doesn't like it. Carina was right; he wants acknowledgment of his crimes, wants her to be upset by what he shows her. He's trying to mentally assault her, and doesn't understand why it doesn't work. What an awful cesspit of a human being.

Mr. Mantel pinged her a few days ago. He said she could progress with her own side project once she and her team could prove that brain recording would work on all four subjects without side effects for five minutes. Just five minutes. The news rejuvenated her, as it was meant to. Mantel knows how to dangle a carrot.

Subject B is up first. All of them have double-, triple-, quadruple-checked Carina's code. In theory, the brain recording should work. Roz shakes with excitement, yet also simmers with a touch of jealousy. She wanted to test her own subject, her own code, but she's been so caught up with the administrative duties of their work and prepping for the real SynMaps project—something that her team can never know about. Her true passion. So Carina beat her to it. And her code is beautiful, probably better than Roz's would have been, much as it pains her to admit it.

They gather around Subject B. None of the scientists can stand the sight of him, with that falsely beautiful face hiding such an ugly mind. Roz has overheard Kim and Aliyah speaking about it through the cameras in the lab.

"They've been tried and convicted," Aliyah said. "But they're here, instead of frozen in stasis where they belong."

"Maybe this is a worse punishment than being on ice," Kim replied.

Subject B gives Roz an oily smile, his eyes too sharp. Bile burns her throat, harsh and bitter. She can't wait to send him right to the freezer where he belongs when this is all over.

Carina takes a deep breath, bringing the code around her head like a crown. Her hands come up, manipulating the last little details. The code hovers over Subject B, its blue light suffusing him in its gentle glow. She sends the command.

Subject B's mouth opens in a silent scream. His back arches, his body bucking against the pain of the implants changing for the brainload to work. Roz fights down the urge to smile at his pain.

Carina does not.

Her face lights up with glee, her teeth bared in a cross between a grimace and a grin. Her whole body seems to vibrate as she watches Subject B in his agony.

Roz's stomach drops. This is not supposed to be happening. Carina is not meant to care at all if she sees someone else in pain. No dread, no sympathetic shiver down her spine. Definitely no pleasure. Muted emotions were key components of the programming, to make her a more efficient and ambitious scientist.

Subject B relaxes as the code completes. Roz wants to dart forward, to pull the plug, but something stops her.

"We will now start the SynMaps procedure," Carina says. "The activation and deactivation switch has been attached to the nerve cluster leading to the hollow of his throat."

She pauses. Swallows. "Assistant," Carina directs the robot, "please press the hollow of his throat three times. Subject B, pay close attention to your immediate surroundings. We will record for five minutes."

Interesting that she asks her assistant to do it. She doesn't want to touch him, is Roz's best guess. The assistant dutifully comes forward and presses metallic fingers to Subject B's skin, between his collarbones. One. Two. Three.

The Adam's apple in Subject B's throat works as he swallows. "I feel sick," he says.

"Nausea is a common side effect," Carina says, still unconcerned.

Subject B turns his head, gagging. One of the other robots grabs a tub and puts it beneath his mouth just as he vomits. Unease prickles at Roz. Subject B has stopped vomiting, but his skin is clammy.

"Blood pressure rising to 135 over 85," Carina's robot assistant intones. "Core temperature rising to 100 degrees Fahrenheit. Heart rate at 180 beats per minute. Danger. Recommend ceasing experiment immediately."

"He'll stabilize. He just needs a minute," Carina says. "Look. It's working."

They all look at the projected readings on the white wall. Subject B's brain is recording.

"Vitals stabilizing," the robot intones.

Carina's lips turn up in a triumphant smile. They all continue to watch the readings. Three minutes. They only need two minutes more. Two minutes, and Roz can start the real work.

"I still don't feel well. I want to stop," Subject B says. His voice is so petulant, Roz half expects him to stick out his bottom lip.

One more minute.

Carina undoes the restraints. She's careful not to touch his bare skin. "Sit up and walk around a little."

He does so. His steps are unstable.

The timer beeps. They've reached five minutes. Roz and the others break into a grin.

Then Subject B's whole body stiffens. He lets out a small sound, almost a mewl. Before the robot assistant can begin to utter its warning, Subject B crumples to the ground. His body jerks, horribly. Grand mal seizure.

The robots circle him. One turns him to his side, sticks a metal finger in his mouth to press down the tongue. Another gives him an injection. The humans in the room hold their breath. Kim's clutching Aliyah close, Mark has both hands over his mouth. Carina's face is smooth as ever.

This doesn't make sense, Roz thinks. He'd stabilized. It seemed like he could have carried on recording with only minor discomfort.

Subject B is still twitching, but less than before. Roz is glad she convinced Mantel the expense of the robots and virtual assistants was worth it. The other scientists have some medical training, but they wouldn't have been able to react as quickly.

One robot carries Subject B through to the next room, and through the clear partition, the scientists watch it set him down on a laboratory table. Roz can only thank whatever luck she has that the other subjects aren't here today.

While the robots continue their dance to save the subject's life, Roz watches Carina. The corners of her mouth twitch. Roz doesn't need a microexpression overlay on her implants to know it's a tiny, suppressed expression of frustrated regret. Something about that glint in Carina's eyes reminds Roz uncomfortably of the way Subject B looked at her, right before he plugged in. She knows Carina has snuck off to Zeal lounges three times after work this week.

The code should have worked. Should have been the breakthrough they so desperately need. There is no doubt in Roz's mind that the careful programming she created in Carina ten years ago is fraying badly. She'll have to fix it, and soon.

Because from everything she's just witnessed, Carina has tried to kill Subject B.

TWENTY

CARINA

The Trust headquarters, Los Angeles,
California, Pacifica

After waking up from her dreams of killing, Carina lies on the floor, cheek against the cool linoleum. She tries to focus on the physical sensations here, in the real world. Her brain still desires Zeal. More than water. More than food. More than air.

There must be Zeal, somewhere in this compound. Vials of it, just waiting to be used to help the Trust brainload, enter virtual reality or have their own catharsis. What does Dax dream in his Zealscapes? Or the others? Is anything in their minds as twisted as in her own?

Eventually, the linoleum beneath her cheek warms, sticks to her skin. She forces herself to sit up. She also wasn't lying to them about her exhaustion. All her limbs are heavy. She catches sight of her new face in the mirror and flinches. Her mind still sees a stranger, and will for a long time. Pressing a hand against that foreign cheek, she turns away.

Carina looks at the bed, debates crawling back under the covers and trying to sleep again. She can't face the thought of more nightmares, so she curls up in the armchair, puts a silly action film on the wallscreen and orders some food from the replicator in the room, rather than bothering to go into the kitchen and risk seeing anyone. The day eases into night. Her eyes grow heavy.

When she finally drifts off, she's fitful. The dead girl from Mark's vision taunts her, over and over again. Those open eyes, staring, as if daring her to bring Roz to justice.

Carina twists and turns. "I can't prove she did it. I can't help you. You're already dead."

The dead girl doesn't care. She only stares, lifeless and pale.

Carina wakes up from her thin sleep. The girl reminds her so much of herself at that age, in that same lab room, with that same scientist. Those memories, locked away and half-hidden for so long, are not what call to her. Instead it's a memory of looking into a mirror and seeing her old face, over a decade ago.

•

She put on makeup in the mirror.

Carina leaned forward, brushing at her lashes carefully with the mascara. There. The finishing touch. She turned her face this way and that, scrutinizing her handiwork. With her blonde hair, brows and lashes and her pale blue eyes, she often felt like a ghost, but now her features stood out in starker relief. She put on a little lip gloss and chanced a smile at the mirror. It still didn't look quite right. Too stiff. Nothing in her eyes. She tried to soften her features, make the smile look natural. Better. Smile like that when you get to the party, she instructed herself.

Carina had been seeing Dr. Elliot for four months. Thirty-two trips from Woodside down to San Francisco, after school. Sudice sent a hovercar to pick her up and send her back after. Four months of scattered thoughts. Her recent short-term memory would stutter. She'd forget where she'd set her tablet, forget to eat breakfast, or she'd eat dinner twice because she hadn't remembered she'd already eaten the same thing.

Her friends would ping her on her implants. Carina had no interest in speaking to them. They seemed distant, formless stand-ins, not real people at all. Her schoolwork improved massively. The only thing that made sense any more to her was science.

Every now and again her head would snap up, and the fog around her mind would seem to clear. Her heartbeat would hammer in her throat, her skin break out in a sweat as if she'd just woken up from a nightmare.

What is happening to me? she'd think, as if trapped in a corner of her own mind. The anger would burn, hot and bright. *Why aren't I doing anything about this?*

She'd access her brain implants to ping her old therapist. She wanted to tell her what had happened, ask her if this was right, if this was ethical. But almost as soon as she did it, her thoughts would spiral away again. Her heart rate would slow, she'd blink owlishly, fall into a sleep. When she woke up, she wouldn't think about the experiments or wonder why her personality was slipping through her fingers like water.

One evening, her friends invited her to a party. She tried various excuses—I have to study, I'm grounded. They were so insistent that eventually she relented. Carina recognized how nervous they were around her. How they were on the verge of speaking to someone at school or to their parents about her strange behavior. This new person Carina was becoming decided she would go, blend in, halt the questions. High school would end in four months. She'd leave them all behind soon enough.

Her one and only high school party.

Leaving the mirror, she put on her coat. Just as she opened

the door, her father came up the drive. He paused. Her stomach dropped.

"What is that on your face? Where do you think you're going?"

She didn't dignify the first question with an answer. She answered the second, albeit with a lie. "I'm going to study group. We have a big project due tomorrow."

"You're not going with that on your face."

She should be frightened—she knew what that look on his face meant. Like everything else, fear was walled away. Her father, the Mana's Hearth apostate, cast out from the cult for breaking the rules. He'd given up their Luddite way of life: he had implants, and he let his family have them, but otherwise, they did not change themselves. It was a strange tenet to cling to.

In the Hearth, no one altered their appearance. Simple haircuts, no changing hair colors. No shifting tattoos. No makeup. No nail polish. Clothing could not be too fashionable or colorful. Her father wore clothes that were little more than homespun. Journalists would always comment on his appearance in interviews, considering his old-fashioned look charmingly anachronistic, and some even mentioned how quaint and touched they were that his family followed his example. He'd give his signature, charming grin and say that his wife and daughter were so beautiful already, they didn't need all the extra "flash," as he called it. The journalist would dutifully chuckle, the smile stretching their surgically altered features, self-consciously touch their own vibrantly hued hair.

Carina had bought the makeup in secret. She'd taught herself from videos on her implants. Her first time sneaking out with a mask of paint, and she'd been caught.

Before she could respond, her father grabbed her roughly

by the upper arm, marching her back into the house. Carina didn't cry out.

He took her to the bathroom and ran the tap of the bathtub.

"I'll take it off," she said.

"Only to put it back on as soon as you leave the house. It's sinful. Sinful."

There were so many things she wished she could say to him in return. That if he still believed in everything the Hearth stood for, then he was in many, many violations with the Impure world outside the confines of the commune. He had implants; their Greenview House had technology far more advanced than the Hearth allowed. They were surrounded by "those who could not hear God's true voice." He had left the bosom of the Hearth. His Mana-ma did not give a damn what he did out here.

Carina said none of this. Logic did not apply in most cases when it came to her father.

He scrubbed at her face with a towel. The mascara smeared around her face until she looked bruised. Still snarling, he held her head under the water of the bath. She had just enough time to suck in a breath before he pushed her under. Human survival instinct kicked in and she struggled, limbs flailing, trying to get her head above water. Precious bubbles of air escaped. She went limp on purpose, and playing possum worked. He brought her up, dragging her, dripping, onto the cold tile floor. She gasped for breath.

I should feel something, Carina thought. *Anger, fear, sadness. I should feel something, but it's all gone.*

He threw the towel at her.

"Finish cleaning yourself up. Then you can go to your study group."

He left, slamming the bathroom door behind him.

Gingerly, she wiped at her face with the towel and wrung out her sopping hair. She took deep, steady breaths.

When she could bear it, she looked in the mirror again. Gone was the careful eyeshadow, the delicate cat-like flick of eyeliner. Gone was the foundation and the powder, the soft sheen of lip gloss. Her pale skin was blotchy, her eyes red, her damp hair limp.

She spent the next ten minutes drying her hair. The blotches on her skin faded.

She put her coat back on, put her books in her bag, so she could still pretend she was going to study group.

Her father looked through her bag and checked her pockets, to make sure she hadn't hidden makeup somewhere.

At last he let her go.

She left Greenview House, took public transport to the main street of Woodside. She walked right past the house where the party was being held, only pausing long enough to gaze at the lit windows. She continued down the path and went to the nearby creek, sitting on a little wooden bridge and letting her legs dangle over the edge.

The fog in her mind lifted ever so slightly as she stared at the swirls and eddies of the water. That night was the first time she seriously contemplated killing herself. She watched the edge of her sneakers kick back and forth, back and forth. The bridge was high enough. The water deep enough. She could stand up, climb over the railing, lean forward, and just let go.

Would it hurt? The water would be cold. Perhaps she'd hit a rock, hard enough to knock her out and let the water do the rest. She didn't like the thought of drowning. Of her lungs burning, vision going dark. It was meant to be painful. Would the river wash her all the way out to sea?

Carina stayed there until late, and then went back to Green-view House. She did not tell anyone what had happened. There was no one to tell. She made herself a cup of tea, made some toast, and sat at the table where she had eaten breakfast every morning with her mother. The food stuck in her throat, but she finished it.

Before she went to bed, Carina looked in the mirror again. And she reached into her secret stash and put on some lip gloss. It shone in the low light. She kept it on for a few minutes, staring at herself in the mirror again, before she wiped it off and pretended to sleep.

And there it is. The image of her looking at herself in the mirror, facial expression unreadable, as she slowly wipes off the lip gloss. The key twists and unlocks the image of the Thorn. It looms, large, pointed, dangerous, barbed like a cat's claw.

It sinks its point into her.

It's not as much information as the first two images. This is a simple, clean snippet that slots into her mind as if it was always meant to be there, settling deep into her synapses.

The name of the girl with different-colored eyes was Nettie Aldrich.

She was sixteen when Roz started experimenting on her. The girl disappeared, but there is no active missing person case. It does not seem Sudice is implicated in any way. A body has not been found; there has been no widespread news cover-age about her. It's as if no one searched for her.

Nettie came from a good family, to outside eyes. Both her parents are pharmacists. She lived in the suburbs across the bay from San Francisco, in Union City. Nettie was bright and showed promise. She was accepted into UC San Francisco, but didn't even start before she disappeared.

Another shot of Nettie's corpse. Blank and staring. Mark

has written scattered notes about the state of her in a hasty pathology report. Did he find her body after Roz was done? Did Roz make him clean up her mess?

Carina skims the notes. It's not easy reading, even for her. Roz had removed part of her skull and put in nanites, sure enough, and though her code had been promising, it hadn't been good enough. The nanites fried Nettie's brain, and she had an aneurysm. It was quick, at least, but from that flash of memory, Carina knows first-hand that Nettie still suffered.

Carina gets out of bed and goes to the kitchen. After she makes a hot chocolate from the replicator, she projects information onto the blank wall in the kitchen. Somewhere, out there, there will be more information on Nettie Aldrich.

She spends hours poring over the notes and then planning how to search for the girl once she has access to the net again, forcing her rusty mind to remember how to search for things hidden and deleted. Carina could ask Raf to help her, or pretty much anyone else in the Trust would be able to search for things more efficiently. But she's still only just met them, and for some reason, feels protective and wants to keep Nettie to herself. Mark tasked her with that mystery, not the Trust. She needs to know what Roz was trying to do to her, and why it failed.

The sound of bare feet swishing along the floor reaches her. Carina sends the information away, but not fast enough. Dax enters the kitchen, wearing a T-shirt and pajama bottoms. He orders a drink from the replicator, then crosses his arms over his chest while the machine hisses and bubbles.

"What were you looking at?" he asks.

Carina should have expected this. He probably has security enabled so that as soon as she left her room, he awoke.

"It's nothing," she says, drawing the empty hot chocolate mug toward her, as if it's a barrier between them. "Couldn't sleep."

"Huh," he says. "So far, you've been a better liar than that."

Carina fights the urge to take the knife on the counter and ram it into his throat. The derisive smirk would leave his face as the warm, iron-scented blood pumped over her hands. She can almost smell it.

It's the strongest urge she's had since kicking Zeal. She lets go of the cup, clutches the edge of the table hard. Her eyes squeeze closed. Don't think of blood. Don't think of sliced skin.

"Carina?" he asks.

She doesn't answer, just hunches over herself, tighter.

"Withdrawal?" he asks, gently.

"Why do you have to be real," she says. "Why does anyone have to be real?"

He sits across from her and waits. Carina's breath drags in and out of her. *This isn't Zeal, this isn't Zeal, this isn't Zeal.*

Eventually, the urge passes, her muscles relax. She's still keyed up, still doesn't trust her body or her mind.

Dax perches at the table with his own drink. Could he have any idea what just went through her mind? He still looks sleepy, eyes half-lidded in the dim light of the kitchen. His long arms are muscled beneath his skin.

Great, Carina thinks. *Now you can't decide if you want to fuck him or kill him.*

"Well. Good night, then," she says, awkwardly. Words are hard to form. She stands, putting the cup in the replicator. Every step is difficult—she still wants to turn around and either attack him or kiss him. Or both.

Lust and attraction have been missing from her life for

years. They'd awaken when called, reluctantly, weakly, but like so much else, they were dampened by SynMaps. Roz would have considered them an unnecessary distraction. How much has been stolen from Carina? Still, most of the time, the anger she should feel about all of that is just beyond her reach.

"You unlocked more information, didn't you?" Dax asks.

She pauses, then turns back to face him. "And you're monitoring my brain activity, aren't you?"

"All your vital signs, actually." He's unrepentant. "You're still healing from surgery. Brain activity spiked three hours ago, but if you have unlocked information, I'm guessing it wasn't much compared to the first two images."

Carina presses her lips together. If she tells him about Nettie, she'll have to tell him about phase one of SynMaps and her own history with it. Mark sent this to her because of the link between them both.

"Come on," Dax says, gesturing to the seat across the table where she's been sitting. "Haven't we established by now that we're on the same side?"

Only until she gives them what they want. This is image three out of five.

"I want to help you, Carina," he says. He stares at her, unblinking, like he truly sees her. Not like the people on the Metro, afraid, as if they could catch her addiction. Not like the orderlies who didn't want to touch her skin in the Zeal lounges over the last year. Even before she grew dependent on Zeal, she's not sure anyone has ever looked at her quite like this.

Carina sits back in her chair. "The trip before I received the full five images, he sent me a girl's dying memory. No information attached. Just her. It didn't save, though it might be in one of the later images."

She projects the image of Nettie onto the wallscreen.

Dax takes her in, his doctor's mind noting her unhealed surgical cuts and the sutures.

"Her eyes are heterochromic," he observes. "Like the last image Mark sent you, right?"

"Yes. They're her eyes. She was a recent experiment for Roz Elliot. She showed this girl, Nettie, an image of a bee on a rose, and somehow it tied into what she was trying to achieve. Maybe it was just distraction, so Nettie wouldn't realize Roz was opening her skull. This is the end result." She glances up at Nettie, then away again. "I unlocked the thorn. It had little more than her name, Nettie Aldrich, and the medical notes Mark took of the state of her body."

"How did he have access?"

"I think he was helping Roz, and this was a step too far."

Dax swallows. "I'll say. Have you searched for her family?"

"Can't. Don't have access to the net down here, and I'm too tired to try hacking it."

"You wouldn't be able to."

"That's probably true. So I've just been studying the notes, trying to get into Roz's head."

"She was your boss." It's a cross between a question and a statement.

Carina meets his eyes. "For a time, yes, but I've known her since before that. Since I was a teenager."

Dax nods.

"You know about it?"

"It was hidden in a previous draft of your employee file. Raf found it this morning."

"What did it say?"

"That you were the main subject to reach the end of phase one of the SynMaps trials. Mark couldn't get the rest of the file out, as it was confidential. Or—" a pause—"he chose not to."

"It was the latter, I think. It's not his secret to tell."

Dax takes both their cups and tosses them into the replicator. "I'm not going to push you right now," he says, still turned from her. "But I think you should consider telling me."

He turns back and pulls up the secure, encrypted net access on the wallscreen. "In the meantime, let's find out more about Nettie Aldrich."

TWENTY-ONE

CARINA

The Trust headquarters, Los Angeles,
California, Pacifica

Dax and Carina stay up until dawn looking for information on Nettie.

They find so little that they are certain Sudice, the government, or both must have erased their tracks. The only information they manage to turn up is on old, archived pages that Dax only discovers because of Raf's past tutelage. Layers and layers of hiding.

"OK," Dax says, rubbing his tired eyes. The false windows mirror the early morning light outside. "I can't stare at wallscreens any more but I'm too keyed up to sleep. You haven't left the compound in almost a week. What do you say to a walk?"

The thought sends a thrill through Carina. "They'll find us if we go outside, won't they?"

"You have an entirely new face and a twice-removed VeriChip identity. They'll flag your DNA if they find it, but wear gloves, glasses, and stay away from thumbprint and retinal scanners and you'll be fine. I find walking while working through problems helps me think. Let's go."

Carina hesitates, then relents. "Sure."

As she goes to her room to change out of her cheap replicator pajamas into the cheap replicator clothing the Trust supplied for her, Carina finds she likes the idea of going outside. It has been longer than a week for her, really. It's been two-thirds of a year since she last sat outside under the sun and enjoyed it. God. The last time that happened might have been that day on Venice Beach, before she walked into her first Zealot lounge in Los Angeles and let herself go.

After dressing, she orders some inexpensive gloves and sunglasses from the replicator. While she waits for those to print, she puts on some makeup she ordered earlier, carefully, suppressing the recent memory that unlocked information on Nettie. She'd worn makeup every day of her life since leaving Greenview House, until she was too addicted to Zeal to care. She's painting a different canvas this time, and it's strange. She needs a darker palette to match her new hair color.

Ting! The replicator finishes. The gloves and glasses won't be too conspicuous. This is Los Angeles, a stone's throw from Hollywood, the land of celebrity. Nowhere else in the world does someone's social ranking matter more. Celebrities no longer have the same vast caches of fortune they did a few decades ago in this (slightly) more egalitarian world since the Great Upheaval, though they never lack for anything. Most live in the Apex, colloquially called the Tinsel, the neighborhood of mansions that float above Hollywood. Celebrity social ranking allows them unimagined privilege, but not without its own costs.

The now infamous antics of Adelmar changed everything. The man who stole celebrity DNA to hack into bank accounts and houses, and then later attempted to use the DNA to make strange, twisted clones of celebrities. His idea of artistic masterpieces. Seven years ago, he displayed his awful work right in front of the Chinese Theater in Hollywood, resting them on the handprints and footprints of the celebrities he'd cloned. He hadn't been able to carry the fetuses to term, and the authorities never found out whether he grew them in artificial wombs or paid transient women to carry them. None of them ever drew breath, though conspiracy theorists still claim the government holds them in secret, and could quicken them if it wanted to.

The twisted infants neatly labeled with the names of the celebrities they could have grown up to look like were terrifying enough, making headlines throughout the world. Adelmar was caught, his other crimes discovered, and he's been in stasis ever since.

Even years later, long gloves are a trend started by celebrities that trickled down to those who don't truly have to worry about their DNA being stolen, or not as much. Short hair and regular exfoliation baths are also the rage. Celebrities and non-celebrities alike regularly DNA-bomb their houses and workplaces, obliterating every dead skin cell. If someone is at a restaurant and notices a hair of theirs has fallen onto a tablecloth, they're more likely to pocket it than flick it to the floor. Just in case.

Carina rolls the gloves up to her elbows and puts on the sunglasses, tying her newly purple hair into a bun at the base of her neck and covering it with a hairnet studded with false jewels. Disguise in place, she leaves the room. Dax is shrugging on a jacket, his long hair also tied back. He looks her up and down.

"The gloves look ridiculous, don't they?" Carina asks.

"They're fine. I'm just admiring my handiwork. You look good. Seems like I've still got the touch." He holds up his fingers and grins.

Carina looks down at her healed and healthy hands, covered

with satin. Blood rushes to her face. When was the last time she flushed with anything other than that deep desire to kill?

She has no idea what she's meant to say. "Will the Trust care that we're going out, just us?" she asks instead.

"I sent them a message. They might be a bit annoyed, but they know I hate being cooped up down here. They wouldn't like you going out alone, but you're with me. We're good."

Out they go through the hidden, subterranean corridors, up steep stairs, until they emerge half a mile from the Trust headquarters at the Metro station by Angel's Knoll Park. It was one of Los Angeles's early parks. After the Great Quake nearly leveled the city and the rest of Pacifica during the Great Upheaval, they re-created it along with Angel's Flight, a short railway that brought people up the hill but kept breaking. The orange archway, edged in black with old-fashioned lightbulbs, and the ticket office at the top were purely ornamental in the days of hovercrafts, but Carina is still glad they rebuilt it.

The light isn't blinding with her sunglasses, but she still squints. The air is warm even though the sun is just rising, not yet cresting the skyscrapers. San Francisco has a lot of domed parks, but this one doesn't have simulated sunlight twenty-four hours a day, like Golden Gate Park.

Angel's Knoll, nestled in Bunker Hill, overlooks the Grand Central Market and older re-created buildings, their stone sides painted with murals. It's much larger than the original park. Carina turns away and looks up at the newer skyscrapers. The floating buildings between them cast occasional shadows, their underbellies glimmering with false UV lights, bridges tethering them to the skyscrapers shifting in the breeze.

Dax chooses a path through the trees and Carina follows. The early morning sun finally rises over the buildings, warming her skin and the crown of her head. She breathes in the smell of fresh-cut grass and new leaves, with just the barest hint of smog and smoke in the background. Her heart beats steadily. Her skin isn't clammy. Her muscles, though still weaker than they were before Zeal, no longer shake and quiver. It feels so strange to feel healthy and walk in the sun.

Yet she's not totally healed. Whenever people pass them—runners zipping through the small park before returning to sidewalks, families, people sitting on the benches drinking coffee and eating their breakfast—she cases them, just as she did over and over in her programmed Zealscapes. Carina imagines the crimes they must have committed that she could avenge. Like that man throwing some breadcrumbs to birds—perhaps he was a kidnapper. If she were alone she could come up behind him, stick him with a needle and drag him into a nearby alleyway between two buildings. Then she could pay the exorbitant fee for a hovercab that wouldn't ask questions and it'd drop her off . . . somewhere. The fantasy ends. There is no Greenview House simulation here. Outside of Zealscapes, she's not strong enough to lift a grown man. She has no needle, no scalpel or other tools. There is no way to kill this man and get away with it.

Thoughts of murder are always a heartbeat away. A desire to maim, to peel back flesh from the bone, to feel the heart stop beating, to watch the eyes go blank. She bites her tongue until it brings tears to her eyes. She really doesn't want to kill on this plane of reality but it would be so easy to ignore that thread of morality. To snap it.

She tries to focus instead on the warmth of the sun. The sound of the nearby fountain. The birds. Life, not death.

As they walk, Dax turns on a White Noise. They're ubiquitous little devices, kept in a pocket, that people turn on when they're in public and don't wish others to overhear their conversation. No implants or other recording devices can penetrate them—all they'd pick up is static. They can still be hacked, but they are sufficient protection against most curious ears.

They make their way up the stairs next to Angel's Flight. "All these people walking past, they look at me and see this new me," Carina says. "The reborn me, rather than . . . who I was." She doesn't say her name, of course, in case the security camera drones that circle the park pick it up. It's hard not to look over her shoulder every two minutes, to see if men in scrambler masks are following her.

"What would have happened to you if Mark hadn't sent you that information?" Dax asks.

"The same as I was before. Throwing myself deeper into the Zeal addiction, letting my body burn away."

"I'm glad that didn't happen to you," Dax says. "That you found us. If you hadn't arrived when you did, the group would have floundered. We were running out of options once Mark went quiet. I'd even tried to convince them that maybe this should be the end."

"It might still be. What I've given you so far is dangerous enough. To use it without getting yourselves killed or captured would be a miracle on its own. And who knows what else is hiding in here?" She taps her temple.

"It must be unnerving, not knowing what else might unlock, or how, or when."

"It's terrifying, but I'm used to being wary of my own mind." Carina's lips thin. Has she said too much?

Dax keeps his face carefully blank. "I've been looking at your brain scans," he says, almost hesitantly. "I compared them to the snapshot they had in your employee file."

Carina gives him a sharp look. "Why?"

"It was idle curiosity, at first. The differences are . . . stark.

But strange. I can't make sense of exactly what's changed, or why. Or how."

Carina takes a few steps before answering. They're halfway up the stairs. Time for the truth. "Dr. Elliot did something to me when I was a teen. An experimental new procedure that she said would help me cope with the loss of my mother. Instead, she changed me. I became smarter, perhaps, more driven. There was a cost. My emotions were gone. My personality shifted. I couldn't care for anyone. They didn't seem to exist as real people. Most people still don't, at least not at first."

They keep walking. The stairs are still hard for her recovering body. They reach the top of the stairs and walk through a large plaza with fountains, skyscrapers flanking either side and a floating office building directly above them, shining soft light into the potted flowers and the gentle curves of water from the fountains. Few people are out this early up here, leaving it strangely quiet and echoing.

They pass the top of Angel's Flight, with its painted orange walls and closed ticket office. Carina's been silent for a few minutes.

"The programming must have started breaking down," she continues. "I started to feel things again. I wasn't prepared. Ten years of being numb, as if everything was wrapped in wool. Then it unraveled. I found myself laughing genuinely at a joke, amazed at how it felt to let go. I started feeling a little burst of warmth when I saw the other scientists in the labs. Friendship was so alien. It was frightening, and then experiencing fear itself was new and overwhelming. I started dreaming again. But then there were the *other* emotions." Another breath. "I started wanting to hurt people I didn't know. It was weak at first. Then it grew stronger. And stronger still."

She doesn't look at Dax. He doesn't say anything. She

wishes she could peer into his mind, figure out what he's thinking.

"And that's why you became addicted to Zeal on purpose?"

"Yes."

"So that you don't actually hurt real people?"

"Yes."

"OK. Did you try alternate treatments? Like Zeal as therapy, or looking into figuring out what she did to you?"

"It's only recently that I found out she *did* do something to me. Before that I tried several traditional approaches. Whatever she did to me, it doesn't respond to regular treatment." Carina reaches into her pocket, takes out the datapod Chopper gave her. She gives it to him. "I've come up with a draft of new code that might help, but I'm not sure." After deciding to tell him the truth, she can't seem to stop. "It's still rough and needs a lot of work. I didn't have the equipment, but I could have found a way to try it. I was afraid, too, I suppose. What if I made things worse? What if I went back to how I was before?" That had been her goal, once. To stop feeling. She's no longer sure that's what she wants.

He nods, a quick incline of his head. "I understand. I think using the Zeal, in any capacity, was making things worse, judging by the brain scan when you left Sudice versus the one I took before I operated on you."

That takes her aback. "I thought it was just deteriorating on its own."

"Perhaps. But Zeal's purpose is to heighten emotion, at least within the dream. It could have accelerated the breakdown. It started happening when you were working for Sudice, right?"

"Yes."

"And you started using Zeal at the same time?"

"Not right away. But yes, I used it there." She remembers sneaking off to Zeal lounges. A lunchtime here, a late-night trip there, until it was part of her routine. Had that really made things worse?

"I'd guess living out those fantasies makes it harder to switch off once back in reality," he says. "Since you've stopped using it, I'd say you've stabilized. Are these . . . urges to kill still so frequent?"

"Frequent enough."

"We could give you something, to even you out."

"It'd either not work or numb me again," she says, her voice soft. "I'd rather fight the urges than feel nothing at all again."

Dax gives her a sideways look, nods. "What about this code? Will you use it?"

A little shrug. "Evidently I can't. Mark's AI told me if I mess with anything before all the information is unlocked, I could delete what's still hidden and most likely fry my brain in the process. So I'm stuck."

"Frustrating." He pauses, choosing his words carefully. "Are the violent urges under control? Are you a danger to us?"

She opens her mouth. Closes it again. "I can't promise you I'm not. But none of you are strangers any more. It's easier to resist if I know people. A little easier. It means I never like to grow close to people beyond a certain point. There's still this . . . film between me and everyone else that I can't seem to break through. That I won't try to cross, because what if I let someone in and hurt them anyway?" She spirals into silence, embarrassed.

His face is closed, considered. "OK. Promise me, though, if it becomes too difficult, you'll come to me, take the mood stabilizers. Temporary numbness might be better than suffering. Deal?"

"Deal." She's not sure if she's lying.

"I'll take a look at your code, if you want. Maybe Raf could, too. We could still try to finish it. For . . . after."

The nebulous future that she can't begin to fathom. Carina shakes her head. "I'd prefer the others not know about this. Not yet."

Dax nods. "Right. It's personal." A pause. "Thank you for telling me."

"It's nice for someone to know. The only person who knew was Mark, and I didn't tell him. He went snooping."

Dax gives her a smile. She returns it. It feels genuine.

"Sometimes I wonder if I'll ever go back to how I used to be," she says.

"Probably not. You were a teenager when Dr. Elliot did this to you. I suppose it's finding out who you'd be now. It's still strange to think that she could have changed you so much." Another silence. He rests his hand on one of the painted columns by the long-closed ticket booth of Angel's Flight. "Do you think she was doing the same thing to Nettie?"

Carina swallows. "Yes. I experienced everything Nettie did when she died. I remember that feeling of someone interfering with the very core of you."

"For what purpose?"

"I don't know. Nothing good. Changing her personality like she did with me, in a way that wouldn't break down."

"What can we draw from what we have?"

Grateful to change the subject, Carina summarizes. Nettie's parents seem to have disappeared in a puff of smoke. Perhaps dead, but there's no sign of death certificates or obituaries. They may have gone into protective custody, or been dealt with for asking too many questions.

When Nettie first disappeared there was that call for information, pleas from her friends for information. What a world they live in. Pacifica pretends it's a haven—no crime, no murders. Peel back a thin layer, and look at what's exposed.

A memorial was held and, Carina was sure, an empty coffin buried. Students from Nettie's high school, who saw her between brainloading sessions, attended. Then, over the past year, any mentions of Nettie Aldrich slowed and finally disappeared entirely.

Dax had found Nettie's deleted social media and the short diary entries. A few photos of her laughing with peers, or awkwardly posing with family in front of monuments, and one serious portrait, with her looking right at the camera, the saturation turned up to showcase her mismatched eyes.

"We know she seemed to be a smart girl with a promising future," Carina says. "Textbook. Nothing out of the ordinary in her home life, unless it was well hidden. If she's in my head, then there must be a link to Sudice. She's not listed as a test subject." The image of the scars and sutures appear in her mind's eye again.

"Not a registered one, at least. The trial subjects were not on the official books either."

"Good point. They never told us the names of our subjects, though we pieced them together during our work, and those experiments were under an NDA."

"Right. And Nettie wasn't an employee, either. No official internships, no relatives or acquaintances who work there. She was planning to study neuroscience, though. They might have recruited her on the sly."

"Recruiting a sixteen-year-old high school student? Seems unlikely. In what Mark sent me, she was preparing for a senior project. Didn't sense anything about her working for them."

"They hired you at, what, twenty-three?"

"Yeah, but I was a precocious little post-doc that Roz wanted to keep an eye on."

"Roz was interested in her, too. Clear parallels."

Carina shivers. That's what has haunted her, from the first time Mark showed her Nettie's death. When he'd taken that memory block off, and she'd remembered what had really happened to her. Roz can't stop molding people into what she wants. It didn't work on Carina. It didn't work on Nettie. What is Roz trying to accomplish and who is she going to target next? Or has it already begun?

"We'll keep digging," Dax says. "There'll be a slip-up somewhere. We'll figure out what's up with Nettie Aldrich."

"Will we tell the others about it?"

"I think so. There may be more information hidden in the images, and they can keep an eye out. Mark found it important enough to send to you."

"If only he'd told us more clearly what she's trying to do. Why go to such lengths to try and change me and Nettie, and why won't it stick?"

"Maybe he didn't know either, not really."

A group of schoolchildren on their way to brainloading sessions walk through the metal plaza, shoes squeaking on the dark imitation marble. Carina pauses to let them pass, White Noise or no. They've reached the museum of modern art with its glass pyramids on the roof, and they lean against the cool brick walls.

Out here in the brightening day, it is hard to reconcile what her life has been and what it is now. A long nightmare in Zealscapes, and she's not sure she has the strength to keep resisting them. There is a Zeal lounge somewhere on the perimeter of this plaza. She accesses her implants. Yes. There. The Rosetta Lounge. Less than 500 feet away. She could go in, pay out of pocket with the dregs of her cash, fall right back in. Kill dozens of phantasms in all the ways she loves best. Maybe she should just let go of it all, let the programming break down further. Stop caring. Forget about Sudice. Forget about Roz. The Trust can carry on without her.

She blinks, focusing again on the here and now. The plaza. The sound of people moving past, on their way to continue their lives. Dax's face, focused on hers, as if he knows exactly what she's thinking.

"It's still a strong lure, isn't it?" he asks, his voice soft.

It frightens her, how easily he can read her. How much she wants him to know her. She's grown so used to pushing everyone away, to protecting them from herself. She moves closer to him, as if seeking more warmth despite the heat of the day.

"Are you afraid of me?" she asks.

"A little. More afraid of what's been done to you." He moves closer, too. She wonders what would happen if she closed the distance between them. Pressed her lips against his. Would it feel as bland and distant as past kisses? Or now, would her new, raw nerve endings light up?

It'd be a sweet kiss, soft, then hard. Opening her mouth to taste him, his tongue slipping into her mouth. Her hands going toward his neck, under his hair. Then she imagines biting his lip, drawing blood, her fingers twisting into claws against the pulse of his throat. Another one of her victims. Another person she can't help but hurt.

She leans away from him, turns her face toward her lap. Bites her own lip, focusing on that pure, clear feeling of pain.

Sudice did this to me, she thinks. She wants revenge. Simple, beautiful revenge.

"I have to stop thinking of it as getting information out of my head just to give to you and the others," she says. "I have to start thinking of Sudice as a target. As a ... victim to be stalked. That's the only thing that will keep me away from Zeal. Sudice gave me a lot—but they also took everything away. I have to make it personal." Her face twists into a grimace.

Dax licks his lips. "I'm maybe a little more afraid of you, in this moment."

She hunches her shoulders. "You probably should be." Now that the sun has risen, it's too bright. The lure of Zeal still sings in her veins, despite her pretty speech.

"Let's go back," she says. "Time to figure out how to rip out Sudice's throat once and for all."

TWENTY-TWO

DAX

*The Trust headquarters, Los Angeles,
California, Pacifica*

The other two members of the Trust are not pleased when Dax
and Carina return.

"You can't just fuck off without telling us, Dax," Charlie
says, still not fully awake and definitely grumpy.

"I did tell you, but you were sleeping. Left a message. Aw,
were you worried that Carina had clunked me on the head
and kidnapped me? I'm touched." He didn't mention that
Carina and violence are things that go together quite naturally.
He's still trying not to think of the look on her face when talking about taking her revenge on Sudice.

"Carina's VeriChip is still new. What if she'd triggered
something?" Raf asks.

"Now you're just being difficult," Dax says. "You checked over
the chip. You know it's sound. Her new face won't trigger anything. She wore gloves. We both needed the fresh air and we're
better for it. Calm down, have your coffee and let's get to work."

He looks at Carina, who has stayed silent during this
exchange, her eyes darting between them. Always listening,
turning everything over to see how best to use the intel.

The Trust grumble, as he knew they would, but the lure of coffee brings them to the kitchen. They load up the Thorn information onto the wallscreen, and Dax tells them about Nettie Aldrich and that information about her was in the third image to unlock. The group look at the still-silent Carina again, each with their own opinions. Raf's still hesitant about her motivations, but is equally fascinated by the idea of so much information spirited away in wetware instead of hardware. Charlie is impatient to retrieve the information and use it. All are wary, and Carina hasn't made it easier for them to like her. Prickly. That's the word for her.

Dax likes her, though he didn't lie when he told her he was afraid of her. She can be cold, but he senses there's a yearning for connection lurking underneath that she tries to hide. Yet he worries about reaching out in turn. She'd either lean into it, or strike out at him.

Charlie is more interested in Nettie Aldrich than Dax would have expected. Carina sends over the information and Charlie sifts through it, frowning, as the rest of the group watches.

"This isn't the first missing teen in conjunction with Sudice," she says.

Dax watches as Carina's focus sharpens. "What do you mean?" Is she wondering if Roz experimented on people before or after her own experience with SynMaps? Dax feels guilty, holding that piece of information back from Charlie and Raf, but it's not his to tell.

"There was a spate of rumors somewhat recently," Charlie replies. "A journalist, Morena Nemec, claimed that five missing person cases were directly linked to Sudice. She compiled some compelling evidence—all of them bright kids, good with science and, even if it was hidden, given scholarships by Sudice. I'll bet somewhere along the line, Sudice gave this girl Nettie some sort of financial aid in return for the internship. With these other five kids, they thought they'd hidden the money trail, but not well enough. Nemec must have had to go through hundreds of cases to find the links. All the kids disappeared in different ways, different places."

"How recently?"

"One to three years ago."

Her lips tighten. The timing meant this would have been going on while she was working at Sudice. Another thing Dr. Elliot kept from her. "What happened?"

"Exactly what you'd expect when Sudice is involved. Nemec was fired from her magazine and blackballed in the industry. She disappeared. The media claimed she'd become a Zeal addict, but I don't believe that."

Carina's eye twitches. There's still a bit of swelling around the left one, Dax's doctor brain notices. He'll have to check it out later.

"Curious and curioser," Carina says, as Charlie finds one of Nemec's first articles on the missing teenagers. "Did she ever have any theories on why Sudice wanted them or what they did?"

"Yes, but she didn't publish them. Raf helped me find this." Charlie draws up some scanned, handwritten notes.

Dax scans the messy cursive. "She thought Sudice were recruiting them to be corporate spies?" Guess his hunch was right.

Charlie shakes her head. "For corporate espionage, they'd surely go for people who have been working in business a few years. Understand the structure."

Carina shoots him a look, as if to say: *Exactly.*

"Nemec didn't publish her article because she knew people would react the same way," Charlie says. "But perhaps it makes sense. Just. Groom them before their brains have fully developed. Teenage minds are still developing and deciding who they are. They can be ripe for manipulation. The Ratel evidently did something similar with Verve before SFPD took them down. Took in young people outside the system, without VeriChips, massaging their personalities."

Carina's jaw has clenched, and she grips the edge of the table. "Brain reprogramming."

"Exactly. Do you think they could do it?" Charlie asks.

Carina gives something like a laugh. "They can, but the last I knew, it was an imperfect method."

Raf perks up at this, not noticing the strain in her voice. "I thought the SF mob Ratel stuff was greatly exaggerated when I heard it, but maybe there was more to it. I suppose it's inevitable, eventually. Pacifica's already tried to control us through Zeal. Calm us down. Troops are less afraid in battle because we change their dopamine supply. We re-route brain neurons to help avoid certain brain diseases. Extra serotonin for depression— we've been doing that for decades now, saving countless lives. If you have the code, you can hack the system."

"None of that is wholesale amending personalities," Charlie says.

Again, Carina's head stays bowed.

"Carina . . ." Dax begins.

She looks up, her eyes narrowed. Then she deflates, the tension leaving her shoulders. "I know."

Charlie and Raf look between them. "What's going on?" Charlie asks.

"Roz is trying to do that. She's been trying for over a decade. I was one of her first subjects. She changed me." Carina takes a deep breath. Dax wants to reach out and take her hand. She hasn't properly told anyone for years, and now three people in one day know. Is it a relief, to let out a secret held for so long?

"It didn't work properly, though. It started breaking down, and that's why I became a Zealot." They ask questions—how did she change, when did she notice her personality shifting? Carina sketches in a few more details, but Dax focuses on the nervous flutter of her hands.

"And so Roz was trying to change Nettie into someone else," Raf muses. "And she died."

"The other teens probably did, too," Charlie says.

"Roz would stop at nothing, and Sudice gave her the blessing to do this." Carina crosses her arms over herself.

Dax shakes his head, slowly. "This is still not enough. We have that image of Nettie, some scattered suppositions. We need more."

Charlie leans forward, her face as determined and vicious as Carina's was in the park. "We'll find it."

TWENTY-THREE

ROZ

Sudice headquarters, San Francisco,
California, Pacifica

Roz hates her temporary Los Angeles office.

Objectively, she should love it. It's a floating office, tethered to Sudice's main Los Angeles headquarters. It has incredible views of the city, hazy in the growing sunset, light glinting from the windows of skyscrapers and the endless stream of hovercars flying past to her left. Potted date palms line the partitions between the windows. The wallscreen behind her large, sleek desk is set to watercolor artwork of Los Angeles, and there's a sofa almost comfortable enough to sleep on tucked into a corner. She's slept on it almost every night since she's been here so far, despite the hotel room Sudice has provided. She'll often get up in the middle of the night, trying another method to find Carina.

No matter how nice this room is, it's not her office. There's a good team in place, but not one she knows. Her San Francisco team thinks she's down here for a conference. There's no lab in sight; she's not here for science.

Roz's new support team are in the offices directly below her. She needs quiet to think, and their very presence annoys her.

The trail to Carina has cooled, and if she doesn't hurry, it'll go cold entirely. The team have their instructions to go through Los Angeles with a fine-toothed comb, aided by Wasps looking for anything unusual. Roz hopes Carina is still in the city—they've been monitoring the outgoings and haven't seen anything suspicious, but if Carina's gotten a good new VeriChip and face, they don't have much hope of finding her unless she's stupid enough to leave bits of her DNA behind.

Roz settles behind her desk, nursing a glass of watered synth whiskey. She's not meant to drink on the job, but she's not meant to do a lot of things she's done under the banner of Sudice over the past few years.

A frantic knock sounds at the door. Roz startles, hates that she does, and answers. It's Niall, one of the underling hackers Mantel assigned her. She schools her face into a bland smile. "What is it?"

"I think I've found something," he says, a little breathless from excitement and the dash up the stairs. He's tall and slender, with black hair slicked back in a hairstyle that makes him look sleazy. He wears clear-lens specs as an anachronistic affectation, which she finds particularly irritating. "Took some digging and reverse engineering on the Darknet, and there's some poor fool in Virginia who thinks he's getting hired by the Atlantica CIA for this—"

"Get to the point."

"Sorry. Sorry. We found a bit of footage of Carina leaving the Metro a few days ago. We mapped the bones of her face, and just a few hours ago, the security drones found another woman whose skull matches the same specifications."

"You think it's her?"

He projects the images onto the screen. "Look for yourself."

There's a woman with dark purple hair. Unremarkably pretty.

She's wearing dark shades, her mouth is twisted as she speaks to a man with long, black hair. Roz doesn't recognize him either, and he's also clad in shades and plain clothing. They're both wearing gloves, which is not unusual in Los Angeles.

Roz takes the snapshot of the woman, puts her side by side with Carina's employee photo. The dimensions work, and Roz recognizes that twist to her mouth. Carina hasn't changed herself enough to be a complete stranger.

"Who's with her?" she asks.

"It's a big leap, but I think it might be a member of the Trust. The one who goes by the moniker of Dax."

"The Trust? That group with Rafael Hernandez? I thought they disbanded." Panic threatens to rise, and Roz pushes it down. There is no room for fear. Forcing it away, she wills her heartbeat to slow. "Any leads on where they're based? Could you follow them back to their headquarters?"

"We tried, but they were clever. Lost them on the way back, moving in between camera drone patrols, taking false trails."

Roz pinches the bridge of her nose. "Keep looking with the rest of the team. Pass on anything you find to me, no matter how insignificant it seems. And for God's sake, all of you cover your tracks. Don't leave a shred of evidence behind for the Trust to know we're looking for them. We want the element of surprise on our side. Am I clear?"

Niall nods, licks his lips.

Roz forces herself to soften her tone. "Good work. This is valuable information."

He brightens. If he were a puppy, his tail would wag. He closes the door behind him. Roz downs the rest of her synth whiskey in one gulp.

She should call Mantel and tell him, but she wants to come with more information than "the woman with dangerous information is with a bunch of hackers led by your blacklisted cousin." He'll be reading all the reports, anyway. If he wants to speak to her, he will. She's not looking forward to it.

Roz stays in her spotless, floating office above the Los Angeles skyscrapers. She sends new commands to security Wasps, trying to find any anomalies. If the Trust are the slightest bit sloppy, she'll find them.

Roz has a chance to hit two birds with one stone: contain Carina before she puts the company in jeopardy, and capture the Trust. A grin spreads across her face as her fingers fly in front of her, weaving the code into the net, calling another software engineer to come up and help her.

"I'm coming, Carina."

TWENTY-FOUR

ROZ

One year ago

Sudice headquarters, San Francisco,
California, Pacifica

Despite Roz's protestations, Sudice replaces Subject B with another stasis candidate. At least the asshole is now on ice. Mantel stalls the greenlight on the next aspect of SynMaps.

Roz has not reported her suspicions about Carina to anyone at Sudice. She's watching her closely, formulating a plan to take the situation in hand. The rest of the team has found a steady balance. They know how each member functions, how they work best. Even Carina seems to have bonded with them, which again puzzles Roz. Yet the scientists are making progress. She can't risk upsetting the equilibrium, even if that means risking the subjects.

It should keep her up at night, but Roz sleeps as she always does: fitfully, rising at dawn to be the first in the office.

The new subject is creatively dubbed Subject E. He's small and spare. Nervous eyes. Something of the weasel or fox about him. Roz dislikes him at first sight, but Carina seems to take to him well enough. Roz should take Carina aside, warn her to be

178

more careful, but she doesn't want to spook her. So Roz observes them all and makes her plans.

A week passes. Another. They stretch into months. Second by second, the subjects are able to brain record for a little longer before they start to exhibit the more dangerous side effects. If they can get to forty-five minutes, *then*, Mantel promises, Roz can move forward to the next stage. Mantel keeps moving the goalposts. She keeps working on her second project on the sly anyway.

Carina is the one who has identified certain brain patterns that are better for brain recording. Specifically, Subject B may have been one of the better candidates for long-term recording because of his reduced frontal lobe. Less empathy and compassion. If this recurs in other subjects with small frontal lobes, it could have some tricky complications. Some Zealot addicts would possibly be the best for Sudice's latest product.

Roz requested a certain type of criminal for Subject E. Mantel hesitated, but in the end, he agreed.

It doesn't take Carina long to figure out what Subject E has done. Roz works slowly on her own subject, watching Carina out of the corner of her eye.

Her shoulders stiffen and she goes completely still. Her eyes shoot up, find Roz's, and Roz can't meet that stare. She adjusts one of her subject's electrodes.

At the end of the day, she expects Carina to come to her office and demand an explanation. She doesn't. At seven o'clock, Carina leaves and goes home. She passes the office and doesn't even give Roz a sideways glance. Roz feels very small, and then annoyed for feeling that way.

Another few weeks drip by. The team makes good progress. A few subjects have had side effects—arrhythmia, migraines, reports of trouble sleeping and apnea. Several are depressed, but are kept off serotonin in case it affects the results. A few have exhibited early signs of stroke, but with quick medical intervention from the robots, they have been all right. So far. She knows it's only a matter of time until there's another problem.

They've managed to have most subjects successfully brain record for thirty minutes now. Today they're aiming for thirty-six. Still so far from forty-five, but Roz will take what she can get.

Mantel is growing impatient, but he won't let her rush ahead. He's a scientist too, supposedly, though his technical knowledge leaves much to be desired. He does little of the day-to-day running of the company. Though he's personable and charming, capable of wining and dining the very best to put them at ease, he's thirsty to prove himself, as desperate as Roz. He didn't inherit the company from his father initially; his father passed it down to his protégé, Veli Carrera. Mantel had to oust the new CEO and possibly order a hit on him to bring the company back under his control. Roz can manage Mantel, but she's wary. He's someone who would throw her to the wolves if anything in SynMaps goes belly up—or just ensure she disappears.

The scientists begin their brain recording for the day. Mark sits next to his subject, head bent so that only his shock of gray hair is visible. His subject, who has developed the unsurprising nickname of "Hollywood," lies supine on the Chair, limbs relaxed. Hollywood has removed all his body hair except his eyelashes and he exfoliates daily, too rigorously, so he always looks pink as a newborn babe. He wears gloves. Even after being captured, he doesn't like to leave any DNA evidence behind.

Aliyah has the arsonist, aka Sparky. He's your stereotypical arsonist—a troubled loner with low self-esteem. His notes show he isn't self-reflective enough to know why he has to light things on fire, only that he finds it exciting in a way nothing else ever is. It's similar to their deceased Subject B. They can't control the urges. They don't want to. Hollywood and Roz's own subject, the thief she hasn't given a nickname to, at least have other motives—monetary gain, mostly. Yet they both still, at heart, commit crimes for that same endorphin rush.

The subjects look around, but don't get up and move. Too much physical exertion can also impact the brain recording, as they learned with Subject B. For now, they're meant to focus on different subjects within the room, let their thoughts and feelings go as normal. It means that when they play the recordings back, the scientists feel and think what their subjects do. Roz finds it intensely uncomfortable, and she arguably has the subject who's done the least terrible crimes. Fraud is bad, but her subject's thefts never even made a dent in the targets' fortunes.

The minutes pass. The fitful San Francisco sun shines through the floor-to-ceiling windows overlooking the bay. The air is full of the soft whirrs and bumps of the machines. Ten minutes pass, inching closer to fifteen.

Roz's own subject starts to show signs of stress. Resigned, she turns off the brain recording. It happens next to Mark's subject, then Aliyah's. Carina's new Subject E is still going, with no signs of stress. Roz finds her hopes rising.

At forty-six minutes, Carina looks up from her code and gives Roz a deliberate gaze. She doesn't blink, and looks as serene as a painting of a saint. Roz looks away first.

Subject E begins to quiver, then shake. His heartbeat rises, his mouth opens in a silent scream, just like with the previous subject. Spittle collects at the corners of his lips, his eyes popping from his skull. Roz freezes, unable to think. The rest of the scientists watch in horror. Roz has grown complacent. She didn't think to send the other subjects out of the room in case something like this happened, and they are just as horrified. Only the droid helpers are unaffected, and they move forward, surrounding the subject, providing medical aid even though it's far too late for that.

He flatlines.

Carina's eyes glitter, even if her mask is in place. She bows her head. "Too much stimuli," she says, voice distant.

The robots congregate, working on Subject E as efficiently as they did on Subject B. Roz holds her breath. She can't afford to lose another subject, not with Mantel breathing down her neck.

The robots restart his heart. One beep. Silence. Another beep. A shorter silence. Soon, his sputtering heartbeat fills the room.

"Subject stabilizing, but calling emergency services for immediate transport to hospital," Roz's robotic virtual assistant, Vera, says. It's just a program, but does she sense a hint of understanding in that mechanical tone? Vera would know what this means for her.

One subject almost dying under Carina's care could be chalked up to bad luck. Twice is suspicious. Carina looks at Roz, her gaze steady, as if she knows exactly what's going through Roz's head. As if she knows all her secrets.

•

Again, Roz doesn't confront Carina.

She works feverishly for the rest of the night on her side project. They did inch past forty-five minutes, so Mantel reluctantly gave her the green light to move into the early stages of production. She's already been working on it unofficially for months, running her side experiments. It's as ready as it'll ever be. She hasn't eaten since lunch, and has that dull ache in her stomach and edge of faintness, but the thought of going through the motions of ordering something, picking up cutlery, chewing and swallowing seems far too complicated. Pouring herself some synth rum, she stands in the middle of the lab, overlooking the bay for a long time, letting her thoughts drift. The moon rises, the bay glows silver and green. In the deep stillness of midnight, all is quiet.

Mantel is livid, but Subject E makes a full recovery and returns the next day. Roz gives the scientists and subjects an extra dose of Verve, telling them it's to help them deal with the repercussions of the day. Really it's so that, though it's not the same as brain recording, she can go in and change how they feel about the day's events. Reduce their horror, their trauma, until it's barely a blip. They remember what has happened, but it no longer bothers them as badly. It's a simpler way of re-creating the emotional block she did on Carina in the early experiments. One by one, she treats all of them except for Carina. When she plugs Mark in, he looks at her as if he knows exactly what she's doing, but in the end, he goes along with it, not wanting to feel that horror any more than the rest of them do.

Roz arranges for a dinner with Mantel. Tells him what she has. What she needs to do next. He lets her have her way. He always does, in the end.

"This is your personal responsibility," Mantel says. "I can't protect you if this goes south."

You won't want to, she thinks. "I understand. Think of what we can finally achieve."

Mantel raises his glass, greed glimmering in the curve of his smile.

TWENTY-FIVE

DAX

The Trust headquarters, Los Angeles,
California, Pacifica

The Trust need a plan.

From first thing in the morning until they can't read any more, Dax and the others pore through the information they have so far. From their briefly planted Viper, they know they can remain undetected, but it's not powerful enough to fully protect them from the Wasps. They'd have to release it from inside and let it move laterally.

In the evenings, when they're all tired from hours of reading and plotting, they unwind. Charlie's urged people to leave the headquarters as infrequently as possible after Dax and Carina's little walk through the park by Angel's Flight. Sudice is looking for them—no camera drone is safe, a dead skin cell could land in the wrong place. No unnecessary risks.

Cabin fever sets in within a few days. Everyone works out in the gym to release excess energy. Raf runs half marathons on the treadmill, complaining that it's boring compared to outside, despite all the wallscreen programs. Charlie is into jiujitsu. Dax does his usual routine, designed to keep him at peak performance. Carina asks him for more muscle implants and avoids the gym. He asks her why but she shrugs, opting to stay in the other room and read instead. Dax doesn't push it.

Carina has told Dax that she's been trying to unlock more images in her mind, to no avail. The first three happened relatively quickly, but the last two images of the drop of blood and the eyes don't seem to be forthcoming. She'll disappear into her room for hours, trying to find them, but no luck. The rest of the group will have to treat those remaining images as bonus information that would be beneficial, but they can't count on it.

Mark has locked up the images so tightly in her that Dax wonders whether they'll ever be liberated at all. Carina has been made into an experiment—first by Roz and now by Mark. As far as any of them know, this much information has never been sent in this way before. What if Mark's plan was only partly successful?

Sometimes in the evening, they'll play cards. Raf will even set aside the security bot he's been dissecting in his spare time. Carina and Charlie are the best—Carina has the best poker face he's ever seen—though in a room of clever people who don't mind breaking the rules, cheating runs rampant. They bet with near-worthless replicated diamonds. Even Carina loosens. Sometimes she'll let out a little laugh, though it feels practiced and forced, as she accuses Raf of cheating and he gives her an innocent look in return. Dax looks forward to these games, where talk of hacking falls by the wayside and they are simply a group of people, laughing and trying to forget everything circling around them. The clatter of dice or the soft shuffling of cards, the clink of glasses or mugs set on the table, the smell of tea and whatever snacks from the replicator they've ordered. The soft dimness of the light in the living room, the stars shining through the fake windows of their underground bunker. Dax could grow used to these nights, though he knows, deep down, they will not last.

Raf has been putting together pieces of a plan against Sudice on his own, possibly with Charlie's input, but he won't discuss it until it's mostly formed. Finally, about three days later, with tensions running high, Raf decides to share.

"I think we need to look for the simplest solution," he says. "We need to go somewhere remote and quiet, and I'll mask the location. We can get in through a two-part plan."

"What are you thinking?" Charlie asks, tearing her eyes away from the wallscreen.

"Spear Phishing," Raf says, throwing a peanut in the air and catching it with his mouth, grinning as he chews.

"Impressive," Dax says dryly, and Raf throws a peanut at him. Dax tries to catch it. He misses, the nut clattering into a corner.

"I've got everything ready. I know where to go. We can do it now," Raf says.

"You have everything you need?" Charlie asks Raf.

He cracks his neck. "Yep. We're all good. I'll lay it all out for you there. Can't show you properly in here. Let's go. Kivon's probably already waiting for us."

They pack up their gear—concealed weapons, hacking kit for Raf's VR, white noises and scrambler masks for extra protection.

"Who's Kivon?" Carina asks.

"Raf's boyfriend. Police officer. He comes along as extra protection sometimes. Don't think we really need him this time, but Raf misses him," Charlie says. "Kivon might have some info. He keeps his ears open. Runs searches for us."

"Another person on the inside," Dax says. "Doesn't hurt.

He's like a half-member of the Trust, though he doesn't know where the headquarters are."

Carina looks wary, as if she's not up for meeting another stranger, but she hefts her backpack over her shoulder without another word.

The Trust enter the hidden corridors, winding their way to the concealed hovercar.

They take the hovercar to the Port of Long Beach, flying on the lane that leads over the old Vincent Stephen Bridge, which looks like a smaller, turquoise version of the Golden Gate Bridge. The hovercar speeds along, overlooking the sprawl. The Pacific Ocean stretches to the horizon, clear and gray, and the skyscrapers and floating buildings of Long Beach rise up to the other direction, where the San Gabriel Mountains are half-hidden in evening fog. In the port, endless shipping containers are stacked on top of one another like a giant's toy bricks. Some companies are so busy that even old cranes have been brought online in addition to the slick hovercranes to help move product, despite the higher operating costs. This late in the day, most regular workers have clocked off, but there are still enough people about to make Dax nervous.

Raf chose the location because it's a mess of industrial debris, a maze that's easy to hide in. There are so many signals in the air from the offices, theirs can easily slip among them. Most of the Trust's work takes place in these edge lands— warehouses and their businesses, shipping containers or silos. Places most people pass without a second look.

Before they took off, Raf lit up some of the side panels of their hovercar with the name of a company, Occamia. They land next to a cluster of squat, round tower silos, skirted with steel supports, with the same boring logo and company name.

Occamia has been shut down for fifteen years, but your average person passing by won't find it strange to see people crawling about long-abandoned silos.

Kivon is waiting for them outside the largest silo. It's been a while since Dax has seen him, but he's unchanged. Six foot five inches tall, black, rippling with muscle, hair cropped close to his scalp. He has a strong, square jaw and thick brows, making it look like he's always on the verge of frowning. He almost has to lift Raf up to give him a kiss. He nods to them in turn, reaches out a hand to Carina, which she shakes firmly. He seems wary of her, and Dax wonders exactly how much Raf has told Kivon about the newest member of the Trust.

Charlie picks the lock to the door and they enter the silo. There's plenty of room for their purposes, and it's dusty but otherwise dry and sound. Dax sets up security cameras around the perimeter while Raf sets up the kit in the center of the silo. Kivon and Charlie assemble the remote generators. Dax notices Kivon's belt bristles with weapons, and he's brought along a veritable arsenal of guns, smoke bombs, DNA bombs and tranquilizers. Dax shakes his head at it all. Kivon may be a man who will steal weapons from his employer or purchase others on the black market, but Dax knows that in low-crime Los Angeles Kivon has never had to kill on duty, nor while helping the Trust.

Raf begins, his fingers dancing as the code projects around him onto the curved walls of the silo, creating elegant commands to move the Trust one step closer to breaking the company that tried to break them.

Raf smiles. "Here we go." He sends the commands, and code scrolls, flashes, goes dark. An inbox appears. Unremarkable, full of boring corporate correspondence—meeting requests, stationery orders, general queries about some sort of charity.

"The inbox belongs to a Mila De Costa," Carina says. "Who's that?"

"Mila is a very real charity organizer for Alacrity, which is for the rehabilitation of Zeal addicts."

Carina gives a snort.

"I really, really wish I could say I did this on purpose, but it's just a fortunate coincidence. In a few weeks' time, Alacrity is holding a one-day party with some of the most exclusive Hollywood celebrities in Malibu. Super-swank, almost impossible to get an invite. It's all been set up for months. Now—" Raf flips to a different screen, and shows a snapshot of an unremarkable-looking man. He looks mid-forties, but that could mean he's older. Thick hair, generically good looks, brown hair with a bit of strategic silvering at the temples, tanned skin, white teeth. A reassuring father figure whom you'd trust with your investments and business decisions.

"This is Harry Mitford," Raf says. "One of the many vice-presidents of Sudice, but pretty far down on the corporate ladder. Managed to eke his way into his spot by being excellent at accounting, but on the management side, being very good at looking like he was doing a lot when really he wasn't doing much at all. My guess is he's done some . . . creative bookkeeping for Sudice, and was rewarded for that, too. I found him through your Rose files, so thank you very much for that, Carina." He gives her a little salute.

She returns it, only a little sardonically.

"So what do we have in store for Mr. Mitford here?" Charlie asks.

"I'm so glad you asked, Charlie. We're not going to do a

thing to Mr. Mitford, at least not to start," Raf says. "For the moment, I've only cloned Mila's email. Dead easy to hack into. Alacrity's security is shit. Any emails sent between Mila and Harry will go straight to me, and I'll be keeping track. So all we have to do is send an email to our Mr. VP like . . . this one."

He brings up the draft, a simple message saying there's been a slight change of plans and to please see the attached flyer. Raf opens the attachment, which is sleek, professional and profoundly boring. It looks just like an older flyer for Alacrity, except it has some additional information about hovercar parking.

"Ah," Dax says, understanding.

"So simple, eh?" Raf beams. "Sometimes old-school is best."

Charlie nods. "Hiding the virus in the flyer?"

"Yup. The personnel files don't have implant serial numbers, and I couldn't find them another way. His assistant might open it first, and we get his access, but I'm betting he'll forward it on, or Mitford will open it briefly anyway."

"I'm missing something," Carina says. "What does the virus actually do?"

"It'll lock onto Mitford's implants," Raf says. "Connect back to the attacked infrastructure. Breaking it down even further: say Attacked System A—that's Sudice—connects to Attacker Infrastrucure B. That's us. We'll also attack System C and connect to B. B will broker connections to A and C, but on C we'll use loads of relays so if they find B, we're still safe from tracking. The hydra will stay in neural pathways in the implants that Wasps tend to overlook because they're so chaotic anyway. So we can see everything Mitford's accessing without Wasps being any the wiser. Hopefully we'll get something we can use right away. If we're unlucky, we'll have to try this again with someone else in Sudice, until fortune favors us. Once we're in, it'll be easy to access sensitive information. Clever little virus."

"It's pretty," Kivon says, giving his boyfriend a little smile, which Raf returns. Dax feels a weird thrum of jealousy—to be totally safe in the assurance that the other person loves you in return. He had that with his sister, in a non-romantic sense. He's never had that belly-deep clench of being in love.

"How does locking onto the implants work?" Carina asks, forcing Dax to focus. "We wouldn't be able to look through his implants for long. If we try to download all he's seeing and hearing on the implants, it's a lot to process. Even if it's not quite brain recording, there's a risk of the same side effects." Carina wouldn't be able to download any of it herself, Dax knows. Her implants are stretched to the absolute limit whenever she unlocks one of the images, though she would never admit it to the others.

"It's going to a remote server and I've written an AI script to sift through it and forward on the relevant info."

"What if it misses something?"

"It won't," Raf says, a little shortly. "And even if it does, we can go in and sort through it manually. Time-consuming, but still works. OK, is that enough questions from everyone? Can I send the ping yet?" He rocks on the balls of his feet, either a nervous tic or a gesture of excitement.

"Let's set your trap," Charlie says.

There's not much for the rest of the Trust to do. Kivon is on surveillance and Charlie, Dax and Carina are the audience.

Raf's code swirls around his head like a crown. He sends the email. Though it's eight o'clock in the evening, the email is opened almost immediately by Mitford's assistant, Gareth. The assistant spends all of three seconds reading it before forwarding it to his boss.

"Bingo," Raf says.

TWENTY-SIX

CARINA

The Trust headquarters, Los Angeles,
California, Pacifica

Since resisting Zeal, Carina has become an early riser.

She likes the quiet and stillness before the rest of the house awakens. Being alone is preferable, even if that means facing her tangled thoughts. At least she's not constantly analyzing the others, second-guessing what to say, how to act, to appear at least somewhat normal. She makes coffee in the replicator and watches the light change in the false windows, wishing it was easier to go outside. Breathing recycled air is growing old.

Nettie Aldrich is a puzzle that keeps niggling at her, just as it does Dax. It's a face to put to the many terrible things Sudice has done. If Carina focuses on Nettie, it's easier than all the other things she has to concern herself with; the Trust leaving her, Sudice finding them, her own weaknesses.

They're all moving forward, barreling into attacking Sudice thanks to Mark's information in her head, and it feels like so much, so fast. Dax is worried about it—he told her about the time they were nearly caught, and then a little about his sister, Tam. Carina did more research on Tam on her own, looking at the information on her from the Rose. Dax doesn't want to lose anyone else.

Raf and Charlie are still wary of her, and when they met at the silo, Kivon gave her covert looks out of the corner of his eye. He's gone back to his squad, slyly using police resources to see if Sudice have circled closer to them. Perhaps they no longer suspect her of being a double agent, or that Mark, or someone pretending to be Mark, planted bad information in her head. The Trust have checked everything multiple times. Carina is still tired of the whispers, the gazes shifting away from hers. She's an addict: violent, a liability. They might be right.

Carina brings up Nettie's information again and searches ruthlessly through the proxy. After drinking three cups of nearly-caffeine-free coffee, she feels her eyes growing dry from staring at the wallscreen.

When she finds something, she turns away, rubbing her eyes. She's afraid to actually open it up and read it. Everything is on the precipice of change. She doesn't want to be alone for this. The kitchen has brightened with the light of early dawn. Draining the last of her coffee, she goes to Dax's door, pinging his implants.

"Found something on Nettie, maybe. Thought you might want to see."

Dax opens the door. His eyes are red—has he slept?

"What'd you find?" he asks, following her to the kitchen and the wallscreen.

"Deleted drafts of a diary entry."

"No shit." Dax gives a low whistle. There are three entries from a year ago, not long after Carina left Sudice. "How'd they miss them?" he asks.

"Nettie never published it, and they deleted the journal, but

I found the drafts on an archive site. Knew someone, somewhere would be sloppy."

"Have you read them?"

"Not yet. I thought . . . maybe we could read them together."

Dax makes himself a cup of coffee and sits down. His hair is still mussed from sleep, and he blinks sleepily, rumpled and handsome. Carina's also disheveled from too little sleep and running her impatient hands through her newly purple hair.

Carina brings up the first draft. All it says is "There's so much."

Carina opens the second one, dated four days later. It's a little longer:

> *There's so much I want to write and want to say. Everything I've wanted is coming together, so neatly I almost don't trust it. I have a scholarship, but that's just the beginning. They said I could join the project.*

"She never posted it?" Dax asks.

"No. I think she used the drafts as sort of a secret journal to herself. Probably couldn't really talk about her work with Sudice publicly. Sure they made her sign umpteen nondisclosures. This is skirting close enough to almost break them." She remembers signing contract after contract, nondisclosure after nondisclosure, before they'd let her into the Sudice building for her first day of work. Little had she known what a bad idea it was to walk into that glass-lined foyer.

"This is the last one." Nettie had deleted her earlier, upbeat draft. All the new draft says is:

> *Maybe I should quit. Maybe this is all just a big mistake. It's boring and strange. I don't see the point of it. Every time I go,*

I say it'll be the last time, but somehow it never is. I've been trying to find out what they're up to, what the point of the project is, but I don't even know where to start. Fuck this.

"This is what, four days before Roz killed her?" Dax asks.

"Think so. So she knew something was wrong, whatever it was."

"Yeah." Dax lapses into silence, fingertips trailing around the edge of his coffee mug. They both stare at the last journal entry, lost in their thoughts. It's strange for Carina to see Nettie's personal entries. She'd seemed almost a figment, but this drove home that she was a scared, lost teenager, just like Carina had been a decade before her. Carina wonders what Dax thinks of Nettie. If he feels that same niggle that she does; that they've missed something that's right in front of their faces. A way to stop the girl from being forgotten and erased. A sense that she is connected to something larger than they know.

They're interrupted by an excited Raf running through to the kitchen.

"I got blueprints!" he yells, darting back out and into the living room. He does a little happy dance, wriggling his butt. "Blueprints! Come on!"

Carina dismisses Nettie's journal entries, making sure to save copies. They go through to the living room. Charlie's already there, crumpled and yawning.

"OK, so Mitford is an early riser," Raf says. "Been watching him since we managed to piggyback, but he hasn't been giving us much to work with, and I figured we wouldn't get much today because he's scheduled to play golf all day, then he has some meetings. Another day of looking busy with networking and shit, but really doing fuck all."

"I knew so many managers like that in my time at Sudice," Carina says.

"I knew many in the government, and Kivon sees them in the force every day," Raf agrees.

"Hospital and flesh parlor administration," Dax says.

"University administration," Carina adds.

"I grew up around them," Charlie says.

"So we're agreed. Everyone's corrupt." Raf fiddles with the button on his pajama top.

From Charlie: "Amen."

"Tell us the good stuff," Carina prods.

"OK. So yeah. Some architect asked for the blueprints of the LA headquarters today, as they're going to do some structural changes to add more floating buildings. He sent them right over. So now I've got the layout of their internal server room. It's all air-gapped, blocked off from the internet to keep it safe, but now we know where it is, how many servers there are. This is promising. We've got a good lug of information we could send out, but I still want to know what else is hiding in that cerebrum." He points at Carina's head. She blinks at him in response.

"We'll upload it all to the server and blast it," Raf continues. "Inside Sudice there's still the firewalls, but with internal to internal transfer, we can connect to infrastructure outside and relay the information. We'll be able to get it worldwide before they know what we've done. Except there's one problem."

"What?" Charlie asks.

"It's basically impossible to get to the servers. More locked doors between the outside and that room than the vault of the Bellagio in Las Vegas. Than the Bank of Pacifica. Than—"

"We get the idea," Dax interrupts.

Raf glares at him. "There's robotic security guards, plus AI

Wasps watching every interface. But that's what we can work on next. This gives us a start."

"And you haven't unlocked anything else?" Charlie asks Carina, almost gently.

"No. I've been trying to sort through memories, but so far nothing since the Thorn." The left corner of Carina's mouth dips. Dax catches it. It's a tell, kept over despite the plastic surgery. She does it when she's lying—she hasn't truly been trying to unlock the information. That makes sense; it means going back to memories best left forgotten. "Mark hinted that they'd unlock at specific times, but this is a longer gap than the first three."

Carina is disappointing them. It's all over their faces. She shouldn't care. A year ago, she wouldn't have. Now guilt twists at her. It's hard to keep this new frayed life together. She's spent a year away from the actual business of living. That diamond-hard exterior helped her appear to be all right, but inside she feels just as flawed as ever.

"Well, while you have fun with that, I'll keep watching Mitford's implants, maybe use them to insert another Viper within Sudice's servers," Raf says. "Might be able to get a wider reach, but I'm still a bit nervous the Wasps might sting me for it, even though they didn't with the first one. Might help me get some of the passcodes, or something else we can use even if Carina doesn't unlock any more images. If I put it in, I'll do it from the silo again, just to be safe. Should I plan for that?"

Charlie and Dax ask him more technical questions, which Carina has trouble following. Dax takes stock of supplies they need—both for the upcoming heist and for life in an underground car park turned secret bunker—and discusses logistics with Charlie once Raf finishes explaining their plan of action. Carina watches them, feeling useless.

TWENTY-SEVEN

CARINA

The Trust headquarters, Los Angeles,
California, Pacifica

Raf has planned his next attack. It's time to send the Viper back to the nest.

As the Trust prepare to return to the Long Beach silo, Carina locks herself in her room. There are two images left from Mark's unexpected gift. Two sections of information she wants out of her head. If they're gone, the Trust won't need her any more, not really. She has nothing to contribute. Her neuroscience skills are out of date and her hands still shake sometimes, even now that the Zeal habit has been kicked, or at least temporarily suspended. Once they have what they need, she doesn't have to look back.

Carina can fall. Fall back into Zeal, to her world of blood and death. She can forget this brief return to reality. There's nothing here but a group of hackers who don't trust her. Dax is the only one who truly interacts with her, and Carina sometimes feels he only thinks she's an interesting case from a doctor's point of view. The rest of them hang back, watching her like a feral dog with a rabid bite. How much do they know about her Zeal dreams? It makes her want to prove them right.

The urge to kill has not left her. It's burrowed so deep that no amount of surgery or abstinence from Zeal will be able to take it away. She's a killer, and has been for a long time.

Carina shuffles through the memories like ragged playing cards, trying to find the two jokers, those hidden wild cards that will set her free.

So many memories don't seem like hers. Once she moved to San Francisco, she actively stopped herself from thinking of her life in Woodside. Life began when she returned to Sudice. After cordoning the memories off for so long, actively reaching for them is strange. Once, she climbed to the top of her school, looked down on the people walking to their brainloading Chairs within, and wondered what it'd be like to jump, spread her wings wide, and pretend she'd fly instead of sink like a stone.

Carina keeps searching through the memories, hunting for the key. None of the memories give her what she wants. Everything's a jumble. The friendships she abandoned once Roz sunk her fingers into her brain. Brief blips of happiness in a childhood tainted by the acrid tang of fear. Standing up to receive the diploma for her PhD, knowing there was no one in the audience clapping for her. Learning she'd be going back to Sudice, unable to fully feel the import of what it meant to return to the place that had destroyed her.

A ping interrupts her. Dax is at the door. Carina comes out of her fuzzy, fractured memories. She opens the door and raises her dry eyes to his calm brown ones.

"You coming?" he asks, holding out his hand.

She stands unsteadily, reaches out and takes it.

•

As the Trust set up their gear in the silo in Long Beach, Raf dances a little jig in the middle of the room.

"I am a magician, and *this*—" he gives a dramatic gesture—"is my stage!"

"Yeah, yeah, let's get on with sawing Sudice in half, then," Charlie says, but she smiles at his enthusiasm.

Kivon is back, and Carina still doesn't know what to make of him. He more or less acts like she doesn't exist, which suits her well enough. He helps Raf set up the kit—location blockers, White Noises, electrodes to attach to their temples for VR access so the rest of the Trust can go in and protect Raf from Wasps. Alarms to sound if anyone gets close enough in the real world to worry them. DNA bombs for when they leave. They're surrounded by metal, like some sort of technological fairy ring.

Carina clicks her teeth together. At least if she doesn't manage to unlock the rest of the crap in her head, if Raf finds enough to take on Sudice another way, then what does it matter?

Kivon stays as the bodyguard. Carina eyes his belt, bristling with weapons, the muscled, agile body. He looks like a cop. Strong, intimidating, but his face is not cruel. It's approachable. It's the face of someone you'd run to for protection.

He meets her gaze, stares at her, deep and piercing, unblinking. *I'm watching you*, he seems to say.

I'm watching you, too, she wants to reply.

"You should stay out with Kivon," Dax says.

She's about to ask why, play innocent, but she doesn't bother.

They need the tiniest bit of Zeal to prep the implants for VR. She's been dreaming about it all day. She can almost taste it.

"I can handle the dose." Carina keeps her voice calm and steady. "It's less than one tenth of what I used to take."

"It could still trigger a relapse. And you know what we discussed."

"It's worth it. I want to see what's happening. I want to help." They all think she's a liability, but she can't sit meekly on the sidelines.

"Fine, but I'll be detoxing you again right away."

"Deal." Her heartbeat quickens with anticipation. She thought Dax would put up more of a fight about this.

Carina hasn't spent much time in virtual reality. The few times she tried, it seemed like a pale echo of Zeal. At Sudice and during university, VR was used for aspects of her work—brain-mapping and other neuroscience. Even then, it'd made her itchy. She should stay out—it's not like she'll be able to do much in the VR if they are attacked.

Even the slightest little taste of Zeal is better than nothing.

The Trust attach the electrodes to their temples, syncing the implants. Dax adjusts her left temple connection; she's placed it a little too high.

"You remember the disconnect password, right?" he asks.

"Yep."

He injects her with the tiniest dose. She can barely feel the Zeal, but even that tiny drop is heaven and hell all rolled into one. Dax shakes his head and quickly doses the rest of the group.

"We should be in and out in ten minutes," Raf says.

"Don't jinx it," Dax warns.

"Focus." Charlie touches the electrodes at her temple. "I don't want any stingers coming to make this nasty. Everyone ready?"

They nod.

Raf holds up his hands. "Abracadabra," he says, and runs the code.

•

Raf's virtual reality is nothing like Zeal. It's a visualization for him to check his code, work with it more interactively than on a wallscreen and share it with the rest of the Trust. People using VR to hack in this way is relatively rare, which is the main reason Raf likes it so much. It spreads around him like an aura without the distraction of the real world. Raf looks just as he always does, but the edges of his body are sharper, lined with electric blue. Carina holds out her own hands, seeing her nails and the outlines of her fingers glowing red as blood. Like softly glowing beacons, the Trust shine in the darkness. Charlie is purple and Dax is green. She wonders what color Kivon would be. A deep red-orange, the color of a sunset, maybe. Did Raf choose the colors, and if so, did they have any significance to him?

Raf's code glimmers, scrolling through the black. Carina understands basically none of it. He creates a window, drawing up the information gleaned from Mitford's implants, and begins to manipulate the code. It comes to life, looking like a snake as it sneaks deeper into Mitford's implants. The snake becomes a hydra, heads forming and moving laterally, tongues tasting for the data they are designed to find and sink their fangs into. So much security is designed to protect from the outside, and they don't anticipate attacks from within the same way.

Their paltry protections are no match against Raf. He has so much information squirreled away in his own brain from years of working with material not meant for his eyes. He knows plenty about Sudice, but not quite enough to take them down. Not without Carina's help.

If Raf could give this hydra enough heads while remaining

undetected, he could download so much information from Sudice's systems that the company would never stand a chance, whether Carina accesses the rest of her symbols or not. Mark found all his intel from these same systems.

Out of the corner of her eye, Carina catches a flash of light in the darkness. Sickly yellow.

<Shit,> Charlie says. <Raf, are you done?>

<Just a little longer.>

<We don't have a little longer. We've got stingers.>

<Fuck,> Dax says.

<OK. OK.> Raf's fingers fly. <Extracting now.>

<No time!> Charlie says.

Carina can sense the giant Wasps made of swarming code. Yellow and angry, their stingers sharp. Trust Raf to make the bots look like Wasps in his VR, larger than life and absolutely terrifying. And Carina can't do anything but watch them come toward her.

Raf dismantles the program, but one of the Wasps hits him. He staggers, the code fracturing. It weakens the thread to Carina's own body. She feels it growing more distant. Isn't this what happened to Dax's sister? She needs to speak the passcode and get out, but she's paralyzed with fear. Raf recovers, yet he's still trying to extract information and cover his tracks. If they pull out in the middle of the transfer, there's a chance they could leave a clue for Sudice to find. They won't be able to try the hydra again.

The Wasp turns and makes for Carina. They know that unauthorized people are in Sudice's servers. Anomalies must be destroyed.

One of the Wasps snags Carina. It's not pain, exactly. The VR simulation is too rudimentary for that. But it feels as though they tear away a small piece of her. She doesn't know how to protect herself. Raf creates a code and flings it at the Wasp, a cascade of binary that forms a wall. Carina stumbles back and the Wasp buzzes angrily.

The Wasps pummel the wall, fracturing it, desperate to break through. If Carina were in her body or a proper Zeal-scape, she'd feel adrenaline and her thundering heart. Here in Raf's VR, she feels as though she floats through cyberspace like a ghost.

<Got it!>, Raf says. Charlie's light-limned form extinguishes. Then Dax. Raf looks at Carina, and she feels herself return to the world, but not before she feels the Wasps break through the barrier and swarm Raf.

•

Carina falls back into her body. She tears the electrodes from her head. Her head is pounding, and she can feel the minuscule amount of Zeal in her system. "Get back in!" she yells at Charlie. "They have Raf!"

Kivon darts over from the main entrance, his face slack with shock and fear.

Charlie starts the process to go back in. "Stop." Dax presses her arm. "It's too late." His voice breaks.

"I have to try." Charlie adjusts her electrodes and slips back into Raf's virtual reality, her body going limp.

"Dammit!" Dax holds her, frantic.

"Charlie's a decent hacker in her own right. We have to hope . . . she can do something." Kivon's voice is strained with grief, his eyes wet with tears. "We have another problem." He points at the security footage projected onto the silo's curving walls. Hovercars come into view, dark and unmarked. "They've tracked us. Disabled the proximity alarms, so it's too late to run."

Kivon passes them weapons. Carina holds the gun in her hand. It's been years since she fired one, at least outside the Zealscape. She still remembers how. The gun is cold and hard in her hand. Kivon's security shows five heat signatures, but there could be more if they are masked.

"What's the ammo?" she asks him.

"Smoke bullets," he says.

"Excellent."

"Be careful. Try to avoid fatalities. We don't need murder added to our list of crimes."

She laughs, harsh and grating. Kivon's eyes turn hard and he looks away.

Raf's body is so still, so silent. The sight of him lying supine, along with the weapon in her hands, reminds her of the Zealscape, and brings all her urges to the surface. She wants to murder each and every one of them. She also wants to get out, stay safe, protect her own skin. Could she use them to do that? Her finger rests on the trigger. Their pursuers start working on the lock. It won't last long.

"We'll have to go through them," Kivon says, shifting his gun and pulling the Kalar hood over his face.

They all follow his lead, pulling the bulletproof hoods down. They should still see through them, but they're now entirely covered to their fingertips. They aren't infallible, but Carina is glad Charlie insisted everyone wear a suit under their clothes, even if it means an extra layer between Carina and her victims.

The Trust take cover behind the metal cases that housed their kit. Not ideal, but better than nothing. Dax guards Charlie and Raf, and his hands, normally steady from his doctor's training, shake. None of them have ever killed in a fight, as far as she knows. Kivon looks grim, determined.

The lock gives, the door swinging open to clang against the silo wall. "Freeze!" a woman in a Kalar suit shouts. They do not identify themselves as police, so Carina wastes no time and shoots a normal bullet, following immediately with a smoke bullet.

The woman falls.

Kalar suits can protect against the bullet, but not absorb all of the force. A well-placed bullet in the throat, the face or the stomach makes them choke, slows them down. Smoke bullets release a small, concentrated burst of smoke for a foot in either direction, and should knock them out.

The smoke bullets are illegal; if someone inhales too much, it can kill them. Carina has spent a lot of time in Zealscape target-practice simulations. Live targets, of course. The deaths were so quick, they weren't much fun. No artistry at all.

This isn't Zeal, though. This is real. This is too much of a test, too soon. Her control, weak as it is, unravels around her. She can't draw back the tendrils and isn't sure she wants to.

Carina shoots a second figure, and Kivon a third. They fall, but Carina's not sure they're all knocked out. Or dead. She should be horrified and perhaps she'll feel it later, when the adrenaline drains. If she makes it that far. At the moment, all is the thrill of danger and the hunt.

There are at least two attackers left, but more are surely cloaked or on the way. Charlie fires, but hits the fourth in the arm, only slowing him. They return fire, and the Trust duck back as bullets rain against the boxes. Charlie darts up again, firing a neat shot into someone's face, at the very least breaking their nose or giving them a nasty concussion. Screams merge with the loud reverberations of shots. One left.

Carina hears a gasp behind her.

"What's going on?" she calls back over the din of the guns. She shoots at the last man, and three more enter. Fuck.

"Raf and Charlie have woken up!" Dax yells.

"Good!"

Charlie says something, but Carina can't hear it over the shots.

"Time to push forward," Kivon yells. He grips the gun, eyes snagging on hers. He nods, once. Carina is a fellow soldier. In this battle, he'll have her back and trust her to have his.

Kivon leans out, fires. He hits one more, then a second, but misses. Carina pops up behind the box, but a bullet grazes her arm. It hurts and she'll have a hell of a bruise, but the pain fuels her. She shoots. She hits the person square in the stomach. Follows it with smoke. The last person falls.

Charlie joins them, looking like hell, but her voice is steady. "Everyone keep your heads up. There'll be camera drones circling the place. We're going to have to dart out to the hovercar and hightail it out of there. Then dump it and find the Metro and ride the trains for hours. If we get separated, we meet back at base no sooner than four hours from now. Do. Not. Let. Anyone. Follow. You."

They all nod.

Raf and Charlie both look decidedly green around the gills, but they can stand. Carina refills her gun with smoke bullets.

"What about the bodies? Has anyone checked if there's any fatalities?" Dax asks.

"Leave them," Kivon says. "No time."

Carina wants to move toward them. She wants to peel back their Kalar hoods and look into their blank faces. She wants to see who they are, and if any of them are dead. She starts moving toward the nearest prone, black-clad body. The head is tilted at an unnatural angle. The person fell and the neck is broken. Carina's breath comes faster, blood rising in her cheeks. Did she do that? She doesn't know whether she's sickened or thrilled by the thought.

Dax puts a hand on her arm. Fighting the urge to shrug it off, she concentrates on its weight. Real.

The Zeal still buzzes in her mind. She grinds her teeth. Wants to turn and run. Run as fast as her body will allow, through the dark labyrinth of the port. To find the dimmer streets of Los Angeles and walk into the nearest seedy Zeal lounge. If she doesn't, no one is safe.

Again, Dax holds her back, and she twirls and snarls at him. Dax doesn't flinch. He holds her arms against her sides. Not hard enough to hurt, but firm. Warm. Again, she tries to anchor herself to it. It doesn't work. She bites the insides of her cheeks. Dax reaches into his medical bag.

"To help detox," he says, and she gives a stiff nod before he presses the needle into her vein. Right next to the mark left by the tiniest dose of Zeal that has undone her completely.

While Dax helps Carina, Charlie reaches into her bag and brings out a DNA bomb.

"Ready?" she asks.

They nod, and Charlie throws the DNA bomb over her shoulder.

They run from the silo, avoiding the supine bodies. Kivon first, Raf behind him and holding onto the strap of his backpack. He still looks woozy. Charlie does too, but she's steady on her feet. All have guns at the ready.

Carina hears a small cry, and then Dax pushes her forward, hard. She staggers out of the silo, turns just in time to see Dax framed in the doorway. Behind him, a Kalar-suited shadow rises, grabbing Dax by the neck and dragging him back into the darkness, kicking the door closed behind him. Carina tries the door. Locked, or something heavy is wedged against it. She bashes her fist against the metal, screaming. They hear the hammer of gunshots from inside.

"Dax!" Carina screams through the door. "I'll fucking *kill* whoever hurts him!"

The Trust run back toward the silo. Charlie is keeping one eye on the horizon in case backup arrives. Kivon yells at Carina to move out of the way. She stumbles to the side and he rams his massive bulk against the door.

Bam. Bam.

The sound is as loud as the heartbeat in her ears. She screams again, a wordless cry of fury, and Raf puts his arm around her shoulders, dragging her back. She strikes out at him, pushes away. It both feels horribly real and impossibly far away. Dax's medicine has not helped.

The door opens and Dax staggers out, his Kalar hood gone, his suit torn and soaked in blood. The bullet hit the suit at such an angle it went right through, now embedded in his shoulder. He falls to his knees and Carina goes to him, hauling him up with effort. She looks at him, burning eyes wide and blank. Blood. Red, beautiful blood.

"We have to get to the hovercar," Kivon says. He pushes Carina away and takes Dax up in his arms, careless of the blood now soaking his own suit.

Charlie glances into the silo. She goes still. Carina edges closer, wanting to see. Charlie pulls the door closed. "Let's go."

"What about our kit?" Raf asks.

"Leave it. None of it will link back to us. No time." Charlie points to the sky. Off in the distance, three hovercars are flying toward the silo.

They dart to the shadows. The sound of gunshots hasn't

drawn anyone else to this deserted section of the Port of Long Beach. No sirens call. The hovercar is still where they left it. Raf is well enough to check it hasn't been tampered with. A bruise is blooming on his cheekbone where Carina hit him. It should shame her. It doesn't.

Charlie's head tilts as she accesses her implants. "Hovercars are landing near the silo now. Let's get in and lie low, see how Dax is doing. They're going to expect we've already left."

They climb in and Raf strengthens security. "Been wanting to try this out," he says, giving the rest of the group a wavering smile. He plays with the controls and then staggers to his seat. "Outside is camouflaged and they won't be able to sense heat signatures or the fact there's a car here. Should be good."

"That's new," Charlie says.

"Accessed military records and retrofitted."

Charlie sees to Dax. He's ashen from blood loss and breathing shallowly.

"Can you stitch yourself up?" she asks.

Dax looks down at his shoulder. He shakes his head. "No. Bullet's inside. I can't get it out." He has his implants run a diagnostic. "Thought so. Hit an artery. Internal bleeding."

"Can you get it out?" Charlie asks Carina.

Carina takes several ragged breaths. She's hung back from the others in the hovercar, back pressed against the wall. She's been concentrating on their conversation to try and distract herself from the blood. It hasn't worked. She sees it, smells it, imagines its texture against her skin. Words fail her. The sight of Dax lying there is too visceral. She wants to dart through and push the bullet in deeper, despite the fact he's one of the few people who has been kind to her. Despite her fevered fear for him when he'd been locked in that silo.

She shakes her head, still gasping, her fingers spasming into fists. At the moment, she does not see any of them as the people she worked with. They are only so many bodies she could tear apart.

"Carina," Kivon says, carefully. "You won't like this, but I'm going to restrain you."

Carina's head hangs low. She wonders if she'll fight him, though she has no chance against his strength. Maybe if she surprises him . . .

The rest of the group is still and silent, poised in case they need to attack. Kivon takes some cable ties from his pocket. He leads her to a chair, her legs stiff as the robot assistants' at Sudice. He ties her wrists and ankles to the chair legs. She wants to kick him, scratch him, but from some deep reserve, she finds the strength not to. It's a little easier when Kivon gives her another mild sedative from Dax's medical kit. The pill is bitter as it slides down her throat.

Kivon's done a good job; the restraints are loose enough not to hurt, but tight enough there's no way she can wriggle free, if the bloodlust grows again. The rest of the group look slightly happier now she's restrained. Carina closes her eyes, imagining breaking bones and drawing them out from beneath the skin.

"What about Dr. Zwiker?" Charlie asks. "He's patched us up before."

"I can try contacting him," Raf says. "It'll take a bit to get through the subfrequency though."

They wait, both for the hovercars near the silo to finish investigating the carnage within, and to hopefully connect to the doctor who can stop Dax's slow, steady dripping of blood. Charlie murmurs to Dax, doing what little rudimentary first aid she can.

She sprays the wound with disinfectant, puts pressure on it despite his low moans of pain. She injects him with a painkiller. Carina forces herself to open her eyes and see what's happening. The pill has made everything fuzzy, taken the worst of the edge off. Raf watches the backup that's arrived at the silo on the wallscreen. They're removing the bodies from within, swarming like ants. So far, they haven't spread out to search for them.

"No response from Dr. Zwiker," Raf says. "Don't think we can wait much longer for him."

"Anyone know anyone else?" Charlie asks.

Through her bloodthirst, Carina thinks of Kim. She could probably help—she did traditional medical training before focusing on brains, but she's too far away, and it'd be too dangerous to reach out to her. Her tongue feels as though it's swollen in her mouth.

Dax shudders.

"He's going into shock," Raf says. "Time to make a decision."

"They're still at the silo," Kivon says. "Only a few, cleaning up, I'm guessing. We could make a quick break, hope they don't have us surrounded already. How's your camouflage work in the air, Raf?"

"Not perfect, but visibility is shit tonight anyway."

Dax convulses again.

Charlie nods. "Start moving us out, Kivon. Raf, you need to wipe Dax's VeriChip, block off access to his implants. We'll dump him at a hospital and hope for the best."

"We shouldn't do that," Raf says, voice low. "They could get to him there."

Kivon starts the hovercar, overriding the automatic pilot. "This is a bad idea, security-wise, but you won't hear me complaining." He speeds up, eyes peeled behind him. The Sudice hovercar is still parked by the silo. They ease up and out, everyone holding their breath and watching the rearview mirror. The hovercar stays camouflaged until they reach the main air road. Traffic is bad, but moving, and within a few minutes, they touch down in front of the hospital.

Through it all, Carina struggles to breathe, to think, to be anything other than a pair of hands longing to curl around a neck or wield a scalpel to cut through flesh. Each heartbeat helps push away a little more of the adrenaline. Not enough.

The hovercar door opens. Raf finishes the final touches of the VeriChip code. Even if the hospital run his DNA or face recognition software, they won't find a thing. They can only hope this is enough. They carefully cut the Kalar suit from him—these things are rare, only seen in the police or military, and would raise even more questions.

Kivon pulls up his own Kalar suit to hide his face, picks up Dax and jumps out. He lays him carefully on the tarmac and climbs back into the hovercar. Carina cranes her neck to peer out the window. Dax looks like he's dead, and is so exposed in his near-naked state. It's only after a few moments she sees his chest rise and fall. Attendants run from the emergency door when they spot him. They wave up to the hovercar, but it's too late. The Trust rise up into the air and into the night, leaving their friend behind.

Carina's head swivels from side to side. Charlie comes up to her with a syringe.

"Dax has this in his medic kit, labeled 'for Carina, in case of emergency.' Think I should give it to you."

"What is it?" Carina asks, muzzily. "Haven't you given me enough?"

"It's a stronger sedative than the one Kivon gave you."

"I don't . . ." Carina trails off, unable to finish the thought.

"It'll help you with withdrawal."

She exhales in a long, forceful breath. "OK."

Charlie wipes the inside of Carina's elbow and slides the needle into her skin. Carina closes her eyes. If only she were going into the Zealscape. As Charlie leans close, Carina opens her eyes. The world is slowly blurring.

"None of you are safe around me," Carina whispers before she closes her eyes again and fades away.

TWENTY-EIGHT

ROZ

Sudice headquarters, Los Angeles,
California, Pacifica

If Roz had been at that silo, things would have been different.
She was sure of it.

There'd been a shareholders' meeting and, no matter how she
tried, there was no way out of it. So she'd taken a hovercar back up
to San Francisco and had an evening of champagne and caviar,
dressed to the nines, subtly accessing her implants and trying
not to scream in the middle of the room of marble and chandeliers when everything went to shit.

Mantel and Roz are trying to keep what's happened with
Mark and Carina quiet and contained. Even telling the shareholders would mean the information leaking to the newscasts
by morning, and then they'd be screwed. Stocks would fall, the
government would come knocking, and all the smooth talking
in the world wouldn't stop an audit and a swift and permanent
visit to stasis.

Roz had thought that eight members of her team, the ones
with military training, would be more than enough to contain
the Trust, along with the coordinated Wasp attack. She and a
few other members of her team had spotted the breach in

Mitford's implants, and Roz was impressed despite herself. The plan had been for the Wasps to attack, leave the Trust unconscious. Have her team go in, grab them and leave.

Instead, by the time Roz left that shareholders' meeting, only half her team survived, and those that did needed quite the patch-up in hospital. They sent three cars' worth of backup as soon as the first man fell. Too late.

The Trust must have had someone guarding them, but Roz hasn't been able to find out who it was. The Trust have slipped away again. So close within her grasp, and gone because of company politics. Raf, despite his brain being half-fried by the Wasp attacks, managed to orchestrate an escape from right under their very noses. At least it doesn't seem like the transfer of information worked—one small blessing.

With all Roz knew, she still underestimated them.

The past few hours, she's been recalculating her plans. Perhaps letting them get away now may have other advantages down the line. There has to be another angle she can use to make the most of this. One of the members of her team pings at the door to her office. It's Niall again. She lets him in and he enters, carefully setting down all of the Trust's kit they took from the silo. Somewhere in here is a breadcrumb for her to follow. Rafael Hernandez is good, but he's also cocky.

She sets to work, multiple screens projected onto the wallscreen, the light of them reflecting off her face. Live feeds of security footage and cameras downtown, where she suspects they're hiding. Aerial shots of the Port of Long Beach.

She'll find the chink and worm her way in. And, unlike the last time, she won't let Carina Kearney get into her head.

TWENTY-NINE

ROZ

Eight months ago

Sudice headquarters, San Francisco,
California, Pacifica

Carina calls in sick the following Monday.

Her biometrics show no illness. Roz could press it, get her in trouble with HR, but she doesn't. It's a brief respite, and she ends up dismissing the other scientists with pay for the week while the subjects remain in their prison apartments. Mantel is impatient, but she holds firm. Everyone needs the break, and she needs the extra time.

Roz makes her preparations while stalking Carina from afar. Carina goes to the Zeal lounge every day that week, for longer and longer periods of time. Roz tries to find a way to access the dream records, but Carina has paid for a top-notch lounge, and Roz can't crack it.

By the time they all reconvene, Roz knows what she needs to do.

The scientists clock in, reacquaint themselves with the subjects and their latest dataset. At lunchtime, Roz brings up the cafeteria cameras on her office wallscreen, ignoring her own

217

replicator-ordered lunch on the desk beside her. Carina's speaking to Mark, Aliyah and Kim, earnest and forceful. Roz tries to bring up the audio, but there's too much interference from the buzz of dozens of conversations, and Carina's not at the right angle for lip-reading software to work. Roz wonders for a second if that's intentional, but decides she's being paranoid.

The rest of the day passes uneventfully. Carina helps the other scientists and assistants with their subjects, analyzing the data. Near the end of the day, Roz drifts to her workstation. Subject E's eyes slide away from hers.

"Carina, stay behind after the others are gone tonight," Roz says, keeping her voice light and unconcerned. "I'd like to speak to you."

"What about?" Carina asks. Brasher than she should be.

"An opportunity," Roz says shortly, aware of all the various ears listening in the room, even as they pretend not to.

They all work late that day. Roz resists the urge to check the time every few minutes. She's calm, emotions safely walled away. If she could feel, it would be a growing excitement, burning through her veins like lava.

Mark leaves first. Then Aliyah. Finally Kim. Carina finishes up with her subject and then sends him away. The lab grows silent and empty.

"Hi Carina," Roz says, her face stretching like tight plastic as she smiles.

Carina seems wary. "Am I fired?"

Roz laughs. "On the contrary. I want to offer you a promotion."

Carina says nothing, her face blinkered. That's what it's meant to look like almost all the time. Smooth as glass.

"Come," Roz says, bringing her to her own private lab. It's the same room where she worked with Carina all those years before. There's another flicker of a nameless emotion on Carina's face, but she settles in the spare chair, crossing her legs and setting her hands over her knee, prim and proper as you please.

"I want to focus less on brain recording in the next few months," Roz begins. "The others will still continue their projects as planned, but as progress is slow, having the full team working on it is not the best use of our resources. Aliyah, Mark and Kim will continue. You and I will do something else."

She's watching Roz, eyes bright and sharp. "Doing what?"

Roz tilts her chin up. "Using Verve and brain coding, we're going to heal Subject E of his criminal tendencies. Make him an upstanding member of society."

Carina blinks once. "That would require a lot of alteration of his neural pathways and personality."

"You know as well as I do that it can be done." Roz is relishing the careful dance of words. All the things between them left unsaid. "This has far greater implications than even brain recording. We could be at the forefront with this!" Her voice is too loud. She reins it in.

Carina chews her bottom lip. "Are you certain it would work?"

Roz stands, moves closer. "There is of course the chance that what we do may not be permanent. Even a brief respite will help the subjects react better to Zeal therapy, integrate back into society. But yes, there is the chance of regression." She's close enough to touch Carina now. She reaches out, tilts up the girl's chin with her fingertips. "Like what happened to you."

"What are you talking about?" Carina asks, flinching back, but Roz holds her tight.

If Carina does remember the earlier experiments, she's playing coy. "Thing is, I think I know how to fix you. If I can, Mantel says I can forge right ahead with this project."

Carina pushes back, but Roz is viper-fast. Her fingers move in the air, fast and smooth. Carina stumbles.

"Your implants are releasing a paralytic and an amnesiac. You'll be awake but unable to move while I perform the procedure, and afterward you'll remember exactly nothing about the previous twenty-four hours."

Carina's legs give out from under her. Roz grabs her under the arms and drags her to the Chair, not bothering to strap her in. She begins to prep the Verve and Zeal cocktail she'll use on Carina's brain for her new code.

"I'm not sure why this programming ended up breaking down the first time around. A fault with my code, or a fault with you?" Roz muses. She brushes the blonde hair back from Carina's face, almost gently. She runs a fingertip over the area of the skull she'll enjoy cutting open. She didn't do that the first time around. Now she'll peel it all back and see what really makes Carina tick.

"You're my patient zero, Carina. I'd be nowhere without you." She keeps stroking the girl's hair. "Every scientist needs a purpose. A calling. As soon as I first met you, I had this thrill of premonition. I didn't know how you'd fit in, but I knew you would. Then your father came, hearing of my earlier work, and when he offered you to my fledgling project, I knew it was meant to be."

Roz sighs. "This is just the beginning."

She moves the needle to the crook of Carina's arm. Carina blinks. Before Roz can register that this shouldn't be possible, Carina rolls to the side, knocking the needle to the floor. The syringe shatters. Roz loses her balance, her elbow clanging against one of the lab tables, the pain reverberating up to her shoulder. She lunges for Carina, but the other woman is too fast. She dodges out of the way again, though Roz's nails leave deep gouges in her arm. Carina's blonde hair tangles over her face and she shakes it out of the way, sweet features crumpled into a grimace. Roz manages to get one punch in—a glorious right hook on the cheekbone. The pain must be exquisite. It doesn't faze Carina one bit.

Though she's smaller than Roz, Carina still pushes her boss to the cold tiles of the laboratory floor. Her hands close around Roz's neck, pressing, pressing. Rather than flailing and wasting her energy and oxygen, despite her terror, Roz struggles a little and then goes limp. Carina's hands weaken slightly, and Roz, dizzy and hurting, manages to twist from her grasp.

Roz has one sweet, deep lungful of air before Carina has her again, pushing her face into the floor. Roz can't scream. Carina straddles her, her slight body heavy against Roz's lungs.

This is it, she thinks muzzily. *I'm going to die. Carina's getting me before I can get her.* The failure is a bitter taste in her mouth. "How?" she manages to wheeze.

"You're not as sly as you think you are. I noticed you locking onto my implants a few days ago, figured out what you were going to do. I did some code rerouting of my own. Let it give me enough of a dose that you thought you would succeed."

Roz looks at Carina's biometric data on her implants. "For the paralytic, you did. Not the amnesiac—you won't remember any of this tomorrow."

"Doesn't matter." Carina's grip on Roz is tight and painful.

"What will you do now, then?" Roz asks, keeping her voice cool and haughty. Show no fear. Feel no fear.

Carina bends close to her ear. "I'm going now. And you will not follow me. You will not send anyone after me. I no longer exist to you. You don't know what I've copied from these servers, hidden away. You don't know how I could take you down. Leave me alone, and I'm a ghost that won't haunt you."

Roz gives another small sigh. "You'll always haunt me, Carina."

Carina's eyes narrow. "Good." She leans back, the movement hurting Roz's hipbone. Roz turns her head, manages to look up into Carina's face. The edges of her blonde hair are lit by the false sunlight, and Roz can barely make out her features. Carina shifts, and her hair covers her face like a veil.

"I should kill you. You're just as much of a criminal as the subjects are."

Roz's heartbeat quickens. The threat of death makes her feel strangely alive. Her own long-walled emotions threaten to break through.

"I wouldn't hesitate to do it if I thought I could get away with it. If we weren't right here in Sudice, you'd be long gone." The tips of Carina's hair brush against Roz's ear. "And how I'd relish it."

Roz manages to swallow.

"So you're not dying by my hand. Not tonight, at any rate. But if you come after me. If you so much as search for my name . . . then some dark night, in some alleyway, you might meet your end. Is that clear?"

Roz pauses. She won't remember. It's an empty threat. Carina presses Roz's head harder against the floor. Her cheekbone burns. "Is that clear?" Carina almost growls.

"It's clear."

"Good." Roz feels the prick of a needle at her elbow.

"What . . ." she begins, before words float away from her.

"Can't have you calling the cops on me. You'd just love to send me to stasis. Maybe slot me into the pod right next to Subject E." Carina grunts as she lifts Roz's limp body and half-drags her to the Chair.

Carina is efficient, strapping Roz in tightly, prepping another syringe. She sees the question in Roz's eyes.

"No, I haven't changed my mind about killing you. I'm sending you off to a nice, long Zealscape. Twelve hours. You'll come out of it right as the other scientists come in for their next working day. And I'll have a great head start."

Another needle slides into Roz's arms.

The last thing she sees is Carina's face, blurred and beautiful.

"Sweet fucking dreams, Dr. Roz Elliot."

•

When Roz wakes up from the endless Zealscape, she's able to access her implants again. Vera, her virtual assistant, borrows a robotic body and releases her. Roz wishes she could be like this assistant. No emotion, no regret, no guilt. Vera follows her processes. Yes or no. One or zero. A binary with no room for gray.

Brain recording continues, though as ever, progress is slow. Yet Roz is not finished. Not even remotely.

Especially when Mark brings in young Nettie Aldrich for her work placement. Roz sees the brain map—so similar to Carina's.

The cycle begins again. And fails. As Nettie Aldrich's last heartbeat fades away into silence, as she holds a piece of the young girl's skull in her hands, Roz knows that she and Carina are far more alike than different.

THIRTY

DAX

San Pedro Hospital, Los Angeles,
California, Pacifica

Dax remembers the sharp pain at his temple from the butt of his attacker's gun. Then that throb of the gunshot, the piercing impact. Right under his collarbone and the fleshy upper chest, missing his heart. The pain excruciating to the point of exquisiteness, so intense it didn't seem as though it could be real, but only a twisted Zealscape nightmare.

He floats in and out. Charlie's face is above him, panicked, asking him if he can stitch himself up. He manages to tell her he can't. Her face recedes. He should care. *Shock*, his doctor's mind tells him. *Exsanguination. Loss of consciousness imminent.* Voices swirl around above him, but he doesn't understand them any more.

His fading eyes focus on Carina. The feral look in her eyes is something he'll never forget. Like she could unpeel his skin and look beneath, to the very core of him, and enjoy every moment.

•

Dax has often wondered what it would feel like to die.

Is it like the stories? A bright light, that tricky tunnel, your deity of choice holding his/her/their hand out to you? He remembers one of the Newe myths his mother used to tell him and Tam, about the trickster Coyote and the Wolf, the Shoshone creator, and how death entered the world. The Wolf and Coyote often disagreed, and always wished to teach each other lessons. Death didn't exist, or if someone died, the Wolf could bring them back by shooting an arrow underneath them. "If someone dies, they should stay gone," the Coyote claimed, hoping the Wolf would listen and then the Wolf's people would turn against him. Yet a few days later, when Coyote's son lay close to death, Coyote changed his tune. Yet the Wolf would not, for he agreed that creatures should not be brought back to life, and so Death entered the world.

Dax feels as though he's floating in the darkness. No arrow passes beneath him. Is he stuck in this dimness forever?

He dies.

He stays dead for one minute and four seconds.

He comes back, and he stays asleep for over a day, in a medically induced coma while his body recovers. Nanobots slip into his bloodstream, working like busy ants to stitch him back together again.

While he sleeps, he dreams.

His childhood rises before him. Salmon fishing in the river with his family. The dances, the fire warm against his face, his heart glowing warm as the coals while he watched and listened. He remembers their mother wrapping her arms around him and Tam before bedtime, telling them stories until they fell asleep.

Home. The home he wishes he'd never left, or had returned to long before they became caught up in Sudice and couldn't go back without endangering those they loved. Have they thrown their lives away to take down a corporation that most of Pacifica adores? At one point, every member of the Trust lived in that same ignorance. Sometimes he wishes the wool had never been pulled from over his eyes.

Dax's memories float among his childhood and teenage years. He remembers correcting Tam one day when they were playing among the redwoods. They played a complicated game with fifteen dolls—all with distinct personalities and complicated interpersonal relationships. An exercise in world-building and government from eight-year-olds. Good against evil, starkly black and white at first, before blurring into hopeless variations of gray.

"I don't want you to call me your sister any more," Dax said, speaking Shoshoni, his mouth dry. "I'm your brother."

"I already knew that, silly," Tam said, picking up another doll. "I already think of you as my brother. Are you going to change your name?"

He hadn't thought of that. "Yes. I will."

The dolls watched them impassively as they brainstormed before deciding on the name he used before he changed his alias to Dax. A few days later, he told his parents and the rest of the tribe. And that was that. If people used the wrong name, they apologized and corrected themselves. When he turned eleven, he began taking puberty blockers. He and his sister, who had been mirror images, began to diverge. They both wore their hair long, but she grew curvy while he stayed flat. She also grew taller, which irritated him.

When he was sixteen, he went to visit several doctors and psychologists. A few months later, he had a testosterone implant. Not long after that, he began seeing Dr. Valerie, who helped him have the body he'd always wanted. That artistry of blending his flesh into his dream inspired him to become a doctor himself.

He has vivid flashes of brainloading at university. Tam desperately wanted to study outside the reservation, for the experience, and he came along. If they hadn't done that, what would they be doing now? He's almost certain they'd be happier.

His thoughts and memories kaleidoscope into bright pieces. He has no idea how much time passes, or if he's still living. Has the Wolf taken pity on him, or is he passing on?

When Dax's eyes eventually flutter open, nothing seems as bright as those pieces of memory. A doctor stands over him, with his white coat and the bottom half of his face covered in a surgical mask that fits to his features like a second skin.

"Hello, John Doe," he says. He's English, voice clipped.

"What?" Dax manages, voice hoarse.

"Your VeriChip has been wiped. No name, no address, no access to implants. Nothing at all. You're the first John Doe I've had in years. Bit of excitement, really."

Dax stays silent. He's still half-drugged, his head pounding. What happened? The silo. The Wasps. People from Sudice in Kalar suits. Pain. Carina's eyes. More pain. Everything is jumbled, interrupted with memories and disjointed dreams. Through the fog comes one clear thought: *you need to think up a cover, and fast.* The best one, the Occam's Razor, is to borrow from a soap opera.

Dax lets his face grow lax, his eyes widen in fear. "Doctor. I don't know who I am."

The doctor considers him, understandably suspicious. "No memories at all?" he asks.

Dax makes a show of considering, gazing up at the ceiling as if trying to remember. "Nothing." He lets his voice quaver, tears pool in his eyes, vaguely proud of his acting skills.

The doctor molds his face into concern, but the annoyance underneath is not quite hidden. Dax can guess the doctor's thoughts: more paperwork. His patient is probably a criminal. He's not wrong.

"How are you feeling aside from a lack of memories? Do you remember being injured?"

Dax shakes his head. "I was hurt? How bad?"

The doctor hesitates. "Gunshot wound. To the shoulder. We've had to report it."

Not ideal. Dax's drugged mind whirrs. The Trust left him here because they didn't have the medical knowledge to help. But how will he get out? They won't just let him leave. The police will be here, and Sudice will probably also be keeping an eye on the hospitals. They must know they injured some of the Trust. *Damn.* Dax raises his hand to his injured shoulder, as if only just learning of it. He makes a show of wincing, even though it barely hurts.

The doctor holds up a mirror and pulls down Dax's hospital gown, tapping just below the collarbone with a gloved finger. "Right here. You'd lost a lot of blood by the time you arrived. You flatlined, which might explain the memory loss."

Dax really did die. He opens his mouth, then closes it, unsure what to say.

"People don't often show up to hospitals at death's door with a gunshot wound these days."

Dax nods, thinking over all the tropes of amnesia. "I seem to remember how the world works, just not how I fit into it." He gives the doctor a sheepish smile. "Thank you for patching me up. What happens now?"

"Well, as I said, it's been reported. The authorities will be coming around to interview you tomorrow. They were going to come today, but I wanted to see how you were faring. I think you could use the time to rest. Perhaps things will begin to come back to you. We'll do a brain scan, to see if the amnesia is a result of brain trauma. If so, I'm sure we'll be able to reverse it." The doctor's surgical mask folds into a smile.

Dax's head does hurt, which he finds strange if they've fixed his injuries. "Thank you again, doctor. I really appreciate it."

"I'll have the resident psychologist come in a few hours as well, after the scan's been processed. Memory loss can often be a side effect of shock. Whatever you've been through has been traumatizing, which is not surprising."

Dax blinks at that. Yes. He's been shot. He flatlined. The Trust left him. Hopefully they returned to the base, but there is a chance they were captured after they dropped him off. His heartbeat quickens. "Thank you." Dax feels like he's done nothing but thank the doctor since he woke up.

The doctor makes a few notes on his tablet. "Lie back," the doctor instructs.

Dax doesn't want to. The doctor has been nothing but kind and courteous, but he's still uneasy. He needs to figure out how to leave, but he can't arouse suspicion, so he lies back. The doctor attaches electrodes to his temples and begins the brain scan. Or tries.

"Hm," he says. "I suppose that shouldn't be too surprising. You can't access your ocular or auditory implants, correct?"

Dax tries. Nope. Raf sealed them off well. "No."

"Looks like they're impacting the brain scanning code. That is a puzzle."

Dax keeps his face blank, mentally thanking Raf. He lets his eyelids droop. "Sorry, doctor. I still feel so tired."

The doctor gives that veiled smile again. "I'll leave you for now. This is a lot to take in at once."

Dax nods. The doctor finally leaves.

Dax investigates the needles of the IV in his arm and the various machines he's connected to. Closing his eyes, he reaches for the implants. Raf has done this to them before. He knows the passcode to access them again. His auditory and ocular implants come back to him, and he sighs with relief.

He doesn't want to contact the Trust right away, on the off chance people are monitoring him. Paranoid, but better safe than sorry. He does try accessing the net, using basic encryption so the hospital can't as easily see what he's researching. He uses the wall controls to project a mindless action film on the wallscreen. If anyone pokes their head in the window, it'll look like he's resting, just as he's meant to.

Forty-five minutes pass as he discovers he's in San Pedro Hospital, roughly twenty-five miles from base. He manages to find basic blueprints from the hospital and has an idea of security. This won't be easy. He double-checks his paltry encryption, belatedly wishing he'd let Raf teach him more. He accesses the subfrequency and reaches out to the Trust.

Holding his breath, he waits for them to respond. If they don't, and they've been taken, all is lost. Raf. Kivon. Charlie. Carina. They can't be gone.

Two long minutes pass as he gazes sightlessly at the explosions on the wallscreen.

"Dax!" It's Charlie. She sounds just as relieved as he feels.

"Hi." He fills her in, knowing the rest of the Trust are listening. He wastes no words and time. Raf sends him better blueprints. Together, they sketch out a plan.

It takes Dax a few tries to stand, the lingering drugs making him woozy. His paper hospital gown ties at the back, at least, but any strenuous movement and he'll expose himself. He grumbles as he tries to tie it tighter. First step: disguise.

Dax rifles through the cupboards in the hospital room, but

unfortunately, no one has conveniently left behind scrubs or a coat in his size.

"Raf," he sends on his implants. "Are the cameras all good?"

"Swapped your room's with a loop of you sleeping from earlier. You're golden. Also, you're an idiot for getting shot. I thought you'd want to know."

"I'd agree with that. Lucky I got you to watch my back."

"Damn straight."

Dax peeks through the small window on his room's door until he sees a nurse about his height and build. He pushes open the door and sticks his head outside.

"Can you help . . . ?" He lets his voice trail off, keeping his face blank, his eyes wide and staring.

The nurse pauses, unblinking. Hopefully he's just checking the time on his implants. "Sure."

Dax backs away from the door. The nurse enters and closes the door behind him. "What's the trouble?"

"I'm really sorry," Dax says, before grabbing the nurse and kicking his legs out from under him. The nurse goes down with a grunt. Before he can fill his lungs for a scream, Dax grabs him in a sleeper hold, pressing the carotid artery. Not having long, he drags the unconscious nurse into the hospital bed, stripping his clothes and tying arms and legs to the bedposts with torn strips of sheet. He presses more in his mouth as a makeshift gag.

"Sorry," he whispers again as he shrugs into his clothes. "You'll have a headache when you wake up, but you should be OK." Dax wipes the sweat from his forehead. He's breathing hard, exhausted already, and he's barely begun.

He consults the blueprints one last time. Opens the door and walks out, head high, not too quickly. As if he's just another one of the few human nurses scattered among the robotic ones doing their rounds. He lets his face take on the far-off look people get when consulting their implants. Less chance of interruption.

Dax turns left at the end of the corridor, then right, making his way through the hospital labyrinth. He keeps waiting for someone to call out. No one gives him a second glance. He approaches the front door. The late evening waits for him outside. The hovercar should be waiting just outside the grounds. So close. He approaches the main doors, waving his wrist in front of the scanner. His VeriChip is still deactivated, but Raf has managed to gain access to the hospital's security. The panel goes green and the door slides open. Dax takes a deep breath of fresh air and leaves.

Someone calls out behind him. Though he knows he shouldn't, he glances back. The British doctor has spotted him, his pointing finger damning. Security bots stationed outside whirr toward him, robotic nurses from within circling his back.

"Shit." Dax takes off, dizzy on his feet, managing to dart between two bots, but he knows he can't escape them for long. Bots fly faster than a human can run. The whirrs of the bots follow him and he hears the Stunners hidden in their torsos slot out. *Come on, Trust. Come on.* The bots avoid lethal force, but he doesn't need to be tranqed and dragged to the police station to fall right into Sudice's hands.

Pfft. He swerves, the dart whizzing past his ear. He's off the lit path, in the darkness of the trees, but all the bots have infrared. He keeps zigzagging through the trees, praying he doesn't trip on a root, his lungs on fire, still weak from his healing injuries.

A dart hits him and he rips it out. Not fast enough. He'll be unconscious in a minute. Maybe two, if he's lucky. Up ahead is the meeting point. If he can just get a few steps closer . . .

He doesn't hear the whirring of the bots any more. Has Raf

figured out how to power them down? He was constantly taking one of them apart and putting it back together again, back at headquarters. The trees begin to blur, but Dax concentrates on putting one foot in front of the other.

Up ahead, the Trust's hovercar dips below the treeline. There is nothing but silence behind him, but he can't spare the energy to turn his head. Hacking hospital security bots: another crime to add to their long list of infractions against the law.

Dax's legs give out and he collapses onto the loamy ground of the artificial forest surrounding the hospital. The hovercar door opens, and Raf jumps out to grab him.

He blacks out.

THIRTY-ONE

CARINA

*The Trust headquarters, Los Angeles,
California, Pacifica*

Carina waits for the Trust to return.

She hasn't gone with them to the hospital. She still feels rubbed raw from her exposure to Zeal at the silo. Lying on her bed, she is conscious of her body twitching and her fingers itching for a sharp blade.

It isn't fair, she thinks, burying her face in her pillow, her skin damp with sweat. She had improved since Dax broke the initial physical addiction. She'd resisted going to the Zeal lounges, though she knows exactly how many are within a three-mile radius. Her homicidal ideation was still there, but she'd started to think that perhaps she wouldn't need to enact it on this plane of reality. She might never return to how she used to be before Roz found her, but she'd found some sort of equilibrium to keep her grounded enough to search for the information hidden in her mind. Now, hidden deep underground in the Trust headquarters, it feels like she's never left the Green Star Lounge at all.

Carina hadn't even known she still had such a thing as

hope. She's wanted to kill for too many years for a bit of detox-ing and flesh surgery to have a lasting effect.

That memory of her first kill looms. *No. No.* She shoves it away. Maybe it has one of Mark's symbols attached—strong memories, he said. She can't look at it. Not now.

Carina can't remember if she ever recorded it during those nights at Sudice, long after the lab work was finished. Did she ever examine that memory from afar, tinging the experience with just enough Verve to prep the implants? That beginning of the addiction that would only grow until it overwhelmed her in that year-long nightmarish dream.

Carina slides sideways into her memories of the months after her mother disappeared. She's looked at these before, dur-ing her ruthless categorization of her life, trying to find the information lurking somewhere in the spools of her brain. Knowing Mark's intel is still in there, hiding, makes her want to saw open her own skull and spoon it out.

She's missed something. It's close. "Mark," she says aloud, voice low. Why has he given all of this to her? She's wondered this a thousand times or more since she woke up from that fate-ful Zeal trip. He knew how broken she was. Is. Why not send this to Aliyah or Kim? The other members of that Sudice team could have done this so much better.

Carina lets herself submerge back into the memories. Maybe something will unlock. Her thoughts open.

One thing punctured Carina's constant apathy: the need to find out what truly happened to her mother.

To the outside eye, she functioned normally enough. Days passed. Carina went to school, brainloaded information, con-ducted experiments in the school lab and went home again. Other students had given up on trying to speak to her. That suited her fine. Already, the students blurred together, feeling like figments created to populate the world she lived in, like those placeholders she'd later create in the Zealscape.

The only person that interested Carina was her father. She tracked his movements—when he left for work, when he returned. She wanted to follow him—she was certain that he wasn't actually working until 8 p.m. each night. Not that she minded seeing him less. It meant fewer bruises.

What was he doing?

It wouldn't be easy. Following him would mean leaving before he headed home on his hovercar. If he came home and she wasn't there, there'd be hell to pay. He didn't let her go to anyone's house any more, and she no longer asked, so she couldn't claim she was spending the night at a friend's.

She concocted her plan. Saved the cash credits of her paltry allowance and bought a microscopic tracking chip in San Francisco, no bigger than one of the freckles on her arm. The man selling it to her seemed uninterested in the fact that a sixteen-year-old with cold eyes was buying something borderline illegal.

Carina attached the chip to her father's favorite pair of shoes, the plain brown ones he wore every day. She'd looked up countless tutorials on her ocular implants, and in the middle of the night, made a tiny slit in the sole where it met the leather of the shoe, inserted the chip and sealed it over. She surveyed her handiwork critically; she couldn't tell the shoe had been tampered with. She could only hope that neither would he.

Carina's father did not seem to, and her hunch proved right. Her father left his work at five o'clock sharp every day. What was he doing for the next two hours before he came home each evening? Most of the time, he went to a few addresses near downtown San Francisco. She looked them up; bars and Zeal lounges. Business meetings or dates, possibly. The thought of him dating made her toes curl with hatred. Once every couple of weeks, though, he went somewhere else on the outskirts of the city. On those days, he came home closer to eleven, when she was meant to be asleep but her eyes were wide open as she listened to him shuffle through the halls of Greenview House.

What are you doing, Daddy?

•

Back in her room at the Trust headquarters, sweat staining the sheets, Carina wants to stop remembering, turn away, yet it keeps coming like a tide. She shakes her head, holding her hands to her temples, groaning.

•

After two months, Carina finally gathered the courage to follow her father. He had always been distant and absent, but in the last few weeks, he'd grown worse. Carina's body was peppered with fresh bruises, from harsh shoving into walls and hard hands around her arms. His abuse had never been sexual, thankfully, but as his abuse worsened, she couldn't rule out those patterns might shift. She'd been studying child abuse, trying to remain remote and clinical. He was definitely escalating.

After school let out, Carina made her way to San Francisco. She went to the Zeal lounge he frequented perhaps once a week, not far from his office. She couldn't understand why he went. Wasn't it against his lingering beliefs from growing up in Mana's Hearth? He'd left that cult, or been kicked out. She never knew which—another mystery relating to her father and what made him tick.

She stared at the Zeal lounge called Galaxy for a long time, at its purple walls flecked with moving stars. People came in and out. It wasn't an off-grid lounge—the clientele were respectable people in suits or loose designer clothes. For a moment, Carina was tempted to enter, take a quick hit. She had enough of her allowance credits left over. Already it felt like a dangerous lure. She managed to turn away. Just.

Carina went to the second location. It took her nearly an hour to get there on public transport, but she still arrived before five. Her father must go to it on his company-provided hovercar. The second address was one of the quiet warehouses in a nearly-abandoned estate on the edge of Millbrae.

Her father arrived half an hour after she got there. Carina had found a way into an abandoned warehouse across the street and watched him from a cracked window. He entered, closing the metal door behind him.

Carina waited. And waited. And wondered. How did her father find this place? Did he own it? What in the world was he doing?

A little over two hours later, her father left the warehouse. His cheeks were flushed, his eyes bright. She'd never seen him like that. He looked almost deliriously happy. He had a small bag in one hand that he hadn't been holding when he arrived. He climbed into the hovercar and took off. Carina had no hope of beating him home. She sent him a message saying she was at a study group and would be home late. It might work. It probably wouldn't. No matter what, she'd have a beating tonight, so she might as well see what he was up to. One benefit of her newly reduced ability to process emotions: she wasn't as afraid of that evening as she should have been.

Carina approached the warehouse, wondering how to enter. On the side of the building, there were no windows at street level that weren't blacked out and obviously alarmed, but if she climbed the fire escape, perhaps she could look in the second-story one.

It was her last chance to turn back. She stilled, wondering if she really wanted to know what was inside or was better off just going home, taking the beating and hoping she'd last until she could move away to university. Though even that wouldn't be an escape—her father would force her to remain in San Francisco. Even after that, she could see him manipulating her to stay close, stay home, stay under his thumb. If she could find something to threaten him with in just the right way, she could break his hold over her. If she dared.

Carina climbed the fire escape. It was old and rickety, creaking so loudly she feared it would fall off the side of the building. Her hands were soon covered in flecks of black paint and iron rust. Upon reaching the top, she stood and peered through the window.

She'd expected to see an empty room, as decrepit as the exterior. Perhaps her father simply liked to go somewhere remote and alone to unwind before coming home and having to deal with her. Instead, the warehouse was still empty, but in the center was a large medical table surrounded by a rod with the curtains pushed back. The sight of it made goosebumps rise on the skin of her arms. The walls were dark and probably sound-proofed. A giant tub was pushed against one wall, with taps and buckets stacked to one side. In another corner was a trunk, tucked away but topped with a globe figurine. She swallowed. They had a similar globe in a trunk in their home, and it doubled as a security device. Her mother had taught her the code, in case she ever needed to access the passports and spare money, the datapods with backups of the house deeds and insurance papers. Her father wouldn't be so stupid as to use the same code, would he? And what would she find inside if he did?

Carina scrutinized the window. Again, if security was similar to how it was in Greenview House, she'd see the tiny green line of an alarm on the windowsill. No line up here, though she saw them one floor up. She peered within and down to the floor of the warehouse. It was a decent drop, but she could make it. Opening the window, she paused. No alarm. She waited ten minutes. If her father had the alarm wired to his implants, he'd turn around and come back immediately to investigate. She should be able to dart into the alleyway and avoid him if so.

She waited. No one came. Perching on the windowsill, her breath steady, she looked down at the very hard concrete of the warehouse floor. On her implants, she searched for the best way to jump from a second-story window. She turned around, hanging from the windowsill by her fingertips, shortening the distance to the floor. Then, before she could change her mind, she jumped.

She bent her knees before impact. The breath left her lungs in a whoosh, and she rolled backward.

Her body hurt, but nothing was broken or torn. At least, she hoped not. She sat up, slowly. Getting out was going to be trickier—she'd have to figure out a way to disarm the alarm from within. She'd worry about that later. Carina checked her father's location. He was still on his way home.

She walked to the globe on the trunk. Every footstep echoed in the empty space. No alarm sounded. She crouched in front of the globe and pulled some gloves out of her pocket. Diffidently, she tapped in the code. The globe glowed orange and rolled out of the way, the lid of the trunk opening.

Inside were torture devices. Scalpels, sharp knives, forceps, pincers, cat o' nine tails and other things she didn't recognize. Her gaze kept snagging on the knives. She wanted to pick one up, but refrained.

Carina's eyes rose to the tub. A horrible theory bloomed in her mind. The tub was big enough.

She knew what had happened to her mother. And now, she feared that her mother was not the only one. Horribly, she felt drawn to the weapons of violence. She reached into the trunk, bringing out the sharpest knife.

•

In her real memory, it is clean and pristine, but now she sees something on the blade: a single drop of blood.

The drop of blood grows in Carina's mind, red as all the blood she saw during her year in the Zealscape. She has missed that color, the gleam of light on that viscous fluid. She wants to reach out and smear the blood between her fingers. Smell it. Taste it. Possess it.

She feels the information release, trickling into her brain like the other three images before it. Mark's face appears, a recorded memory, just for her.

•

Mark looks thinner than the AI she saw in the Zealscape. His cheeks are sunken beneath prominent cheekbones, and shadows gather beneath his eyes that not even gene therapy could erase.

"I'm glad you've made it this far, Carina, though I'm also grieved that you have." Mark stops and coughs. It's wet, deep in his lungs. He's sick. Very sick. "You see, I've left things out. Vital pieces of the puzzle. I should have made this information the first image. If it didn't motivate you to stop Sudice, nothing would." More wet coughing. "But it's not easy to confess to such crimes. After you see what I show you, you will think so differently of me. You looked up to me, I think, in your own distant, disconnected way. You shouldn't have. I won't ask for forgiveness. I don't deserve it." Mark looks at her, eyes ringed with purple bruises. "Stop this before it's too late." His image pixellates and dissolves.

One of Mark's recorded memories plays from his point of view.

He is in a plain, white-tiled room, the bright lights harsh and unforgiving. The Sudice labs in San Francisco. He looks down at an operating table, so similar to the metal table in her father's warehouse that it startles her. On it is Nettie Aldrich. Her head turned to the side, her eyes closed. Her skin and skull have been cut and peeled back. Carina, through Mark's eyes, sees her brain.

The image zooms out and Carina finds herself standing next to Mark. He seems healthier and also . . . not quite like Mark. With a jolt, she realizes it's Mark's AI ghost who convinced her to dive headfirst into this mess in the first place.

"Plug into the Trust's brainloading Chair. They've likely kept it from you, but it's in a storage cupboard at the back of the compound." A map flashes in her mind's eye. "What I need to tell you can't be fully transmitted in this manner. It means more Zeal, but the risk is worth it. I promise."

•

The drop of blood blooms in her mind, the information still pooling into her brain. It pours through Carina, the torrent gaining momentum. She balls her fists over her eyes, struggling to breathe. Her heart beats an arrhythmic staccato in the chest. It's the information on the subjects before Carina joined the brainloading project. The heart attacks, the strokes, including the ones she created on her own subjects. Mark has dumped more information into her brain than the previous three times. What if it's too much? What if she goes the same way as all those nameless people before her and she dies right here, right now?

She should ping Dax so he can help her, but she can barely hold onto the thought before it flies away again. Then she remembers she doesn't even know if he's back from the hospital, or if he even survived his wound. Lying there, the information coursing through her, she's vaguely surprised to find that she doesn't want to die. Not yet. Not today.

After a time—how long, she can't begin to guess—her mind quiets. Carefully, she sifts through a little of the information. Raf will be so happy. It has information on the subjects Roz's team worked on, yes, plus lots of information about Sudice's experiments on other criminals who should have been put in stasis. It also contains information about the remote server, unconnected to anything, in the heart of Sudice's Los Angeles headquarters. Carina feels her face crease into a smile, the dry skin of her lips cracking. She tastes blood.

She has no mental fortitude to look through it all more closely, especially when her mind burns with curiosity.

The Trust have been hiding a Chair from her. They told her they brainloaded directly through their implants. She knew they had Zeal somewhere in the compound, but not where it was.

Carina tiptoes from her room, hoping the rest of the Trust hasn't put sensors on her door like Dax did. The room with the brainloading Chair is locked, but after a bit of careful sifting, she finds the passcode hidden in her head. *Thank you, Mark.* Raf should change the internal passwords more often.

She walks in. The Chair is small and lonely in a small and lonely room. How many times has she lain back against a headrest like that? In Sudice, in slick Zeal lounges in San Francisco and dingy hovels in Los Angeles. Losing herself, finding herself, and wanting to lose herself all over again.

Do the other members of the Trust come here to fall into Zeal? They never mention the drug. Carina thought none of them used it. Perhaps, like her, they need to lock themselves in a dream to scream at the top of their lungs, to let out that anger and fear. What do they dream? Who do they hurt? Unlike her, they can seemingly release that darkness without it consuming them whole.

She opens a cabinet on the far side of the room. Clear vials of Zeal are lined up neatly, as though waiting for her. She reaches out with a shaking finger, touching the tips of the vials. So much of it, all in one place. Zeal isn't a drug you can overdose on, or not in the traditional sense. The more you take, the longer you stay in the dream, but if you take enough to keep you in for a week without any fluids or nutrition, your chance of dying increases. Zealot lounges, no matter how seedy, never put in a client for longer than twenty hours.

There's enough here that she could stay in Zeal for months. If she could somehow lock herself in so they couldn't open the door, no matter what, she wouldn't hesitate to do it. Even with all she needs to do. Even with the promise she gave Mark.

She would still let go.

Instead, she takes one half-full vial, preps the dose. Her hands shake. She shouldn't—one drop nearly undid her completely—yet here she is, unable to stop herself. Mark's AI will tell her something important. She feels it deep in her bones.

Lying back on the cushioned Chair, she doesn't strap herself in, hoping she won't flail enough in her dreams to hurt herself. Once she slipped out of her restraints at the Green Star Lounge and scratched deep gouges into her cheeks, as though she'd been attacked by a large cat. They didn't leave scars. Sometimes she wishes they had.

She starts the machine, presses the syringe into her vein, and falls back into that warm, deep void.

THIRTY-TWO

CARINA

The Zealscape, the Trust headquarters, Los Angeles,
California, Pacifica

Mark does not appear right away.

Carina is back at Greenview House. She missed the depravity that happened in its various rooms of her own creation. She walks through the hallways. She could open any door, walk in, create a victim and kill again.

Behind the first door of the hallway is her father's room. She stumbles back. In her old Zealscapes, she never went there. She wanted no reminder of that monster. In the corner, a shadow rises, hulking, larger than life. It glides closer to her, and she almost imagines his laugh. Fear closes her throat.

Instinct takes over. A knife appears in her hand. Long, sharp, another limb. She hefts it, checks the sharpness with a thumb.

A drop of blood wells up, crimson bright.

Greenview House disappears. She knows that nightmare will never leave her.

•

Mark is still in the lab with Nettie's corpse, on a Chair just like the one where Carina now sleeps. It's as though no time has passed.

Carina's in the throes of murderous rage. She flies at Mark, but her hands move through him. He's as insubstantial as the phantom that he is.

She tries to conjure up another victim. Someone, anyone that she can kill. But in this section of the Zealscape, she's powerless. Nothing happens. She pants, her hands empty of that knife, clawing at air. Mark comes forward, places his hands to either side of her face. She can't feel it.

"Breathe. Breathe. You control more than you think."

She tries to follow his instructions, but her breath only comes faster.

"Close your eyes. Breathe. In. Out. This is all in your mind. You are the master here, not your urges."

It takes an age, an eon, but eventually, her breathing slows, her heart finds some semblance of a steady beat. The urge to kill is there, as it always is. She's driven it back, for now. Out there, in the real world, it's only a matter of time before she snaps.

"This is too much for me, Mark," she says. "You placed your bets on the wrong person. I'm only going to let you down."

"You're strong as iron, Carina."

"Iron rusts."

"Then you will be reforged." He takes his hands away. "Come. You're getting closer. I have every faith in you, even if you haven't yet found it in yourself."

Mark disintegrates, appears again beside Nettie. Carina drags herself to the corner of the lab.

"Nettie," he says. "The girl whose death I caused, even if unintentionally." He shifts, moving to her other side. "From this angle, she looks like she's sleeping, doesn't she? Just a patient etherized on the table, to borrow a line from T. S. Eliot." He reaches out, fingertips hovering over Nettie's hair. Blonde, like

Carina's once was. "I brain recorded this memory, and have overlaid it with this AI code so I can speak to you. I've sent you just the brain-recorded memory as part of the information associated with the drop of blood. That one is completely untampered with, the memory clear enough you should be able to use it as evidence against Sudice, if you can manage to send it. Just the police won't be enough. Too many internal moles that'll sweep it under the rug. Get it out wide enough, and everyone can't look the other way. Roz killed her within Sudice walls. They still never managed to have brain recording work easily for longer than an hour. It matters little, though. Brain recording was never Roz's main goal, as you must have known. That's why you left, isn't it, Carina?"

Carina nods. "Yes. My memories of that day are fuzzy from the drugs she gave me. I only remember that she wanted me to do something else with her, and I refused. The facts aren't solid, but the emotion was. I needed to run. So I did. I left the rest of you there. I'm sorry for that."

"Don't be. I wish I'd been as strong as you." He pauses, sighs. It's the same AI ghost as in the Zealscape, but it feels so much like him. Carina wants to reach out and touch him, but he'd only be air between her fingers.

"After you left, she gave me the same job proposition she offered you. And, God help me, I took it. She asked me to get in Nettie, an intern I'd brought in for work experience. She'd seen her scans and thought she'd be a good candidate." He looks at Nettie, small and silent below him. "I followed Roz's instructions, mapping Nettie's reactions to images encrypted with proto-code Roz'd been developing. She's grown so much more sophisticated since she first meddled with your brain. She tried to amend your coding, didn't she?"

"I think so," Carina says. "I don't really remember. It was another thing I didn't really think about because she didn't want me to."

"If she'd managed to pull it off, the new code would have been ironclad. You'd have been back to being as robotic as she is."

"Did . . . she program herself?" Carina asks, a dawning dread seeping through her.

"Of course she did. To improve her concentration and focus, to dampen emotions and to become utterly ruthless. She literally made you in her image. As she tried to make Nettie, but failed."

"Why did it fail with Nettie? And why has Roz's held up?"

"Not entirely sure. I never gained access to all her notes. My guess is with Nettie, it was like brain recording. Too much stimulus at once and the brain short-circuits."

"You're still evading something you need to tell me, aren't you?"

"Merely laying out the various steps," he says. "There's another reason I had to have you carry on my work after I no longer could . . . it's what Roz plans to do next."

Carina says nothing, waiting for him to continue.

"Sudice are planning to roll out an implants software upgrade in two months' time. It's meant to have faster download speeds, fewer glitches, the ability to run more applications at once. So far, so normal. Those happen every few years. This time, though, there will be an optional add-in."

Mark's AI ghost gestures, and Nettie's body and the lab disappear. The drop of blood blooms brightly in Carina's mind's eye again, and then, with another sickening lurch, it turns into an advertisement. It's designed for virtual reality, the colors hypersaturated. Her vision is split down the middle, with the same man on the left and the right. It's a quick montage of two very different versions of his day. There are flashes of different decisions from the mundane—one skips breakfast, the other doesn't—to larger—one accepting a promotion and one turning it down, or one accepting a date and the other putting it off. It flashes forward to several years later, one version of the man happy and successful, the other in the same rut as before, in a job he doesn't like, living alone. "Make the right choices," the voiceover says, firm and confident. "Let Pythia™, the optional Sudice upgrade, guide you on your path."

It goes dark, Mark's AI appearing again. They seem to sit in Carina's old office at Sudice. Her skin ripples with fear. "She's hidden personality programming in this Pythia upgrade?"

"Right," he says. "She's done it very cleverly. Very slow, very gradual changes to everyone's personality. Zeal helps make people more complacent, but it's not perfect. Zealots are proof enough of that."

Carina suppresses a flinch. It all fits, though. She should have seen it. They all should have seen it.

"Once she had access to Verve, she realized she could roll out the personality reprogramming on a larger scale. Lower side effects, but not foolproof. There will still be a percentage of people who are significantly at risk by using Pythia. I don't know how she finally convinced Mantel to release this," Mark continues. "It's been brewing for a long time, before you even arrived at Sudice for the second round of SynMaps. She's had the code prepared for ages. She tried to roll out a similar initiative after your seeming success as a teenager, but it was deemed too experimental. You were a long-term subject to be studied, and she must have hidden the fact it failed."

"I'm not stable and I'm too small of a sample."

"You weren't the only one, back then. Neither was Nettie this time around."

In this strange dream-memory, her mouth does not go dry, as it would in the real world. "What?"

"That journalist, Nemec, nearly stumbled across it. There have been many people who have disappeared into the depths of Sudice, but the path is well hidden. I couldn't find any other proof save you and Nettie, and only because I knew to look for it." Another pause. "Have you accessed the information I just sent you before coming back in here?"

"No. I came straight here. I would have been too exhausted if I let it all unravel."

"When you're out, take a look through it. I think it'll be enough if you can manage to send it out wide scale."

"We're still trying to figure out how to do that. How to gain access to the servers."

"The Trust will figure it out. Send it far and wide. This should be enough, just. The last image will have that bit more. Once these brain recordings of mine go public, my memory will be tarnished. My family will be shamed to know what I did with my life." His head bows.

"It's worth it, yes?" Carina says. "Doing the right thing, even if it's too late."

"My previous self would hope so."

Carina wonders where Mark is now, in whatever afterlife waits for them, if any.

"Thank you, Mark," she says.

Mark reaches out to Nettie's still face. "Don't thank me for doing the bare minimum of common human decency. Just finish them."

"I'll try, Mark. I really will."

He stares at her, unblinking, until the dream fizzles and burns away.

THIRTY-THREE

CARINA

The Trust headquarters, Los Angeles,
California, Pacifica

Carina gasps as she comes out of the Zealscape, looking up into the face of a very irate Dax.

Her head feels full. She transfers the information to the Trust's servers, wanting it out of her head. Dax's lips tighten and he narrows his eyes in disappointment.

If she wasn't dosed up with Zeal, she'd feed off his anger and lunge for him. Instead, she feels the dopey, soporific effect she's been craving for so long. He's safe around her, at least until the drug leaves her system. Then no one will be safe. She doesn't let herself think about that.

"I missed this," she says. "Sometimes I think this is what it must be like to be normal. I still feel, but it's not so . . . big. And I'm not numb. I'm just . . . warm. I wish you hadn't hidden this from me. Even taking tiny doses might have been better. At least until this is over, I could have had these little respites." She blinks, dreamily, reaches up and touches his cheek. His color is good, though the dressing peeks over the collar of his shoulder. The gunshot wound is probably already nearly healed. "I'm glad to see you looking better.

And see, I'm not afraid of touching you," she says, half-wonderingly.

Dax's face stills. He doesn't pull away, but he doesn't lean into the touch, either. Carina lifts herself off the Chair, moves closer to him.

She presses her lips against his. They are soft, and warm. Normally she'd be afraid that she'd lose herself, that she'd dig her fingernails into his skin until drawing blood, but for the moment her mind is blissfully silent.

Dax returns the kiss, but doesn't move it forward. He doesn't draw her close, doesn't run his fingers through her hair. Instead, gently, he pulls away. His eyes are sad.

"I'm sorry we lied to you about this. I wasn't lying about Zeal breaking down your emotional connections further. This dose, even though it's small, will do damage. You're not yourself at the moment," he says. "When you're sober, you may not feel as you do right now."

She wants to tell him that this is how she's felt for days, beneath her fear. That desire for closeness, for connection. That she's attracted to him physically, and also drawn to his kindness, so different from all her sharp edges. And now she's dulled enough from cutting them both, she wants him.

She says none of that. She shuts down, clams up.

"Why did you take Zeal? How did you get in here?" he asks, neck stiff. Carina has grown to know him well enough that she can guess at his thoughts, his emotions, but he's completely closed to her.

"Mark told me to."

"I thought Mark was dead."

"He is."

They stare at each other. Carina resists the urge to bring her fingers to her lips.

"His AI ghost. He wanted to explain what was in this image himself. He was ashamed."

"Why?"

"See for yourself when it transfers. We've got bigger problems than we thought."

Carina forces herself out of the Chair and the world tilts and blurs. Blood rushes to her head and her vision darkens. She holds onto the side of the Chair until the worst of it passes.

"Are you all right?" he asks. He takes her hand, and her hopes rise, but he's only given her a pill. A beta blocker, like Chopper gave her the night she became Althea Bryant so briefly. "Take this when the withdrawal starts to kick in again. It'll help."

"Fine," she says, curtly. Talk about harshing her buzz. She leaves the room with the Chair behind, making her way back to her bedroom. Dax does not follow her.

Carina hobbles to the shower, thinking of all she's learned. Roz is no longer content to change one person here, another person there. Her ego is such that she wants to change the whole of Pacifica.

Carina can understand the reasoning. Hell, if Roz's programming hadn't broken down, she'd probably be right at her side still, and it's a sobering thought. Would she have thought of this grander scale? If the population could just be guided that little bit more to avoid violence, or bigotry, or jealousy, could Pacifica move closer to that utopia it pretended to be?

Mark was right, though. Seeing that he knew about Nettie, that he was in a way complicit in her downfall, makes her see him in a different light. She had looked up to Dr. Mark Teague. Thought he was one of the good guys. A little selfish, a little childish, but ultimately someone she could count on. Instead, he'd been a coward and let a teenager die right in front of him. He'd ended up collecting this information and sending it to Carina, but more to assuage his own guilty conscience than because he felt it was the right thing to do. She's not exactly doing the right thing for altruistic reasons, either. Her own sins haunt her.

After stepping out of the shower, she towels herself off. The reflection in the mirror still looks like a stranger's. Will she ever grow used to this new face? Her old face bore bruises from her father. That's the face she wore when she experimented on humans at Sudice. That's the face that she wore in the Zeal-scape, enacting countless horrors.

Snarling at her new features in the mirror, she pulls her lips back from her teeth like a wolf. Then she turns away from the mirror, drying her hair and slipping into more replicator-ordered clothes. She looks at the face long enough to carefully apply makeup.

She finally forces herself to leave her room. The Trust are awake and gathered in the lounge, and they look at her as if they know exactly what she's done. The last time they saw her was in the hovercar, when she was a wreck in withdrawal from a small dose of Zeal. It's going to be worse this time. It already claws at the edges of her awareness. Time to get it over with before she locks herself in her room and muffles her screams into a pillow. She doesn't remember what she did, just the confused thrum of want and need. Did she hurt any of them? She can't meet their eyes, instead perching in an armchair a little out of the way.

Raf and Charlie are tinkering with new kit they ordered after losing everything at the silo, making sure it's all in working order. Dax is resting on the sofa, eyes closed as he reads something on his tablet. It'd be a cozy scene, except for how keyed up everyone is. Carina, as usual, feels like an interloper.

The black sheep of this family. Someone they're only tolerating until they've received everything they need from her. One image left. If she unlocks the information from Nettie's mismatched eyes, will they kick her out, and will she still want to leave? She could finally try her code and see if it helps or fries her neurons into dust.

"I take it the fourth image has finished downloading," Carina says.

Charlie nods. "Me and Raf went through a bit of it. Decided to wait for you and Dax. He just woke up. We need to accelerate our time plan. They'll start testing early versions of those new implants for reviews any day now, if they haven't already. We can't let them roll out Pythia large-scale."

"Those memories Mark sent are going to give me nightmares for weeks. That poor girl." Raf bends his head, turning a piece of metal over in his hands.

Charlie projects the information onto the wallscreen. Carina is still tired, and the beautiful afterglow of Zeal is starting to recede. She's taken the pill Dax gave her, but it'll only buy her so much time. Her fingertips are already shaking. She stumbles into an armchair, massaging her temples. She has the beginnings of a migraine, a warbling aura wisping through her vision. She wants to go back to sleep even though it's only mid-morning.

They all give an involuntary intake of breath as Nettie's corpse flashes onto the screen again. It's a difficult image for those who aren't used to the sight of blood—and for those who are. Even Dax glances away from the unhealed sutures.

"Were you involved in this?" Charlie asks, gesturing to the frozen image of Nettie.

"No," Carina manages to say. "Mark found her after I left. She was supposed to be an intern. She was interested in the project. I think Mark let her try a brain map. Roz must have seen it, or I think Mark showed her. Roz realized Nettie would work for her next step. I think it's in those memories somewhere." Her head throbs, but she forces herself to rifle through the information. "There."

She wonders if Nettie's brain map was similar to Carina's teenage brain. Is that what drew Roz to her? Nettie looked like an echo of a younger Carina, except for those mismatched eyes. She can't help but feel guilty.

"So Mark was confessing his sins to you," Charlie muses, tapping a finger against her lip. "It was calculated, though. He's also, very deliberately, given us a human angle." Charlie brings up Nettie's school photo. Cute, smiling, heartbreakingly innocent. She'd never smile again.

The light from the wallscreen falls on Charlie, highlighting her red hair and the column of her neck. "We have plenty of intel and ammo from the images he's put in your head." Charlie moves closer to the wallscreen. "Humans need something concrete to focus their horror. Like Anne Frank's diary and the Holocaust. Like Lucas Hollander, a five-year-old boy who died of radiation poisoning and became the poster child of the Great Upheaval. Humans can't picture thousands of horrors; they can be very good at sticking their heads in the sand. Even if it's going to happen to them. Pythia would be so gradual, they wouldn't notice. Give it a personal angle, one person they connect to, and it's harder to ignore and push away."

"Hmm," Raf says. "You definitely have a point. We have evidence of Sudice tampering with stocks, of driving other businesses to bankruptcy and tightening its monopoly. Patenting everything. Umpteen white-collar crimes. They experimented on people in Carina's old project, but since they were criminals due to go into stasis, it won't have the same impact. Nettie, though—she had her whole life ahead of her, snuffed out for corporate greed. It's an angle the media can't ignore. Sickening, isn't it? She's already been killed and we'll have to hold up her image to help the world do the right thing? Add the threat of personality changing before it begins to happen. A combination of guilt and self-preservation is just the recipe for action."

Charlie nods. "It is. Poor Nettie. We send this out, with everything else, though, and I think we've got a shot."

"The other stuff is useful, too?" Carina asks. Dax gets up and goes to the kitchen, asking if anyone wants a drink. Everyone dutifully gives him their orders. Carina can tell by his slow steps that Dax is still feeling weak. She tries not to think about the kiss. Fails. The Zeal withdrawal is kicking in more strongly now. Her hands ball into fists.

Raf doesn't answer her right away. He's still flicking through the Blood information. "You've given me a golden ticket, Carina. Lots of information on servers. I think I can get us in, and we can blast it all across the world before Sudice can blink."

"Go in . . . ?" Carina asks. Mark had perhaps hinted at that.

Charlie nods. "This has been Raf's plan for a while. We have access to a lot of information thanks to that earlier Viper and your images, but any moment now, Sudice could discover Mitford's been compromised. It's better to delete it now so there's no chance of them tracing it back to us. We've copied as much info on the infrastructure of the Los Angeles headquarters, but their server's so cut off, the only way we can access it is to physically go in and blast it ourselves. If we connect to that server, there's no government or Sudice firewalls. Our information will go everywhere."

"Then we have to hope we can find a way out again," Carina says, voice quiet. With Nettie's image projected above them, none of the Trust can avoid wondering if they will make it out alive. Carina hopes they do. If she dies, though, life will go on. The world will not stop turning on its axis; barely anyone will miss her. She'll have done something worthwhile with her last few months. There are worse ways to go.

If she's gone, she won't feel that inevitable disappointment when, even confronted with cold, hard facts, people try to make excuses for what Sudice have done. The apologizts will come out in full force, or people will pretend their support of the company didn't directly lead to this being possible. Maybe it's better not to be around for that.

Carina blinks. She's recently found the thought of living not so bad, and now she's back to thinking impassively of death. She clenches her hands into fists again, the fingernails digging into the soft flesh of her palms, grounding her. The Zeal is already getting to her, dragging her back into those dark spirals of thoughts when the withdrawal wraps around her.

"Do we have a definite way to get to the server?" she asks, trying to distract herself from her humming body. "That place is a fortress." She remembers the specs. The San Francisco office is huge, and the Los Angeles one is not much smaller, especially when you consider the recently added floating offices. There are security bots that run Wasp AIs, VeriChip checkpoints on every floor and at every door, including elevators. There are also Wasps within the servers if anyone tries to access the system from inside. Raf's Viper might be able to mitigate those. Not many human guards, though—why have fallible humans susceptible to bribes, when you can have perfect, Sudice-made machines? Unless Pythia works, and Roz can mold loyal employees to her will.

Raf smiles. "We'll find a way. Every safe can be cracked. Every castle can be stormed. No one else has been stupid enough to go after Sudice like this. Physical breaking and entering is so last century."

Carina manages something resembling a smile and heaves herself off the chair. "By all means, continue the plan for storming the castle. But my head is killing me. I'll go check on Dax in the kitchen, maybe see if he has anything for it, then go lie down."

Charlie and Raf murmur their goodbyes, but their eyes are sharp. They know she took Zeal. Surely they can see how she's unraveling.

Carina walks into the kitchen. Dax already has the tray loaded with drinks. He takes one look at her. "You need another pill." He takes it from his pocket, hands it to her. Always prepared.

She swallows it dry. "I'm not the one who's just made a daring getaway from the hospital after being shot."

"True," he says. "I was very daring." He flashes her a smile that makes the world seem to tilt beneath her. Carina takes her mug and sits at the table, staring into its milky depths.

Dax takes the other drinks through and returns a few moments later. An apology for the kiss is on her lips, but she can't feel sorry for it. In many ways, it had been her first real kiss, Zeal afterglow or not. One she'd wanted, rather than simply accepted and endured. Just a kiss. Yet so much more.

"You OK?" he asks.

"The pill's helping, but I have a migraine."

"I'm not surprised, with what you've just had shoved into your head. That'd have killed most people."

"Mm."

Dax leads her back to his room. His movements are slow. "How are you feeling?" she asks him. "I mean, really?"

"Not that bad, actually. The doctors at the hospital did a good job patching me up, but running at top speed to escape the hospital wasn't really ideal for still-healing muscles. In a few days, I should be back to normal. I have some headaches, though not as bad as yours, I'm guessing."

"That's good." The pain of the migraine rises again, drowning out thought. She groans.

"Lie down in my room and I'll get you something for it."

"Thank you, doctor." She's not been in his room before, but she's in too much pain to investigate. She crawls under the covers, not even bothering to take off her slippers. She lies down, eyes shut. Dax dims the lights to spare her eyes and she hears him rummaging through his medicine bag.

He asks her questions about her symptoms and she gives quick, terse replies. On hearing her vision is affected, he places small electrodes on her head. They tingle.

"Are you shocking me?" she asks.

"It's just TMS. Less invasive than intense painkillers. You don't need more drugs in your system if we can treat it another way."

Electrodes remind her of so many things. She used them to plug into the Zealscape, placing the rounds on her skin to hear Mark's last message. She used them on her subjects at Sudice. She attached them to her skin before slipping into VR at the silo, resulting in Wasp attacks, her killing and Dax nearly dying. Used electrodes to transfer Mark's information to the Trust's servers. Electrodes have caused her so much pleasure and pain.

The tingling against her skin does soothe the static of her mind, chasing away the tension and anxiety. Dax brushes a lock of hair away from her forehead when it falls too close to an electrode. She startles.

"Sorry," he says. She's not sure if he's apologizing for startling her or for pulling away from that kiss.

"I never choose to touch people usually," Carina says. It's not an accusation, but an explanation. "Before, it seemed useless. After, it felt like too much. Like I can't hold myself together so close to someone else." She lies there, muscles stiff again, the electricity irritating rather than calming. Tentatively, she asks, "Could you do that again?" She regrets the words as soon as they leave her mouth.

She's certain he'll turn her down, but instead, he moves closer. His fingertips dance gently over her scalp, then slide lower to knead at the stiff muscles of her neck and upper shoulders. Her eyes close. After a time, his hands move back to her hair, gently removing the electrodes. While she dozes, not quite asleep and not quite awake, Dax strokes his fingers through her hair. It's the most comforting thing she's felt in years. Maybe, even, in her entire life.

THIRTY-FOUR

CARINA

The Trust headquarters, Los Angeles,
California, Pacifica

Carina wakes up in Dax's bed, confused. Dax sleeps in the arm-chair, curled up on his side, legs against his chest and arms loosely around his knees. His face is relaxed, open. Vulnerable. Her hunter instincts rise—he would be so easy to surprise, to take. More deliberately than she ever has before, she pushes those thoughts away. Dax is not prey.

Carina's headache is gone. It's evening, the time she should be thinking about settling down to sleep, but now she's wide awake. They slept through dinner. She wonders what the others must have thought.

Carina stretches, deciding Dax's bed is far more comfort-able than hers. She hasn't felt so well rested in years. She inves-tigates his room. It's tidy, but personalized. He has a beadwork medallion necklace hanging over his bed. She wonders if it was his sister's. Carved redwood figurines of animals line the shelves. There are no holographic images of his family, though. It takes her a moment to realize why: if this place is ever com-promised, why telegraph images of your loved ones to whoever breaks in?

Dax shifts in his chair, his features wrinkling. Should she wake him or let him sleep?

One of his legs falls from the chair, then spasms. He grimaces, his eyes pressing together tightly. His muscles jerk in a way that's disturbingly familiar. Her mental alarm bells sound.

"Dax," Carina says. "Dax, wake up."

His eyes snap open. He blinks rapidly, but his eyes are clear. "We . . . fell asleep."

"Do you feel all right?"

"I feel fine."

She frowns, but lets it go. His muscles have calmed. Perhaps it was only a bad dream.

They leave the room. Carina is the hungriest she's been in ages. Dax orders mac and cheese with sliced hot dogs for both of them. He says it was his favorite comfort food growing up, and Carina practically inhales it. She still watches Dax closely. The skin below his left eye twitches, once, then stops.

"Dax," she tries. "Can I double-check something with you?"

"Check what?"

"When you were sleeping, you started twitching. Has that ever happened to you before?"

He frowns. "No. Not as far as I know, anyway. No one I've shared my bed with accused me of kicking." He gives her a half-smile.

She stays serious. "How long have you been having headaches?"

"Ever since the hospital."

"Upset stomach?"

He frowns. "A little."

"That's what I thought. Let's get you into that Chair, then."

"Why?"

"Just trust me. Please."

"OK." He leaves the rest of his food. He stands, stumbles, his eyes unfocusing.

"What's wrong?"

He tries to speak. Can't form the words. Aphasia.

"Shit." She grabs him, leading him out of the kitchen. He keeps stumbling, closing his eyes against the dizziness he must feel.

The Trust are still awake in the lounge.

Carina strides through, and they watch her. "What's going on?" Charlie asks.

Carina doesn't answer. "She wants . . . to check something," Dax manages to say, his voice slurred.

"Check what?" Charlie asks. "What's wrong?"

"Just trust me," Carina repeats. Her heart hammers in her throat. "Open up the room with the Chair."

Charlie and Raf follow, and Raf opens the door. "I've changed the codes," he said. "You won't be getting back in here without me."

"Fine," she says, though the addict part of her mind wants to snap at him.

She straps Dax in, working quickly. His arms and legs are twitching again.

"I want to know what you're doing to Dax," Charlie says.

"I think Dax is exhibiting early signs of a stroke."

"I could check myself over," Dax says. "I am . . . a doctor." He's speaking as though his tongue is swollen.

"I have more experience with the brain than you. Do you have a recent brain scan stored on the servers?"

He thinks. "S-s-six . . . months ago." He pauses as she accesses his implants, and then projects the scan above their heads. Carina's face tilts as she examines it, memorizing its shape and the locations of the implants. "OK. That seems normal. Lie back. I'm going to take another."

"But what—" Raf starts.

"Shut up," Carina snaps. "Let me work."

"You like to kill people. And we all saw how you were in the hovercar. You almost turned against us."

The room falls silent.

Carina pauses in her prep. Charlie and Raf both seem suspicious. The tension grows.

Dax opens his mouth, but words have fled again. Not a good sign.

"She wanted to kill you on the way to the hospital, Dax," Raf says. "She might have tried if Kivon hadn't tied her up. He's worried about her presence here. We all saw it, and it's hard to pretend we didn't. What's to stop you from simply frying his implants? Isn't that what you did to your subjects at Sudice?"

"Dax's are going to fry of their own accord if you don't let me do my job," Carina says. They look stricken. "If I was going to kill any of you, you'd all be dead by now. Starting to reconsider you, though." She narrows her eyes at Raf, and blood drains from his face. Carina gives him a brilliant smile. "Joke!"

Dax lies back. "Not . . . funny. Go. Trust . . . you."

No one else says a word. Carina starts the scan.

Dax's new brain map appears above them, overlaying across the old one. Everyone gives a quick inhale. Dax opens his eyes.

"M-my . . ."

"Your implants have doubled because," Carina says, slowly, "someone put extra ones in."

Complete silence in the room.

"You've been turned into a sleeper agent. My guess is for

Sudice." She crouches in front of Dax, glaring into his eyes. "Hello, Roz."

Dax's eyes widen. "I'm . . . n-not a spy." His breath catches. He looks around at them, pleadingly. Carina wonders if he's thinking of Tam, and how he'd been afraid she'd given up information that resulted in her coma.

"We know you're not a spy," Charlie says. "Not willingly. Jesus Christ. Has she changed his personality, too?"

Carina shakes her head. "No evidence, and that would take too long. She would have had to be there herself. The implants were injected when he was unconscious."

"What do we do? How long has this been happening?" Carina sees the gears in Charlie's head turning. How much have they said in front of Dax? Is their entire plan blown?

Dax swallows, shakes his head from side to side.

"The hospital. At least, I think so." Carina checks his vital signs. So far they're fairly stable, considering the amount of impetus his brain is getting.

"Two days. It has to be. Otherwise I guess it'd be months ago." Charlie bites her lip.

"Or someone else within the Trust did it," Carina forces herself to say. Raf looks at her. "It wasn't me, for the last time. I'm the one who pointed it out."

"Cut it out, Raf. It wasn't any of us. It had to have been at the hospital," Charlie says.

"I'm inclined to agree," Carina says. "The implants look like they're rejecting. And if they'd put them in months ago, they'd be stable, and Sudice would have already nabbed us long before the silo. One well-placed bribe at the hospital, though, it's comparatively easy."

Dax shivers. Tears fall down his cheeks, but he doesn't sob. Carina can't imagine what he must be feeling. Someone hacked into his brain without his knowledge. Violation of the highest degree. "F-fix," he says, staring at her, unblinking.

"I will. I promise. I'll have to put you under."

He takes a steadying breath. Manages to give a jerky nod.

Before she inserts the needle, Carina looks deep into Dax's eyes. "I'm going to kill you for this, Roz Elliot. Really fucking slowly and painfully." Dax's eyes narrow in satisfaction. *I'll help*, is what he would say if he could, but the aphasia is growing worse.

Carina sends him under.

•

"OK. We need to get out of here five minutes ago," Charlie says.

"We should operate now," Carina protests.

"No. If they've latched onto his implants, they'll probably have put a tracking device in him, too. They're coming. Raf, grab the essential kit. I'll carry Dax and start up the hovercar. Carina, come with me. Raf, you'll start scanning Dax for tracking devices as soon as we move out."

"We should check no one else has been compromised either. Everyone needs a brain scan once we're in the hovercar," Carina says. "Check me, too."

"Right. OK."

Raf rushes back to them, arms full of metal.

"Let's move out!" Charlie calls. Raf, Charlie—holding Dax—and Carina all pause at the door of the garage. They realize at the same time that they're leaving these headquarters and not coming back. Carina will take nothing with her, just as she arrived. Charlie dims the lights.

"Goodbye, Technodrome," Raf says.

"Maybe we can come back again," Carina tries.

"Maybe," Charlie echoes, but they all know it's a lie.

•

They've put Dax in the back partition of the hovercar, on the long padded bench seats, wrapped in a sensory deprivation helmet Raf remembers they have. Just in case Sudice can still access his implants when he's unconscious.

The hovercar rises above the Los Angeles skyscrapers. It's still full night, a few stubborn stars shining through the clouds. Below them, the world is a lit mosaic. She wonders which lights are grimy Zeal lounges. A few dozen in a city of millions. So many people below, living their lives, not knowing their very autonomy is at stake. Some of them might even welcome it. Ignorance is bliss.

Raf has scanned for tracking devices and finds none, on them or within the hovercar. Sudice must have thought the extra implants would be enough. They all take brain scans, but their implants seem unchanged. One small relief.

They fly higher, leaving the other hovercars behind. The dashboard beeps as they cross the Hollywood hills. A calm, robotic female voice says, "Proximity warning."

Charlie keys in a sequence on the control panel and sends it out to the sky. The hovercar pauses, engines near silent. Carina looks down through the wisps of clouds. They're almost directly above the Hollywood sign, and the rest of Hollywood is laid below them in another glittering tapestry. Carina feels something resembling a smile cross her face as she realizes where they're going.

A few people live up here in the Apex, among the clouds. The crème de la crème of celebrities. It only opened a few years ago, when technology allowed the creation of floating mansions. The elite did not hesitate to move in and design their own palaces. Passing this invisible sky gate to their floating neighborhood is harder than getting into the most exclusive gated community on the ground. The only people who live here have a social ranking within the top three hundred. To compare, Carina's ranking is somewhere in the thirty-eight millions, not that she cares.

"Friends in high places, Charlie?" she asks.

Charlie flashes her a smile. The control panel beeps. "Proceed," the robotic woman instructs.

They fly through, the force field temporarily lifted. All the floating mansions are miles apart, glowing softly through the clouds. Every one they pass seems to defy belief. One seems to be a futuristic fairy-tale castle of ice, crystal and chrome. Another is low and long, black and red, the perfect evil villain's stronghold. Another looks like a jungle tree house and another like a strangely luxurious army bunker, complete with a full submarine out front. The sky is the limit, here.

Charlie navigates between the houses. Carina's stomach drops as she remembers something. "Charlie, doesn't Alex Mantel live here?" She remembers reading an article complaining about it—he was the only non-entertainment celebrity up here.

Raf hisses as he inhales.

"He used to," Charlie says. "Moved out a few years ago. Lives in an even more exclusive patch of sky all his own."

"He'd still have access to get in, though?" Carina asks.

"Yeah, but again, this is his old backyard. I don't think he'll look here, especially if we get Raf to set up some false trails."

Raf nods. "I can do that."

Charlie turns the hovercar and they pull in front of a mansion made all of smooth white stone, as if the clouds have shaped themselves into a modern Olympus. Carina half expects an angel to emerge, large wings spread.

Charlie pulls the hovercar in front of the wide drive. There is a second invisible force field around the house, and again, Charlie types in a code and waits. If she tries to go through it without approval, the hovercar will stall and reverse. The robotic woman soon welcomes them, and they fly through. Charlie lands in the drive and kills the engine. The place is huge— acres of floating house and grounds. There are gardens, pools, garages full of the best hovercars on the market. How many Greenview Houses would this mansion fetch? Carina guesses at least a dozen.

Who lives here?

The front door opens, a robotic droid flying out and standing sentry. They file out of the hovercar, cautiously. Charlie carries the unconscious Dax, his head still covered by the deprivation helmet. Just in case.

Charlie leads the way to the grand, sweeping stairs and the front door. The butler droid bows to them all, which strikes Carina as a little over the top. One droid takes Dax in its arms and floats away. Carina watches him go, nervous to have him out of her sight. They step across the threshold, and the sense that they've left the real world behind only grows. The Apex is another realm entirely.

Inside the house is as pale and pure as the outside. White marble floors and columns, like the interior of a Grecian temple crossed with a starship. There is no dust anywhere, and white vases filled with magnolias ring the round, bare walls, the only ornamentation besides the columns and the sweeping double staircase to the rest of the house. Its simplicity telegraphs wealth.

Whoever lives here has no human servants. More droids, as white as their surroundings, flit through the white ballroom to the doorways leading to other wings of the house. One peels away to assist the butler droid in taking their coats and few belongings.

Charlie's face turns up, and her face breaks into a radiant smile. Carina has never seen her wear one like it before. The rest of the Trust follow her gaze to the figure at the top of the grand stairs. Carina's mouth drops open.

"We're meant to be lying low and you take us to Isaac fucking Clavell?" Raf asks, the words too loud, echoing in the empty ballroom.

"Because Isaac fucking Clavell is the only man in Los Angeles with security to rival Sudice's," he says, descending the stairs for his grand entrance. "And that's exactly what you need just now."

Carina blinks as he comes closer. They move forward to meet him in the middle of the grand ballroom, following Charlie like nervous ducklings.

Isaac Clavell is the prime actor of cinema. Plug into the VR at any theater, and one of his many films will be in the selection. Action, romance, nail-biting thrillers, thoughtful character pieces, tear-jerking biopics—he's done them all, and will do many more. He's been headlining films for the last twenty years, and probably has another thirty or forty years in him. When people tire a little of his face and image, he goes to the best flesh parlor in Hollywood and emerges with a whole new face, takes a different role from his recent fare, and lets the audience fall in love with him all over again.

Isaac's been wearing his current face for a few years. Carina remembers seeing some of his films in San Francisco while she worked at Sudice, and it's so strange to see that same face right before her. Like most people, she'd enjoyed his movies, especially after a long day of SynMaps trials and having to look into Subject B's brain.

Isaac Clavell is tall, but not too tall. Trim, but neither too skinny nor too muscular. His features and skin seem like they are from everywhere and nowhere, impossible to place. An aquiline nose, eyes that tilt up a little at the corners, a high fore-head and cheekbones, a generous mouth and a little cleft in the chin. A dazzling smile, teeth impossibly white. He's uncommonly beautiful, even for a world where everyone looks their best. He's dressed in a suit that seems simple, all cream and pale blue, but she's sure it's worth more than she made in a year at Sudice.

"Charlie," he says, his voice colored by his warm smile. He holds out his arms and she gives him a firm hug. He squeezes her back just as tight, his winning celebrity smile softening into something resembling a true one.

"Where have you taken Dax? Do you have a Zeal Chair and a wallscreen?" Carina asks. "That's all I need, plus Raf and Charlie to lend extra hands."

"Of course. Please follow me." He makes his way across the marble floor, Italian shoes clicking compared to the duller thumps of the Trust's practical rubber soles. He leads them down wide white corridors that remind Carina—painfully, sharply—of her old Green Star Lounge.

Isaac opens one of the doors and motions them inside. The room is gray. A blank palette for Isaac's own fantasies, if he ever plays with Zeal in here. What would the man who has everything dream about?

The robot has laid Dax in the Chair already. His blindfold and earplugs have been removed. Charlie brushes the hair back from Dax's face, her features concerned.

"Don't say anything incriminating. You." Raf gives a pointed look to Clavell. "Don't speak, in case they recognize your voice."

Isaac gives them a bland smile.

"Someone strap him in and prep the Zeal," Carina says. She leaves the rest of the words unspoken: *I don't trust myself enough to do it.*

Charlie prepares the syringe expertly. It's a tiny dose, just enough to prep the implants to make it easier for Carina to manipulate the code. To find out what Roz has done, find the link back and sever it. After, she'll want to flush his implants and put in new neural dust entirely. Can they trust Isaac to order that for her without detection? She wants to know why Charlie's put their lives in Isaac Clavell's hands, but there's no time.

Focus. Focus. Carina turns away as Charlie slides the needle into the crook of Dax's arm. She wants to take his place and disappear. It would take less than three minutes once she's back in a Zealscape to create and kill a victim. Three minutes until that sweet release.

Focus. Focus.

Dax's body relaxes. Carina takes a deep breath, feeling as though she's almost slid back in time to when she was a brainhacker at the top of her game. She draws up Dax's new brain map taken in the Trust headquarters and compares it with the old one again. Algorithms count the neural dust implants, highlighting the new ones. She'll start with these, deactivating and setting them to self-destruct and flush from the system. They blip off the map, like stars going out. Within twelve hours, they'll have dissolved. No trace left.

The Trust and Clavell are watching her every move. She can't think about them. She can't think about that deep, throbbing desire she still has for Zeal. She can only concentrate on the code. The letters, the numbers, the commands. No mistakes.

The code floats around her, transparent and multicolored. She could have gone full VR for ease of seeing the relationships, but that would require Zeal. She has to keep her head together. Carina steps from side to side to access different parts of the code, fingers moving through the air almost as if she's conducting a symphony. She remembers this dance. It's both soothing and electric. Once, she knew the steps so well she could do it in her sleep.

Now, it's so much harder. The implant interfaces are slightly different than they were over a year ago. Sweat gathers on her temples. Her muscles shake as badly as they did during her Zeal withdrawal. One mistake, and she could fry Dax's brain. Like what happened to his sister. Like what she did to Subject B and Subject E. Dax's brain could be so overexposed to data that it gives him a heart attack and a stroke in front of another room of witnesses.

At the thought of those long-ago, real-world kills, her face flushes. Isaac Clavell even reminds her slightly of Subject B, in looks if not in manner. That old-school Hollywood charm, perfectly styled and coiffed, a smile that shows too many teeth. What would Carina find in his memories, if she peeked beneath his skull?

Focus, goddammit. Focus.

Carina moves through the code. It feels so slow, so clumsy. Dax's new implants are gone, but she still hasn't found the link back. It's as if she's tiptoeing through his brain, and it's so full of trip wires that one wrong move and all alarms will sound with disastrous consequences.

There. She's found the threat. Carefully, so carefully, she begins to dismantle it, like untying a particularly tricky knot in a necklace chain. Pull the wrong way and it only grows tighter, until your fingernails find no purchase.

Finally, it unravels. She snips the code. Back at Sudice headquarters, Roz will know. It's the middle of the night, but Carina guesses she'll likely be sleeping fitfully on the hard sofa of her office, like she did for so many nights in San Francisco. Right now, alarms are sounding, and Roz will blink sleep from her eyes and go on the hunt. She'll be desperate to find them, and Carina has to hope that Clavell's security is as good as he claims.

Dax's heartbeat speeds, slows and then stops.

Carina wastes no time. An implant is anchored to the medulla oblongata, the area of the brain controlling heart rate, blood pressure and respiration. This is new—she didn't know Sudice were capable of doing something like this. She works at the code around the section of implants, trying to stop it, but everything seems to snap. Dimly, she can sense the others' distress. Raf is crying, Charlie is doing CPR, Clavell stands well out of the way.

Carina types, hoping her intuition is right, and then slams the code into the implant area, restarting the neural dust.

Dax's heart starts again, fitfully at first before settling back into its usual rhythm. He gasps, eyelids twitching, mouth opening and closing, but he's still unconscious. Raf laughs and Charlie joins in. Carina doesn't.

Dax's eyes are open, his mangled implants still able to project a recording onto the white ceiling for all to see.

It's a recording of Carina in the Zealscape. It's an older one, Carina thinks, which is no less unnerving. Roz must have known where she was in LA and bribed an orderly to record a dream, something they weren't meant to do in the Zealot lounges.

How long has Roz been watching her dreams?

Now, the rest of the Trust are witness to one of her darker, depraved fantasies. It's a slice of Carina cutting open a middle-aged woman, mouth open in a rictus scream. Carina carefully snips the arteries of the heart and draws it from the open sternum, the ribcage spread like wings, blood slick in her bare hands.

To clear any potential confusion, Roz chose the clip well. Carina looks up at a mirror on the ceiling of the room in her dream Greenview House. There's her old face and blonde hair, cheeks flushed, pupils wide. The recording ends and Dax slumps against the Chair. A sting in the tail, like Mark's first image.

Dax groans, waking up. He missed the recording, at least. Everyone else stares at her in fear, though Clavell's is tinged with confusion—he doesn't recognize her older features in the recording.

No one says anything. Carina shuts down the programs, the code disappearing in the air. Charlie unlaces Dax from the Chair and he struggles to his feet.

Carina leaves the room. She can hear them murmuring, hesitant and hushed. Isaac is silent, but Carina knows he's taking everything in.

She ignores them all, walking through those stark corridors. Something stirs in her for the first time in a long while: shame. It's keen enough to cut her. She didn't kill that woman in real life, but what does that matter? The intent was there. It still is. They saw how close she came to losing it after Dax was shot. They're all terrified of her. She can't blame them.

One of the robot assistants floats to her in the hallway.

"Would you like me to show you to your room, Madame?" The robot asks in its smooth, modulated voice.

"Yes."

She follows it through the hallway, up the grand set of stairs, to the east wing of the house. The robot shows her a room and leaves, the door clicking shut behind her. She falls face first onto the white, clean bed, leaving her shoes on. Freshly replicated clothing is folded neatly on the dresser. She has no other possessions in the world. Once, she'd had savings, an entire wardrobe of designer clothes, a career, an apartment all her own, a life. A flawed life, perhaps, with everyone kept at a distance.

The withdrawal pulses through her, hot and intense. She balls her hands into fists. It's more manageable than the night of the detox, but she still feels as though ants crawl underneath her skin.

She'd let herself grow closer to her team at Sudice than anyone else. Mark. Kim. Aliyah. Even Roz, in her own way. Look what had become of them. Mark murdered by Roz. Kim stuck working for a company she knows is evil. Aliyah is on the other side of the continent in Boston in Atlantica, hoping it's enough distance that Roz leaves her alone. And Roz is determined to kill Carina, their once almost-friendship turned to the purest hatred.

Closing her eyes, she tries to quiet her mind. She doesn't want to think about Sudice, her team, the SynMaps brain trials. About all the Zeal dreams she still misses. About the look on the rest of the Trust's faces when they saw, in high definition, exactly what she is.

THIRTY-FIVE

DAX

The Apex, above Hollywood, Los Angeles,
California, Pacifica

The first thing Dax sees when he wakes up is Isaac Clavell's face, and he thinks he must surely be dreaming. He thinks it until Charlie takes the needle from his arm and it hurts like hell.

Charlie fills them in. He grew worse. They came to Clavell's. Carina helped him.

"Where is she?" he asks.

"In her room." A pause, a sidelong glance.

"What aren't you telling me?"

"Roz Elliot put in a booby trap. Once Carina severed the link, we all got a front-row seat to one of Carina's Zeal dreams."

"Oh." Dax's stomach clenches.

"Oh," Charlie agrees, grim.

"Where is she?" he asks again.

"One of my bots will show you," Isaac Clavell says, all smooth charm. "She's in the east wing."

"Um. Thank you." He's never really met anyone famous before. He's not starstruck, but he doesn't know how to act around someone who holds their lives in his well-manicured hands.

Dax follows the bot through Clavell's lavish home. He's too tired, his head too tender, to be amazed at the luxury surrounding him. He focuses instead on trying not to think about what has just happened. When he reaches Carina's door, he gives a tentative knock.

"Not now," he hears faintly, as if her face is pressed into the pillow.

"Carina," he says.

A pause. Then: "Fine. Come in."

The door slides open, and Dax slips inside. The room looks like the rest of the house: pristinely pure. There are no sharp edges; all is oblong and smoothed. Bookshelves are built into recesses in the walls, a low bench topped with satin pillows emerging from another. Carina draws herself up from the oval bed with effort. Her face is smooth; he has no idea what she's thinking or feeling. He finds the stillness unnerving.

"I'm a bad neuroprogrammer," she says, voice flat. "Running off without doing tests. I'll check you over now."

Dax's nerves spike. "Did you get everything? What if this is still recording? They'll know exactly where we are."

"Shh, don't worry. I got it all. I'm checking your basic physical responses. You're up and moving and speaking, so that's good." She holds up a finger. "Follow this."

His eyes dutifully move side to side.

"Your pupils are normal. Good. Any headache? Auras, warbling vision?"

"No. That all seems fine."

"Can you access your implants?"

He tries. "No."

"Good. I blocked them. You won't be able to access them until we flush your neural dust and put in new ones. I need to figure out where to get it. Clavell might be able to help, but . . ."

"But you don't exactly trust him."

"No. Do you?"

"No."

"Good call." She pauses. "Well, most things seem fine from my end. What're your doctor senses saying?"

Dax pauses, closing his eyes and focusing inward. He checks his heartbeat. Goes to the bathroom and looks in the mirror at the whites of his eyes (a little bloodshot, but not too bad), and his skin (a little paler than usual, but nothing to worry about). He comes back. "I'm OK. Physically and mentally sound, at least until the next catastrophe comes along." Dax leans against the smooth, white wall of the room. He feels his face crumple. "They went into my mind, Carina. They let the doctors heal my body and they ravaged my brain." It is a violation of the worst kind. They had brain recorded his thoughts, his memories, his feelings.

"Looks like Roz managed to finally finesse brain recording. I guess she'd have had to, to have Pythia up and running smoothly. Similar amount of processing required by the brain. If they manage not to overload most people, then it's an acceptable level of risk."

Dax shudders.

"Sorry. Old habits. But I am sorry. That it happened to you." The words sound stilted, empty. She's trying.

"I don't know if you can fully understand how horrible this is for me. My body . . . has always been important to me. I mean, it is to everyone, but *especially* to me. I fit it to match my identity. I made it mine, in a way most people don't. I treat it well. It took time for me to be comfortable in it, but now I am."

"I understand, though I can't pretend I treated my body well."

The side of his mouth quirks. "No. Not particularly. But

to learn someone's been in my head, done whatever they wanted . . ." He trails off, unable to find the words.

"You've never doubted your mind. Your mind always knew you were Dax. Your mind is a doctor's. Strong, smart, capable. Your mind has shaped everything."

"Yes. I could always trust it, even if I couldn't trust my body. I feel so exposed."

Carina hesitates. She's not used to comforting people, Dax realizes. She's never had the cause. Never really let herself grow close enough. The fact she's trying, even if she's doing a monumentally bad job at it, is actually comforting.

"What they did to you . . ." she tries, "is inexcusable."

"It's not surprising," he says. "It's what Sudice do, isn't it? They think of people as expendable, to use or destroy in pursuit of profit. I was lucky compared to Nettie." His throat closes.

Carina grabs his hand, clutching it hard. "We'll make them pay, Dax. We'll make them pay for what they did to you. To Nettie. To me. To the others. We won't let them do it to everyone else."

His hand hurts, but he doesn't pull away. His eyes sting, filling with tears he doesn't want to let fall. They do, though he doesn't sob. Carina sees, but she doesn't look away in embarrassment. Her eyes may be dry, but they blaze. She moves closer to him. She doesn't kiss him, but she does embrace him.

It's an awkward hug. She's stiff and not sure where to put her hands. He pulls her closer to him, burying his face in her purple hair, his arms around her back. He feels her breath against the collar of his shirt. He slows his own breath, steadies it, breathing in her scent. It helps him come back to himself. She gradually relaxes, too.

"I can't remember the last time I hugged anyone," she murmurs against his neck.

Dax gives a strangled laugh. It's tinged with pity. He hugged Tam every day before she was injured, and the rest of the Trust are fairly affectionate, giving hugs or slaps on the back. He can't imagine living life an arm's distance away from everyone, never touching.

"I think I do remember," she says after some thought. "It's been seven years. The last person to hug me was my mother."

Dax sobers. He wants to ask, but senses she might not respond and is too raw himself to have a request rebuffed.

"We will get Roz Elliot and Sudice," he says instead. "For what they did to me, and for what they did to you."

She pulls away a few inches, looks into his eyes. They're about the same height. "What she did to me wasn't near as bad. She has good reasons to be pissed off at me."

"What did you do?" He's desperate to stop focusing on what Sudice did to him. He wants more fuel for his hatred of the company.

Carina sighs. "The short version is that, when we started SynMaps, brain recording was killing people almost one hundred percent of the time, usually within a few minutes. I think Roz probably started that when she first experimented on me, and the project stalled for ten years. When she convinced Sudice to start it up again, they sent us criminals who should have been put in stasis as subjects. Sudice bankrolled it all. Two subjects almost died. Under my care." She pauses, staring into space.

"You tried to kill them."

A slow blink. "I did."

Dax suppresses a shiver. He is glad he didn't see the Zealscape recording. "How?"

"I induced strokes or heart attacks."

He swallows. "Like what could have just happened to me."

"It's probably where she got the idea, yeah." At his wince, she adds, "Sorry."

"Do you regret doing that?" he asks.

She considers. "I should lie and say yes, but I don't. The subjects were hardened criminals. A serial rapist and a serial killer. I had to leave before I got caught or my . . . impulses grew worse." Her voice is rough.

"You don't kill innocent people."

She opens her mouth. Closes it. She's acutely aware of his arms looped around her. "No. But I want to."

He shies away from that topic. "Tell me more about Roz."

"She's driven. A total perfectionist. Once, I liked and respected that drive. I thought she'd get results. If anyone could get us all to work together and solve brain recording, it'd be her. Then I realized that to do that, she'd stop at absolutely nothing. It scared me back then, and I left. I didn't put together what Roz did to me until Mark unblocked it from my mind. You didn't see the Zealscape recording Roz sent?" she asks.

"No." He'd overheard the others talking about it in hushed voices in the kitchen, though. Carina had cut a still-beating heart out of a woman. He's glad no one had the courage to tell him directly.

"OK."

He thinks about his words before speaking. "You don't have to be that person."

"I am that person." She pulls away then, perching on the bed. He sits next to her. Her fingers clench on the bed sheets. "You keep thinking of me as someone better than I am. Don't. It's dangerous. The others are right about me. I can't be trusted. I have one last image to unlock. If I can find it hiding in my memories, I'll give it to you guys, and then I'm out. My skills won't help break into Sudice's headquarters. You know that. I know that. Sudice knows that."

"You didn't feel for so long that you're still pretty good at pretending you don't care. I see through that."

"You've seen how my brain is breaking down."

"You're using that as an excuse. There are ways to work around it. I've looked at the code you designed. I think once the information is out of your head, it'll hold."

"You're not a neurologist."

"No. You are. I have faith you'll find a way to patch up the worst of what Roz did to you and become stable again."

"I think you're good at putting too much faith in me. And maybe I'm afraid of changing again. What if I don't like who I become?"

"You've already been self-medicating yourself with Zeal. This is simply a different, steadier approach. You'll still be you, just hopefully less . . . murderous. Is there a reason you were so reticent to pursue actual treatment and chose Zeal instead?"

She recoils from him, and he curses himself. He's struck a nerve. "Do you know how easy it would be for me to kill you right now?" she asks him, all sharp edges.

He raises his chin, exposing his neck. "Anyone can kill. You're very good at using that as an excuse to keep yourself withdrawn from the world. You literally ran away from the world and nearly killed yourself."

She looks like she's about to fly at him.

He stands. "I'll go. Maybe I spoke out of turn, but I think you needed to hear it."

She says nothing as he leaves. He wanders the hall for a second before a robot comes to lead him to his room. It's as pale and impersonal as Carina's.

He lies down on his bed, and misses Tam with a sudden intensity that takes his breath away. If only she were here. She'd sit at the side of his bed, take one look at him and know everything he was feeling. She would wrap her arms around him, squeezing tight. Dax would cry, as he is crying now. Tam would understand that this was his worst nightmare come true. No words would need to be said. She'd be there for him, as she always was.

She's not here now.

He lets himself feel all the emotions—the rage, the fear, the sadness. When they've all run their course, he's drained himself until there's nothing left. He drifts off into sleep, mercifully dreaming of nothing at all.

THIRTY-SIX

ROZ

Sudice headquarters, Los Angeles,
California, Pacifica

Roz works through most of the night, but it's no use. Carina has managed to snap the connection in Dax's brain and hide where she and the rest of the Trust are.

Roz was so close she could taste it. She switches off the wallscreen, screwing her eyes shut tight. She's in the main room with her team, deciding that completely cutting herself off wasn't helping morale. Around her, some of the most promising Sudice employees work, trawling through internet traffic with the Wasps, looking for anything they might have missed. Others search the Trust's headquarters. They are throwing so many resources into finding the hackers, and yet it's still as though they've disappeared off of the face of the planet.

At least she's had a small measure of revenge. Roz only found the memories from the Green Star Lounge a few weeks ago. Some orderly recorded all of Green Star Lounge's dreams on the side for a bit of extra profit. There's a small but growing black market of people who want to experience dreams they can't quite create themselves. It can give them ideas for new depravity when the old stuff grows stale.

Roz is proud of how she laid the trap, even if it didn't spring perfectly.

After the failed mission, she made sure the Wasps were sweeping hospital records for any John or Jane Does checked in. Sure enough, there was a John Doe at the hospital in the Port of Long Beach, and there was Dax. Lying right there in a bed, unconscious, as the doctors stitched him up. A perfect, helpless offering. She thought it would be easy.

"Should we bring him in?" Niall asked. "Get him to tell us what he knows?"

"No," she said. "I have a better idea." He could lead them right to the Trust. An inside viewpoint, to know exactly what their plans are.

She already had a draft of the code for extra brain recording implants, developed from SynMaps. It didn't take long to brush it up and fit it for her purposes. Roz slipped into the hospital herself to perform the procedure. She didn't have to cut him open. A simple connection of electrodes, drawing up the code for his implants and twisting it for her purposes. As she took off the electrodes, she pushed Dax's hair back from his forehead. "I'll find you, Carina Kearney," she whispered into his unconscious ear. All the while, Dax's attending, greedy doctor watched with hungry eyes.

She killed that doctor the following day, of course. Just to be safe. Poison in his coffee. Simple but effective.

She's now seen the world through Dax's eyes. In some respects, she actually experienced being Dax. She felt his love for the others in the group. Their closeness, their connection. His attraction to Carina. It made her uncomfortable, and still does, to feel those emotions, even secondhand through her own implants. The whole reason she's shut herself off from any feelings in the first place is that they're so . . . messy. It makes the world more logical to be without all that angst. So she watched impassively as Charlie cracked a joke with Raf, as Dax went to the kitchen to make drinks. She focused on Carina's face when she joined him, now changed entirely. Even though Carina's body has been brought back to health, Roz would still recognize her in a heartbeat.

And now all that work has been made redundant after only a few hours. Dax went to the kitchen just when the Trust were starting to discuss their plan. She managed to catch a little bit here and there, but Dax clattered the cups so much that he drowned out most of it. Fate's a fickle bitch.

Still, though, she has some crumbs. She can use those, and she will.

Roz needs a break. She leaves her team, eyes glazed as they stare at wallscreens and direct the Wasps. Back in her office, she collapses on the hard sofa. Her whole body is exhausted. She hasn't slept properly since coming to LA. The odd catnap here and there, but any longer periods of rest have her brainloading information that could prove useful.

Roz brings up Carina's Zealscape files. She's only been able to watch a small percentage of them so far. Every few hours, when she starts swaying from exhaustion, she comes up here and watches a few more. They sustain her. Carina's violence is almost beautiful in its cruelty. It's artistry, of the darkest kind. It rejuvenates Roz, and after a few minutes in these fantasies, she can return to work again.

She brings up another, leaning back her tired body to slip into Carina's mind. It's not a brain recording—Roz can't know exactly what Carina felt or thought during her trips.

She can imagine, though.

THIRTY-SEVEN

CARINA

The Apex, above Hollywood, Los Angeles,
California, Pacifica

Carina feels ill at ease in Clavell's sprawling mansion.

Every time she leaves her small room, she becomes lost in the endless corridors. There are areas of the house none of the Trust are meant to enter, and whenever they accidentally wander into them, the blank faces of the droid servants calmly usher them away.

The Trust are still formulating the attack on Sudice. They've all looked back at everything they said in front of Dax, and they don't believe they said anything too incriminating during his brief period as a sleeper agent. Just in case, though, they're shifting their plan. Originally, they'd thought to hit the Los Angeles headquarters. They have the blueprints, the air-gapped server layout, a way to get in. Trying to corrupt the air-gapped server remotely would take months, and they don't have months. They've evaded Sudice so far, but it's only a matter of time before they find them. Deep pockets, and a government in said pockets, will do that.

It makes sense, though traveling most of the way across the state as fugitives is risky. With luck, they can hit somewhere that won't be as fortified. Roz Elliot will still be in Los Angeles hunting for them. If Sudice did overhear anything through Dax's brain recording or implants, then they will probably be protecting the wrong headquarters.

They make sure Clavell doesn't know an iota of their plan. They have a room with no cameras, and not even a wallscreen. Raf shows them all the information on a retrofitted older tablet, practically an antique.

Clavell seems to enjoy the intrigue of it all. He gives the Trust their space, but in the evenings he invites them to elaborate meals in the grand dining room. They eat the best food Carina's ever eaten off expensive china, served by silent, faceless droids. No one seems particularly comfortable with the sumptuous surroundings except for Charlie. She's back in her element. Her table manners are impeccable, and Clavell has gifted her with designer clothes from the replicator, which she wears with flawless ease. Sitting next to Clavell, she'll tilt her head toward him, smiling. Carina is nearly one hundred percent sure that they were lovers before, and may or may not have fallen back into bed together. Sometimes one of them will rest a hand on the other's arm, or they'll make sure their shoulders brush as they walk along a corridor together, despite there being more than enough room. Carina wonders what it's like to feel comfortable around a person like that, so that a casual touch is as easy as breathing.

Four days pass. Their knowledge of the San Francisco headquarters is still not as thorough as the Los Angeles one, but they're hesitant to dig too deeply in case it sets off any sort of alarm.

"What about speaking to someone who still works there?" Carina asks, after a particularly frustrating afternoon trying to plan their entry point. "I might know someone. She could give us the passcodes or her employee badge. By far the simplest solution."

"That'd be hanging herself out to dry," Charlie says. "And I'm not sure if her employee badge would get us in so late. Might be a starting point, though. Who is she?"

"Dr. Kim Mata. One of the people I worked with on the brain recording project. She helped me escape from Roz before I met you." She fills them in on her street encounter and triggering both parts of the Bee. She's never gone into much detail before about that night she joined them.

"And you trust her?" Charlie asks.

"I think she's only one of a few people I do. The last time we spoke, though, she said that it would be hard to contact her directly, and she told me not to unless she could find a way to send me a safe word. I've never gotten one, so she must not have found a secure line. I used a subfrequency to contact her that first time, but perhaps she feels it's been compromised. So she could give us stuff, and I know she would; but meeting her would still be chancy."

Charlie wriggles her nose, thinking. "I might have an idea. Let me run it by Clavell."

"You said we weren't going to tell Clavell anything," Kivon says.

"I'm not going to tell him anything about what we're doing, obviously. I think there's a way we could get her and a few others here, though. A suitable disguise, enough of a cover that they wouldn't notice her sneaking in here as well."

Dax's eyebrows rise. "You're going to ask him to throw a party, aren't you? One of his over-the-top lavish ones, with hundreds of the biggest celebrities in Hollywood."

Charlie's face breaks into a wide grin. "You betcha."

•

Clavell lives alone in his house, rarely inviting guests. When he has a party, he throws the doors wide open to those exclusive enough to enter the Apex. He doesn't compromise security—he only invites people he knows. No plus ones allowed. Most of the inside of the mansion stays well locked, and guests know not to go looking for the keys. For them, this type of social event can mean a golden ticket of new film roles, and so his wishes are respected.

"I'm long overdue a soiree," Clavell says, flashing white teeth. "I've had several people pinging me asking when they might expect another. Are you sure you think it's a good idea?"

"Yes, but how would we sneak in some decidedly non-famous members?" Charlie asks.

"Might take some finagling—usually everyone at these parties more or less knows each other, but we can reinvent her as a potential new film star. Oh! Or I can make it a masked party, where everyone has to wear false faces. That'll be fun. I'll have their VeriChips scanned at the door for security, don't worry. And I do love a good party, don't you?" Again, that megawatt smile.

Carina's been spending some of her free time researching Clavell. She's never been one for looking up random titbits of celebrities' lives. She doesn't care who dates who, who has what ranking. He's made about fifteen films in the last two years. That seems to be a lot, but she's unsure what's considered normal.

Isaac Clavell was not born to Hollywood royalty. He grew up in the Great Plains area of the Formerly United States, not too far from Minneapolis. Clavell was scouted on a visit with his family to Los Angeles. He starred in his first film, *Actually, Love*, where he played a misogynist internet troll who falls in love with a feminist online, and that star continued to rise.

He's managed to stay away from the worst edges of celebrity gossip. No one could ever find proof of him cheating, or drinking to excess. No penchant for drugs, except for the occasional Zeal trip. Doesn't speak badly of those he works with, though several of his films have been associated with hefty lawsuits and scandals. Somehow, though, he manages to dodge these, no mud landing on his flawless shoes. He gives the right answers, the perfect smile, but underneath it, Carina is certain he's just playing another role, just like she has most of her life. Only he plays his a hell of a lot better, and gets paid for it.

Clavell begins to plan the party. Carina doesn't want to give him Kim's name initially. She chances the same subfrequency she used before to call Kim, when Roz confronted her after the chop shop; Raf helps her mask the location three times before she uses it, just in case. He sits cross-legged on the bed, resting his cheek on one hand, his old tablet balanced on his knee so he can follow along.

It takes a while, but Kim accepts the ping.

"Is this safe?" Carina asks. "Last time we spoke, you said you'd send me something, but you didn't."

"A safe word. Yeah. I tried, but I couldn't risk it, even with quantum cryptography. You changed your implants and Veri-Chip again, didn't you?"

They were all flushed when Dax changed her face. "Yeah."

"I can only promise it's me, and hope that's enough. I think this is safe, or reasonably. Call me back in five so I can make some safety arrangements on my end." Kim hangs up.

Carina brings up a timer in the corner of her ocular vision. As it counts down, she tries not to think about the fact that Kim could be pinging Sudice and turning her in at this very moment. She knows Kim well, or thinks she does. The timer beeps. She tries the subfrequency again. "Hi."

"Hi. I see they haven't caught you yet," Kim says.

"Not yet."

"Are you safe?"

Carina glances around at her surroundings. "Safe enough. I'm in a veritable fortress. We have a plan. We need your help."

"We? Wait, never mind, don't tell me over this line."

"Can we meet?"

"How? Where?"

"Can you get to LA?"

"I'm already here."

Suspicion flares within Carina. Raf raises an eyebrow. "Come again?" she asks.

"I know how that sounds. I'm here for a tech conference."

"When did you get here?"

"Yesterday. The conference starts tomorrow down in Anaheim. It's going to be mind-bogglingly boring. I'm meant to attend a lecture on VeriChip ghosts—people sending out false signals for bogus locations, that sort of thing. The guy giving the talk is an idiot, though. I could give a better presentation while half-asleep."

"I can't leave where I am for long, it's too dangerous. You'll have information we need, but to give it to us we'll need access to our tech. You can come to me. Tomorrow night."

"How?"

Carina tries to think of a way to phrase it so only Kim would know where she meant. Ah. Kim grew up in Los Angeles. "Remember the Christmas party?"

Kim laughs. "I'm missing bits of it from that home-brewed alcohol. And I remember the pain of it the next day."

"Remember your first memory? And where your mom took you after?" Santa Monica Pier.

"Yeah."

"A hovercar will meet you there. At the . . ." Carina tries to remember what's actually at Santa Monica Pier. "The closest cafe from the parking. Wear an evening dress."

"An *evening* dress?"

"Or a tux, whichever. Wear a coat over it so you don't stick out. And one of those masks to obscure your features and make you look like someone else."

"OK then. You've got me interested. Are you sure I have what you need?"

"God, I sure hope so."

"Can I bring a friend?"

That stops her. "What? Who?"

"Someone else you know is out here for the tech expo. The other member of our team." She's avoiding names, just in case.

Carina laughs. "OK, I think we can do that. The gang's all here."

"Not all of us."

They both quiet, thinking of Mark.

"See you tomorrow."

"Yes. Tomorrow."

The line goes dead.

Carina rubs her hands over her face. "I hope they can help us."

"We've got just enough without them that I think we can swing it, but anything they can offer will be helpful. Who's the other member of the team?" Raf asks.

"Aliyah. She still works for Sudice as well, but at the Boston branch."

"What was it like for them, after you left Sudice?" Raf asks. "My colleagues had a hard time of it when it was discovered I'd been the leak at the government. There'd been suspicions for months, but not many actually suspected me. I was pretty good at staying under the radar. Still, though. If it hadn't been me, I wouldn't have wanted to be in that office after I left."

Carina sighs. "I doubt it was particularly fun. The project limped on for a few more months. Roz got a stay of execution. Little did I know she was doing her experiment with Nettie. Creating Pythia. I wonder if Kim or Aliyah knew about that . . ." She trails off. "I hope they didn't. I don't know. I lost touch with them, did everything I could to forget about Sudice." *By then I was addicted to Zeal and didn't care about much of anything in this plane of reality,* she finishes mentally.

Raf lies back on the bed. He's wearing a T-shirt with a band on it Carina's never heard of. There are bags under his eyes. His dark hair falls into his eyes and he blows it out of the way, looking at her.

Carina's not sure what to do here. The only member of the Trust she really spends time with alone so far has been Dax, unless it's passing each other in corridors or ordering tea and coffee from the replicator at the same time. Especially after they all saw Roz's little gift, after Carina got rid of Dax's brain malware.

Carina fidgets. Raf opens an eye. "Do you want to watch a Clavell movie?"

Carina snorts. "In his house?"

"Why not, it'd be sorta funny. He has them all, of course. Vain man."

"You don't have work to do?" *Don't you want to run as far away from me as possible?*

Raf's mouth quirks up in a half-smile. "I'm here. You're here. Let's just watch the movie, OK? Don't overthink it."

"All right." She settles down into the bed, drawing the covers around herself and making the pillows comfortable.

Raf brings up the list. "Any particular request?"

She takes a few moments to look through them. "Not action. I feel like I'm living in enough of one recently."

"Fair enough. How about a romcom? Ooh, this one is perfect for being in the man's very lair."

They settle on *Everyday Normal*, a story about a man who is so famous he feels he never connects with people any more—that they only see him for what he is, not who he is. He spends more and more time in VR, using a completely average-looking avatar. There he meets a girl, and they fall in love. There are the usual twists and turns, the suspense of who she is and whether she'll accept him. The betrayal of a friend; the moment he makes a mistake and it seems he'll lose the girl forever. There's the usual happy ending, the passionate kiss.

Carina watches it all with her usual detachment. The acting is fairly decent, the plot OK. Raf ends up teary-eyed, but Carina's never cried at a film in her life and can't imagine doing so. Sometimes she wishes she could, though. Raf seems to enjoy it so much more than she does.

Afterward, Raf says good night and leaves her alone. Carina's still not sure what to make of it. He could have masked the subfrequency location, and then left her alone. He didn't. He never mentioned the Zealscape memory the rest of the Trust had to witness. By spending some time and watching a film with her, though, he made his opinion pretty clear: he's not holding it against her.

She's not sure if his trust is misplaced or not, but she appreciates it all the same.

THIRTY-EIGHT

CARINA

The Apex, above Hollywood, Los Angeles,
California, Pacifica

Carina is impressed with how quickly Clavell can turn around a party. The droids are busy bees, darting about and adding understated white decorations to the grand marble staircase. The pool outside is cleaned, the protective dome around the house ensuring that the water temperature is always optimal. She's gone for a few swims in it, like a shark in the shallows.

The invitations have gone out to some of the most famous people in Hollywood and the rest of Los Angeles. Carina worries that this means those who are friends with Sudice will attend.

"Of course they will," Clavell says, with an unimpressed flap of his hand. "But you'll be sufficiently peacocked and disguised, your two friends included. I'm sure the president of Sudice himself could come and wouldn't recognize one of you."

"You haven't invited him, have you?" Dax asks.

Clavell gives him an eyeroll in response.

"Why are you doing all this for us?" Carina finally asks the question they've all been wondering, but were too afraid to ask.

"It's hardly a surprising story. I owe a debt to Charlie. She got me out of a spot of trouble a few years back, but I don't fancy going into it now, so don't bother asking. And like the rest of you, I have my own bone to pick with Sudice. They're nasty, but so good at pulling the wool over everyone's eyes. In fact, hasn't it seemed like over the last few months, public opinion of Sudice has even been on the rise?"

Carina hasn't been paying close attention, but Charlie nods grimly. "Yes, the polls are rising steadily. We've been watching. We're not sure why there's a sudden upswing but it might work all right for us. A longer, harder fall is more difficult to return from when they trusted you."

"Or they're still blinded by their own ignorance," Clavell says. "I've seen first-hand how brilliantly people can bury their heads in the sand, if they're so inclined."

"True enough," Charlie says.

"Well," Clavell says, all brisk business. "The party's tomorrow, and there's much to do!" Clavell gives them a farewell wave. As soon as he leaves, the group sobers.

"Has public opinion really been rising?" Carina asks.

"They've rolled out new products people are content with, but I'm starting to wonder if they've already been rolling out Pythia on the sly in small, controlled groups. Perhaps without even telling the subjects that's what they were doing." Charlie shakes her head. "If so, this is only the beginning."

Dread spreads through all of them. They bend their heads back to their work.

·

About an hour later, Raf snaps his head up, gasping.

"Raf?" Charlie asks, half-rising.

"Kivon just messaged me on the emergency line. The police or Sudice have found him out. He's busted."

"Shit. Have they caught him?" she asks.

"What about Tam?" Dax's voice is tight. Carina remembers Kivon is hiding Tam.

Raf holds out a hand. "He's managed to give them the slip and put the security measures I left him in place. His implants are blocked and he's en route to get a new VeriChip. I don't think they know about Tam. It's not under his name. But we'll check and move her somewhere else. I promise."

Dax nods, jaw muscles working.

"Does he have a safe place to hole up? We can't bring him here easily without arousing suspicion," Charlie says.

"I know that," Raf snaps. Carina's never seen Raf so stressed, and that's including the time she saw him stung by Wasps in virtual reality. "He has a hideout. But we've got to sneak him in with Kim and Aliyah. Now he's out, he's in the Trust completely. We clear?"

"You'll hear no argument from me," Charlie says. "Isaac will add him to the guest list. Is he removing his police mods?"

Raf scoffs. "No way. Too useful, especially if we're going to break into Sudice. Plus, you've got to hear what he's told me."

Raf's fingers move and he projects Kivon onto the wallscreen. Kivon looks remarkably calm for someone on the run from both the law and Sudice. Not even a bead of sweat glimmers on his brow. He's hard to read, but Carina would guess that he's furious. She can't tell where he is—some other underground bunker or abandoned warehouse, she's guessing. Probably not comfortable, but well hidden.

"You're secure?" Dax asks him.

"As sure as I can be. But look, we're going to have to change our plans," Kivon says. "Drastically, and fast."

"Why?" Charlie asks.

"You heard Sudice's stock is rising fast, right? Lots of positive stuff in the media, and there's that huge press junket in San Francisco in four days' time?"

"Yeah . . ." Charlie says, her face tightening as if she's guessing his next words.

"They've been rolling out Pythia on some high-end reporters, tech gurus, the like. For months now. Without telling them. I was searching on servers at work and found records of extra security for the press junket, and a deleted message trail." He licks his lips. "They're going to release their standard implant upgrades the night of the junket. We thought they'd mention Pythia then, right?" Kivon says. The others nod, cautiously. "Nope. Pythia is no longer optional, but will be embedded in that update. Large-scale personality control is set to go live in less than a week. Everyone in Pacifica will have an automatic update alert. Imagine how many people will simply click 'accept' without thinking about it." He gives a shaky sigh. "I legged it out of there as soon as I found the info, but I must have triggered something from within, no matter how much you taught me, Raf. I'm sorry. I couldn't get it off the servers, but I figured you would believe me."

"It's exactly what Roz would want to do," Carina says. Their eyes turn toward her. "She's been working toward this for so long that she'd want to go as wide as possible. She's already started, setting the stage so even if people find out what's happening, it will be too little, too late. I wonder if she got the idea from what the Ratel did with Verve."

"Very possibly," Kivon says. "Except the Ratel wanted to use Verve to cause chaos, swapping it out in all the Zeal lounges. Tear down society so they could rebuild it. Messy. Roz is more considered in her approach."

"Just as ruthless," Carina sighs. "Her and Mantel both. So we have to accelerate our plan?"

"It seems that way. Three days instead of seven weeks. Just brilliant."

"We'll do it," Raf says. "We don't have a choice. Better hope your friends come through for you, Carina."

Carina swallows, nerves wound tight. She hopes so, too.

THIRTY-NINE

CARINA

The Apex, above Hollywood, Los Angeles,
California, Pacifica

It's time for the Trust to don their disguises.

Luckily, living with the most security-obsessed celebrity in Hollywood, there is no shortage of the things they need. They have masks to change their faces, and Clavell orders them all clothes.

"I hope you don't mind," he says. "If there's anything not to your taste, let me know and we can exchange it for something you prefer."

After so long in show business, though, Clavell's taste is impeccable. For Charlie, he has chosen a long evening gown the same vibrant red as her hair, with little cut-outs in the torso that show flashes of pale skin. Charlie wears a longer wig and a mask over her features to subtly change them, along with violet contacts. Dax offers to change her iris color for her, but she waves him off, saying it's far too much work for just an evening. Dax is wearing an orange bow tie and cummerbund, and Raf is wearing blue. He's given his hair a blue sheen, which looks quite rakish.

Clavell has chosen a deep green dress for Carina. It trails

along the ground, and the sleeves leave her shoulders bare. The torso has a built-in corset, and the overall effect is of a dress borrowed from the 1700s. Dax brightens her hair from deep purple to lavender, and one of the droids twists it into an elaborate updo studded with false green roses. She paints her altered face herself, with blue, green and purple eyeshadow and a neutral lip. She dons a lacy purple eye mask and smiles at the mirror. It's still not quite right—too stiff, and doesn't reach her eyes—but it'll do. All told, the Trust brush up pretty well.

Isaac Clavell has deliberately made this a masked ball so that they don't have to come up with false names. They each have their roles to play if prodded—they'll hint that they're newly discovered stars, not yet known to the public eye. Carina and the others don't plan to spend much time at the actual party, but they've decked themselves out to fit in. She feels powerful, with the swish of her skirts along the pale marble. Her father would have found her get-up unbearably offensive, and the thought only makes her eyes narrow in satisfaction.

She stays in the corridor above the main ballroom, watching the people arrive and waiting for Kim and Aliyah. The hovercar has picked them up and Clavell sent her confirmation that there were no difficulties, so they should be here soon. Kim knows enough to send a false location ping for both herself and Aliyah, so Sudice shouldn't be able to follow. Even if, somehow, they do, they won't get through Clavell's security, even with an arrest warrant. The Apex is a law unto itself.

So many celebrities are below her. The net wealth of the attendees is more than the GDP of many countries. Clavell gave the Trust an exclusive implant overlay so that they know who the true people beneath the masks are. There is Ada Khan (social rank: thirteen), the female equivalent of Isaac Clavell (rank twelve, he just squeaks ahead). She's been in more than three hundred films, several starring alongside their illustrious host. There is Randall James (rank twenty-one), one of the most eminent film directors, and his wife, Marina James (rank eighteen), one of the most sought-after producers.

Carina hopes no one will speak to her beyond small talk. She's pretending to be a new starlet who's just landed a big role, but of course neglecting to say which one and give away her identity. She's no actress—she can, at a push, fake normalcy, but it's never perfect. Trying to play a bright-eyed, innocent ingénue is beyond her.

There. Kim and Aliyah have arrived, and Kivon is close behind. He met them at Santa Monica Pier without mishap, then. Like everyone, they're wearing masks to alter their features, and they're dressed up far more than they ever would have been at Sudice's labs. But their height and colorings are both the same, and they don't match anyone from the guest list when their fake names pop up on her ocular implants. Clavell swoops in to greet them and leads them to a side room. A few curious heads turn to watch them go.

A droid comes to meet Carina, and she follows it down a side hallway.

She doesn't enter immediately. Aliyah and Kim have been led to the Chair room where Carina operated on Dax. Raf is there, in his masked disguise, to screen them both, ensuring they don't have the same malware in their heads. They'll already have been scanned for trackers when they entered the hovercar that brought them here. Carina watches on her ocular implants.

Carina sends Raf a ping, letting him know that Kivon is here and safe. He's also brought Tam, and Clavell has hidden her in one of the many rooms of his fortress. Carina feels a little bad she's keeping Raf from his boyfriend, and then absurdly pleased her empathy is working well enough for that.

Kim and Aliyah hesitate. She knows they're both thinking of other Chairs in San Francisco. Their respective subjects. How Carina's subjects had a tendency to nearly die, and how they were meant to meet her in just a few moments. They can't hide that flash of suspicion.

Kim volunteers first and clambers into the Chair. Raf maps her brain within a minute, scrutinizing the implants. He doesn't see anything unusual, but he reaches out to Carina on his implants, just in case.

"She's clear," Carina pings back. "At least as far as I can tell."

Raf disconnects Kim and she sits up, patting her elaborate hair and clambering down from the Chair. Aliyah climbs in next, Raf rolling up her jacket sleeve to slide in the needle. Another brain map. Another few minutes of scrutiny. Aliyah has some extra memory mod implants, more than Carina remembers from her Sudice brain maps. She spends extra time looking through her former colleague's brain.

"I think we're good," Carina says, finally.

"But you're not totally sure?" Raf asks.

"I'm about ninety-seven percent sure. Is the three percent enough of an error margin for you?"

"OK." He takes her out and leads them both to Clavell's lavish, empty yoga studio nearby. Carina waits a few moments. Raf comes out to meet her.

"You want me in there with you?"

"No, you go enjoy the party. Go see Kivon. It'll be easier to speak to them if it's just us. Old camaraderie, you know."

She doesn't need to tell him twice. "All right, but we're all a ping away if you need us. And come for a dance after. Let off some steam." He mimes a boogie.

Carina manages to swallow a scoff. "I'll think about it. Thanks, Raf."

He flashes her a smile with his disguised face and heads down the corridor.

She enters the studio. It's long and thin, curled around the edge of the house, looking directly into the clouds and the stars. Kim and Aliyah sit on plush, soft chairs by the windows. Kim's dress is black with white jewels clustered at the hem, like stars. Aliyah's wearing a woman's tux in a deep blue-purple.

"Who are you?" Kim asks, blunt as ever.

"It's me."

Kim startles. "Damn. I don't recognize you at all."

Aliyah whistles. "Neither do I. You're completely transformed."

"Not sure if that's good or bad. I do have this." Carina takes off the mask.

Aliyah blinks. "Yeah, I still don't recognize you."

"You should have seen her a few weeks ago, Ali," Kim says. "One step away from death's door."

"Um. Thanks," Carina says, awkwardly.

They remove their masks. Seeing their true faces is easier, though Carina's shoulder muscles are still wound tight.

It's been eight months since Carina has seen them in person. Aliyah has swapped her vermilion hair for turquoise, but otherwise is unchanged. Kim still looks the same as when they video-chatted, except her face is dotted with false jewels around her eyes and her hair is in a complicated updo.

"So," Kim says. "I can guess why you want me here, which is why I brought Aliyah."

"Can you?" Carina asks, gazing out the window at the stars, impossibly bright this far up above the cloud line.

"You're planning to break into Sudice," Aliyah starts. Carina turns back.

"What makes you say that?" she says, choosing her words carefully. She desperately wants to trust Kim, but she also knows that Sudice have deep pockets, and Kim still works there. She has become a very rich woman thanks to them. Is she a friend or an employee first?

"Because it makes sense. You've found lots of dirt on Sudice, I'm guessing, right?"

Carina pauses, then nods cautiously.

"Good. I hope you found some really foul stuff. What were you checking for, in the Chair just now?"

"Sudice have evolved brain recording enough to create sleeper agents. They turned one of our own."

Both Kim and Aliyah's eyes widen. "Shitting hell," Aliyah says. "They actually cracked it?"

"Not completely. The person they tampered with had the usual side effects. They obviously didn't care if they killed him."

"Fuck," Aliyah says. "And you thought they might have done it to us? How?"

"If you'd been put under at a hospital. Maybe even a Zeal lounge. They're even more ruthless than we thought."

The silence grows between them.

"I was never able to thank you all, properly," Carina says. "For helping me escape." They had helped her disappear from Sudice, leaving no trail that Roz could follow. They'd stuck their necks out for her, and she in turn had abandoned them to deal with Sudice on their own. They'd both pinged her and she'd ignored their calls, too ashamed by how far and how quickly she was falling into her Zeal addiction.

Until Mark had sent her the message she couldn't ignore.

Kim waves her hand dismissively.

"It was nothing," Aliyah says.

"It was more than that." Carina coughs.

"Anyway, enough with the emotional heart-to-heart, though Lovelace knows I love you both dearly," Kim says. "You need help with the three-step verification to get into Sudice, don't you?"

Time to delve into some specifics, but not too many. Just in case. "We have some passcodes," Carina says, delicately.

"But you don't have an employee VeriChip, and it's not as easy as you thought to create one," Kim says.

As ever, she catches on fast. "Not really, no. We could probably do it, but it'd take longer than we'd like. The code is complex."

Aliyah reaches into her tux pocket and brings out a VeriChip. She drops it into Carina's palm.

"What's this?"

"I've transferred to Sudice in Boston, and I managed to create a backup of my employee profile in San Francisco. This is a clone. If I showed up with that in my wrist tomorrow at the front doors, it'd let me in, not even pinging that I'm an out-of-Pacifica employee. No alarms."

"Why'd you do that?"

"I had some vague notion of doing what you're trying to do," Aliyah says. "Then I never moved forward with it. Too afraid of them in the end, I guess, and I never found anything really good."

"Well, I'm pretty certain we're on a path to getting ourselves killed." Carina inspects the VeriChip. She'll have Raf double-check it, but this could be exactly what they need. Carina had been hoping they could borrow Kim's or something, but this is much better. Roz will have flagged Kim's employee file, but she might not think to look for someone who's moved across the continent.

"It's one step of three," Carina says, then pauses delicately.

"Yes. The other two steps are not as straightforward," Aliyah says. She holds herself straight and stiff.

"We . . . we have a flesh doctor. Who could do what we need. It's entirely up to you. I know it's a big ask." Carina stares at Aliyah. She hopes she doesn't look hungry, and is blinking frequently enough.

Aliyah licks her lips, nervous. "You'll destroy it after, of course? Turn it all back?"

"Immediately."

She gives a twitchy smile. "OK, then. Yeah. I'll do it."

Carina sags a little in relief, her skirts rustling. "Thank you, Aliyah."

"Can you do it here?" Aliyah asks, looking at their ornate surroundings.

"Yes. One of the other members of the Trust will come in a moment." Carina forces herself to reach out and squeeze both their hands. *Don't think about the tendons and bones beneath the skin. Don't think about how easy it would be to break those fingers, one by one.*

She pings Dax, and he leaves the party to come to them. They all put their masks back on. Letting Dax in, she introduces him. He nods at them. He has prepared a room in case Aliyah agrees.

Carina comes along, partly because she's a familiar face— well, so to speak—and might make Aliyah more comfortable, and partly because she's curious. Her face has been changed by a flesh doctor, but she's never seen it done.

Dax doesn't let her stay.

"You don't need to see me with a scalpel," he says.

Carina's mouth twists, but she has to admit he's right. Her urges are still there, as strong as ever. This kind of plastic surgery won't require much blood, but still more than she'd be able to handle. Kim stays instead to watch over Aliyah.

Carina waits in the yoga studio, staring out at the stars, arms wrapped around her torso. She feels left out. Aliyah and Kim are actual friends, who keep in touch, meet up for lunch or drinks whenever they're near each other. Carina has never been able to do that. Probably never could. Sit and pick at food, make small talk. It's her idea of torture. For a moment, though, she wishes.

Mentally, she toys with the patches in the code that could help regulate her urges. It would be almost frightening to let them go. What if she ended up going back to how she was before? Does she still want to be that cold, emotionless automaton? That total distance kept her removed from people, but it also kept people safe.

Shit. She can feel it building in her mind. The memory rising, ready to open and reveal its hidden secrets. The last image. Of course it's tied to the memory she both pushes away as far as she can, yet picks up in her darkest moments, twisting it and turning it from different angles. She's thought about it a few times since Mark put so much information into her head, but it wasn't ready to release, not yet. Here it is, inevitable, almost welcome.

Carina had the beating of her life when she arrived home late after following her father into the warehouse.

He hit her where it never showed. Ribs, stomach, back, legs. The bruises bloomed, and later in the night she rubbed bruising cream on them to help them fade. This was unlike any of his violence before.

She wished he'd hit her in the face. Just one shiner, right to the cheekbone. She wouldn't use the bruising cream, and the teachers would ask questions. He was too careful.

She wished she was strong enough to hit him back.

Carina's understanding of him had changed. She knew why he kept to his exact schedules, guarded his privacy under lock and key. Why he isolated her, just as he had isolated her mother. She knew so many of his secrets, but not what to do with them. Not yet.

Her father was a killer.

Carina's mother had not been his first victim. He worked his way up to her. Carina hadn't been able to find much information on his suspected victims. He had hidden his tracks very well. Probably women, or mostly women. Carina brainloaded as much information on serial killers as she could find. She couldn't do it at school—they monitored the information you requested outside the normal curriculum—so she researched how to hide her trail and did it at home, hoping her father wouldn't look too closely. He'd never expressed much interest in what she downloaded before, but if he had even the slightest suspicion of what she was really up to, he'd go through it with a fine-toothed comb. The information about killers did not frighten her. Perhaps it would have, if she could feel.

Weeks stretched past. Her father became less abusive after a kill, Carina decided, her horrible beating the other night an aberration. One week out of the month, he grew disinterested in hitting her. He didn't become pleasant by any means, but he became distant and easier to be around. She tried to think back to his patterns of abuse over the last year or so. She couldn't pinpoint a pattern then. Maybe once every six months or so? After her mother disappeared, though, it had been about once a month. The last month, twice. He was growing worse. And her indecision meant others were dying.

Pacifica prided itself on a lack of crime, but her father was getting away with murder right under their very noses. Countless times, she debated pinging the police. Yet she had no proof. He kept the warehouse deliberately pure. She didn't even have a record of him hitting her. She needed to be careful. If she so much as brought up 911, he would know, and he would start monitoring more closely.

One night, her father did hit her in the face. She stared at the mirror for a long time that night, looking at the swollen left eye, already purpling. She wasn't sure whether her cheekbone was fractured or not. Stars of pain pulsed across her face every time she moved. Her lip was split and puffy. She couldn't straighten her right arm all the way. That girl in the mirror looked weak. This was not going to get better or go away. Numbness would not protect her.

"I'm not a victim," she said to the mirror. "Not any more."

She documented those injuries, storing the images deep within her implants. She smeared on the healing cream, and over the next few hours, the bruises faded from her skin. Gone but not forgotten.

Carina had a few possible courses of action. She could upload the photos and call the police while at school. Maybe it'd be enough proof that he merited a closer look. None of his victims were likely logged as official missing persons. He probably found those who had slipped through the cracks—Zealots or the like. No one had noticed them missing, at least not yet.

She had no idea who exactly he had hurt. Too many. She didn't care about the people he'd killed, not really; they were too abstract. But she wished she did. Didn't that count for something?

Slowly, she pieced together her plan. Thought out every aspect, imagining the various ways it could fail and finding ways to fix the flaws. When it seemed as foolproof as it could be, it was time.

She drugged her father during dinner and helped him to bed before he passed out completely. She even tucked him in. He groaned and fell back on the pillow, his mouth opening. A dribble of drool fell from his chin. She stared at him for a time. This man who had killed her mother and terrorized her throughout her life seemed so pathetic and small. Just a sad, middle-aged man who had never had a lick of waxworking done to his features.

Carina could leave. Pack her bags, break into the safe and take the credits he stored there for an emergency. It would be enough to help her go far from Greenview House.

She was tempted. If it wasn't for what she'd found in that warehouse, maybe she would have.

When he woke up, she was going to terrorize him until he pinged the police and confessed, there and then. Details of every kill. If he kept souvenirs of each death, like many serial killers did, where they were. He'd be frozen in stasis for the rest of his natural life, and she'd finally be free of him.

There was always the fear that he wouldn't play nice. That no matter what she did, he'd find a way to wriggle out of justice. She could only hope she'd planned this well enough that he couldn't escape.

At that time, Carina was still a minor. No matter what happened, the media were obliged to leave her name out of the papers. They'd spit out the details for greedy readers, but she wouldn't be mentioned. She could legally change her surname in a few months and sever the last link between herself and her father. The chance of freedom.

She disabled the house's security, so he wouldn't be able to ping for help once he regained consciousness. She would record his confession and ping it to the police herself. She cut the power. It was just him and her now.

She took a slow walk through Greenview House. With any luck, this would be her last night here. The corridors were silent. This house was full of so many secrets, she could choke on them.

Finally she went up to her father's room. Her pocket held a knife—something to scare him into finally telling her the truth.

There was her father. Still sleeping. Still unaware that the last chapter of his life had closed and a new one leading to stasis was about to begin.

She sat at his bedside, crouched on the stool, waiting for the drug to wear off. Two hours she stayed there, unmoving, almost in a trance.

Her father eventually groaned, moving his head from side to side. The sedative should still make him sluggish and weak. She tied him up anyway, with padded shackles she'd later destroy. They shouldn't leave ligature marks. It took him a few moments to realize where he was. Another moment to take in his daughter, now crouched on the end of his bed like a spider, holding a very large knife.

"Carina," he said, his voice thick with the drugs.

"Father."

"What are you doing?" He tried to stay calm, but even beneath his fog, the anger was bubbling, ready to break. His breath came faster, his hands clenched into fists.

She didn't answer him directly. "It's long past time for the truth."

His eyes widened. "Carina." His voice held the promise of violence. It would have cowed her a few months ago. Now, she was unmoved.

"I'm no longer afraid of you. I'm not afraid of anything." She hefted the knife. Time to scare him into telling the truth. She switched on the datapod in her ear. All of his words from now on would record. Some would say it wouldn't hold up in court. That it could have been artificially created, or tampered with. Again, though—as long as it turned the eye of the law toward him, they'd find something. An errant smudge of DNA evidence in the warehouse. An instance of him being too close to one of his victims at the time of their death.

"Carina," her father says again. "Stop this."

"Did you stop for my mother?"

His eyes closed. Tightened. Opened wide. He said nothing.

She placed the tip of the knife against his throat. Deep within, below that eternal numbness, came a thrill of excitement. It startled her so much, she almost dropped the knife. Her father swallowed and the knife nicked the skin. Carina couldn't look away from the two bright drops of blood dripping down his neck.

"What happened." She didn't ask it as a question. She pressed the knife a little harder. A third drop of blood appeared. Her cheeks flushed with warmth. Something within her was unfurling, rising to the surface like a tide. She should stop, back away, but she had come too far.

"She wasn't meant to die," her father said, his voice hoarse.

Carina froze. She'd almost wondered if she'd made it all up in her head. If her father had hurt people, perhaps that hadn't actually extended to her mother. Yet with those words, there could be no turning back.

"She found me . . . with someone." He didn't mean an affair. Nothing so banal.

"Did. You. Kill. Her." Each word tore itself from her throat.

"Yes," he whispered. "Yes." The second word was more forceful.

"Why?" she asked, and her eyes filled with tears for the first time since she'd visited the San Francisco Sudice offices. They slipped down her face, unnoticed.

"I see it in you," he said, not answering her question. "That same thirst."

"Liar," she spat. "I was a sad girl who had lost the only person who loved her. You tried to control my mother, and when it didn't work, you killed her like the others. Then when I wouldn't conform to how you thought I would be, you let them change me."

Carina could feel it, almost breaking through. The certainty that going to Sudice had transformed her, in some way. She knew that feeling wouldn't last, that it would sink down back into the numbness, but she held it to her while she could. She'd forgotten how powerful emotions could be. They threatened to drown her.

"I see it now," he said. "You were always like me. Now it's even clearer. You are your father's daughter." He had the nerve to give her something resembling a smile. His teeth glinted in the dark. "Think of what we could do together. A bond that cannot be broken. God still speaks, despite all that has befallen me. You are my clear sign."

She didn't dignify him with an answer. The hypocrisy was baffling, but then, her father had long since lost his grip on sanity or morality, even if he could present a decent façade to the outside world.

The emotions bubbled up inside of her. An urge growing within her, twining through every atom of her, every beat of her heart.

Kill. Kill. Kill.

After being cut off from her emotions for so long, she was completely unprepared for this torrent. The fear grew. What if she was just like him, doomed to destroy all she touched? What if, somehow, he had made her this way? Serial killer tendencies were not meant to be hereditary, or not solely so. They could be genetics and environment. Nature, nurture or both.

Her arm raised, almost as if it were controlled by someone else. The knife slid across his face, a thin line of red blooming on each of his cheekbones. They were symmetrical, except for when he tried to twist away, making the left side deeper and more jagged.

"Don't move," her voice said.

He complied. He thought she only wanted to hurt him, to frighten him.

That had been the plan. Now, she was not so sure.

"Tell me all of your sins," she said. "Every kill. Spare no detail."

Information given under torture would not hold up in court. Oh, they might find out what her father did now, but if she ever gave this datapod to the police, she would follow him right into stasis. She would be deemed just as much of a threat to society. And she was. She knew it in her bones.

Dutifully, her father told her of the crimes he'd committed, urged on by the edge of her knife when his words trailed away. Each drop of blood only fed her fascination. It was the ultimate satisfaction. The warm feel of blood. The easy give of flesh. She took her careful, measured revenge against the man she despised, foreign feelings swirling through her.

"How many?" she asked him, near the end.

"How many what?" His face was covered in a thin sheen of blood. His injuries were all superficial.

"How many deaths?"

"Thirteen," he said. No hesitation. His thinning hair was plastered flat to his skull.

Carina wasn't sure if it was higher or lower than she expected. Thirteen lives that might still be lived, right at this very moment, if not for her father. In so many ways, great and small, life for those affected by those thirteen people would be different. In a way, he'd changed the course of the future, even if in all likelihood he hadn't made any lasting, large-scale changes. Still, the thought of that power, that control . . .

"Does that include Mom?" she asked.

A hesitation. A short, sharp nod. "Please," her father begged.

Carina closed her eyes, breathing in the iron tang of blood and acrid sweat. When she opened them, the knife was deep within her father's throat. Warm blood gushed over her hands. Her hand moved the knife, back and forth. Cutting a throat was not easy. The throat was grisly, the skin slippery. Her father gurgled, his back arched. Air whistled in and out of his severed windpipe. Where was the carotid artery? Had she hit it? There was so much blood.

It took four minutes for her father to die. He never looked away from her, until his eyes went still and glassy.

This had not been the plan.

She was breathing as hard as if she'd run for miles. Her heartbeat hammered. Her apathy was in shreds around her. Turning away from the bed, she ran to the bathroom. Threw up in the toilet, her throat raw with acid, her cheeks still burning.

She flushed the toilet and crawled back into the bedroom.

The sheets were already soaked. She could smell the iron in the air. As her heartbeat slowed, the emotions that had overwhelmed her receded. A few minutes later, she was wrapped back within her protection of numbness.

She'd never been more grateful not to feel.

.

Carina needed a new plan.

She peeled off her clothes and bundled them in a clean cloth. She found some gloves and pulled them on over her hands. She went to the back of the house, to the barbeque pit, throwing the clothes in and watching them burn to ashes while standing in the cool night air in her underwear. All was so quiet. She threw the datapod after them, and it popped and sizzled as it melted. The proof of her sin vanished.

She went back inside. Showered, washing her hair three times to make sure all the blood and smoke was rinsed out. After toweling herself off, she put on pajamas. She threw several DNA scrubbers around the house.

The next part was harder, but she didn't know what else to do.

Once her hair was dry, she threw herself against the walls of her bedroom, until flecks of her own blood splattered the white walls and she had the beginnings of a beautiful black eye.

Next, she fell down the stairs, making sure to scuff her arms and legs against the wall and banister. She stumbled, as if drunk, until she reached the basement. She threw herself back against one of the support pillars and slid down it. She might have hit it a bit too hard—she felt dazed. At the base, she'd already laid out the ties. She put her hands back around the pillar and the robotic rope slithered up her hands and tied tightly, before moving around the pillar and the torso, pinning her in place.

All she could do now was wait.

•

It took the police over sixteen hours to find her.

When her father didn't show up for work that morning, his boss pinged him. Carina could imagine how it all played out: no answer. Very unlike Mr. Kearney. He was always in like clockwork, and never took a sick day. It'd have taken a few hours for his boss to obtain special dispensation to look up coordinates via VeriChip. At lunchtime, he'll have had a spare moment to enter them in. At home. He'll ping again. Still no answer. He'll huff. Disciplinary action the next day, no doubt.

Meanwhile, Carina had not shown up for school. This was also irregular. She did not skip because her father would find out, and that'd mean an extra beating. Her lead tutor pinged home. No response. They pinged her father. No response. Because of her reputation as anti-social (but not quite anti-social enough to merit disciplinary action), they were the ones to ping the police.

The authorities arrived at around 4 p.m. She heard the sirens approach, the hovercar set down. They noticed the disabled security right away. The door opened. They checked the ground level. When they cried out, stumbling upon the telltale small smears of blood on the stairway, Carina lifted her head. Opened her mouth and tried to scream. No sound came out. The movement caused the scab on her split lip to break open. Blood leaked down her chin.

It tasted like copper. Like freedom.

She heard their boots on the main staircase. They found her father first. Someone threw up. That wouldn't be good for the crime scene.

"Where's the daughter?" she heard someone say. Carina had left the basement door open, but she had a thrill of fear that they might not realize she was down there.

She opened her mouth to scream again, but it only came out as a squeak. She'd pissed herself three hours ago, and it was cold and unpleasant. She swallowed a few times, and then she opened her mouth and let out the most bloodcurdling scream of her life.

•

Carina's memories after that grow fractured. They found her, tended to her wounds and gave her fluids. They interviewed her, and she managed to keep it together enough that they never truly considered her a suspect. She doesn't like to think of those days spent wondering if she'd say the wrong thing, or they'd find some sort of evidence. But that didn't matter. She'd remembered enough. Nettie's green and blue eyes rose in her mind's eye, staring at her, unblinking, accusing. One long, slow blink, and the information unlocked into her brain.

Mark had uncovered even more crimes, leading back to the very beginning of Sudice. Proof that they undercut other companies to make sure Sudice was the sole company working on tech during the Great Upheaval. Sudice had stolen technology from other companies in order to fulfill contracts. Every year was an elaborate exercise in tax evasion. Government officials were regularly bribed. It's all plenty of ammunition to add, if the Trust can manage to send it all out into the world.

The last image also has information on Nettie's family. Her parents' new names, where they live. It's a chance to reach out and explain what happened to their daughter. It's Mark asking Carina to apologize on his behalf for what ended up happening to the girl.

"Oh, Mark," she sighs.

The last of the information settles into her brain. A shiver runs through her from the top of her skull to the tips of her toes. She stumbles back to her room to grab her electrodes. Once back in the yoga studio, she sticks them to her head and begins transferring the information to Raf's servers. All the information in her brain has released. She has done what she set out to do, and fulfilled her promise to Mark's ghost.

Carina returns to the hallway that overlooks the party, resting her elbows on the railing. It takes her a few minutes, but she finds the rest of the disguised Trust down below. Kivon and Charlie are chatting and eating nibbles. Raf and Kim have just entered. Aliyah is probably resting and recovering. Charlie gestures them over. A faster song plays, one ideal for dancing. Most of the perfectly coiffed, masked celebrities move in a careful, measured way that doesn't muss their hair. The Trust, instead, lose themselves in the music. They've been so pent up for so long that they let themselves go. Raf twirls Kim, and Kivon lifts Charlie above the crowd. Aliyah enters in the middle of the song, seeming fine, and does a very good pirouette on one foot. Dax follows behind and does some silly moves. They jump, they dance, they ignore the sidelong glances from the celebrities. Carina finds herself smiling as she watches them, wondering if it's actually a genuine expression.

Dax's head swivels, searching for her. Carina watches them for another moment and then turns and makes her way to the front door. A drone asks if she wants her coat, and returns with it. She wraps the dark fabric over her finery, even though the night is relatively warm. Carina walks through the garden, a mile above Hollywood, scented with rare, engineered flowers.

She finds the Trust's hovercar, takes out the keys from her

coat pocket. She took the spare ones from the Trust headquarters before they left, in case this moment presented itself. Here it is.

She opens the hovercar and climbs into the driver's seat.

The five images have been unlocked. Raf has all the information. They don't need her any more. She won't be much of an asset, breaking into the headquarters. Charlie will be the one to use what Aliyah gave them. Carina is free to go find the closest Zealot lounge. She'll just have to get her hands on enough credits for a hit first, as she can't access her bank account and government money. She'll find a way. Selling the hovercar would do it. The Trust will be annoyed she stole it, but surely it's fair payment for all she's given them.

She's just about to start the engine when there's a knock on the hovercar door.

FORTY

DAX

The Apex, above Hollywood, Los Angeles,
California, Pacifica

Dax pushes open the door to the hovercar. Carina's guilty face looks back at him.

He sighs and climbs in, the door shutting behind him. "Leaving already?"

She looks away. "How'd you know?"

He pauses. "Raf stopped mid-dance and said you'd uploaded a bunch more information from the last image. They're all looking through it now."

"Aw. I killed their party buzz."

"I think they're more excited now than when they were dancing."

"But you knew to come looking for me."

"I remembered you saying you only planned to stay until you unlocked everything. I wondered if that was still true."

"Well."

"Well, indeed." Dax leans back in the chair, crossing his arms across his chest. He looks out into the clouds and stars, the white, smooth mansion glowing like a pearl with the lights of the party. "Is it really worth throwing away everything you've gained?" he asks her.

Carina's lips purse. "I'd ruin it anyway. Sort of my specialty."

"Cursed to loneliness and self-destruction?" Dax's voice is sardonic.

"Something like that." Her shoulders hunch, and he sees her force them to relax, to seem unconcerned.

Dax keeps his voice soft. "Well, I don't believe that."

"It doesn't matter what you believe." She stares ahead. "You've never really asked me which memories Mark's images were tied to. Were you ever curious?"

"Of course I was. Still am."

"I told you the first image, the Bee, was tied to my first memory, but never what it was."

Dax waits. She doesn't speak. "Do you feel like sharing, then?" he prompts.

A hesitation. "They all revolve around my father. I guess Mark pegged I had daddy issues. Might have mapped them deliberately after finding them in Roz's data." She gives something approaching a laugh. "Still don't know how he did it, not really."

She pauses, licks her lips. "My father ended up making me who I am today. If he'd not been a monster, maybe I wouldn't have become one either. It's hard not to wonder—when the programming broke down, did I become violent because it's hidden in my nature, or did I become that because I feared it so much?"

"Are you saying your father was violent?"

"He killed my mother. He killed thirteen people over ten years. Pacifica had its very own serial killer, as it prided itself on its lack of murder. I looked beneath his façade and found out we're mirrors."

Dax looks at her, eyes wide.

"They never caught him," she continues. "He was so careful, only targeted people who wouldn't be missed. Except my mother."

"You're not a serial killer."

"It depends on your definition." She bites her lip, then answers his unspoken question. "Only one. My father. I killed him when I was seventeen. The first little break in my programming. I only . . . I only meant to frighten him. To have him confess what he did." She stops, thinking. "And maybe those people at the silo. Let's say three."

Dax lets that information sink in. "You haven't killed anyone innocent."

"No one's innocent."

"Nettie was."

"Please. Teen girls are just as varied and complicated and full of flaws as anyone else."

"She didn't deserve to die, is all I mean."

Carina nods. "I know."

Dax stares out at the stars. "I might have killed people, too. At the silo. In past altercations with the Trust."

"How many?"

"Two. Maybe."

"You don't kill like I do. In the Zealscape, I killed hundreds. In every way you can imagine. You want to avoid speaking about that, to pretend that didn't happen. But it bothers you. It's why you pulled away from me when I kissed you."

"That wasn't why." Again, Dax is glad he never saw that Zeal recording. "I pulled away because you were off your face on Zeal, and I wasn't sure if it was what you wanted. Or I figured perhaps you were projecting emotions onto me, a sort of transference after the trauma of the Zealscapes. I didn't want you to feel pressured into anything you weren't ready for."

Carina sighs. "I don't know how I feel. That's the whole goddamn problem. I feel too much, or it snaps back to nothing. You were probably right to pull away, but I can't pretend it didn't hurt." She shifts in the hovercar chair. "Well, we've shared our respective body counts. Let's say our goodbyes, and you head back to your party. I'll be on my way. I wish you all the best, Dax. The best in the world."

The words sound hollow.

"You're running away in that dress? That's really unobtrusive."

She looks down at the crumpled silk emerging from her coat. Her lilac hair is falling out of its hairstyle. She shrugs.

Dax moves from his chair and spins hers toward him. He crouches in front of her. "Do you really, actually want to leave before seeing Sudice take the fall for everything they've done?" He wants to say more, to apologize, but the words feel clunky and stick in his mouth.

Carina's eyes close. "I don't know. I can watch from afar." They both know she wouldn't. That she'd be in a Zealot lounge before morning. Even though it would likely mean Sudice finding her, if they can find Zealot recordings. It's a death sentence.

Dax chances reaching out to take her hand. She does not pull away. "Stay."

Her eyes open. "Why?"

"I want you to. I'm serious. I want you to stay if you really do, deep down. I want you to choose the harder option because I think it's worth it."

"You're not afraid of me?"

He considers. "A little. I'm far more afraid of letting you go and never seeing you again. Of never knowing what could have happened."

She moves forward, the dress crinkling. He opens his mouth to ask a question, but she presses her lips to his. Dax stays still and shocked for a moment before he moves to respond, his lips opening, his hands resting first on her upper arms, before moving one arm to her waist and the other to the back of her neck. Before the kiss fully takes hold, Carina pulls back. Her cheeks are flushed. "I'm afraid of feeling too much."

"So am I. That's OK."

"Or what if I can't give you what you want? I don't know if I can give you a relationship, that closeness. What if I can't?"

"I'm not asking for that."

"Aren't you?"

He pauses, considers. Emotions swirl through him, heady like wine. "I'm not asking for anything you do not wish to give."

She takes in his words, processes them. Dax says nothing, waiting for her. She leans close. He wonders what she's thinking and what she truly wants.

"It doesn't have to be some grand gesture, does it?"

"No." He doesn't ask her the questions on his tongue. *Are you staying? Will you want to leave again after Sudice? Will you always be playing this game—of reassuring yourself that you can leave whenever you want to, that nothing is ever permanent, because that's too dangerous?* He knows these questions. He's asked himself the same things, so many times before. As soon as she kisses him again, he lets all those uncertainties fall away.

Carina's kiss deepens, and Dax's mouth opens. He pushes the hair back from her face, holding the back of her head. All the nerves of his skin awaken, until he feels as lit up as the stars outside the window. Dax stands, taking her with him, pressing her tight against his chest. He feels the hard stays of her corset.

She turns, holding her arms out from her sides. He unlaces the stays, slowly, carefully, while kissing the back of her neck. He bites her, not hard, and she arches back against him. He lets out a low groan.

Her dress is not easy to escape from. It takes some maneuvering, including some low laughter, before the rustling silk finally falls away.

He already knows what she looks like naked, from his time sculpting her flesh back into health. This is entirely different. She reaches up and takes out the pins in her hair, her newly lilac hair falling around her shoulders, framing her breasts. His eyes travel over her, to the nip of her waist, the flare of her hips, her long legs. She's pale, like marble threaded with a pink blush. He steps back, feeling her eyes on his.

Carina reaches out, pushing his hair back from his face. She takes off his jacket, removes the bow tie. She's close enough that he can feel the warmth of her skin, but she doesn't touch him as she unbuttons his shirt, one button at a time. He takes an awkward moment to kick off his shoes and peel off his socks. She unzips his trousers. They stand across from each other, taking in the sight of one another. He always feels a little exposed at this moment. She's gazing at his modded muscles. The scars from those long-ago surgeries are long erased. Does she look at him through the film of wondering what he would have looked like without flesh parlors, or does she see him, in this skin he's suited to fit who he is?

It occurs to Dax that he could be afraid of her. She's admitted to killing, to loving it. She could be looking at him and mapping the bones beneath his skin, deciding how best she'd murder him. Yet he doesn't think his death is on her mind.

Pushing him down on the chair in the hovercar cockpit, she straddles him. As she kisses him, he grabs her waist, fingers tight against her flesh. Her lips move to his neck, and his hands travel lower, between her legs. He trails his fingers gently, almost tickling, before pressing the heel of his hand against her. She rocks against him, lips parting as her head tilts back. She drags her nails along his chest and he gasps. Her hands move between his legs, mirroring his moves. Kissing him even deeper, she lowers herself onto him.

Carina moves, agonizingly slowly, rubbing herself against him. Her long hair tickles his shoulders. He grabs her waist again, helping her move. They speed up, finding that perfect rhythm. Carina's eyes are open, unblinking, pupils wide as she focuses within. She licks her lips, just once, and it nearly undoes him. She shudders, tightening against him, and Dax lets her set the pace, pulsing faster and faster, keeping his fingers between their bodies so she hits them each time she shifts, until she kisses him and moans against his mouth in release.

"The back," she says, angling her chin to the room where Dax had been transported to the hospital. He stands, carrying and putting her down on the bench seats. She positions herself on her hands and knees and they begin again, and this time he sets the pace, reaching around and again helping her with his fingers. Her back muscles clench, her shoulder blades pressing together like wings. He makes sure she comes again.

They take their time. Different positions, different rhythms. Exploring expanses of skin with tongues or fingertips, murmuring instructions to each other. She's under him, hands on his back. The tension builds and they move together, fast and frantic. Carina bites his shoulder, hard enough to draw blood, and he finds his own release. His head tilts forward and he closes his eyes. He loves that moment of pure pleasure, when all thought leaves and he just exists, in his body, in this moment.

Dax moves off her and lies against her side, wrapping his arms around her in a hug, and she hugs back. There's only just enough room for them on the seats. They don't speak. They don't lie there and cuddle for ages, and whisper sweet nothings. Something between them has changed, even if they do not put a name to it. A crack in their defenses that lets in a bit of light in the dark.

They pull on their now sadly crumpled finery. Their hair is a sight, and they try to smooth each other into a veneer of propriety. The devilish smiles that pass between them mar any pretense of that.

They leave the hovercraft and walk back to the glowing house in the stars. They do not touch, but that new awareness crackles between them, a promise that it may very well happen again.

FORTY-ONE

CARINA

The Apex, above Hollywood, Los Angeles,
California, Pacifica

They don't have enough time to prepare before Sudice rolls out Pythia to everyone in Pacifica.

The Trust do as much as they can. Kivon fills them in on everything he saw from the database. He's a wanted man—there are posters asking citizens to keep an eye out for him, flashing through thousands of ocular implants throughout the city. The police claim he's a spy, thought to be armed and dangerous.

"Fucking bullshit," Kivon mutters. They're in the room Clavell gave them, with no cameras or networks. All planning still takes place on old tablets that link to Raf's stored intel.

"They're making it seem like you sold state secrets to a rival government or something," Raf says. He's swapping out Kivon's VeriChip, lifting it from below the skin of his wrist with tweezers. He drops it into the replicator to be destroyed. "Technically you *are* a spy, though."

"Shut up."

Carina still doesn't know Kivon particularly well, but he's seemed especially grumpy. Understandable. She has been deliberately not looking at the small cut on his wrist, but almost imagines she can smell the blood even from the other side of the room. Dax knocks his knee against hers, lending wordless comfort.

"Don't be rude when I have sharp implements near you," Raf says, waving the scalpel. Carina flinches.

Carina has not left the Trust, though the urge to flee is still there, lurking behind her thoughts. In her tiny bit of spare time, she puzzles with the neuro code to try and undo some of Roz's damage, but it's still a long way from being safe enough to run. In the meantime, she has to try and keep herself together.

Clavell helps them with the last of their supplies. They pack everything into their hovercar, and then it's time to go. The sun is just beginning to set, outlining the clouds in soft golden and pink light. By the time they arrive at Sudice in San Francisco, it will be the dead of night.

Clavell shakes each of their hands solemnly, though he gives Charlie a long, lingering hug. Something has passed between them. An old love or an old attraction rekindled. Is it difficult for Charlie to say goodbye, knowing she might never return?

"Thank you for hiding us, Isaac," Charlie says.

"I was happy to have you somewhere safe. I hope you enjoyed your time at my humble abode." He gives them all his far-too-perfect smile, tinged with a bit of self-deprecation. He knows exactly how incredible his home is. If he's nervous about the fact that he hid them from Sudice, that he opened his home to strangers, it doesn't show. The perfect actor.

"We'll always be in your debt," Charlie says, her eyes a little wet.

"No, my dear. No. I'll be far more in yours when you are all successful tonight. The world is about to change. I, for one, am looking forward to having a front-row seat."

Carina still isn't quite sure what to make of one of the most well-known celebrities in the world. They've stayed with him for about two weeks, and she is sure he never dropped the role of Isaac Clavell, ultra-celebrity, to reveal whoever he is underneath. As Charlie says, they are in his debt; but she still hopes they've covered their tracks, just in case.

Clavell stands in front of his mansion. The wind of the hovercar taking off ruffles his immaculate suit and hair. He lifts his arm, in either a wave or a salute. Then they're gone, weaving their way back through the other mansions of the Apex.

"All these people up in Tinsel," Kivon says, using the slang term for the floating neighborhood. "How their lives will change if we actually pull this off."

"A lot of them will go tumbling down, to live with the rest of us on ground level," Charlie replies. "Maybe it'll be better for them." Her smile is sad. She's turning against her own family once again, bringing the Mantels down into total ruin. It must in a way be hardest for her, out of all of them.

The Trust fall into silence. They're all tense, nervous. They should have had weeks longer to plan, and instead it's been a hasty, last-ditch effort to send out information before it's too late. Dax reaches out and takes Carina's hand and squeezes it. She keeps it for a moment, then pulls her hand away.

"When are you two going to stop pretending you haven't fucked?" Raf asks bluntly.

Dax clears his throat.

"Really?" Charlie asks. "That's interesting. When?"

"Ah. The night of the party." Dax sounds sheepish.

"Where?" she continues her investigation.

An awkward silence. They both glance at Kivon's seat, then away.

"Augh," Kivon says, jumping up.

It startles everyone into a laugh, breaking the tension at least a little.

They fly to San Francisco, eyes on the horizon. Sometimes there are random sky checks, where a driver has to pull over and present their credentials to a police bot. They have false papers, just in case, and they're wearing scrambler masks to boot, but it's still a worry. Yet with every mile they travel away from the city of Hollywood and the urban sprawl, Carina finds she breathes a little easier. No matter what, they are doing something. They're flying over the coast. Carina looks out at the dark patches of forest, the zigzag of the coast. It's so dark compared to the ever-lit sprawl of Los Angeles. Down below, people sleep, unaware that tomorrow morning everything might be different.

Raf and Charlie murmur in the corner, going over the last details for the umpteenth time, and the rest of the Trust half-listen to their conversation.

"There's no going back," Carina says, softly.

"No. There's not," Charlie agrees. "We have no idea what will happen tonight."

"Either this will work or we will all die spectacularly," Raf says, remarkably cheerful.

"Not the best angle for a pep talk, Raf," Kivon says.

They've discussed the potential consequences many times. Sudice is tied into so many elements of Pacifica, its fall could mean an unraveling of society. Or other companies, just as corrupt, could sprout up in its place.

"We can't do it all," Charlie says. "It's not up to us to fix every-thing that's wrong with Pacifica and the rest of the world. We do what we can, and hope everyone else steps up."

As the hovercar slices through the sky, they draw ever closer to Sudice. They enter San Francisco from the south on the San Mateo flight path. In front of them, the city glitters and glows. The bay is its signature luminescent green, the orchard towers reach toward the starred sky, flanked by apartment blocks. There's the TransAm Pyramid. There's the Bank of Pacifica Center. The usual clouds have fled, and all is cool and clear.

They park the hovercar a few blocks away from the Sudice headquarters on the Embarcadero. Kivon has been listening on all the subfrequencies, and there's nothing from the police that hints they're on alert. The Trust have been locked out of Su-dice's servers for the most part since the silo, though, unable to risk another Viper to try and get in. Raf's been able to get enough scraps that they're fairly certain there's been no emer-gency changeover of all their procedures, especially not at the San Francisco office.

Carina glances in the direction of the Omni Hotel, where Sudice are having their press dinner to announce the upgrade and several other products—banal things like a new type of replicator and hovercar. Harmless and designed to distract from the real threat.

It'll be an evening of tuxedos and ball gowns, real cham-pagne and wallscreens screening carefully curated versions of what they want Pacifica to think Pythia will do. Roz will be there, decked in her finery, hopefully nice and distracted from what is about to happen right beneath her nose. Kim and Aliyah will be there, ready to record watching it all fall. If the Trust make it that far.

The monolith of the Sudice headquarters towers above them. Even the building looks evil—all black glass and chrome. Up near the top, in those state-of-the-art labs, Carina nearly killed two people. She chose to leave her work, her career, to run away from her problems. Now she must try to stop a woman from pushing the limits of humanity, and hopefully gain a little redemption for herself.

Dax has mapped Aliyah's cornea and fingerprints onto Charlie. Her eyes are now darker, but you can't tell a thing from her fingertips, of course. It's still strange to think that her identity, in a way, has shifted. It's what all the celebrities in Hollywood like Clavell fear: someone taking pieces of them, becoming them, right down to the cellular level. It's not easy to do that detailed level of flesh work. Dax made it look easy.

Time for the first step. They're all dressed in military-grade Kalar suits, which even Clavell struggled to secure for them. With the hoods pulled up, they'll be cloaked from the infrared sensors. Kivon still has his extra ocular implants, and he's able to see in the dark. They all have weapons—guns, knives, small hand-held tranq dart guns.

With any luck, they won't need them.

They wait. Security drones make their occasional rounds of the perimeter, in a seemingly random pattern. Raf has cracked it. If they enter from that direction in two minutes, they'll have a two-minute-thirty-six-second window.

"Go," Raf whispers. They dart forward under the cover of night. Kivon carries most of their kit slung across his back. The Trust move like shadows. Carina feels alive. Her fingers tingle. It's not the same as hunting a person, but it's still thrilling. She's killing a company. An idea. She's going to watch it all bleed out.

They make it through the first ring of security. Now it's getting into the building itself. The Trust make their way toward the entrance to the underground parking structure. They go to a side entrance. Kivon unhooks his backpack from his shoulders and passes Raf a piece of kit, which he places over the controls. He can't quite jimmy the lock, but he can prep it for Charlie. Raf spends a few minutes entering his meticulously created code. The Trust wait, eyes constantly roving, keeping a sharp eye out for Waspbots, camera drones or anyone else. Carina rests her hand lightly on her gun. It comforts her.

Raf gives a muted "Yes!" Raf notices that all of the internal systems and bots are synchronized to a Network Time Protocol server. NTP keeps clocks aligned over various data networks. Sudice has the NTP servers linked to cesium atomic clocks that are precice to the millisecond. Raf finds a flaw in security—they did not cryptographically sign the NTP packets for authentication. It is a fairly simply matter to spoof the NTP message and flip the clock on all systems from PM to AM. They can enter and security will think it's normal working hours and not sound the alarm. He's made a few other modifications to the system, too—motion detection within the building is now turned off, along with heat sensors, just in case they have to take off their hoods for any reason. Raf is nothing if not thorough.

Charlie reveals her face. She scans Aliyah's VeriChip, presses her thumb to the panel, then crouches down to present her false eye. A few tense seconds as the machine processes. Then the small red light turns to green. Charlie pushes the door open and the Trust sneak through, the special Kalar suits making them almost invisible. Charlie closes the door behind her. She takes a deep breath before pulling the hood back over her face.

The underground parking lot is completely empty of hovercars. They keep to the edges, the only sounds their echoing footsteps against the concrete and their ragged breaths. At the next door, all they need is Aliyah's employee badge and they're through again. The main building of Sudice is all clear windows, cold metal and marble. They stand at the very edge of the grand lobby. Being here again is strange. Carina's been here many times in the dark of night, when she was working late. It's almost as if she's stepped back to her time in the SynMaps project. Almost.

They've all studied the blueprints countless times. Single file, they edge around the lobby and make their way to the head security room. There's a ring of Waspbots watching it, dead to the world thanks to Raf. Kivon takes out three small orbs and throws them. They hit the Waspbots in quick succession, spreading out along the metal casing. The bots jerk and then fall to the floor, short-circuited.

Raf gives Kivon a high five, and then a little kiss.

They break into the security room. The wallscreens are full of cameras throughout the building. Control access points for human guards to be able to override aspects of the security system. Just what they need. Raf begins his work, with Charlie and Dax offering advice in low voices. Kivon covers the door. Carina stands next to him but ultimately feels a little useless. She should have made better use of her time at the compound— brainloading how to fight, brushing up on hacking. Something, anything. Instead, she focused on clinging to sobriety.

"Um," Raf says. "It's not working."

Dax swivels his head toward the shorter man.

"What do you mean?"

"We're locked out, even though we shouldn't be. These are controls anyone's meant to be able to change—in case of an emergency or something," Raf says.

A buzz sounds in all of their implants.

"Good evening, Carina and friends," Roz's voice says pleasantly.

They all freeze. Carina checks her implants. The outside signal is blocked. If Kim noticed Roz leaving the Omni Hotel, there was no way to sound an alarm, even through subfrequencies.

"Oh fuck," Raf says. Carina agrees.

Even now, through the small window of the security door, she can see Roz walking down the hallway, flanked by men and women in Kalar suits with guns. A flock of AI Waspbots circles above them, ready to strike. She's changed out of whatever ball gown she wore to the press expo, and is clad head-to-toe in Kalar.

"How many of those bot killer things do you have?" Carina asks Raf.

"I only have five more." His eyes narrow as he takes in what's happening outside.

There are at least seven Waspbots, and an equal number of guards for Roz. Fifteen people and bots versus their four, plus if Roz knew they were coming here instead of the LA headquarters, then the whole building could turn against them.

Kivon passes the information to the others. Raf's shoulders are hunched as he works at the controls in the security room. Kivon bars the door with one of the metal chairs, in case Roz can override the locks. It won't stop them for long, but it may slow them down.

"I have an idea," Raf says. "It's risky as fuck, though."

There's an aching hesitation, but Charlie gives a terse nod. Raf's fingers fly as he calls down code from his offline implants.

The server room is two floors above them. They are meant to have finished here and be there by now, sending out all the information, looking out those clear windows to the glowing bay and knowing the world is about to change. So close. So impossibly far.

"Come on out, Carina," Roz says. "There's no point fighting. You don't have a chance. Come out with your hands up and I won't shoot your friends."

"Liar," Carina spits at her through the bulletproof glass.

Roz laughs. Carina can't see her face beneath the Kalar suit. If she could, she's certain it would be creased into a feral grin, her eyes bright. An expression not unlike Carina's in the Zealscape, so many times before.

"There!" Raf cries behind him, and a second later, the Waspbots begin to fire on Roz and her human guards. "Reverse engineered the command key from the—"

"Now is really not the time, Raf," Charlie says, loading her gun.

Roz screeches, and several of her guards scream. They duck for cover.

"Come on, to the server room," Charlie says.

They open the door and dart out. Roz is near the end of the hallway, ducked down, firing back at the Waspbots. One bot is hit and it falls, crashing to the floor in a fountain of sparks. She shoots in the Trust's direction, and bullets from the other guards follow. They ricochet against the walls, the noise so loud it seems to vibrate within Carina's skull.

Someone behind her cries out. She can't afford to look back. All she can do is put one foot in front of the other as fast as possible. They turn the corridor and start running up the stairs. A lone AI follows them—Roz has somehow turned it back, perhaps, or it's one from another part of the building. Kivon throws one of his weapons and the Waspbot halts then tumbles down the stairs. As they all turn back to watch, Raf stumbles.

His hands go to his stomach and come away darkened with

blood. He looks to Kivon and falls. The bullet shouldn't have gone through at that angle. Carina grows cold, wondering if Roz has access to bullets specially designed to pierce Kalar suits.

Kivon catches him, holding him in his arms. "Come on," he says. His face is harsh. He shifts Raf and uses his hand to press against Raf's wound. Raf screams. Carina reaches into the pack on his back and takes out the remaining bot killers. Footsteps sound below and they all sprint to the server room. It's locked.

Charlie takes out the kit to break in. Her hands are shaking. Raf's breath is coming in ragged gasps. It's like the silo all over again.

It's a disaster in the making.

As they cover Charlie, the first of Roz's guards crest the top of the stairs. Kivon takes aim and fires. The guard staggers but does not fall. Carina takes aim next, her heart aching as she aims right for the throat.

She fires. He falls, his scream cut silent. There's a chance that's another kill to add to her tally.

The next person appears. She fires again, three times.

Carina and Kivon do most of the shooting. Dax gives Raf first aid, smearing Amrital onto the wounds, and she doesn't have the heart to ask Dax what the prognosis is, especially with Kivon there. It doesn't look good. Dax injects Raf with something that will slow his heart rate, something else to help with blood clotting. It might buy him time, but only if they can escape this building within the next hour.

Four of Roz's guards lie sprawled on the floor among bullet shells, broken glass from the windows. One body is pooled with blood, and the warm, iron scent reaches Carina. It feels just as thrilling as a Zealscape. Or more. This is real danger.

Carina doesn't know where Roz is.

"Yes!" Charlie cries out behind them. The door swings open. They shuffle into the server room, but Carina stays behind.

"Come on, what are you doing?" Dax asks, eyes wide.

"I need to go find Roz," she says.

"I'll come with you."

She shakes her head. "You're not a fighter. You should stay with Charlie. She has to do this on her own now, and she doesn't have the skills that Raf does. You and Kivon have to help." Another guard comes up the stairs. Carina pushes Dax back into the server room and takes cover behind the open metal door just in time. The bullets blast against the door.

She takes aim and hits the man in the gun arm. It knocks the weapon from his hand, giving her time to aim again and hit him in the throat. She twists and looks at Dax, who gazes at her with his mouth open, a hint of fear in his eyes that he can't contain. Good. He should still be a little afraid of her.

"This is between Roz and me."

"Be careful," he says. "Try not to go down in a blaze of glory." The words are meant to be flippant, but his tone is not.

She flashes one of her stiff smiles at him. "I'll do my best."

There's no lingering last kiss. There's no time, and they're not in one of Isaac Clavell's films. There's an instant of eye contact, of understanding. And then Carina turns and walks down the stairs, gun at the ready in her hand, only pausing to rip the Kalar hood off of the fallen soldiers and shoot them in the head to make sure they're truly dead. She doesn't turn back to see if Dax is watching.

FORTY-TWO

DAX

Sudice headquarters, San Francisco,
California, Pacifica

Dax hears the gunshots against the closed door. He cracks it open, sees the corpses, but not Carina. He stares for a few precious moments at the fallen bodies. Is it any worse, seeing the blood rather than a prone, Kalar-clad form, or knowing that it is Carina who has done this? He closes the door again and turns away.

The server room looks as he expected. It's small, the servers black and glowing with blue light. The machinery whirrs gently. It seems almost peaceful in here after the gunshots, the crash of glass and desperate run for their lives.

Charlie has already started trying to link the server to a connection. They've brought an older piece of tech with them, a router that will work with a secure line. Another one of Raf's ideas. Their own relay to bypass the safeguards. Everyone's so used to everything being synced wirelessly and accessed by implants, they might not have a good defense against something old enough to actually need wires. Raf created a converter, and Charlie's trying to plug it in.

Dax looks at Raf, worried. He's fully unconscious. His

347

vitals are steady, for now, but they need to get him to some-where with medical equipment. He has all he needs back at the Trust headquarters, but who knows if that's safe, or if Sudice found it and trashed the place? They might have to drop Raf off at a hospital like they did for Dax, and the thought fills him with terror. What if they do the same thing to Raf as they did to him, and use his mind for their own purposes?

Charlie is shaking, but she's managed to attach Raf's device. She starts to prep the connection. Dax puts a hand on her shoulder and squeezes for reassurance.

Kivon saves their lives. "Duck!" he screams, opening fire.

Dax glimpses one of the ceiling tiles moving, and a Kalar-swathed head peeks down along with the point of a gun. He falls behind a server, panting. Kivon's firing. Charlie's some-what shielded by the column of servers as she works franti-cally. She's shaking so much she can barely type and keeps having to go back and rewrite sections of code. What if a bullet hits the main server? Several of the backups are already down, the blue lights extinguished. Water pools on the floor where some of the bullets fractured the water lines cooling the serv-ers. If it all goes, then they're trapped. All this for nothing.

Kivon is protecting Raf, and at this angle he has no hope of hitting the shooter. Or is it more than one person above them? In the melee, Dax can't tell. He's never been so fucking afraid in his life. Kivon cries out and crumples.

Dax clutches his gun, moving closer to the other man. Kivon's been hit in the shoulder, but it's a graze. It doesn't seem to have breached his Kalar, but he's broken his clavicle. He'll be in so much pain he won't be able to see straight.

It's up to Dax. He tries to find his focus. He darts around a wall of broken servers and fires upward. He hits the man in the face, and their attacker falls from the ceiling down to the floor, landing on his neck. The crack is loud in the silence. The man does not move.

The Trust all stare for a moment. He was trying to kill them, and it's not the first corpse they've seen tonight, but the aftermath of a death still leaves them stricken. Dax crawls over to Kivon and rummages in the first-aid kit. "Any other injuries for you or Raf?"

Kivon shakes his head, his lips clamped shut in pain. "Fucking rookie mistake. Shouldn't have gotten hit."

"You're protecting Raf. Hard to keep your head when the person you love is hurt. My only advice is to take that fear and pain and try to turn it into rage."

He nods, features tightening. Dax takes the painkillers and sticks one in Kivon's neck. Kivon's tight muscles relax, and he gives Dax a nod. Dax moves closer to Charlie. He's not been hit but all his muscles feel like they've taken a beating.

"You hurt?"

She shakes her head, frowning over the servers.

"Any luck?"

"Some. I'm just so slow compared to Raf. And I'm worried I'm going to miss something vital. Is Raf totally out?"

"Fully unconscious. I'm sorry, but you're on your own here."

"I got you and Kivon. Better off than most. Where's Carina?"

"She's gone after Roz."

"Hope she buys us some time. I need all I can get."

Dax leaves her to her work, knowing what he has to do. He takes his gun and creeps closer to where the hit guard lies, keeping cover when he can. When he reaches the body, he kicks the extra gun over to Kivon. He aims his weapon up toward the ceiling, making sure no one else is there. He's in the open—if anyone is there, now is when they'll fire. To be safe, he shoots into the ceiling a few times, the sounds ringing in his ears. No cries of pain.

Dax reaches out and pulls the Kalar hood off the guard who tried to kill them all. He looks heartbreakingly young. He's not dead. He blinks slowly. By the way the blood runs out of the corner of his mouth and ears, though, Dax knows he doesn't have long. He presses the gun against the boy's temple. The boy closes his eyes.

Dax fires.

FORTY-THREE

CARINA

*Sudice headquarters, San Francisco,
California, Pacifica*

Carina sees no one on her way back to ground level. She feels exposed despite the Kalar suit. The bodies of Roz's guards are below. She counts five. Gunshots sound above from the direction of the server room. Her steps slow. She should help. What if any of them are hurt?

The low beep of the intercom sounds. "Carina," Roz's disembodied voice says, low and clear. "Come on, Carina. We have unfinished business, don't we?" She gives a laugh and it sends a shiver down Carina's spine. Of anticipation or fear, she's not sure. Both.

"I'm coming," Carina mutters, and makes her way up the stairs.

•

The entrance to the lab is just as she remembers it. Shiny, clean and untouched by the gunfire and fighting below. Carina holds her gun. She's low on bullets, but by her calculations of the bodies downstairs and the one in the server room, there could still be one guard unaccounted for. She should be able to manage one more guard and Roz. She hopes she can.

She walks down the corridor, opening each door and checking it with her gun. There's her old office. It looks similar— Carina never bothered personalizing it, and whoever works in there now hasn't done much to it either.

Carina reaches the end of the corridor. There is the lab. Beautiful instruments, that sprawling view of San Francisco glittering below them. This was almost her home once. Where she came right after waking up, and left just before she went to sleep. Her life was here, with Mark, Kim and Aliyah. With Roz at the helm, for a brief period Carina had felt she was doing something worthwhile. Then it all fell apart and shattered.

Roz is standing there, in her dark Kalar suit. Though Carina can't see her face, she'd know that confident stance anywhere. Roz's gun is aimed right at Carina's throat.

"Let it go, Roz," Carina says. "You're not on the right side in this and you know it."

"The right side is all a matter of perspective," Roz says, words clipped. She's frightened but determined not to let it show. Carina can use that.

"Why haven't you brought the full force of Sudice and the police on us?" Carina asks. "Just a small selection of guards. A few bots. What are you afraid of? Does Mantel know what you're really up to?"

"It does not take the full might of Sudice to take you down. Don't get ahead of yourself."

"Your bots are dead. Your guards are gone."

"Not all of them, Carrie."

Carina feels strong arms wrap around her, one hand knocking her gun to the ground and the other crushing her windpipe. The last guard, silent as a shadow, and she curses herself for a fool.

Roz walks up to her and pulls off the bulletproof hood. The guard presses something against her neck, but she can't tell what it is. It doesn't feel as sharp as a knife, it's too thick.

"Oh Carrie, you have caused me so much fucking trouble," Roz says, voice sweet as sugar.

"The Trust will send all they have out," Carina says. "No matter what you do to me."

"Oh, please. Do you think I'm an idiot? We've dropped an extra firewall as tough as a Kalar suit around the building. Nothing's going to get out tonight."

Carina sags. All this work. All that effort getting the information, dragging it from memories best left forgotten, for nothing. She'll die here tonight, with the rest of the Trust.

"No one will even know you're here," Roz says in a soft whisper, her hand coming up to cup Carina's cheek. "Downstairs, the bots are at work repairing the broken windows, removing the bodies, sweeping up shattered glass. Tomorrow all will go on as normal, except the world will never know your name and what you tried to do."

"Just like Nettie," Carina whispers, and Roz jumps at the name. She gestures at the guard.

Carina's entire body jerks and goes limp. He has a Stunner against her neck, but it hasn't hit her off-center, like that dark Los Angeles night just after Mark dumped the info in her head. The guard drags her along the lab and deposits her in one of the Chairs. Not just any Chair, either, but the one she used to study Subject B and Subject E. At least it's not the one that Roz used to mold her into someone new. Scant comfort. The Stunner hasn't affected her adrenal glands, and terror rushes through her. She's lying right where two of her victims lay during those SynMaps trials. Trying to speak, she only manages a rough moan.

Roz puts on the various electrodes, though she doesn't bother strapping Carina in as she can't move anyway. "Now," she says, all brisk business, "I can't pretend I haven't been looking forward to this. I can't tell you how many hours I've spent planning this moment. So many ways it could go."

Carina wishes she could warn Dax and the others. Carina wants to ask Roz what her plan is. Roz likes evening the scales, meting out her own form of justice. In that way, they are the same. Carina has humiliated her. Threatened to destroy her work, her career. Carina has failed Roz by not keeping that code perfect in her head, by daring to become human again, even if that humanity was scarred with the monstrous. Roz is not the type to let anyone forget they've wronged her.

"Are you going to kill me, then?" Carina says. The thought of death does frighten her now, when a few weeks ago it wouldn't have. She has more to live for. The hope of a life.

"Not yet. That'd be too easy for you." Roz leans against the edge of the Chair. Carina imagines her hands unbound, reaching out to scratch out the other woman's eyes. She would enjoy every scream. She'd pop Roz's eyeballs like blueberries.

Focus. Focus.

"I debated killing you quickly. Or giving you seizures like the ones you gave Subjects B and E. Seemed fitting. I found all your dreams. I know exactly what your worst nightmare would be." She leans over Carina's face, grinning. On the Chair, Carina shudders.

She holds up a syringe. "I'm going to do what I tried to do at Sudice that day you left. I'm going to reset you."

Carina's pulse spikes. "You are *not* dampening me again."

"This is ironclad. It won't break down. In fact, you'll be so loyal to me that if anything does go awry, I'm the first person you'll come running to. I've learned so much, Carina, and it's thanks to you, in a way. I've never hated anyone as intensely as I've loathed you."

"Thought . . . emotions made you weak," Carina grinds out through numbed lips.

"They do. I locked it away, in the end. The memory of it is still there. That hate made me stronger. It made me willing to do anything to win."

"Like butchering a teenage girl," Carina says.

Roz does not flinch this time. She's close to Carina again. If Carina could move, she could arch up and bite her. Carina craves the taste of Roz's blood against her teeth and tongue, the satisfying scream the woman would give.

"You see, Carrie. Watching all your dreams at the Green Star Lounge means I understand you, perhaps more than anyone else ever could."

Carina feels a strange rushing in her ears. She knew Roz had found some dreams when she planted one of them in Dax's head; but she hadn't anticipated that she had seen all of them.

"It's time to leave all that behind. Emotion is a weakness. Aren't you tired of it overwhelming you, clouding your decisions?"

Carina can't help it; she lets out a sob. Roz reaches out and presses a fingertip against the tear that has leaked down her cheek. "Oh, Carrie. I will make you strong again. And, side by side, we will do such great things. Now it's time to go back to Greenview House, just for a little while. And while you're screaming in your mind, I'll go kill your friends."

Roz begins to prep the code. Carina struggles against her inert body, the panic rising. The emotions frightened her, the urges almost overwhelmed her, but they didn't. She kept them under control well enough that she didn't kill. She was able to grow closer to the Trust, to Dax. She doesn't want to look at him and feel nothing. The idea of being trapped at Roz's side, her cowed lackey, is worse than any nightmare within Greenview House.

Roz presses the button.

•

Greenview House feels like the actual house, not the re-creation she made for her Zealscapes. It seems so real and solid, like she's there as a child again. The afternoon sunlight filters through the windows, dust motes like golden glitter in the warm air. The fear she felt in the Sudice headquarters is all gone, as if it never existed. It's as if she's gone back in time, to before everything went wrong. When her father hid his violence behind the closed doors of this house, and her mother tried so hard to protect her from the reality of the monster in their midst.

She smells toast and honey.

"Mother?" Carina calls. She walks through the hallways, small as a child. She wants to find her mother and curl up with her on the couch in that warm patch of sunlight, have those arms wrap around her and breathe in that scent of peppermint.

Her mother is not there, yet the wallscreen in the living room has switched on.

Carina perches on the sofa, wrapping her arms around her knees like she used to do as a child.

Her memories roll out on the wallscreen, slow and steady. They're out of order. One moment she's seven, turning up the music in her auditory implants so she can't hear her parents fighting. Even as she watches, the vestigial fear she felt on that day disappears into nothing. Another memory of her mother helping her with a school project, spending ages gluing together the parts they'd ordered through the replicator to make a small spaceship she'd be able to launch with the other children in the field behind the school. Her mother had glue on her cheek and Carina had reached out and pressed her fingertip to it.

"Oh no," her mother had said. "You're stuck with me."

"That's OK," Carina had said shyly, with that hint of a lisp her father hated so.

The warmth around that memory extinguished, until she felt nothing. More memories went by, and Carina watched them, feeling more and more impassive.

No, some part of her thought. She ignored it, watching a memory of her father hit her, feeling it no longer sting. Perhaps this wasn't so bad.

No. The voice is a little louder. Then: NO.

"This isn't real," Carina says aloud. "This isn't real. I don't want this."

Nettie appears on the wallscreen. Her lips draw back from her teeth. Her sutures are weeping. "You don't get to escape my fate," she says. Some cruel part of Carina's subconscious, punishing her.

Greenview House twists, buckles, becoming just like it was in her Zealscapes. The colors are darker and harsher. Shades of gray instead of gold. Carina stands up from the sofa and wriggles her fingers and toes. She lets herself take one small moment to pretend that this is just another Zeal trip.

Everything has changed. The house is no longer that sanctuary rebuilt from her terrible childhood memories. She knows she has to go through the corridor and open the door, to see what Roz has left behind, to reach the front door. Maybe if she leaves the house behind, she can wake up. She doesn't know how she knows this, or if it's true, but it's all she has to go on, so she moves forward, doggedly.

She holds out her hand and tries to call forth a gun from thin air. In any of her Zealscapes, it'd only take a fraction of a second. No gun appears. Her empty hand falls to her side. Her fear roars to life, but she's pathetically glad she can still feel it.

She feels so small. So alone. Like that little girl watching the bonfire out back behind this grand house, seeing that burned skull of her childhood pet. The first memory that set all of this in motion. She no longer feels that fear at the sight of the cat skull in the flames. Are her emotions still breaking down with every moment she spends in here?

Carina opens the first door. There's one of the victims she created in the Green Star Lounge. A man based on her father's physiology, but changed enough that the sight of him didn't make her shudder. She'd peeled off his skin, inch by inch. He staggers around the room, muscles weeping old blood, his empty eye sockets staring at her, his mouth open in a scream. The white room is splattered with blood and connective tissue. He points a finger at her. She slams the door shut.

Her breath rushes in and out. She's changed since she was in her personal Zealscapes like this. The sight of that old victim did not fill her with delight at violence, but sickness and guilt. Do all of these doors contain the reanimated ghosts of her fictional kills?

That is what Roz has decided to do to her while she files away all the rough edges of Carina's personality. She started the program sweetly, but if Carina dares to fight back, it will turn into a nightmare.

Carina opens the next door. There's the woman Roz showed

to the rest of the Trust after Carina neurohacked Dax and stopped him from being a sleeper agent. Her chest is a gaping, dark red hole, and she can't stop screaming, high and pure as a banshee. There's a tall, skinny man with old-fashioned glasses. Carina had smashed the lenses and pressed the glass shards into his flesh to kill him. They're still there, half-submerged in his skin, dripping blood.

They shouldn't scare her as much as they do. They are not real. They are only her creations, brought forth just to be destroyed. Yet their screams hurt her in a way nothing else ever has.

She has to find a way out. She has to return to reality, to save the Trust. To save herself.

"Wake me up!" she cries. Of course, nothing happens. No failsafe. She doesn't know how else she can break through, or how big a dose of Zeal or Verve flows through her system. When she does wake up, if Roz doesn't simply kill her while she's under, the drug is going to mess with her. She'll be worse than that night at the silo, when she wanted nothing more than to kill anyone who crossed her path. Even if she wakes up, there's no guarantee she'll be able to do anything to help the Trust. And she's fast running out of time.

The reanimated corpses of her Zeal kills scratch against the closed walls of the hallway. She fears that soon they'll break through and overwhelm her. Is that what Roz plans, to have her killed by her own creations? A fitting way to go, Carina supposes. Not that far off her original plan of staying in the Zealscape until she starved to death. This, though, she has no control over, and emotions are still roaring through her, sharp as scalpels.

Falling to the ground, she curls up, wrapping her arms about her head. Everything's too loud, too bright, too real in a world she knows is made of pixels and code. The doors are opening, the dead trailing through Greenview House, coming for her.

Something shifts and turns. She feels someone standing over her.

It's Nettie again. She's uninjured this time and she offers her hand to Carina.

"You're another one of my victims, too," Carina says, voice hoarse. "If I hadn't broken, she wouldn't have broken you."

"Neither of us is responsible for what she did to us," Nettie says.

"You're just my subconscious," Carina says, her voice thick with tears.

"Yes, but that doesn't mean I'm wrong. Go home, Carina. You know how."

With Nettie's help, Carina pulls herself up to standing. She moves forward, passing through Nettie, who disintegrates into a flood of pixels. Almost like Mark's AI, but dredged up from her own fear. A phantom that appeared when she needed it most. She reaches the front door and pushes it open, leaving behind her nightmare childhood home.

She collapses on the front path, surrounded by rose bushes. A bee lands on a blood-red bloom.

"Wake me up!" she whispers, and closes her eyes tight.

•

Carina wakes up, alone in the lab. They've left her unattended. She was meant to be asleep for hours yet. Her face is wet with tears. She's shaking with fear.

"I'm still me," Carina whispers. She breaks down into sobs. "I'm still afraid. I can still feel. She didn't win. She didn't win."

Some damage has been done. Many of her childhood

memories feel remote and distant, including the ones Mark tied information to. There's no time to mourn.

Carina can move her muscles again, but only slowly. It takes too long to sit up and find a way to stand on shaky feet. Her gun is gone, but at least she still has her Kalar suit. Her body thrums with leftover emotions from the Zealscape. The urge to kill is dampened, as it should be. One scant comfort, but as ever, she's not looking forward to withdrawal and the urges that come with it. As soon as she seems to kick the habit, back into the Zealscape she goes. With any luck, this will be the last time, and not because she dies tonight.

She looks around the lab for something to use as a weapon. In the process, she finds a bottle of beta blockers, similar to those Chopper gave her the night she briefly became Althea Bryant. The scientists used them on subjects sometimes, and they're still stored in the same place. She downs one, hoping it helps her shaking hands.

The knives are in the same drawer as always, and though the drawer is locked, with a decisive tug she breaks the cheap replicated wood around the lock. She chooses a nice, pointy knife, and feels better with a weapon in her hand. Then she totters to the frozen cupboard and opens it. *Aha.* The liquid nitrogen is still where it was when she worked here. They didn't need it often, but it was always on hand. There was even a small, handy portable dewar. That'll do. She tucks the knife into the belt of her Kalar and takes the cryo-gloves from the hook outside the cupboard, slipping them on before picking up the canister.

She stumbles from the lab, the dewar of nitrogen unbalancing her. Though she's still not exactly sure how she woke herself up, she's glad to be away from Greenview House. If she never sees that fucking place again, it'll be too soon.

Trying to ping the Trust is useless; her implants are still blocked. She's alone inside her head.

Carina takes the stairs, trying to remain quiet. Her heartbeat is still pounding like a drum in her ears. She hears the gunfire long before she reaches the level with the server room. Keeping to the darkest part of the hallway, she peers around, afraid of what she might find.

Roz has taken cover behind an open door opposite the server room. Carina is at a terrible angle and can't see the remaining guard. Someone's shooting at Roz from behind the door, back and forth in a metallic standoff.

Carina starts to crawl along the hallway, as low to the floor as she can. She has an idea, though it might only get her a bullet in her skull for her trouble. She's out of options, and out of time. The Trust can't have much ammo left. When she's close to the door, she unscrews the top of the dewar. She takes a deep breath, holds it, narrows her eyes to slits, then twists around the door and throws the liquid nitrogen at Roz.

Kalar suits are bulletproof, but not immune to corrosives. It burns through, and Roz begins to scream. Carina sets the dewar down and grabs her arm, dragging her into the server room, not breathing in case the liquid nitrogen turns to nitrogen gas in the hallway.

"Fucking hell," Dax says, looking at them both before darting for his med kit.

The shooting has stopped. Carina hopes that means the last guard is either dead or knocked out. No Waspbots have swooped down on them, so Raf's patch on them must have held.

Dax sprays medicine onto Roz, neutralizing the acid. He begins to clean the cold burns. Carina personally wouldn't bother, but she leaves him to it, although not before ensuring Roz's hands and feet are tied. Her Kalar suit has partially disintegrated. There are a few blisters on her neck and along her jaw, but the worst injuries showing are the angry burns on her stomach and left leg. Dax rummages in his pack again and begins spraying an epithelial autografting spray onto the wounds. The mix of keratinocytes, fibroblasts and melanocytes will protect the burns and promote rapid healing. So Carina's little trick with the liquid nitrogen won't kill Roz, but it definitely hurts like a motherfucker. Good.

The beta blockers have kicked in, and between that and the Zeal after-effects, Carina feels calmer than she has in a long time.

"Roz said that even if you can send things from this server, it'll be caught by another firewall," she says to Charlie, who's crouched in front of a small screen connected to the server, tapping onto an ancient keyboard. She didn't even know those things still existed.

"Extra work for us then," Charlie says.

"Where's Raf?" Carina asks.

"Injured," Kivon says. "And badly. We need to get out of here."

"I think I found the recent block they've done," Charlie told them breathlessly. "It's a little messy. I might be able to unravel it."

"How long?"

"Probably longer than we have. That press junket is going to start any minute now, and the implant upgrades are set to instantly download in about half an hour."

"Shit." Carina takes in the damage. Charlie seems relatively unharmed. Kivon's face is badly bruised. Raf is alive, but desperately needs medical attention. Most of the servers are dead. No alarms sound, and no police have arrived. Was Roz really so determined to catch the Trust on her own that she didn't notify anyone of their presence?

Carina is surrounded by death and gore. She can smell the blood. She hopes the Zeal and beta blockers hold. She doesn't want to turn feral, like the night of the silo. She wants to help, not have to be tied up right next to Roz to prevent her hurting anyone else.

"Let me see," she says. "I'm rusty but I might be able to help."

They puzzle through it, carefully unpeeling the new layers, trying to find a way to break the firewall. It's going too slowly, but they have to keep calm and avoid mistakes.

"I think I got it," Charlie says. "This new firewall they plopped down is hyper secure, but they haven't updated to the latest version. Too hasty. This version has a stack-based buffer overflow in their DNS client resolver. Just give me a minute. Still means it'll be hard to get out intel quickly, but at least it'd start."

"Almost everyone in Sudice already has Pythia, right? And we have their names and ways to ping them from the intel dump."

Charlie's eyes widen. "Brilliant."

"I've missed something," Dax says.

"We can relay the information through their implants. It'll be the first point of contact, then it'll relay out from there. I'll also target that damn press junket."

She creates a quick exploit code to attack the flaw. The problem is, they haven't been able to prepare for this or run simulations. If this doesn't work, they won't have a second chance. They won't be able to access implants before Pythia digs its claws into Pacifica.

She gives Carina a nervous look. Carina nods. It looks as good to her as it could.

Charlie blasts through the last bit of code, and there: the connection is completely open. Charlie turns to the others. The whites of her eyes are bloodshot, and there are cuts from flying debris on her cheeks.

"Send it," Kivon says. He smiles, and blood from a split upper lip coats his teeth.

"Sorry, cousin." Charlie gives a little shrug and begins the upload.

"Let Sudice burn," Carina whispers.

FORTY-FOUR

KIM

Omni Hotel, San Francisco,
California, Pacifica

"Stop fidgeting," Aliyah hisses under her breath. "You're completely failing at acting natural."

"How can you be so calm?" Kim demands. One of the other women at their table—Donna Harker, the CEO of Silvercloud Solutions—gives them a look out of the corner of her eye. Kim takes a deep breath, digging her hands into the skirt of her dress.

"Inside I'm screaming." Aliyah smiles serenely. She leans closer, pretending to refold her napkin. "No word?"

"Not a peep. Totally blocked." Kim tries not to think about the fact the Trust could all be dead. She only saw Roz very briefly during canapes, and as soon as she disappeared, Kim's stomach dropped. She should have tried to put a sedative in Roz's champagne, risks be damned.

Old Mr. Mantel, the brother of Gregory Mantel's late father, is up on the podium, droning on. Kim has managed to block Aliyah's and her own implants from downloading the upgrade, but the thought of so many people having tech in their heads they didn't consent to makes her sick.

Come on, Carina. Don't let us down.

The old man continues to espouse the virtues of Sudice, how they are the forefront of any innovation within Pacifica since the Great Upheaval. Everyone else in the room is praying for the speech to end, but Kim and Aliyah hope it goes on for as long as possible.

Kim crosses her fingers under the table, begging every female scientist for help, despite not believing in any sort of afterlife. Aliyah reaches out and takes her wrist, squeezing for reassurance.

Old Mantel finishes his speech to applause. Kim has hardly heard a word of it. Mantel steps onto the stage, his hair so gelled it reflects off the light from the glowing chandeliers.

"Thank you. I'm sure if my father were here today, he'd be so pleased to see Sudice still on the cutting edge of technology. My eternal thanks to everyone for coming this evening. You've seen our excellent new replicators, which will be featured in all new builds from this point forward, and our latest model of hovercar. However, in a few minutes, we'll be unveiling our routine brain implant upgrades. It'll include faster downloads, smoother integration into VR and Zealscapes, and more. I'm so excited to see how you find it, as our early feedback has been unanimously positive!"

More applause. *Yes*, Kim wants to say. *Because you already snuck Pythia onto those early reviewers, so it'd never even occur to them to question their reactions.* She wishes she could stand up and scream at them all, tell them this is a trap and Pythia is a lie. She'd only be escorted from the building, sacked from her job and unable to help anyone.

Mantel continues, the large logo for Sudice behind him. There's the tiniest flicker on his wallscreen, so quick Kim isn't sure if it's real. Mantel's hesitation makes her lean forward in her seat.

Mantel tries to recover, but with a screech, his mic cuts out. Behind him, the logos disappear, replaced instead by a young girl, dead, open, mismatched eyes seeing nothing at all.

"Nettie," Aliyah whispers.

"They did it. They fucking did it," Kim says. The CEO of Silvercloud hears her, but in that moment, Kim doesn't care one bit. Kim sets her ocular and auditory implants to brain record. She knows she can do it safely for up to twenty minutes, and she'll want to relive this moment.

The image zooms out and shows Roz, lifting the section of the girl's skull. Roz asks her the emotions she feels regarding certain images. The girl says she feels nothing. Then she dies.

The image wavers. Someone appears on screen, features obscured by a scrambler mask. A shifting kaleidoscope of generic faces stare at the dumbstruck audience of the Omni Hotel.

"This is what they've hidden from you, from the very start," the figure says. Despite the disguised voice, Kim knows it's Carina. Her shoulders are tight. The server room of Sudice flickers behind her. In the lower corner, Kim spies a blur of dark-blonde hair. She'd bet her entire fortune that's the top of Roz's head. Did Carina kill her?

"All of this information was released by a Sudice employee from the inside. Someone who could no longer stand by idly as untold crimes happened in this supposedly crime-free country of Pacifica. This person entrusted it to me, and with the help of some friends, we send this to you. The only things we have omitted are our own personal details, and details of Sudice employees who were not involved in these crimes."

The advertisement for Pythia plays on the large screen. Kim winces as she watches. "Make the right choices," the voiceover says, firm and confident. "Let Pythia™, the optional Sudice upgrade, guide you on your path."

The mask's features flicker again. A man with green eyes. A woman with a tattoo of a dragon on one cheek. An androgynous person, as pale as the moon. "Are you wondering why you never saw this advertisement? They binned it. Do not, under any circumstances, download the Sudice implant upgrade. Pythia is not optional. Pythia is mind control. Its main goal is to rewrite personalities. They tried to do it to me, and it almost broke me. They will try to do it to you, too. Sudice has been working on this deliberately for years. Mantel knew of this. At least a few officials in Pacifica government knew this would happen. We are unsure how widespread it is.

"Watch. Listen. Don't turn away from this. We can only deliver the message. What the people do with it is up to each and every one of you."

The screen goes dark. At the first few words, Mantel tried to slip from the stage. His bodyguards surround him, paving the way to the exit. It's useless on their part; he'll be picked up immediately. There is nowhere left to hide.

Behind Mantel's bowed head, all of his crimes appear. Nettie's death. The scant details of the other people involved in Dr. Roz Elliot's Pythia plans. Memos showing many people in the higher echelons of Sudice knew exactly what it would do. Nondisclosure agreements. And earlier crimes, dozens of them, dating back to Sudice's start during the Great Upheaval. Fraud. Extortion. Tax evasion. More missing people. So many crimes. Too many to ignore.

The silent audience erupts into frightened or excited murmurings. The journalists are one step away from rubbing their hands together with glee, fingers wriggling as they tap into the algorithms that the media bots will use to generate headlines. Donna Harker jerks next to Kim. "This isn't just happening here," she says, her voice shaking. "It's everywhere. Every wallscreen. Every implant. Within Pacifica and in the rest of North America. At least."

"Why, Dr. Harker," Kim says, mildly. "Do you have anything to fear?"

Dr. Harker gives her a wild-eyed stare and stands up, grabbing her things. Many others are also making a getaway. By the call of sirens outside, they won't get far.

Kim wonders if there's anything in those flashing images on the screen that will implicate her and Aliyah. They worked on criminals. It wasn't technically illegal, but it was on the dark side of morally gray. She hated every moment of it, but that doesn't matter. She still did it. So did Aliyah, and Carina, and Mark. If Kim comes under fire for it, then so be it. Helping to undo these wrongs, even in a small way, was completely worth it.

Aliyah grips her hand under the table. "I know one of the workers here. He might be able to get us out," she says under her breath. "The Trust are going to need our help now more than ever."

In the melee of Sudice breaking down entirely, Kim and Aliyah slip away.

FORTY-FIVE

CARINA

Sudice headquarters, San Francisco,
California, Pacifica

The information is still uploading, spreading like a virus through-out Pacifica, the rest of the formerly United States, and soon, the whole world. Their job is done. Almost.

"We did it," Charlie says. "We actually pulled it off." She sounds unbelievably tired.

"And that is definitely our cue to leave," Dax says. "Police will be here in moments, and we desperately need to get Raf better medical attention."

Kivon carries Raf. Charlie wraps up the code, but leaves the wallscreens up. Dax grabs some of the kit, and his medical supplies.

Carina doesn't move. She stares down at Roz, who moves and rolls her eyes up at her former mentee, her co-worker, her rival, her enemy.

The numbness breaks like a dam. Carina feels everything. She turns to the Trust. "You go ahead, I'll follow in a moment."

"Carina—" Dax starts.

"Don't," Carina cuts him off. Roz begins to moan, trying to

move away from Carina, trapped by her bonds. "This is between me and her."

The rest of the Trust look at them both, then they turn and walk away. Dax goes last. "Two minutes," he says. Carina nods.

Carina crouches in front of Roz. The med spray has stopped her bleeding. The burns are still a livid red, covered with a sticky, pale layer of culture.

Roz stares at Carina, unblinking. She doesn't beg, she doesn't fight against her bonds any more. Carina's eyes burn, and her fingers twitch.

Roz seems resigned. If she dies, Roz won't have to face Sudice and lose the career she's given up her morality to gain. She won't need to answer the endless questions from Sudice, or be put on trial with her face blasted on all the media casts. If she survives, everyone will know her for the monster she is. Then she'll be put in stasis, frozen like the subjects used for phase two of SynMaps.

The need to kill rises up in Carina again. It would be a just death. Roz fits her profile so perfectly—a criminal who has done unspeakable things. She killed Nettie. She killed Mark. She tried to kill Carina and the Trust. How many others? Roz is probably responsible for more deaths than Carina's father, either directly or indirectly. And, had this all worked in Roz's favor, she'd be responsible for so many more.

Carina raises her hands to Roz's ruined neck. "The things I would do to you, if I had all the time in the world, all my tools at my disposal," she murmurs, almost gently. "There have been so many times I've imagined this. It's a pity I never brought you forth in the Zealscape, but then I didn't know all you'd actually done to me. And I promised I'd make you pay for what you did to Nettie and to Dax. Would anyone miss you? Would anyone come penalize me, considering the whole world has now seen your sins?"

She takes her hands away from Roz's neck.

Roz closes her eyes. "Spare me the long, rambling speech and simply do it already." Her breathing is ragged, and the burns still weep a little beneath their bio bandages.

Carina takes out that knife still tucked into the small of her back, bringing it up to Roz's face, slicing just beneath her eye on the unburned side of her face. Roz winces.

"Do it quick."

Oh, how she wants to. If only she could take that metal edge and slice it across Roz's throat. She'd be better at it since her first kill. She's had lots of practice in her mind.

"You don't deserve to die quickly." Carina deepens Roz's cut. A few drops of blood well from torn skin. Carina licks her lips. Her heartbeat echoes in her ears. She still wants it, but she doesn't need it. She's stronger than it, and killing no longer defines her.

Dax wanted Carina to choose the harder option of living. Now she's choosing it for herself.

"Kill me," Roz says. "You have to kill me."

"No, Roz. I don't." Carina throws the knife behind her.

Roz screams, rocking her head from side to side. "Don't leave me here! Don't do this to me!"

"You did all this to yourself, Roz."

Roz's screams turn to muffled sobs. Carina leaves her staring at the wallscreen, a witness to Sudice's crimes.

•

The Trust make it to the hovercar just before the police arrive.

No one asks Carina what happened in the lab. They'll find out soon enough when Roz is put on trial. It's quenched something in her, leaving Roz alive, in a way she thought only killing could. She is stronger than her urges. Even if the code she's working on never undoes what Roz did to her, maybe she can come to terms with who she is now. Her heart still pounds, but it's different to that night at the silo. She tilts her head back and laughs, low and controlled.

Dax gives her a look out of the corner of his eye. "You didn't do it."

"She'll be frozen soon enough."

Dax nods. "So she will."

Her laugh does not put the others at ease. Charlie clears her throat. Kivon keeps his eye on the sky. Dax is using the better medical supplies in the hovercar to work on Raf. He's still in terrible shape, but Dax says he shouldn't be in any immediate danger. They should really drop him at a hospital, but Dax thinks he can patch him up on his own, even with limited supplies. The bullet missed the vital organs, but Raf has some internal bleeding. Kivon bows toward his chest, bandaged, muscled shoulders heaving with silent sobs. Dax pats him on the shoulder comfortingly. "He'll be all right."

"He'd better," Kivon says, voice thick.

They take off, weaving away, and watch Sudice, lit up by flashing lights, police sirens wailing in the night. Lights in nearby apartment buildings switch on, people peering out at the stark glass-and-chrome Sudice tower. Wallscreens flicker in each window, still transmitting the information the Trust sent out.

"Welcome to life after Sudice, world," Charlie says, softly.

They take off and circle the city. Charlie works on wiping all their VeriChips and giving them new identities, just in case. They contact Kim on her subfrequency. She tells them she's left the Omni, and sends them the access codes to an empty property she owns in the city. It should be safe enough for them to consider their next plan. Kim says she and Aliyah can get Dax more medical supplies, too.

"Kim," Dax says. "Where's Tam?"

"Still at Clavell's. We'll go to his in a day or two, once the worst of the dust settles. Don't worry. We'll work together and see what we can do. I hope we can wake her up."

Dax sniffs. "I hope so, too."

Carina clutches her arms around her torso, head bent. She's bruised and scratched. Her neck hurts from the Stunner. Yet she's whole, alive, and the rest of the Trust are as well. She's still amazed, having expected that surely at least one of them would die, but it seems they'll all survive to fight another day. Or stop fighting and quietly disappear.

Pacifica and Sudice won't let them fade away easily. It'll be another game of cat and mouse. There's only the hope that the company will have too many other things to worry about to put their full force behind searching.

Kim's hideout is a house on historical Bradford Street, one of the steepest hills in San Francisco. The house is forest green, three stories and in a faux Art Deco style, like most of the other houses on the street. Nothing about it stands out. They circle and then park the hovercar a few streets along and walk the rest of the way, slipping into the house. There is a cherry tree out front, full of buds just about to flower.

The inside of the house is almost completely empty. It's all polished hardwood floors and feature fireplaces. As they lock the door behind them, the security alarm beeps reassuringly. Carina only hopes they're safe here. She has no more energy to run.

Dax continues helping Raf, setting him up in one of the bedrooms while Kivon brings in blankets from the hovercar, making Raf a nest and sitting by his side. Eventually Dax comes out to patch up Charlie and Carina's minor wounds. Afterward, they all sit around Raf, staring into space. They should order food, but no one is hungry. They turn on a wallscreen. Every channel flashes news of Sudice falling.

It's the triumph the members of the Trust have been working for, some of them for years. Yet looking around at them all, to Carina they all simply seem tired and drained, and a little wary. What happens now?

Carina can't bear to look at the newscasts any more. There's a little patio out back. She goes outside, wishing for something to drink. So many lights are on in the windows, despite the fact that it's three in the morning. People are glued to wallscreens, sifting through all the information the Trust have blasted around the world.

Kim and Aliyah arrive. Carina forces herself up and joins the others. They're still dressed in their finery, but they both look exhausted and worried. Kim holds up a bottle. "I brought bourbon. Real bourbon, none of the synth stuff."

Charlie grabs it, hugging it to her. "Bless you."

Aliyah orders glasses from the replicator, as the cupboards are completely empty.

"I didn't send anything that would implicate either of you—or Mark," Carina says, hoping to put them at ease. "Mark wanted me to contact Nettie's family. Pass along his apology. His last, last request."

Kim sighs, takes a slug of bourbon right from the bottle. "I was ready to face the consequences of my actions. Still am, if it comes to that, sweetpea. I never felt right about it, but I did it anyway."

"Same here," Aliyah says, passing glasses around.

"I felt no compunctions. If my programming hadn't broken down, I'd have followed Roz straight to hell," Carina says.

"But you didn't," Kim says, passing her the alcohol. Carina downs it in one burning gulp.

"What do we do now? Where do we go from here?" she asks, hating how forlorn she feels.

"Now we pick up the pieces," Dax says, clinking his glass against hers.

•

The Trust drink until the bottle is empty. Kim produces another bottle, and they drink that down, too. Kivon curls up next to Raf, closing his eyes. Their hacker is stable, the internal bleeding stopped. It'll take him a few weeks to heal, but he should be all right. Charlie leans against the corner of the room, either sleeping or pretending quite well. Kim and Aliyah return to their own homes, promising to come back tomorrow with more blankets and some basic furniture.

Carina can't sleep. Every time she closes her eyes she sees those few drops of blood welling up beneath Roz's eye. Those weeping bandages. Part of her desperately wishes she hadn't left her there, that she'd claimed the kill that was so deserved. Too late now.

Near dawn, she goes back out to the patio. The sirens throughout San Francisco have quieted. The wallscreens in other houses have darkened. It's quiet and peaceful.

She turns at a rustle behind her. Dax comes out, bearing two mugs of coffee from the replicator. She accepts one gratefully, and he sits down beside her.

"How are you?" he asks.

Somehow, she laughs. "Fuck knows. Still trying to process everything. I feel like I should be dead, yet here I am."

"I know the feeling."

"What are we going to do now?" she asks.

"I suppose we'll all have our own personal goals. I want to see if we can wake up Tam." A pause, a flick of his eyes.

"I'll try to help with that. Kim and Aliyah, too, I'm sure. We need medical-grade equipment, but we'll find a way. Kim probably has a lab stashed away somewhere."

He lets out a careful breath. "I can't get my hopes up too much. What if even after all this, I can't help her?"

Carina thinks. "Then you've done your best. She wouldn't begrudge you that." She sips her coffee. "After you two wake up, will you return home?"

"To Timbisha? I wish we could. It wouldn't be safe to go back. My tribe would give us asylum, I'm sure, and I'd love to see my family, but I don't want to put that pressure on them. Maybe one day, if we can stop running."

She hasn't thought about it. "This isn't the end. We still have to tiptoe around the law, stay hidden." Her head bows. She'd hoped that if they could unpick Roz's mess and she could fix her own brain, there could be a semblance of a normal life for her. She's never had that. Something like grief wells up in her, then passes. She was never one for normal.

The idea of a future is still strange. Just a few weeks ago, she'd been so ready to throw it away. If Mark hadn't sent her that information, if she hadn't kicked Zeal, she'd be well on her way to being dead by now. She didn't expect to fight for life. To want to live.

"Maybe Pacifica will give us a pardon," Dax says.

"Hell will probably freeze over first. Even if we did the right thing, we broke several dozen laws in the process."

Dax shrugs. "A few months ago, I thought hell would freeze over before Sudice could fall."

"It hasn't crashed yet. We've only given it a push. I don't

think we changed the world tonight." Out here, in the quiet, the world seems relatively peaceful.

"No. But we gave the world the tools to try and right a wrong. Hopefully they take it." He sighs. "I wish we could have told Nettie's family before all this went down. They're going to wake up and see the murder of their child, if they haven't already. Hope someone else sees it first and braces them for it."

Carina's emotions stutter. After feeling so much, she has nothing left for strangers. "At least now they know, I suppose. Maybe they can find closure. I'm going to send them Mark's apology, as soon as I can figure out how to do it safely. I don't know if it'll help."

"It might." He drains his cup, then changes the topic. "Charlie still has more money than she knows what to do with. She's setting each of us up. It won't last us forever, but it should buy us time to ride out the worst of it."

"Charlie's the most generous rich person in existence, I'm pretty sure. Rarer than a unicorn," Carina says. She drinks her wine. "Is the Trust splitting up?"

"Some of us. Charlie's probably going to lie low with Clavell. Kivon and Raf will probably peel off on their own. I'll definitely stick with Tam. So. Where do we go from here?" Dax asks.

"Go into hiding . . . like you said." She trails off as he shakes his head and gives her a meaningful look. Time to stop dancing around it. "You mean me and you?"

He nods.

She takes a moment to think through her words. "I don't know. I'm still pretty messed up. I don't know how to begin to unravel all that Roz did to me. I killed my father, even if my emotions were walled up, so I never processed that. For years, I could never develop friendships, much less relationships. I'll probably end up hurting you, either mentally or physically. I can understand if you don't want to sign up for that."

Dax smiles at her, softly. "I'm willing to take the risk if you are. What do you actually want, Carina?"

She tries to empty out her mind, the swirl of confusing emotions that can still overwhelm her. She looks at Dax and doesn't case him as a potential victim. Does not focus on the pulse of blood at his neck, whether she could surprise and overpower him. She does not want to hurt him, and that is still a strange and precious feeling.

There are no words. So she stands, sits on his lap, facing him. He looks up at her. Unguarded, open. She presses her lips to his, and his arms come round her. She forces herself to keep the kiss gentle, sweet.

Tears form behind her eyes but do not fall. It's the first time she's cried since her mother died. She kisses him as the sun rises.

CARINA

The Apex, above Hollywood, Los Angeles,
California, Pacifica

The Trust camp out in Kim's empty house for a few days, and then take a hovercar back to Isaac Clavell's mansion in the Apex. Kim and Aliyah had left crumbling Sudice and come with them, swapping out their VeriChips for new identities. No one's come after them yet, but if they do, Kim thinks it only prudent to be one step ahead. She hopes she can go back to her true identity soon.

"I have people I don't want to lose touch with," she says sadly. "Even if they don't particularly want to talk to me." Carina presses her for answers, but Kim simply evades them. Carina knows that Kim has a somewhat estranged daughter she rarely speaks to, though she always holds out hope that they'll find their way back to each other.

Clavell greets them in his grand foyer, exclaiming that he's only too delighted to have them back, but Carina does not think she can ever grow comfortable in these cold, pale hallways.

Dax, Carina, Kim and Aliyah work for two weeks on waking up Tam and perfecting Carina's brain code. Raf helps a little, but he's still weak.

"You've all got it covered, and I'm useless at human systems anyway," he says with a half-smile, alluding to Carina's words not long after she first joined the Trust.

Once reports show Carina has not, in fact, murdered Roz, the Trust relax slightly around her. Carina sends an encoded message to Nettie's parents, but does not hear anything back.

Kivon tends to work out a lot. He's bored and doesn't know what to do next. He's been a cop since he was sixteen. He'll figure it out. They all will, or so Carina hopes.

They finish both Tam's and Carina's sets of code at almost the same time.

"Who first?" Kim asks, rubbing her hands together.

The last two weeks have been difficult for Carina. Not that it's been a picnic for any of them—all of the Trust have symptoms of PTSD, and Aliyah has been treating them individually, keeping track of their mental health and helping them heal.

Carina's emotions still surge, and going through withdrawal and kicking Zeal addiction once again has not been fun. She has nightmares and her moods swing wildly, even with mood stabilizers. Whatever Roz has done to Carina, her brain has shorted many of its serotonin receptors; hopefully, the code will restart them and make her moods easier to treat.

As desperate as she is to finally try and undo Roz's mess, she's afraid, and only too happy to try and wake Tam up first. Dax is absolutely desperate to see his sister again.

Clavell has hidden Tam's stasis facility well within the depths of the mansion. It's in an empty, chilled room. The stasis pod is like an elongated silver egg, the front of the pod clear blue glass. Carina's never seen a pod up close before Tam's. It's a sobering reminder that she and the others could be frozen in one of these, just now, if they hadn't escaped. That they still could be, if they're captured. Tam is inside, vertical, eyes closed, skin glowing blue in the light of the pod. It's hard to tell what she looks like—her face is mostly hidden by tubes—but Carina guesses she looks a lot like Dax.

They begin by bringing Tam out of cryo. They rotate the pod until it's horizontal. The machine does it all automatically—within an hour, she's almost ready to be woken. They keep the breathing tube covering her face, the tubes like snakes.

Kim and Aliyah prep the code, attaching electrodes to Tam's temples. They've done it more recently than Carina, and their hands are steadier. Carina's can still tremble sometimes, especially when she's nervous.

"Are you ready?" Kim asks Dax.

"Yeah," he says. He reaches out and strokes Tam's cheek. They've gone over the risks together, several times. She may not wake up. Her body may live, but her mind may still be somewhere unreachable. Carina had asked Dax what he'd do then. He wasn't sure. Killing her body seemed cruel, but was keeping her body frozen indefinitely any better? Carina hopes he does not have to make the choice.

"OK, sleeping beauty, let's wake you up," Kim says, and sends it through.

Tam's body jerks, then releases. It only takes a few seconds for the code to settle into her brain, but it'll take a few minutes for the full effect. With luck, Tam's cortex and brain stem should be repairing the damage inflicted by the Wasp attack in VR. The cause of Tam's coma was complex—the attack made the Zeal in her system surge into almost overdose-like systems, although it's meant to be impossible to OD on Zeal. The shock resulted in a lack of oxygen and—*voilà*—a coma. A very stubborn one.

Tam's eyes begin to flicker. Her head moves from side to side. Her eyes open wide, the whites around the irises stark, and she claws at the breathing tube.

"She's going to be confused," Kim says. "I've given her a light sedative, but it'll still take a while for things to settle. Don't be alarmed if she doesn't recognize you right away. That's normal."

Dax swallows hard. "Get that thing off of her."

"Tam," Kim says. "I'm removing the breathing tube. Try to stay calm."

Tam keeps scrabbling at Kim's hands. Her eyelids droop. When the breathing tubes are removed, she sucks in great, uneven breaths. Her fingers reach out. Dax takes her hands.

"Tam," Dax says, his voice breaking. "It's me, sleepyhead. It's Dax. You might not remember me yet, but I'm your brother. We're twins."

She blinks at him, frowning. She opens her mouth, closes it. Without the breathing tubes, the resemblance between Tam and her brother is clear.

Carina stays out of the way, watching it all. There's so much emotion in the room, it's still difficult to handle. And what if Tam doesn't recover properly? Her eyes are open, but that doesn't mean she's aware. What if she does recover, and hates Carina? That'll be awkward.

Carina leaves Dax to his moment, feeling as though she's intruding. Going to the gardens, she stares at the misty clouds beyond the temperature-controlled perimeter of the floating island. Down below them is Hollywood and the endless sprawl of Los Angeles. The city she'd run away to, that now might be something resembling a home.

•

Carina's fears turn out to be baseless. Tam recovers well, and the next day when they meet, she lurches waveringly toward Carina and gives her a shaking hug. Carina returns it, a little stiffly. Tam's memories are fractured, and her short-term memory is still settling. She'll ask a question, nod and seem to understand the answer, only to ask it again a few moments later. Kim says it'll pass, but Dax is still worried. Tam slips back into the weave of the Trust and makes fast friends with Kim and Aliyah. Carina largely keeps to herself. It's easy in the maze of Clavell's house.

Raf and Kivon leave, deciding to stay with some of Raf's friends in Chile. Saying goodbye to them both is strange. Carina forces herself to dole out more hugs.

"You can reach me if you need to," Raf says. "Take care of yourselves, all right? We've had enough bullets thrown our way to last a lifetime."

No one else is in a hurry to leave, and for such a reclusive man, Clavell seems to love having extra people around.

The day after Kivon and Raf leave, Dax comes to Carina.

"The code's been ready for almost a week now, but you haven't asked us to use it. Are you having second thoughts?"

He sits next to her. She takes his hand. "Of course. I'm worried I'll be changed. Silly, though. Isn't that the point? To even me out, make it a little easier to exist in this brain." She taps her temple. "It's been through a lot. I wanted to leave it alone for a little while."

"Do you think you need it?"

"I don't think it's a question of needing. I think I can function like this, but it's harder."

Dax nods. "I'd hoped you'd say that. Look at it more like a myopic person having laser eye surgery, or someone depressed evening out their brain chemistry."

"We don't even know if this code will hold. Aliyah thinks it will, but there are no guarantees. At least she's almost certain it won't completely cook my brain, so that's reassuring. Sort of."

"Nothing's a guarantee."

Carina stands. "Let's do this, then."

•

Kim attaches the electrodes to Carina's temple, settles her into the Chair. The restraints fall over her wrists and ankles, in case she lashes out when she's under. If she closes her eyes, Roz looms above her. She knows Roz is frozen in stasis, convicted of her crimes, but that does nothing to quell the spike of fear.

"No. No, no. Take these off."

Dax understands, and immediately removes the bonds. Carina tries to slow her breathing.

"Sorry," Kim says. "I didn't think."

Carina waves it away. "I'll be fine. Let's do this."

She lies back on the Chair. Dax takes her hand, holding it tight. Aliyah and Kim take a last scroll through all the numbers and symbols that will help unpick the web Roz wove. Time to break free and discover who she'll become.

Carina closes her eyes. She's looking forward to waking up.

ABOUT THE AUTHOR

Laura Lam was raised near San Francisco, California, by two former Haight-Ashbury hippies. Both of them encouraged her to finger paint to her heart's desire, color outside the lines, and consider the library a second home. This led to an overabundance of daydreams. She relocated to Scotland to be with her husband, whom she met on the internet when he insulted her taste in books. She almost blocked him but is glad she didn't. At times she misses the sunshine.

Lauralam.co.uk
@LR_Lam